THE
WAYFARING
SWAN

ROSE SCHMIDT

ISBN 9780995161511

Self-Published by Rose Schmidt

acatandahorse@gmail.com

www.riderwhowrites.wordpress.com

In memory of Judy Bovaird,
my dear friend and inspiration.

Sweet Dreams

"The future belongs to those
who believe in the beauty of their dreams."
Eleanor Roosevelt

Howling down the mountain slopes, a ferocious wind blew the thin covering of snow across the frozen lake. It was a blur of feathers and fur as the pack of winter-starved wolves chased down the hapless swans. Slipping and sliding across the glassy surface, birds with clipped wings did not stand a chance. There would be no escape.

Liana's breathing quickened and her heart pounded a frantic rhythm through her mind. The wedding would be ruined and all eyes would turn to her.

She sought comfort by stroking the small rosewood box sitting in the middle of her black lacquered desk. Its contents served as a reminder to protect what was hers with everything she had. The Wayfaring Swan was more than a highly respected name in the world of travel; it was Liana Taylor's heart and soul. From iceberg diving off the coast of

Newfoundland to recreating Lawrence of Arabia's epic ride through the desert, she was the fairy godmother who made her client's wildest dreams come true.

Unfortunately, this particular dream was fast becoming a nightmare. Liana envisioned meeting the same gruesome end as the graceful swans, only her demise would come at the hands of a ballerina bride who would be after blood when she discovered there will be no swan lake on her special day.

For the first time in her career, Liana had no idea how to proceed. A winter wedding in a fairy tale castle called for the expertise of her provocative assistant, Scarlet Channing. Liana glanced at the leather mini and red sweater clinging to her friends curves and then back to her own modest cream coloured blouse and skirt. Scarlet screamed blonde bombshell while Liana whispered modest and subdued. Even though it seemed like an unlikely pairing, their close friendship laid the foundation of a thriving business. Scarlet's creativity and affable personality were the perfect complement to Liana's relentless determination and attention to detail.

"The interior on this one looks right, but the front view could use a few more turrets." Scarlet tapped her chin with a blood red nail while scrutinizing the image. "A drawbridge would be fun. I wonder if you operate them with remote controls like garage door openers?"

Liana knew her friend was trying to cajole her out of her disagreeable mood, but it was as impossible as their current task. "It's not going to work. The last mile is inaccessible by car. We would have to carry everything along a footpath through the woods."

"Enchanted forest." Scarlet whispered absentmindedly while lost in another of her idyllic daydreams. "Can't you just picture it? The handsome prince rides in on a magnificent white steed and whisks the lovely princess bride away. It sure beats driving off in a car trailing tin cans. Hey, he could even save her from the clutches of an evil stepmother. Brilliant, right?"

"I think having our sweet mother of the bride assume the role of villain would give the woman in white one more reason to hunt me down."

A wicked grin stretched across Scarlet's perfectly made up face. "I know just the person. We can rope Delia into the role. I'm picturing her bound and gagged. It works for me."

While the thought of dulling her aunt's sharp tongue was very appealing, this conversation was getting them nowhere.

"Scarlet, why did I ever let you talk me into this? I swore off destination weddings because of the pretentious spectacle, overwrought emotions, and general insanity."

"The perfect wedding is every girl's dream. It has to have crossed your mind at least once."

Liana scowled at her well meaning friend. "Marrying a man means falling in love, and that means believing someone out there won't abandon you and break your heart. Do you see where I'm going with this?"

Scarlet knew when to leave well enough alone and dove back into the task of sorting through endless photos. Their companionable silence was eventually shattered by a high pitched trill.

"Liana, Liaaana, I need to see you immediately. Where is everyone?"

"I'm not here, and you haven't seen me all day. Go!" Liana hissed.

Her assistant leapt into action, heading for the reception area. Liana's stomach twisted in unpleasant anticipation as she frantically searched the room. While aesthetically pleasing, the minimalist decor left her with no place to hide. Fairy godmother her ass, where was a magic wand when she needed it? She was desperate to poof herself anywhere but here. The best she could do was secure the entry and maybe erect a barricade with an arm chair. She had just put a hand on the door when it swung open, hurling her onto her backside.

As usual, her mother was oblivious to the role she played in Liana's mishap. "Whatever are you doing down there, dear?"

"Mom, most people book a time to meet with me. You know I run a very precise schedule." Liana dusted herself off and gingerly moved back to her desk.

"Nonsense. Mothers never have to bother with appointments, and this will only take a minute." Jillian dragged a tufted, leather armchair across the room, making herself entirely too comfortable. Her mother's tenacity was matched by a surprising physical strength.

"I stopped by to tell you I made a few alterations to our itinerary. We are still flying into Miami, but I have something very special planned for us after we land."

Liana gave her mother an incredulous look and managed to sputter out, "What?"

"Teensy, tiny changes, nothing to worry about." There was no opportunity for further comment. Jillian gave her a quick pat on the hand before making her way to the exit.

"We can talk more tonight. Supper will be waiting when you get home." She jangled a set of keys in one hand, blowing a kiss with the other.

Liana turned on her traitorous friend. "Scarlet! You let her have the spare keys to my house?"

"The word 'no' vibrates at a frequency your mother can't hear. She grabbed them off the hook and kept moving. I tried to block her, but it's like holding your own against the Patriot's offensive line."

"There is no stopping Mom when she is on a mission. I know you did your best."

Like the unsettling jack in the box she had as a child, her mother popped up when least expected. Surprises had always been disconcerting, and Liana needed some air. "I'm going on a coffee run, be back in ten."

As she grabbed her coat, the company slogan adorning the front window caught her eye. *Happy*

5

endings begin here. It had immediately drawn the attention of Jillian on her first visit and sent her imagination into overdrive. Securing Liana's happiness consumed her thoughts. Instead of drawing her daughter closer, Jillian's obsession only served to drive them further apart.

She set a brisk pace to ward off winter's chill and ease the tension from her shoulders. Containing her emotions in Jillian's presence was becoming increasingly difficult. Liana had defied the odds, leaving the past exactly where it belonged, behind her. There would be no looking back, only ahead.

If she had been looking ahead instead of contemplating her mother's intrusion, the icy patch on the sidewalk would not have caught her off guard. She groped at the nearest brick wall in an attempt to regain her balance as her feet slid along the pavement. Given the precarious angle of her body, the signage for *Buy the Bottle* was directly overhead. Serendipity at it's best. An entire evening spent in her mother's company called for some wine. Perhaps a bottle of red and white since she had no idea what her mother had cooked up for supper or the holiday from hell.

*****

Liana poured herself more liquid relief while silently thanking stemware manufacturers for the ever increasing size of glasses. Gulping the fruity Merlot was helping to drown out the litany of complaints coming from the kitchen. Something about an empty fridge—

blah, blah—you should be taking better care of yourself and on it went. The pleasant buzz she was developing evaporated when she heard her mother mention the way to a man's heart was through his stomach.

"Seriously, Mom? No more blind dates. We agreed."

Jillian emerged with dessert and a baffled expression. "This has nothing to do with me pointing cupid's arrow in your direction."

"Pointing? It is more like impaling." The rest of Liana's snappy comeback was cut short when she noticed the butterscotch happy face decorating her plate.

"I thought it would be fun to leave hints about our trip with every course. Any guesses?"

Liana tilted her head and furrowed her brow. "So you were not labouring under the delusion that I'm five when you put the goldfish crackers in my tomato soup?"

"I did no such thing. And yes, it was the first clue."

"I am guessing the flag in the mashed potatoes was the second one." Another very unladylike swig of wine was overlooked by her mother.

Jillian twirled the item in question between her fingers. "It is a square top sail. I also served the gravy in a boat." She drew out the vowels as if her enunciation would lead to enlightenment. It did not.

"And this is?" Liana suspiciously eyed the fluffy confection she had been served.

"Meringue in creme anglaise, better-known as floating islands." Jillian bit her lip in eager anticipation. When no answer was forthcoming, she could not contain herself any longer. "We will be sailing around the Florida Keys on a tall ship. Isn't that exciting?"

Liana drained the rest of her glass. Two weeks on a boat with her mother, exciting was not the word that came to mind. Trapped. Yes, that was it. "So, we sail during the day and then retire to separate rooms in the evening. That's the plan, right?"

"Don't be silly. Where is your sense of adventure? We will be staying on the boat the entire time. I have cancelled the hotel in Miami and reserved our spots on board. Two of my friends have accepted an invitation. There is room for one more. I thought you could close up shop and ask Scarlet. She seems like such a daring individual."

Liana took deep steadying breaths. "Wow, this is certainly unexpected. I had no idea sailing was an interest of yours. Isn't most of your spare time spent with your treasure hunting group?"

"Sweetheart, it's called geocaching. Tom is trying to incorporate it into our holiday."

"Tom is coming with us? You said no poison darts—I mean matchmaking." Liana could not believe her mother had invited him. Tom had been smitten with her since they first met at one of Jillian's excruciatingly painful Sunday brunches. It had taken months for Liana to shut down his amorous pursuit. There was no way this could get any worse.

"You might as well know your aunt Delia is also coming along. Now, before you say anything, she is going to try and make this a pleasant trip for everyone. She promised to be on her best behaviour."

Liana was certain her aunt's best behaviour would send most people to prison for life. In fact, she would not be shocked to see a fiery tail peaking out from underneath Delia's perfectly tailored suits. It was all too much, and she needed it to end.

Faking a yawn, she stretched her arms. "Mom, it's been a long day. I think we should get some sleep and talk about this in the morning."

"You're disappointed. Don't bother to deny it because I can hear it in your voice. I did not want you to make the arrangements because it's what you do every day. I wanted you to relax and enjoy yourself."

"The work I do at the agency does make me happy. I wish you could accept that and focus on your own peace of mind. Do not base your happiness on mine." Liana was tired of defending her choices in life and held out little hope her mother would ever accept her as she was.

Jillian began fidgeting with her pearl necklace. "You spend every day trying to secure happy endings for other people. Liana, what about your own dreams? I just want you to give someone a chance even if it's not me."

"I can't. You know I no longer gamble on anyone. Stop feeling guilty. I do not need you to atone for what happened thirty years ago. I have a good life." Liana pushed herself away from the table. "I'm going to bed."

Easing into sleep was impossible as Liana replayed the day's events. She needed something to help her relax and reached for the pile of reading material accumulating on her nightstand. It now contained a lone volume. Her mother was at it again. She rolled her eyes at the image of a scantily clad couple on the cover and the title, *The Pirate and The Princess*. Jillian's childhood fascination with fairy tales had evolved into an adult predilection for romance novels. Since there was nothing else within arm's reach, Liana opened the book to a random page.

The stubborn princess never imagined she would find herself so exposed and out of control. Head thrown back and bosom heaving, she cried out in ecstasy. She felt the throbbing need of the roguish pirate pressed against her as he began to ravish her against the mast.

"Oh my God!"

She slammed the book shut knowing her mother had read the same words. No, no, no! Now the image of Jillian in the throes of passion was seared into her brain. This was bad, really bad.

Liana switched off the light and buried her face in a foam pillow. Bedding filled with feathers was strictly prohibited. The ergonomically designed cushion did not prevent her from tossing and turning. Insight suddenly dawned with the morning light. Clues about the trip.

She grabbed the bodice ripper and thumbed through the pages trying to uncover her mother's devious plot. A princess finds her true love in the pirate who absconds with her. Smut ensues. They have grand adventures on the high seas followed by more sexy times and a happily ever after. It was all pretty standard fairy tale stuff except for the smut. Damn! This holiday was not about mother and daughter bonding. Someone was going to be plundered by a pirate.

Caught Unawares

*"Our brightest blazes of gladness
are commonly kindled by unexpected sparks."
Samuel Johnson*

She had a need only he could satisfy. The silky voice purring those words lured Taron Royce out into the biting cold of a January afternoon. While his rugged good looks and easy-going manner often attracted intriguing requests from the opposite sex, none had ever been so direct. Meeting the mysterious caller sight unseen was a risk worth taking if it meant providing relief to a woman who had been left wanting.

It had been an enjoyable afternoon at his favourite pub. Time slipped away as he tried to imagine who might make such a brazen offer. A voluptuous temptress came to mind. 'Good things come to those who wait' was a phrase his mum often repeated to her impulsive youngest son. A tousle of his black hair was followed by a hug that felt like she would hold him close forever. Her words of wisdom had always rung true until now.

The cheery blonde bounding toward him with a swish of her woollen poncho exuded conventionality. The only other word that came to mind was motherliness. She introduced herself as Jillian Barton. She was the woman he had been waiting for, but she was not at all who he expected. He hoped his disappointment was not obvious. The likelihood of being tucked into bed with some milk and cookies was far greater than the night of sinful indulgences he had been anticipating.

Given his hastily revised impression, when Ms. Barton asked him to captain her ship, he choked. Yes, he was seriously choking on his scotch.

She sprang into action, taking charge with a calm sense of authority. "You'll be alright, dear."

The vigorous pounding his back was receiving would put his rugby mates to shame. "Do you need me to do the Heimlich thing?"

A sudden gulp of air came as welcome relief. Taron quickly raised his arms, fending off any further attempts at resuscitation. Receiving mouth to mouth from a Mary Poppins wannabe would require more than a tumbler of hard liquor to overcome. Sadly, a spoonful of sugar was all that would go down this evening. The peculiar little woman perched herself on the edge of a bar stool and appeared ready to continue her medical assault if necessary.

After a few sips of his amber elixir, Taron was composed enough to respond. "I am sorry to disappoint you, but Ocean Odysseys is closed for the season. There is a scarcity of hardy souls willing to brave a sail at this time of year."

"Oh my goodness, your voice is perfect." Jillian seemed inordinately pleased by the rich timbre of his British accent.

He raised a quizzical eyebrow. "Excuse me?"

"Someone who uses ye olde words and phrases is very rare in a world filled with modern slang. People talking only in letters and LOLing all over the place are even worse. No one has the time for proper diction anymore." She encouraged him with a nod of approval.

"I think some enlightenment is in order, Ms. Barton. My speech patterns are important to you because…?" Taron was bewildered.

"Please, it's Jillian. I'm not asking you to sail around Boston's harbour during this cold snap. It would be very impractical, and well, brrr!" She mimicked a shiver while rubbing her arms.

"I want you to captain the boat I have chartered for a two week tour of the Florida Keys. I have run into a bit of trouble finding the right man for the job, and that is where you and your delightful manner of speaking come in. I have a flight booked for next Thursday which gives you time to acquaint yourself with the boat and the crew before the rest of us arrive. It is a tad larger than you are used to sailing, but I'm sure it's nothing you can't handle." She leaned in and added, "I hear you are quite the captain."

Taron had not agreed to anything, had he? "Bloody hell woman, what are you going on about?"

"There is no need for such language, and it's Jillian, remember?"

Getting straight answers from Ms. Barton was like trying to hold onto a fish bare handed in a hurricane. Throwing a net over her would be the most satisfying way to end things, but the more practical method was to verbally take charge. "I will not agree to anything until I fully understand your proposal." Taron downed his beverage, motioning to the bartender for a refill.

She launched into a well rehearsed sales pitch. "The ship is every sailor's dream. It is a two masted, square topsail schooner. They were very popular in the nineteenth century, and this replica is a beauty. While its original purpose would have been to carry cargo, the modern design allows for all the comforts of home. There will be six guests, including myself. We will be assisting the crew with the day to day tasks. The boat is usually leased for films and season-long charters but I have managed to…"

Much to his surprise, Taron was able to stop her in mid sentence with the raise of a hand. "Ms. Barton— Jillian, while I am impressed with your knowledge of antique sailing vessels, I cannot offer you my services. I would advise you to contact someone who has experience sailing her."

Jillian squared her shoulders while waggling a finger at him. "Now you listen carefully, Mr. Royce. You are the only one who can command this boat. If you turn me down, I will be forced to abandon the entire trip, forfeit my deposits, and disappoint my friends. My life long dream will die with me." The words 'will die' were uttered as tears welled in her eyes.

Taron sputtered, "You're dying?"

"No, but it's always good to look ahead and make plans. Like the girl guides say, be prepared."

"Boy Scouts," Taron corrected.

"How wonderful! You were also a scout. A boy who performs good deeds inevitably matures into the ideal man. Loyal, loving, and level headed."

It was more like lewd, lusty, and libidinous. Before Taron could correct her misguided conclusions about his character, she slid a large manilla envelope toward him.

"You will find everything you need to know in here. Time is of the essence, Captain. I need a decision at the beginning of next week."

The exasperating female was half way to the door when she glanced over her shoulder with a final comment. "Do give this some serious consideration. It could change your life."

Taron rubbed his hands over his face and groaned. The unthinkable had finally happened. He had badly misjudged a woman.

*****

Taron's pulse was pounding as he watched the image on the big screen TV. The sails of the agile vessel were billowing in the wind as it sliced through the water. He would never tire of documentaries about tall ships.

"I'm guessing, unlike most of Boston, we won't be watching the Bruins and Habs tonight?" His roommate handed him a beer.

According to their unspoken agreement, Wednesday was hockey night. While Taron still preferred a game of football or rugby, he had come to appreciate the finer points of chasing the puck down the ice during his twenty plus years in America. There was also the added bonus of comforting disappointed puck bunnies after attending a live game.

Greg took his usual spot on the couch, helping himself to a slice of pizza. "Even though I'm off the clock, my uncanny detective skills tell me you are seriously considering that crazy woman's offer."

"Was it the film on tall ships or my nautical collection that solved the case?" Taron tipped his beverage toward the photos and memorabilia scattered across the coffee table.

"Hey, there is no need to pretend with me. I know how hard this month is for you. The anniversary date has passed, and it only gets easier for both of us." Greg inspected the perfectly executed model of a square rigged brigantine. "Daniel loved the time you two spent putting these together and he was always so proud of his little brother."

Taron winced at the reminder. "It was his dream to sail down the coast and through the Panama canal. I can't remember a day when Daniel didn't talk about our grand adventure. My brother always said life was too short. He was right."

"I miss him too, you know. He was my partner on the force and my best friend."

"And now you are stuck with me, a sorry substitute. Daniel Royce was a far better man than I am or ever will be."

The winter months were always a struggle for Taron. As the days grew shorter so did his temper. The Odyssey was in dry dock, severing his bond with the sea until spring. He preferred whatever mother nature offered, be it the pristine waters on a calm summer morning or the lashing waves of a fall storm, to the anguished memories waiting for him on shore. He needed to get away, and Jillian's offer was too tempting to turn down.

Greg seemed to read his mind. "Tell me more about this Barton woman. She sounds like quite the character."

"You don't know the half of it. I am surprised she is not camped outside the door awaiting my decision. She strikes me as the very persistent sort." Taron helped himself to another slice of Boston's finest deep dish.

"You already said yes, didn't you?"

"Only if I have back up, Detective Sloan." Despite Jillian's best efforts at swaying his decision, Taron insisted a crew member of his choosing accompany him. The man sitting next to him was the only person he trusted.

Greg was the one who stood by him when his life degenerated into superficial relationships and aimless pursuits. Taron was adrift in a sea of despair when his friend towed him back to the security of a familiar routine. Greg had been divorced for over a year and insisted Taron move in with him. He reasoned the companionship would be good for both of them. Greg also encouraged him to purchase the Odyssey, and in doing so, Taron turned his hobby into a vocation. Sailing became the one constant in his life. It was the balm that soothed his bruised and battered heart. This was also a chance for Taron to repay his friend's kindness. Greg had spent the last few years working every available shift on the force. He needed a reprieve from his grief as much as Taron did.

"I know Chief Beckett has been encouraging you to take some time off. You must have amassed the most overtime of anyone in the Boston police department by now."

Greg did not take kindly to having the tables turned. "That is not the issue. Two weeks would be the longest I've ever spent at sea. This is not like our weekend sails to Portsmouth or Cape Cod. I am comfortable with basic tasks, but I'm not the expert sailor you are. It still sounds dodgy to me. I don't understand why she wouldn't hire the ship's regular captain?"

"I asked her the very same question, and she insisted it had to be me."

While Taron remained unperturbed, his friend was skeptical.

"It's a hell of a ship given what we are used to sailing. Ms. Barton did say an experienced crew was hired?"

"I think she did, but you try spending five minutes with her and see if anything makes sense," Taron said with a wry smile.

"I think some undercover work is exactly what's needed. Give me her number, and I'll arrange a meeting."

"Be careful. While she seems innocent enough, the woman definitely packs a wallop." Taron would have liked nothing more than to watch Greg unravel the mysteries of Jillian Barton, but he had a plane to catch.

The Best Laid Plans

"Once you make a decision,
the universe conspires to make it happen."
Ralph Waldo Emerson

Jillian handed the menu to the waitress after placing her order. The Thursday special at Bruno's Burgers was always 'Meatloaf Monster Mash.' She loved the homey atmosphere of the family style eatery, and the food related puns on the menu added a quaint touch.

Not everyone was as charmed by the place. Jillian glanced over at her sister who was waging a losing battle with the worn covering of their booth. Delia's attempt to remain inconspicuous by slouching down as far as she could resulted in an unavoidable slip and slide. The molecules of her expensive silk suit seemed to repel those of the discounted vinyl upholstery, and she found herself at eye level with the table. Delia looked like a plate of jello with a case of the shivers as she wiggled and wobbled her way back into a seated position.

"If you really wanted to avoid being spotted, head to toe black was not the way to go with bright red seating." Jillian managed to suppress her laughter by taking a sip of her drink.

"Sorry, Sis. I should have asked to borrow some sensible pants and a button down sweater. I'm sure there are a few suitably dull items in your closet," Delia mocked.

Even though the preliminary tasks were very suited to Delia's talents, it had taken a great deal of convincing to gain her support. Her approach was very thorough, spending hours poring over potential targets until she found her bullseye. Ogling photo after photo of eligible bachelors provided Delia with endless hours of entertainment, and it allowed Jillian to put the finishing touches on her plan. The internet was a wonderful thing, but a stake-out was also a must to guarantee no photo-shopping had taken place. While shopping through photos to hunt down a man might not be very respectable, it needed to be done.

She had to give her older sister credit. Captain Royce was too good to be true and exactly what Jillian had imagined. He would hopefully be the temptation Liana could not resist just like the 'Don't Trifle With Me' Jillian was having for dessert. The problem with her daughter was literally staring her in the face. Liana did not take any of her mother's attempts to develop their relationship seriously. While she appeased Jillian by conceding to superficial requests like calling her 'Mom,' Liana normally kept her heart well guarded.

Jillian's guilt had fuelled the idea for this holiday. It was a last ditch effort to get her daughter to open herself up to the possibility of love. Liana was going to get the happy ending her mother envisioned come hell or high water. She hoped the water would not be very high. Sea sickness was not attractive, and it would interfere with her romantic machinations.

Jillian surveyed each person entering the restaurant while she continued to mull over her thoughts. She was looking for a man with brown hair, dark jeans, and a navy parka. The first spoonful of custard barely touched her lips when her eyes locked with his. As the man in the sensible winter coat made his way over to them, she made a mental note to tell him it was much to cold to be walking around with it unzipped.

Delia's interest was immediately piqued, and her head swivelled in his direction. She peered over her shaded eyewear. "Well, hello there!"

Ignoring her sister's outspoken appraisal, Jillian shook his outstretched hand. The necessary introductions were made, and a tentative exchange of information began. Greg talked about his friendship with Taron and modestly described working with the drug control unit of the Boston Police Department. Jillian was mesmerized. If he had announced that he was in the mounted unit as well, he could actually be her knight in shining armour. Although, a bullet proof vest was probably the safer option and not as clunky when chasing down criminals.

Jillian tried to ease into a more serious subject, but she was thwarted by Delia's characteristic candour. "Detective, you obviously came here to interrogate us and make sure we don't pose a threat. Get on with it."

Greg did not seem offended and handled the situation graciously. "For starters, I was hoping you lovely ladies could tell me more about the motivations behind this trip."

Jillian was impressed. Judging by the narrowing of Delia's eyes, she was not.

"Let's cut to the chase shall we? My sister is trying to connect with the daughter she gave up for adoption as a teenager. The low life who got her pregnant disappeared when he found out about the baby. Despite Jillian's best efforts, Liana is still rather distant. We thought a change of scenery might help. My niece is a workaholic, and there is no better way to relax than taking some family vacation time. Am I right?"

Delia waved off Greg's attempt to respond. "Rhetorical question, no need to answer. Rest assured, we are not going to rob tourists, smuggle drugs, or commit any of the other crimes crossing your mind right now. Taron has already agreed, so we really don't care if it's you or someone else who tags along. This trip is happening."

"Delia!" Jillian screeched. "Please accept my apologies on behalf of my sister, Mr. Sloan."

"No need, and please call me Greg. I am sorry if I seem overly suspicious. It's in the job description for a detective. I know you ladies are not telling me the whole story, but you are innocent until proven guilty. Am I right, Delia?"

He gave Jillian a wink as he stood. "I won't push this any further right now. I am definitely on board and will be shipping out with the rest of you."

Jillian watched Greg depart and then leaned toward her sister. She kept her voice down, "You don't antagonize the best friend who just happens to be a police detective. Let's hope he doesn't dig any further, or this whole thing could blow up in our faces. The boat better be out to sea before anyone figures this out."

"Sis, if no one has caught on given your obvious attempts to hide the truth, I think we're good. By the way, don't think I didn't notice how you and Mr. Detective were making eyes at each other. It's about time you were getting some as well."

Before Jillian had a chance to express her outrage, Delia disappeared with a flourish of her Burberry coat.

*****

Liana's schedule had been cleared for the vacation months ago. With Scarlet's help, she managed to reschedule her appointments so she could leave earlier then planned. There was more to this voyage than her mother was confessing, and she needed to gain the upper hand before they were all confined to the ship.

Everything was moving smoothly until she reached the Miami rental car counter. After waiting in a line that stretched halfway across the terminal, Liana was in no mood to have her plans challenged by the agent. He told her the fastest way to the Keys would be to hire a boat. The Overseas Highway linking Miami to Key Largo had sections that were being resurfaced. There would be inevitable delays during peak tourist season. Liana turned down his offer to arrange a boat charter. She needed a getaway car if the trip went even further south than their geographic location.

As predicted, traffic ground to a halt a few miles into the crossing due to an accident in the construction zone. Perfect. Her lap top was buried in the trunk with the luggage, and accomplishing anything on her tiny cell was impossible. All Liana could do was stare at the glassy surface of the water. Yup, nothing moving out there or on this damnable bridge transporting her to the holiday from hell. Her fingernails dug into her palms as she repeatedly banged the steering wheel with her fists.

After an hour, air conditioning became a luxury she had to do without. The last thing she needed was to run out of gas or have the car overheat, so she turned off the engine. Rolling down the windows, she hoped to catch a cool ocean breeze, but luck was not with her today. The air was as stagnant as the water.

The quiet solitude of Liana's thoughts was interrupted by the roar of a fast moving power boat. Bouncing along at maximum velocity, it seemed to skip along the ocean like a joyful child on a playground. There were no ocean traffic jams, and the two thrill seekers on board would arrive at their destination long before she would. As she rested her sweaty forehead on the steering wheel, she knew there was only one person to blame for her predicament, her mother.

Liana was a damp and disheveled mess when she finally arrived at her destination. All she wanted was a cooling shower and a comfortable bed. What she got was a desk clerk who told her the room she had reserved was no longer available. Yes, she was horribly late given the infernal traffic jam, but it was her room. He then regretfully informed her that there were no more vacancies at the Sea Ahead Inn.

She stormed out and began the process of googling and dialling. A path led to the bay which was, as the idiotic name implied, directly in front of the Inn. Ten minutes later, Liana was still furiously pacing the dock as she tried to explain her problem to another oblivious mind.

One wrong step was all it took. She found herself windmilling her arms in a useless attempt to stay balanced on the weathered boards. A cry for help barely escaped her lips before everything went black.

*****

Taron made his way from the airport to the boat launch at Convoy Point with the assistance of the beautiful flight attendant who had served him only too well on the trip to Miami. No need to wait in the horrendously long line for a car when you had such a willing chauffeur. He was met at the dock by a friend who had agreed to ferry him to Key Largo.

Ferrying was definitely not the right word for a 300 horse power Monterey sport boat. It was not the most direct route to the Keys, but the weather was perfect, and he was at the helm of an agile, high speed vessel. Taron reluctantly geared down when he noticed the snarled traffic on the Overseas Highway. Rubbernecking an accident was to be expected whether you were travelling on land or by sea. He couldn't help but feel sorry for the unfortunate strangers stuck in their sweltering cars as he sped past them.

After a light meal and a few drinks at the Inn's bar, Taron settled into his room. The nautically themed decor definitely had the Jillian Barton quirky feel to it. He was just nodding off when he heard a commotion at the front desk. Some lunatic was harassing the poor kid staffing the night shift. Taron fought the urge to barge out of his room and let the pretentious woman know the sun did not rise and set on her. There was no need. The one-sided argument ended as quickly as it began, but not before he found himself irritated and wide awake.

He poured himself a generous measure of his favourite scotch and stepped out into the night air. A gentle ocean breeze whispered to him with a salty breath that caressed his face. He inhaled deeply while listening to the rhythmical sound of the waves softly lapping at the shore. Taron closed his eyes, indulging in the fond memories his senses evoked. The hushed lullabies of his mother, the throaty laughter of his brother, and the sea shanties sung by his father. A shrill voice jarred him back to reality, and his eyes popped open. It was the belligerent woman who had disrupted his sleep.

Stomping along the path toward the marina, she was shouting something about, 'how dare they,' and 'didn't they know who she was.' She was precariously close to the water. Rather than startle her by yelling, Taron raised an arm in a futile attempt to get her attention. His waving became frantic when another turn took her closer to the edge of the dock. The blasted woman was so caught up in her rant that she took no notice of his increased efforts to warn her. Another step and she would be finished.

He turned to set down his drink and go after her but dropped it with loud crash as her arms flailed in his peripheral vision. He was already running when she went down hard, hitting her head on a piling and disappearing into the water.

"Son of a bitch!"

Taron raced down the pier and dove in after her.

Doctor's Orders

"If you obey all the rules, you'll miss all the fun."
Katherine Hepburn

Retiring to his room and donning a dry set of clothes would have been the sensible thing to do after his valiant rescue. Instead, Taron found himself in the ambulance transporting the ungainly woman. The unexpected events of the evening once again reminded him that life was governed by chance and coincidence. Anyone who thought they were in control of their own existence was a fool.

A soft moan shifted his focus to the immobile form on the stretcher. Her slim build and brown hair were a far cry from the buxom, raven-haired beauties he coveted. The freckles dusting her cheeks were even more pronounced against her dreadfully pale skin, and she still wasn't moving. Shouldn't she be coming around by now? The EMT assumed Taron was directly related to the patient and answered his question with reassuring words. He had heard them all before. There was little comfort in the half-truths and hopefulness.

Taron tried not to worry, but she looked so frail and vulnerable. When her hand slipped out from under the blanket, he reached for it. He was seized by the intense urge to protect her as his fingertips trailed over her skin. Taron pulled back. He was not that man anymore.

The ambulance came to an abrupt halt, and emergency room staff hurried to evaluate the incoming patient.

Taron stepped back and caught the eye of a tantalizing young nurse. Her eyes clung to him like the wet clothes adhering to his skin. She was eager to help the dashing hero, pulling him along to a storage closet when he asked for something dry to wear. His numb fingers fumbled with the buttons of his shirt, and she reached out to help, making her intent very clear. Normally, a partner willing to conduct amorous acrobatics in tight confines would be worth the effort, but tonight, something held him back. His thoughts were focussed on the patient being evaluated down the hall.

After returning to the reception area, the nurse requesting the accident victim's identification and insurance was not as impressed by Taron's charms. The necessary information was neatly tucked into the purse he had retrieved from the dock. The recipient of his gallantry finally had a name, Liana Taylor.

The medical centre staff continued to labour under the misapprehension that the two new arrivals were somehow connected. They allowed Taron access to

31

Liana's room, and he settled in next to her bed. His determination to discover more about her led him to conduct a thorough search of her purse. The contents were supremely organization. Credit cards and money were in a case secured inside a plastic bag. It was as if she planned to be underwater for an extended period of time.

Taron grinned. The object of his fascination was a cautious, straight laced type, and he would be more than happy to help her loosen up. He continued his bedside vigil. Taron was absentmindedly thumbing through the pages of a magazine when she began to stir. The first words escaping her inviting lips were not the generous thanks he was expecting.

She blinked several times and yelled, "Who the hell are you?"

"Ah, sleeping beauty awakens. I am disappointed that I will not have the opportunity to kiss you into consciousness," Taron smirked.

She rubbed the bump on the back of her head with a shaky hand. "Oh, shit! I was at the marina. I was falling and then—" Liana slowly turned her head, taking in the white walls and stark surroundings of her hospital room. "Where am I?" She tried to sit up and grimaced, most likely regretting her decision.

Taron stilled her with a gentle touch. "Easy there, darling. You took a nasty spill and hit your head."

"That explains what happened, but not who you are?" She sounded very ungrateful considering all he had done for her.

"Taron Royce, at your service."

As her vision cleared, the look of adoration he had grown accustomed to seeing was decidedly absent.

"Enough with the come-ons, doctor. Tell me about my injuries so I can get out of here."

Taron glanced at his scrubs, realizing her mistake. It was the perfect opportunity to help her lighten up. After witnessing Liana's earlier tirade, she definitely needed more amusement in her life.

"Let me start by taking some vitals, and I can answer your questions more accurately." He feigned taking her pulse while softly stroking her wrist. "Your pulse is strong, but it appears to be quite rapid for someone at rest. Are you agitated or excited by anything right now, Ms. Taylor?"

Liana snatched her hand away and glared at him. "Great bed side manner." Her voice was dripping with sarcasm. "Are you always this intimate with your patients?"

Ignoring her protests, Taron continued with his bogus physical examination. He gradually lowered her hospital gown. "Given your powerful vocalizations, it is safe to assume that you did not ingest any water into your lungs, but it would not hurt to double check."

His gaze lingered on the rise and fall of her breasts. "Breathe deeply for me, darling."

"Are you going to do it with your ultra sonic hearing, or did you need to get a stethoscope, Dr. Casanova?" Liana huffed through gritted teeth.

Before Taron could respond, the door swung open.

"Hello there. Glad to see you've come around. My name is Dr. Halibut. I hear you took a quite a fall."

"Wait, you are the doctor?" Liana threw a withering look at Taron as the qualified physician checked her chart.

"Ms. Taylor, you seem to have sustained a mild concussion. I will be sending you for more tests in the morning to rule out anything more serious. As for tonight, it looks like you will be our guest."

As the doctor spoke to the confused and irritated patient, Taron made a swift exit before she could object any further. The lusty nurse who had loaned him the dry clothes was waiting and offered to give him a ride back to the Inn. Clutching a set of keys, he glanced back at Liana's room. He would definitely be seeing her again.

*****

Liana was livid. Her unwelcome visitor had slipped out of the room before she could confront him. Having him arrested sounded like the most satisfying option, if she knew where to find him. The creep.

She pounded her pillow before carefully lowering her aching head onto it. Even though Liana had a comfortable bed for the night, sleep eluded her. Her dark haired visitor preoccupied her mind despite her best efforts to forget about him. The iridescent blue green of his eyes was something she had only seen in the glacial lakes of the Canadian Rockies. The colour defied description and took her breath away every time she saw it. The water always called to her, and she was unable to resist plunging her hands into the icy depths. The shocking cold jolted her back to reality. It was a vivid reminder that danger often hid behind the most beautiful of facades. Nothing was ever what it seemed.

After a night of fitful sleep and an early morning CT scan, Liana was discharged. She ran through her to-do list while waiting outside the hospital's main entrance for a taxi. Her first priority would be to search the docks for her missing car keys. She hoped that a kind soul had stumbled upon them and returned them to the Inn.

Several blasts of a horn startled her out of her thoughts. The window rolled down, and she was about to tell off the jerk when an all too familiar voice resonated in the morning air, "Hello, beautiful. May I offer you a lift?"

Thankfully, medical treatment was still at hand. The surge of anger engulfing her would very likely cause a stroke. The lecherous fake physician was back and he was driving her rental.

He was quick to get out and open the passenger door, beckoning her with a wave of his arm. "Your chariot awaits, my dear."

There was no way she was going anywhere with the womanizer. Liana crossed her arms and stood rooted to the pavement, staring him down.

Her stark perusal was met with fervent interest as his gaze swept over her form. "No need to be surly. I realized you might have misconstrued the liberties I took last night. It was all in jest, and I intend to make amends for any perceived misdeeds." He put his hands up in a gesture of innocence, his expression the picture of virtue.

Liana exercised as much civility as she could given the circumstances. "So now you're going to try and convince me you are a gentleman?" She took a calming breath. "In the light of day, you look more like a car thief."

Well, maybe not a car thief, but definitely someone with a mischievous past. He rested against the hood of the car, long legs encased in dark jeans and crossed at the ankles. Liana had to firmly remind herself that he was an annoying pervert. He was not at all attractive, and definitely not available.

"Your distrust wounds me, Ms. Taylor. I took charge of your vehicle so it could be safely returned to you. Forgive me if it was unreasonable to assume you might be unfit to drive. Rest assured, you are in capable hands." His lips turned up in a wide grin, eyes glinting.

"And I know exactly what those hands were going to do last night." Liana fumed, unaffected.

Taron wiggled his fingers at her. "These were also the hands that pulled you out of the water. I saved you. Remember, darling?"

Liana weighed her options and decided she could not risk losing her vehicle. She would have to take a chance on Royce and hope for the best. He tried to help her into the car, but she shoved those nimble hands of his aside.

Taron attempted to engage her in conversation on the drive back to the Inn. He was also staying at the Sea Ahead and volunteered his continued assistance. Liana made it very clear she could manage on her own. She always had and always would. He began to ask questions about her life in Boston, what had brought her to the Keys, and so on. The man never stopped talking. The dull pain at her temple was now a throbbing headache. She encouraged him to be quiet for the sake of her recovery, but it may have come out more like, "will you just shut the hell up!"

He pouted like a champion two year old, and it was not adorable. Nope, not at all. Shifting his attention to the radio, he was about to turn it on when she grabbed his hand. "Too loud, my head hurts."

Of course the stubborn idiot would not back down. He smiled at her and then began humming an upbeat tune for the rest of the drive.

Once they arrived back at the Inn, the owner profusely apologized for the events of the previous evening. He assured Liana a room was waiting for her, and staff were ready to attend to her every need. She doubted their help would extend to getting rid of the nuisance standing next to her. After a thank you and goodbye, have a great life, never want to see you again, she retreated to her room.

Much to her relief, she found her luggage at the foot of the bed. The trinket box that accompanied her on every journey was still safe and sound in her carry-on bag. As she began to unpack, a sudden bout of dizziness forced her to sit on the floor. Dr. Halibut warned her the after-effects of a concussion might linger for several days or weeks. He encouraged her to rest and refrain from driving until she was certain any light-headedness and confusion had passed. Driving. Royce still had the keys to her car. She would need to see the insufferable man again. It would all have to wait until tomorrow. Right now, all she wanted to do was to get into comfortable pyjamas and crawl into bed.

Accidental Tourist

"There are no accidental meetings between souls."
Sheila Burke

As Taron watched her teeter down the corridor, it reminded him of a ship trying to ride out a storm. He rarely found himself chasing after a woman and was confounded by Liana's outright animosity towards him. He wondered if she generally approached life in such an adversarial manner. Taron had grown complacent about the fact that the opposite sex found him attractive, and while he had no idea how to rectify the current situation, Liana Taylor had become a challenge he could not resist.

The cool metal pressing into the palm of his hand alerted him to the fact that he still had her car keys. In her rush to depart, the keys guaranteed they would meet again. He was more than confident in his ability to gain her affections. In the meantime, he set off to inspect the ship he would be captaining. One good deed deserved another, and the lovely Liana would surely not begrudge loaning him her car for the day. After all, he had saved her life.

Less than fifteen minutes later, Taron was awestruck as he stood in front of the magnificent vessel. Every detail had him enthralled as he slowly made his way onto the deck. Years stripped away until he was just a young lad reliving every sailing fantasy he had ever imagined. As he ran his hand along the burnished oak of the railing, he thought of Daniel and the grown-up adventures they had planned, but would never be achieved.

The sound of a throat clearing drew him out of his reverie.

"She is a beauty, isn't she? I've had the privilege of manning the helm for ten years. Captain Morgan, pleasure to meet you."

Taron shook the man's hand and managed to quell his laughter. "You are named after a brand of rum?"

"Actually, the brand of rum is named after the legendary Caribbean privateer, Henry Morgan. I am also his namesake. Captain a ship or tend bar? Life has a way of steering you in the right direction. I chose well and couldn't ask for more." He winked and then clapped Taron on the shoulder. "You are going to have the time of your life young man. Let me show you around."

The Captain guided Taron through a comprehensive tour of the grand lady. Her outward appearance fit the bill of antique schooner, but below deck lay the mechanics of a state-of-the-art ship. She was equipped with an engine to back up her sails and a generator allowed for modern amenities like hot water and electricity. Taron would need to make adjustments for steering a larger vessel, but sailing her was well within his expertise. The missing element was the manpower needed to manipulate the additional sails and rigging.

"When can I meet the rest of her crew?" Taron's practical question drew a frustrated sigh from Captain.

"My sailors have not been hired. Didn't Ms. Barton tell you?"

Taron was surprised to hear the regular crew had not been employed, but Jillian did not seem like a woman who made rash decisions. The two men parted company, and Taron's thoughts returned to the wooing of Ms. Taylor.

He soon found himself standing in front of a 'Do Not Disturb' hanging from the handle of her door. He carefully examined the signage to ensure Liana had not added his name anywhere. She seemed like the type of woman who would be precise about such things. Rather than risk her ire again, he opted for a sound sleep in his own room .

Taron was reliving some very pleasant dreams as the grey light of dawn filtered through the sash windows of the small dining area. He had finished breakfast and was nursing his third cup of coffee when he saw her. She was fresh faced and casually attired, wearing jeans and a plain white T-shirt. Her pony tail swung to and fro as she scanned the room for an available table.

The room was at capacity, and Liana was about to leave when he stood and called her name. He hoped she would not back down from a public challenge, and she did not disappoint him. Taron needed a new tactic and tried to think back to a time when he had been a more honourable man. The only thing that came to mind was blatant flattery.

Pulling out a chair, he gave it his best. "I am delighted to have the pleasure of your company this fine morning. You look radiant."

"I look and feel like shit." Liana rolled her eyes as she sat down. "Let's not add to my suffering. I believe you have my car keys."

Taron knew he would regret it, but containing his baser impulses would take some practice. "Getting right down to business, I do like that in a woman. I prefer to set a more leisurely pace, but I aim to please. Take it as fast you like, darling."

"Do you ever stop with the innuendos?" Liana scowled. "And just so we are clear, the pet names are not endearing. They are annoying."

He paused, unable to maintaining his teasing. "Why are you so unhappy, Ms. Taylor?"

Liana seemed startled by his simple but forthright question. She looked away without replying. When she reached out for the keys he slid across the table, Taron did not relinquish them. He softly squeezed her hand and saw a flicker of confusion in her brown eyes before her dispassionate expression returned.

"I think our business is complete." Liana grabbed the keys and stood. "Thank you for everything, Mr. Royce."

She was gone before he could utter his own good-bye. It was all beginning to make sense, the look in her eyes and her need to flee. Liana's anger was a mask which hid the truth. She was afraid. Fear had been his unwanted companion for far too long, and with her hasty dismissal, he would never have the chance to discover how it had come to rule her life. Hoping to catch one last glimpse of her, he turned to the window overlooking the table.

Liana rushed to her car in set determination. Yanking the door open, she dropped behind the wheel. In her haste, she failed to notice the cargo van as her car sprang into reverse. The collision wedged her between its front bumper and the car in the adjacent parking space.

"Bollocks!" Taron was out of his seat before either driver fully realized what had occurred.

He tapped on Liana's window and was greeted with a look of forlorn resignation. "Are you alright?"

She was glassy-eyed as she spoke. "I got dizzy for a few seconds and forgot to check my rear-view mirror. I didn't see the van."

Taron offered his arm as she staggered out of the car. "Don't blame yourself. You are recovering from a head injury and haven't eaten. A bout of lightheadedness is to be expected."

The van driver did not appear irritated by her negligence. He seemed more concerned with making his delivery on time and sped off.

Liana exhaled a heavy sigh. "Wonderful, my first back and run."

Taron escorted her back to her room before spending the rest of the day aimlessly wandering the town. He should just leave well enough alone and move on. The lass clearly wanted nothing to do with him, and yet she continued to preoccupy his thoughts. Stubborn arse that he was, he decided to make one last attempt before they went their separate ways.

As the long shadows of early evening began to form, he gently knocked on her door. He was greeted with a brusque, "What do you want, Royce?"

"I dropped by to see if you needed anything. I have an abundance of scotch and thought it might help dull the pain."

The door opened, and he held out the bottle. He hoped she would see him as a lost puppy pleading to be let in, and not the big bad wolf she should be keeping out.

Liana eyed the liquor while considering her response. "You win," she said tiredly. She sat back down on the bed, leaving him to pull over a chair.

"Is it always a contest with you, Liana?"

"You made it a contest when you tried to seduce me despite my big fat no."

She downed most of the generous portion he poured for her and held out her glass. He promptly replenished it.

"I won't deny the thought crossed my mind. I am also very aware that you do not find me desirable in the least." He took his own sip, savouring the taste the way he wanted to savour a kiss from the woman sitting next to him. "I did not come here with carnal intentions."

"You didn't?" She looked shocked, but her words held a note of longing.

44

"I am here to offer comfort and companionship." Taron swallowed the rest of his drink, pleasantly surprised to find he was absolutely sincere. "I thought you might enjoy some cheering up after the misfortunes of the day."

"I'm all for more cheer." Liana held out her glass. When he did not pour her another drink, she jiggled it. "My whiskey is gone."

He reluctantly complied but lessened the amount he dispensed.

"If we are to spend the evening imbibing spirits, perhaps you could start calling me Taron. I think we should be on a first name basis since we keep bumping into one another. Although, you have been doing most of the bumping," he grinned. "Are you always this accident prone?"

"I am not an accident waiting to happen," she admonished. "I am very competent in all aspects of my life. I built a successful business from the ground up and have a long list of satisfied clients. I don't think I've ever disappointed a single person. I have a steady and reliable routine. It works for me."

"Steady and reliable. Are those qualities that you also look for in a man?"

"I think I've made myself pretty clear. I'm not looking for a man," Liana snorted.

"I see." He hesitated and began fidgeting with a small wooden object on the nightstand.

"Hands off, Royce" Liana's attention was riveted on the box he was holding. "Put it down!"

45

He could not resist finding out what she was safeguarding and popped the latch with a quick flick of his thumb. She was on him in an instant, snatching the keepsake away.

"Why the devil are you carrying around a white feather?"

"None of your business. I wouldn't expect someone like you to understand. Touch it again, and you lose the hand."

"Quite the passionate response." He looked at her expectantly. "Is there someone back in Boston who arouses such intense emotion? Someone you love?"

"I —It's not something I need in my life," she said softly. "It complicates things and it's messy." There was a slight catch to her voice.

He watched her while carefully gauging his response. "I would have to agree as I have managed to avoid that particular fate myself."

She seemed bewildered by his confession, but soon recovered and renewed her efforts to rebuff him. "No kidding, you're so the 'love 'em and leave 'em type.' Can't imagine you staying around for very long. Gone before the morning, right?"

Taron could not deny the truth when it was so painfully obvious. He was guilty as charged. "When both parties are agreeable, no harm is done. Have a bit of fun before moving on to other conquests. If I were inclined to ponder it more deeply, which I'm not, it might seem like a lonely existence."

He gave her a small smile as he made his way over to her bed and sat next to her. She edged away and tried to get up. Tried was the operative word. Taron steadied her with a hand on her hip as her upper body swayed.

"Hey, hands off. I'm not the klutz you think I am. Not that I care what you think." She looked at her empty glass and shoved it forward. "More pu-leez."

Taron held the bottle out of reach and cautioned, "Perhaps you better call it a night?"

"Who are you now, my mother?" Liana flopped down on the bed and groaned. "You should haf jus let me drown. It would haf been quicker."

"You can't be serious, darling. I am very perceptive, and there is something that you are not telling me. I've been told I am a good listener if you want to get it off your chest." She exhaled a dramatic sigh, and he found himself staring at her lovely breasts. He was a man who readily yielded when temptation called.

Much to his relief, she was past the point of caring and rolled over onto her side. She propped her head on one hand. "You know the thing about mothers, Royce?" She paused while pushing a finger into his chest. "They are just so smothering. Smother mother, thas what she is. Hey, it rhymes. Thas really funny don't you think?" A weak chuckle was all she could muster.

Even in her inebriated state, Taron saw through the dismal attempt at humour. It was a ploy which had also served him well. "So this frustration is directed at your mother? What heinous act has she committed that has you so willing to sacrifice yourself to the sea?"

47

"This whole trip is her stupid idea, not mine. She wants to make things better, but my life is fine the way it is. Fixing things means I'm not good enough, not for her or anyone. It hurts."

She closed her eyes, grabbing a pillow and hugging it. "Pretty sure I'm done with all thisss. Unless there's more booze, I'm gonna sleep."

Taron felt her pain, and a chink formed in his own emotional armour. He told himself to walk away, but he could not turn his back on her. He waited until her breathing evened out before reaching over to wipe away the single tear on her cheek with a delicate stroke of his thumb. He would likely never see her again and felt the unfamiliar pang of regret.

Taron made it as far as the door before pausing to take a blue gem out of his pocket. He always carried it with him as a reminder of all that he had lost. He had once been a decent man, a man with principles. Perhaps the stone could also be seen as a glimmer of hope for the future. Tucking the talisman into Liana's purse, he prayed it would keep her safe and bring her the happiness she deserved.

Tell No Lies

"Few are those who see with their own eyes
and feel with their own hearts."
Albert Einstein

Taron could not resist passing Liana's room as he left the Inn. His thoughts were swirling with unresolved emotions. While his mind told him to move on, his body refused to heed the command. Liana had given him no indication she was interested in the man he was, and the road back to his former self was an impossible journey. The only choice was to forget her, but he remained motionless. Minutes passed before he pressed his palm to the door and whispered, "Good bye, Liana. Find your happiness."

He ran through the list of tasks that needed to be accomplished before setting sail during the short cab ride to the ship. All thoughts of Liana were pushed aside as he transitioned from unsettled landlubber to confident sailor and captain. He noticed the ship was oddly quiet as he boarded. There was no answer when he called out, but he heard faint noises coming from the ship's galley. He went to investigate and found a young women stowing away provisions.

"Good morning," he said, perusing her assets as she bent over a box.

Taron's greeting must have startled her, and she jerked herself upright.

"Goodness, I didn't hear you come in." She wiped her hands on a towel before offering him one. "I'm Claire Danvers, and I will be managing the household chores on board."

"Pleasure to meet you, my dear." He smiled warmly while shaking her hand. "Taron Royce, and I will be captaining the ship."

"Captain. Oh my, it's nice to meet you too. I have almost everything put away, and the cabins have been readied for our guests. A package addressed to you is in your quarters, and everything I was unsure about is in the salon. That is what you call the living room area on a ship?" Claire was staring at her shoes while she spoke.

"Yes, it is. I commend you on being familiar with such nautical terminology, well done."

"I did a fair bit of reading when I found out I would be sailing on such a majestic and historical ship. I was hoping you might allow me to learn more about her. I would love to help above deck if I could." She quickly added, "That is in my spare time, and only after I have completed all of my own duties satisfactorily." Claire nervously shuffled her feet while waiting for him to respond.

Taron smiled warmly. "It is always a pleasure to welcome someone who has a passion for sailing."

"Um—to be honest, this is my first time on a ship, but I am eager for an adventure. My life has been kind of dull. That's why I am here."

Claire carried on after a moment of hesitation. "I am a research assistant in the History Department at Boston University and spend my time looking up information for students and professors. Most people don't know Boston's Public Library houses one of the largest collections of rare books and manuscripts in the country. I could spend all day in the stacks, reading about people's lives and all of the marvellous things they accomplished."

"It sounds like you found a job you love, why leave?" The slumbering brunette he had left behind was in the forefront of Taron's mind as he asked the question.

"Are you sure you want to hear more about this, Captain?"

Taron nodded.

"I began to feel restless, and it dawned on me that I no longer wanted to follow in the footsteps of the past. I felt compelled to see the world and start a story of my own. I called an employment agency specializing in temporary and unusual jobs, and this one caught my eye. So, here I am."

Taron admired her courage. Claire wanted more from life and had willingly sacrificed the contentment in her grasp for a chance at something better. He would see to it that this trip was an experience she would not soon forget.

"I look forward to seeing you at the sails. Speaking of which, I need to check on the whereabouts of my crew."

After performing a final inspection of the ship, Taron could accomplish nothing more without his missing deck hands. He retired to his cabin and found the package Claire had mentioned on his bed. Tearing open the envelope attached to the brown paper wrapping, he found a note from Jillian. As he skimmed over her words, he was certain the meddlesome woman would be his ruination.

He reread the letter several times to ensure he clearly understood her intentions. While Taron was reluctant to take part in the shenanigans Jillian had planned, he was curious to see where her little game would lead. A mischievous grin emerged as he examined the contents of the parcel. His decision was made.

*****

Liana awoke to another pounding headache and more pounding on the door. Was it too much to ask for just one morning where her head didn't feel like it was going to explode? She clambered out of bed and shouted, "Just a minute, Royce."

She released the lock and was caught up in Jillian's powerful embrace.

"Sweetheart, it's good to see you. I've been so worried." Jillian placed a hand on Liana's forehead and swept back her hair. "You're not feverish, but you don't look well. I'll bet you haven't eaten. We will grab a bite on the way to the boat. Everyone is waiting in the van."

"Mom, slow down." Liana tried to focus on what her mother was saying. "What time is it?"

"It's nearly ten, and we are running late. Didn't you get my texts?"

Dammit. Liana meant to replace the cell resting on the bottom of the bay. "Give me a minute, Mom."

Her mother was already on her way out with both of Liana's suitcases. Damn, the woman was strong.

Liana tried to smooth out the wrinkles in her clothes as she stepped into the bathroom. She leaned over the sink, allowing a wave of nausea to pass and then splashed cold water onto her face. If only she hadn't had drinks with Royce last night. Like everyone else in her life, he was probably long gone. She would not allow herself to think about the care he had shown her or the compassion she saw in his eyes. She did not need anyone to hold her hand. Yes, he had held her hand, and she remembered the spark she felt. It was both thrilling and alarming when their fingers touched.

Taron Royce was dangerous, and she shied away from anything that was not safe and predictable. He had come precariously close to uncovering truths which were best left hidden. She looked at the face reflected in the mirror and wondered who she was deceiving the most, Royce or herself? There was no point in thinking about it. Grabbing her sunglasses, she walked out into the tropical glare.

Scarlet was tightly squeezed between Tom and the van driver, making little effort to hide her enthusiasm. The man behind the wheel introduced himself as Greg Sloan. Jillian was beaming with motherly love as she held the van door open. Wonderful. The only seat available was between Delia and her mother. There would be no way to open the door and fling herself out of the moving vehicle. It was sure to be the most unpleasant trip in the history of motoring.

Delia immediately began her badgering, "Lia, it looks like you had a rough night. I hope whatever you drank loosened you up enough to finally have a good romp between the sheets. The only thing that makes a hangover worthwhile is a post coital glow. Am I right?"

"I have a name, and it is Liana. It's not Lia, Ana, or Li Li . I have told you this at least a thousand times, Dee." There was no known universe where a splitting headache and close proximity to Delia would ever go together.

"Yes, Liana." Her aunt dragged out each letter in her uniquely derisive manner. "It is just like you to count and then carefully log the number somewhere. Do you have a specific journal for all of my offences? It must be the size of War and Peace by now."

Liana caught Greg's eye in the rear view mirror, and he gallantly tried to redirect the building tension. "It's nice to finally meet you after hearing your mother sing your praises. I see the old adage 'like mother, like daughter' is very true when I look at two such beautiful women."

Delia looked like she was going to regurgitate breakfast while Jillian stared appreciatively at the back of Greg's head. Her mother then tipped forward, inhaling deeply.

Oh my God! Was Jillian smelling him? Liana could see the cause of death on the coroner's report; accidental, acute embarrassment by mother.

Greg seemed oblivious to the goings on behind him and continued his conversational efforts. "I hear that you run a travel business back in Boston. If you ever need to book a boat trip, my friend sails a—"

Jillian rudely interrupted, "Sailing means the boat is moving on the water. I hope no one is going to get queasy. Tom, did you remember to pack your Dramamine?" She exchanged a panicked look with Delia.

Tom turned around and gave Liana a knowing smile. "I did. If there is stormy weather, I might need to confine myself in a cabin and rely on someone's tender loving care to get me through the worst of it." He licked his bottom lip in anticipation as Liana closed her eyes in disgust.

She definitely needed something to dull the pain. "Speaking of medication, does anyone happen to have anything for a headache?" Tom and Jillian jumped into action, racing to see who would be the first to assist Liana. The win went to her mother.

"You can always rest your head on my shoulder while I massage it for you," Delia offered.

Liana flinched and tried to move away as best she could in the close quarters of the back seat. As Delia leaned toward her, she noticed the small markings on her scarf. Liana took off her sunglasses and examined them more closely. "Are those skull and crossbones?"

Jillian grabbed the end of the scarf and looked as though she was going to strangle Delia with it. Liana wanted to ask why the hell they were all behaving so strangely, but was interrupted by Scarlet 's quip.

"I'll bet Delia has plans to wave it as a flag of surrender in case we meet any hot pirates at sea. If we do, I plan to take quicker action. I'm pretty sure I can tackle one if a chase is required."

The only sane person in the van seemed to be Greg. "I'm afraid the days of pirates are long gone, and the best you ladies can hope for are sailors on shore leave. I hear there are some great bars when we dock at Key West."

A hush descended on the occupants when they pulled into the marina and caught sight of the ship. Liana was blown away. Seeing her on the water, in her full glory was like being transported to a bygone era. She glanced at Jillian who was busy giving the boys instructions on where to put the luggage. Maybe, just maybe, she had misjudged her mother, and this wouldn't be the excruciating ordeal she had anticipated. It might even be fun.

After making sure the Luis Vuitton steamer trunk holding her precious cargo was properly secured, Delia sidled over to Liana. "Lia, take a look at the ship's name. I'll bet we're in for some sexy times. Am I right?"

Liana looked in the direction her aunt was pointing and saw *The Wicked Wench* emblazoned on the ship's bow. Images from her mother's novel flashed into her mind, and she felt her stomach lurch. She knew you couldn't get seasick until the ship was actually moving. It must have been the scotch.

As they made their way onto the ship, Liana noticed two crew members standing at the railing. What was it they were wearing? Pants were tucked into long boots, chests were covered with puffy shirts, and knitted caps were on their heads. Were they supposed to be pirates? This was far worse than anything Liana could have imagined. Her mother was going to subject her to some type of costume drama.

"Welcome!" A man wearing an inflatable vest was the first to greet them. Wait, why was he wearing a life vest? Liana could barely keep up with each distressing revelation.

The second man introduced himself, "Good morning. My name is Shane Redmond and this Charlie Oliver." He motioned to the other man. "We will be your crew for this voyage. Our captain should be here soon. He is probably checking last minute details before we put out to sea."

All eyes turned to the aft of the ship as a figure emerged from below decks. The captain self-assuredly strode toward them. A long coat billowed around him as he walked. Its open front allowed a glimpse of form fitting black pants and a matching shirt. The closer he got, the more Liana felt there was something oddly familiar about him.

"Hello, my lovelies. Welcome aboard the Wicked Wench. I am Captain Taron Royce, at your service."

"Hell, no!" Liana desperately looked for an escape route. Her mother was blocking the exit to the gang plank and would most likely tackle her to the ground if she tried to bolt. Jumping overboard? She knew Royce would just leap in after her. Shit, shit, shit!

"Liana, is that you?" The captain sounded as stunned as she felt.

Jillian furrowed her brow, turning her head from her daughter to the captain. "You two know each other?"

Nowhere to run and nowhere to hide, Liana was trapped. She slowly took off her sunglasses and looked at Taron. "I see you've met my mother."

A Fine Mess

"Get your facts first,
then you can distort them as much as you please."
Mark Twain

Jillian was aghast. She could not utter as much as a single syllable. There were confused looks all around and a cackling sound coming from her sister.

"This is perfect. Jillian, isn't this just perfect?" Of course, Delia would love this unexpected plot twist.

Jillian found none of it amusing. "Liana, please explain this."

"Mom, there is no this." Liana gestured between the captain and herself. "He pulled me from the ocean and tried to get into my pants. Then he stole my car and got me drunk. End of story."

"Captain Royce!" Jillian had never given superpowers much thought, but she wanted one right now. Death ray vision would work nicely, incinerating the horrible man where he stood. The added bonus would be no untidy clean up afterward.

Ignoring her yelp, Taron directed a disapproving glare at Liana. "Evidently, our tale continues. For the record, there is more to our shared past than your quick rendition suggests. I am happy to account for the gaps in your memory, but we need to make haste and depart."

Jillian struck what she hoped was an intimidating pose by widening her stance and planting her hands on her hips. "We are not going anywhere until this is settled."

Taron checked his watch. "The owner of the marina requires this berth for a vessel docking later today. I have instructions to leave port by noon which means we have twenty minutes to weigh anchor. Getting acquainted will have to wait."

He strode past Jillian and barked out his orders. Greg hustled over to the sail on the mainmast while the other two men sheepishly looked at each other before turning to Jillian.

Shane scratched his head. "We're expected to pitch in and work the ship? You hired us to create an authentic pirate experience. We don't have any real skills. We're actors not sailors."

"Neither of you know how to sail?" Taron asked, appalled. He bristled with indignation as he advanced, forcing Jillian to take a step back. "They don't know how to sail. You hired a crew who do not know how to sail a ship!"

This was not her fault, and Jillian self-assuredly replied, "I arranged for your earlier departure so you could teach them all about sailing. What happened?"

Taron's outstretched arm was heading for her throat until a loud cough from Greg saw him change course and vigorously massage his scalp. "Ms. Barton, I can assure you that one does not learn how to sail a ship like this in a few days. It also seems your bogus crew is a tad late. This is the first time we have met."

"What!" Anger was making the rounds and Jillian was up next. "What have you two been up to for the last three days?"

The pretend pirates hung their heads. Shane was the first to volunteer an explanation. "One of our pals from the pirate show in Miami was having a bon voyage party. It might have gotten a little out of hand."

"The money you gave us was spent on booze and—um—stuff. We were drunk and hung over for two straight days," Charlie blurted out his version.

Fists clenched, Jillian marched toward the hapless pair.

Greg managed to cut her off before she could inflict any damage. "Looks like we have a few things to sort out, but we have to get this ship out to sea first."

There was something down to earth and very practical about Greg. They were excellent qualities in a husband, er—man, Jillian thought. "That sounds like a splendid idea," she said, briefly losing herself in thoughts about the dreamy detective.

The captain scowled at her as he spoke. "The ship has enough engine power to get us underway, so there is no need to man the sails. Greg, we drop anchor as soon as we are a reasonable distance from shore."

Jillian was still trying to think of a way out of her predicament when she heard the anchor chain release. There was no way this voyage would end less than a mile from where it began. Adopting her cheeriest smile, she addressed the group. "I'm sure everyone is excited and wants to have a look around. I have a map of the ship and everyone's cabin assignments." She held out the colour-coded schematics.

When no one stepped forward to collect the pages, she carried on undeterred. General apathy was no match for her relentless enthusiasm. "Lets all settle in before we enjoy the delicious lunch Claire has prepared. We will meet in the dining room at one o'clock."

Jillian grabbed Delia by the arm and retreated below deck.

Once they were safely behind closed doors, Jillian vented her frustration. "They hate each other, don't they? To be honest, right now I'm not very fond of our captain either. He tried to get into her pants. Oh my God, what if he's some kind of pervert, like a sex addict? How could we not have known?"

Delia wrapped her in a bone crushing hug. "Remind me to tell Liana to wear skirts more often. Getting into pants seems to be a barrier to our master plan in more ways than one."

Her sister continued to administer her own unique brand of emotional first aid. "I'll admit it's not the best start to our 'Romancing Liana' project. I always thought 'Getting Liana Laid' was a better title. Given these new revelations, it is a more realistic goal than falling in love."

"Be serious, Delia. We have to think of a way out of this. Maybe, we can substitute Tom. After all, he is crazy about Liana."

"This is not like coaching a football team. You can't just send in a replacement. Tom is attractive, but he would be second string at best after seeing our captain in that outfit. Let's not do anything rash and see how this plays out. This is only the first quarter, and a lot can change before we reach the two minute warning."

Jillian sat dazed and confused. Months of meticulous planning were ruined. "Why did Liana have to leave Boston ahead of us? They were not supposed to meet until we could gently guide them toward each other. Her defences are now sky high, and that is exactly what we wanted to avoid."

"We have an even bigger problem, Sis. Given the lack of skilled manpower, this trip may not happen. You know, it really has been an all too common problem in our lives. I think even you would have to agree that we need a few good men or nobody sets sail."

Jillian's lips curved into a smile. "Alright, let's absorb all of this new information while we unpack."

She watched Delia unlock the antique steamer trunk. "You did remember to bring along a sensible pair of shoes? Something with rubber soles is the best choice for a slippery deck."

A showcase of pricey designer footwear was revealed when her sister stepped side.

"Delia! How many do you think you need?"

"Getting the number down to twenty was an excruciating ordeal. Choosing a favourite pair would be as difficult as a parent choosing one child over another." Delia's face twisted into a pained expression.

Jillian knew her sister's demons all too well. It was her turn to provide comfort. "You know Dad loved us both with all his heart. It was never about favourites where he was concerned."

"Pops was the kindest person to ever grace this world." Delia rested her head on her sister's shoulder. "Grieving the loss of his wife made him such an easy mark for my mother. Once she set her sights on him, the poor man was doomed."

"He didn't see it that way. I truly believe he loved Eve as much as anyone could. Don't you dare feel guilty."

"Why should I feel guilty? You were tormented by an evil stepmother, and I gained the most exceptional father in the world. Sounds like a fair trade to me." She took Jillian's hand in hers. "I'm so sorry."

"Stop apologizing. I always dreamed of having a big sister, and I would not change a single thing. I can't imagine my life without you."

Revisiting the wrong-doings of the past would change nothing. Liana's future was all that mattered. The little girl she lost all those years ago would have her happy ending. Jillian would make certain of it.

*****

Standing at the window of his cabin, Taron gazed out at the tranquil water while contemplating this strange turn of events. Liana was here on the ship. It was nothing short of miraculous. While Jillian was giving providence a heavy hand, it seemed Liana and he were destined to be together. Sorting the mess they were in would be a formidable task, but he was determined to make it work. There was no way in hell he was going to say goodbye to Liana for the second time in as many days.

Greg walked in just as Taron turned his back to the sea. "I guess the perks of being the captain are getting your own quarters. Jillian decided I should be roomies with Tom since we hit it off on the flight from Boston. He seems like a decent guy aside from his quirky obsession with geocaching. Jillian says…"

Taron stirred at the mention of her name. "Jillian says, does she? Do you honestly think whatever the duplicitous woman has to say would make a damn bit of difference to me? Lies and more lies, she has been dishonest with everyone. Hells bells, nothing makes any sense. I thought you were going to meet her and find out more about this trip. You were supposed to have my back, mate."

"Hold on a minute! I did meet with her and that disagreeable sister of hers. I sensed something was off, but I didn't get very far. Interrogations with hardened criminals have gone easier than having a conversation with those two." Greg cast a dubious look at Taron's sudden change in appearance. "It looks like there is a bit more to your story as well, black leather man."

"I would be happy to explain my leatheriness but I cannot. Our disingenuous employer left a note to join in the fun by donning this outfit. I think Ms. Barton owes everyone an explanation, especially her daughter."

"Liana, isn't it? I would love to know how you and Jillian's daughter crossed paths. Care to tell me what you two have been up to?" Greg seemed entirely too pleased with himself.

"Nothing is up." Taron's lips twisted into a roguish grin. "She has proven to be immune to my charms."

"What? Taron Royce struck out." Greg looked confused before coming to an unnerving conclusion. "Don't tell me Boston's most notorious bachelor actually cares about a woman? You should warn a man before you deliver such shocking news." He plopped himself into a chair. "I definitely want to hear more about this."

"There is nothing more to tell. The story has not begun as far as the captivating Ms. Taylor is concerned, and it may end much sooner than I would like." Taron was not a man who gave up easily when he fancied something, and he could not remember ever wanting something this badly. He would find a way to make this all work. He had to.

*****

Liana was staying in the cabin next to Taron's and overheard him shouting her mother's name. She desperately wanted to do the same thing, over and over again. Collapsing onto a bed, she flung her arm over her face in a fit of despair. Scarlet seemed to think the whole thing was hilarious. Her attempts to suppress her giggles only caused her to laugh harder.

"Let's get this over with, Scarlet. Just say what's on your mind. I would like to think this can't get any worse, but given the last few days, I think it probably can and will."

"Liana, how can this not be a good thing? The Captain is the hottest man I have seen in—well, ever. In fact, I'm surprised the ship hasn't already burst into flames. I may just spontaneously combust if I stand near him, and I really want to get closer to that piece of ass."

"Scarlet, enough! Let me tell you what my life has been like since meeting him, and maybe you'll see things differently."

"The only way I want to see Taron Royce differently is without all that leather in the way. Liana, did you see those hip hugging pants and all of that black. He nailed the sexy bad boy look."

"Yes, he is attractive. He also has heartbreaker written all over him. Thanks, but no thanks, I've had enough heartache to last several lifetimes."

Scarlet listened intently as Liana recounted what had happened in Key Largo.

"I don't think he's as bad as you make him out to be, but let's leave the captain out of the picture for now. Liana, you never do anything special for yourself. I don't remember you ever taking a holiday even though travel is your business. Your schedule is clear, and we are talking about two weeks of tropical vacation. Besides, Jillian and Delia are going to be really pissed if you jump ship."

Scarlet grabbed her hands and pleaded, "Please don't leave me with the gruesome twosome."

Her friend's playful banter always managed to lighten Liana's mood. "I'll give it some thought while I take a walk above deck. See you at lunch."

She was almost at the stairs to the hatch when she ran into Greg and Taron as they emerged from the ship's mechanical room. Greg excused himself while Taron followed her onto the deck.

Liana pondered her decision as she scanned the blue expanse of water stretching to the horizon. The shocking revelations were an emotional tsunami, and she had already survived a near drowning. She needed to regain her equilibrium before she could make sense of it all.

A contrite voice sounded behind her. "This is a first. Shouldn't you be taking offence with something

I've said or done today? There seems to be an abundance to choose from."

Liana had questioned Royce's role in all of this, but there was no way he could have known or been in cahoots with her mother. He was as visibly shaken as she was when they were reacquainted. Evidently, Jillian had kept her daughter out of any conversation. And there it was. The ache of rejection encompassing every part of Liana's being and the empty room in her heart that she kept locked at all times. Her mother was looking for a key she would never find, and no one in her life had ever been determined enough to break the door down. She would never be worth the effort.

As the hurt settled in, she felt a comforting warmth radiating near her. Royce was standing beside her.

"Liana," he softly called her name while putting a hand on her shoulder.

He gently turned her to him, and she was immediately caught up in those blue eyes. No words needed to be exchanged. There was no mistaking the kinship of loss and pain etched on his features. Liana felt her chest constrict and breathing became difficult.

Taron took a step back. "Liana, just breathe. It's going to be alright. Tell me what you need."

"Nothing." She couldn't tell him because she didn't know the answer herself. "You've been conned by my mother just like the rest of us. I should have looked into all of this when I was still in Boston. I came down to the Keys to try and find out what she was planning, but it was too late."

She could blame no one but herself and her self-deprecation continued. "It seems I've again miscalculated where my mother is concerned. I don't know if I have ever really caught her in a lie. It's more like an evasion and not so much what she tells you as what she leaves out. You could lose your mind trying to keep it all straight."

"Don't sell yourself short. It would seem your mother had an accomplice and the two of them made quite the formidable team. Delia seems, well…"

Liana jumped in, "Wicked, sinful, heartless, pick a word because they have all applied to my aunt at one time or another. This whole thing is insane, and now it's not just me, they've screwed this up for everyone."

She peeked at her watch and saw their time of reckoning was drawing near. "I guess we better go deal with the two troublemakers. I hope walking the plank is still considered part of the authentic pirate experience." She gave Taron a hesitant smile.

"Care to do battle with the enemy, Ms. Taylor? Two against two should make it a fair fight."

"Lead the way, Royce." A sinking feeling took hold in the pit of her stomach which was definitely not a good thing when you were on a ship.

Ship of Fools

"Surprises are foolish.
The pleasure is not enhanced,
and the inconvenience is often considerable."
Jane Austen

Taron and Liana were the last to join their fellow travellers in the salon. He tried to take her hand as they walked into the room but her fingers slipped through his. He had to settle for a reassuring glance. Delia had already opened the bar and was pouring drinks for everyone. Their newfound alliance would be sorely tested. Liana positioned herself as far from mother as possible, leaving him to address the group.

"Given the unforeseen events of today, I think the most pressing issue is whether our journey begins and ends right here. Continuing onward will require dedication and hard work from each of you." Taron turned his attention to the sisters. "I have devised an alternate plan, but you must respect my command."

The co-conspirators remained tight-lipped as he continued, "The original navigational charts must be abandoned because they put us too far out to sea. Sailing an island chain like the Keys works to our advantage. We will be able to maintain a safe distance from shore while teaching those who are interested the basics. Greg and I are willing to try, but we all must to work together if this voyage has any chance of succeeding."

Claire was the first to offer her assistance. "You can count me in, and I can loan people the sailing books I brought with me."

Taron gave her a grateful smile. "We will be relying on the sails as we move parallel to the coastline, but we need the engine to get us into and out of port. Docking a ship this size is too great a risk for a novice crew in a busy waterway. The safety of everyone on board is paramount. I suggest we all sleep on it and let clearer heads prevail in the morning."

Taron slowly scanned the room. "Before we adjourn, I think we should clear the air. An undertaking such as this requires crew members to have absolute trust in one another which means no more secrets." He turned to face Jillian. "Ms. Barton, let's start with you. Is there anything else you have neglected to tell us?"

Jillian ignored his question entirely. "Just how well do you know my daughter, Captain Royce?"

The woman was a menace and Taron carefully crafted his reply. "I have had the pleasure of your daughter's delightful company for only a short time. It would seem circumstances have put me in the role of dashing rescuer more than trusted confidant."

"Well, let me explain a few things. I wanted to do something special for Liana since she is always giving so much to others. Her happiness is the most important thing in the world to me." Jillian rushed over to her daughter, folding her in a tight embrace. "I'm so sorry. I just want you to be happy and I thought this was the best way to make it happen."

Taron recognized a guilty conscience when he saw it. He was ready to toss the sodding woman overboard for whatever hurt she had caused her daughter, but Liana bravely confronted her mother.

"You thought reliving days of yore as pirates and wenches was something on my bucket list? Are you confusing your dreams with mine again, Mom? It does happen quite often." Liana held her own, and Taron was impressed.

"I may have a slight inclination to read a romance novel or two, but don't we all deserve love and a bit of whimsy? Must life always be so serious, Liana?"

"Yes, real life is serious. We do not live between the pages of some fairy tale. There is nothing playful or romantic about the situation we find ourselves in thanks to you." Liana flushed with anger.

"You're blushing. Stop! I can't take blushing, it's red."

All heads swivelled in Shane's direction, and he was forced to explain his outburst. "I have erythrophobia which means I'm afraid of the colour red. Before anyone says anything, it is a very real condition, and I'm getting therapy. It's not usually a problem unless you plan to wear 'that' colour, eat something 'that' colour, or if someone bleeds. No bloodshed is allowed on this trip."

His confession was greeted with bewildered expressions, forcing him to continue. "I was hopelessly in love with a woman who adored all things 'that' colour. Hot damn, she looked amazing in it. Things were going great until one day she just up and left me. I have no idea why, but my therapist assures me once I get over the loss I will be fine."

Delia pounced before Taron regained his wits. "I'll bet having the last name Redmond is a problem. Ever consider changing it?"

Shane covered his ears. "Don't say it out loud. I could barely say it when I introduced myself. Dr. Krane, my therapist, thinks changing my name would be a setback. I need to accept every part of myself. Call me Shane and everything will be fine."

"Looks like therapy is going swimmingly for you." Delia swung around to face Charlie. "What's up with you and the orange vest? Let me guess, you can't swim?"

Charlie's lower lip quivered as he looked up at the ceiling. "It's a bit more serious. I'm afraid of the water."

Delia howled with laughter.

Shane jumped into the fray to defend his friend. "There is nothing funny about any of this. Charlie has a very real problem called aquaphobia and has come a long way. Look at him. He is out here on a ship in the middle of the ocean."

Taron watched the colour drain from Charlie's face at the sudden reminder. Shane quickly clapped a hand on his friend's shoulder. "No worries. I'm here for you, and Dr. Krane would be proud."

Delia turned to Jillian. She was grinning like the mad hatter. "Sis, you managed to find two pirates who can't sail a boat, and they are both bonkers. I'm not sure if you should be reading comedies or tragedies, but romance is out of the question."

There was no longer any doubt in Taron's mind. This was the ship of fools, and he was their beleaguered captain. He suspected Jillian had not provided her pirates with swords in order to prevent the inevitable execution. He took several steps toward the person he would most like to skewer with the pointy end of a blade. "Delia, we have yet to hear from you."

"Unlike most people here, I have nothing to hide. My motto in life is tell the truth and nothing but the truth. My testimony is an oath that will hold up in any court."

Taron was sure he felt the ship moving on the waves of tension emanating from everyone. "Since dead men tell no tales, honesty means very little. I assume the same applies to dead women, Delia."

Jillian tried to diffuse the situation with another about-face. "Captain, perhaps you could tell us where you acquired your delightful accent and the charming diction you use when speaking."

He braced himself for another round of verbal dodge ball. Taron's only choice was to play or be sidelined, and he would not allow Liana to face this insanity on her own. "I was born in England and moved to the States when I was ten. Most of my schooling was completed at a private British academy. I went on to complete a degree in historical linguistics. If that satisfies the ladies, I would like to get back to the matter at hand."

"Oh, I'm sure you always leave the ladies satisfied." There was a predatory gleam in Scarlet's eye, and it did not sit well with Jillian. She shoved the younger woman aside as she made her way over to Taron.

"I think the captain is right. We should be trying to figure out how to get on with our journey." Jillian side-eyed her daughter's lusty friend.

A sword. What Taron wouldn't give for a sword right now. "Ms. Barton, you do realize the only reason we are in this impossible situation is due to your artifice? You have single handedly managed to disable this impressive vessel and render her dead in the water."

Tom ended his self-imposed silence by coming to Jillian's aid. "Hey let's just ease up on Jilly. She has everyone's best interest at heart, and I am not giving up on a romantic holiday. I agreed to this trip because I am in love with Liana."

Taron raised his eyebrows in surprise. It never occurred to him that he might have to battle an adversary for Liana's affections. The woman in question was closely examining the carvings on the oak bar while Tom continued, oblivious to her disinterest.

"I know you don't have feelings for me yet, but things can change. I will never give up. My heart beats only for you."

Liana made her position abundantly clear. "Tom, we've been over this so many times. It's never going to happen. Never!"

Delia turned to her sister and guffawed, "Told you, second string."

"Don't listen to any of them, Tom. My name is Scarlet. I'm here for the hot men and good times. I'm sure you and I can work something out." She wet her bottom lip while checking him out.

Shane smacked himself on the forehead. "Your name is—I can't say it, and don't you say it again. It's 'that' colour."

"Well, you can call me bunny instead. It's a pet name my mom came up with, and that should work for you." Scarlet winked.

"Bunny? Is that because you jump every man who—"

Greg stood up, brandishing his weapon before Delia could finish her salacious remark.

"For anyone who has forgotten, my name is Detective Greg Sloan. If I discharge my weapon to shut up the next person who says anything, any judge in the country would deem it justifiable homicide."

A deathly silence descended upon the room. Taron looked at his friend and mouthed the words, "Now what?"

The frustration in Greg's voice said it all, "I think we have had enough truth for one day. Those who think they can help sail the ship will join Captain Royce for a quick orientation. The rest of you will stay here with me.

Liana demonstrated her faith in their recently established collaboration by immediately crossing the room to where he stood. Taron let out a breath he did not know he had been holding. Tom was about to follow her, but he reluctantly stayed put when Jillian pointed out his geocaching experience would be best suited to mapping a new course.

Liana's mother positioned herself inches from Greg and shamelessly ogled his weapon. A man with a revolver might be exactly what was needed to redirect Jillian's unrelenting focus away from her daughter. As Taron predicted, Delia's loyalty was never in question. The bastion of truth walked over to join her sister.

The two phoney deckhands had to decide whether they would fulfill an obligation they had clearly not signed up for. Taron felt badly for poor Charlie who had an impossible choice. Asking him to help work the sails would put him in close proximity to the water, but working below deck with Delia would be an equally terrifying choice for a man so riddled with anxiety. After a whispered exchange, the two men joined his group.

Scarlet checked out the men on both sides of the room before strutting over to Taron. Sadly, Claire opted to stay behind. She chose to honour the duties she was hired to perform rather than pursue her dream. Taron recalled how ebullient the young woman had been at the thought of sailing and silently pledged to try and make her wish come true.

While the solemn faces around the room spoke volumes, there was always that one exception. The ear to ear grin on Delia's face signalled she was entirely too pleased with this unanticipated turn of events. She raised her glass and tipped it toward Taron as if issuing a personal challenge. He gave her a withering look in return. The teams were chosen. Let the games begin.

All The World's A Stage

"The lady doth protest too much, methinks."
William Shakespeare

Liana woke to the gentle snores of Scarlet. A quick check of the time confirmed it was too early to emerge from the cocooning warmth of her blankets. Her headache had returned which was not surprising given yesterday's disastrous developments. She tried to will the pain away. It would not surrender, so she grudgingly got out of bed.

Rummaging through her purse, she found the bottle of aspirin her mother had given her and something unexpected. A small gem was nestled among the items. The icy blue sparkled and shone as she held it in the narrow stream of light coming from the porthole. The colour reminded her of Royce's piercing eyes. Liana massaged her shoulder while recalling the warmth of his touch during their private moment on deck. If eyes really were the window to your soul, then there was something more to the innuendo-laden man.

Something that spoke of comfort, belonging, and home.

She tried to blink away the tears that were threatening to break free. Home had never been more than some bricks and plaster where you began and ended your day. A car crash took the lives of parents who had supposedly loved her dearly. At five years old, she was left to face life alone, shuffled from one foster family to another. Family. It was not a word she ever used because it meant someone cared and she belonged. No one in her life ever stayed, and she would not delude herself into thinking otherwise. She set the gem next to the trinket box on the dresser. An explanation would have to wait until after her shower.

Grabbing some toiletries, she tried to glide out of the room as noiselessly as possible. The ship was equipped with two small bathrooms at either end of the passage alongside the cabins. It would make sense to designate one lavatory for the men and the other for the women, but nothing had been discussed. Knowing her mother, there was a detailed chart posted somewhere with scheduled times for each person and their requisite bodily functions. Delia would be incensed at the thought of sharing a bathroom with five other women. It would hit the fan alright and lots of it.

The space was small but not as cramped as she had imagined. Liana wasn't sure how much hot water was available, so she resigned herself to a quick clean up. After towelling off, she realized her clothes were back in the cabin. Without coffee, she was suffering from a severe case of early morning brain fog. The only option was to scurry back as she was.

She had just set foot in the hallway when she collided with Royce. Liana froze. In her rush to move away, she pitched sideways, clutching at her towel. Taron's arms encircled her waist as he tried to keep her upright. She could feel her face turning as red as the material that enclosed her naked body. Naked! This was not happening. Nothing but a skimpy piece of cotton was separating her from Royce. His arm tightened around her as the moment lengthened. He was holding her tightly, and she was not struggling because it felt good. Not good. What she was feeling was bad, very bad.

Royce set her more firmly on her feet. "It seems life has once again put us on a collision course. I am only too happy to cushion your fall."

"Sorry, I was—I mean—thanks for the hand."

Royce was staring at her with an intensity that suggested he could see right through her cotton covering. The emotions surging between them left her feeling more exposed and defenceless than her current state of undress. She was not the prude Delia believed her to be and recognized the look of unadulterated need when she saw it. But this was more, so much more. His gaze spoke of tenderness and genuine affection.

The only sure fire way to defend herself against the assault on her senses was to break cover and run. To her utter shock, Royce moved aside the very instant she stepped forward. She entered the safety of her room and leaned her back against the door as her legs threatened to give way. What the hell was happening to her?

*****

The group of discontented travellers were slowly preparing for what would surely be a day to try everyone's resolve. Jillian had already been the recipient of Delia's foul temper after her sister discovered the washroom restrictions. Captain Royce expeditiously escorted his fledgling crew above deck after receiving one of her sister's scathing glares. Greg was interrupted by Delia when he stood to address those who remained in the salon.

Her sister clearly stated her intentions, "I think you men should get on with the mapping thing while the rest of us get into the spirit of the trip. I'm thinking a little sun tanning above decks. Wouldn't you agree, Jillian?"

Delia's skin was fifty shades of white. Prolonged exposure to the sun did not happen without hats, cover-ups, and the intensive application of sunscreen. Even during the hottest Boston summers, she would wear hosiery with her dark skirts and slacks. Staring at her sister in a swimsuit would require polarized lenses and likely blind the crew working the sails. Lounging around above deck would also not ingratiate them with those working hard to solve a problem which was largely her doing.

She needed to ensure the rest of her plan was brought to fruition and that meant some girl talk. "Delia, I think it would be unfair if we did not pitch in and help. We should all be able to contribute if we think about this hard enough. You boys should get on with the charting." She shooed Tom and Greg along with a wave of her hands. "Off you go."

The two men eagerly departed, and Jillian turned her attention to Claire. She hoped the meek young woman was tougher than she appeared.

"Delia and I have been thinking about how to make this trip a fun and interactive experience for everyone, and we have come up with some creative ideas. Think of us as cruise directors in charge of the entertainment on board. We are hoping to tap into your wealth of historical knowledge to help us achieve the atmosphere we are looking for."

Claire choked out a reply, "Um—what exactly did you have in mind?"

"I think it's best if we show you." Jillian hauled a trunk out from behind the bar. "We should move this to a more private location."

She proceeded to manhandle the beastly baggage down the hall as Delia put a hand on Claire's back, giving her a push in the right direction. The eldest sister locked the door to the cabin and Claire's eyes widened in fear. Jillian was reminded of a rabbit caught in the ravenous gaze of a fox, and she redirected the wary young woman's attention back to the trunk.

Jillian flipped the lid open and began unpacking the period clothing she had ordered. Wait, something wasn't right. These were not the outfits a respectable lady of the time would wear. What she found was more likely to be worn by women working in an eighteenth century brothel. The luggage contained shifts, corsets, and scandalously low-cut gowns in all manner of styles and fabrics.

Claire seemed equally bewildered by the contents. "Those are very —um— colourful." She examined one more closely. "Don't you think they might be a tad too revealing?"

Why had she let Scarlet be in charge of the costuming? Jillian mentally chastised herself for not having checked on the items before they were packed. The dresses would definitely appeal to the captain, but getting Liana to wear one was going to be a bother. This could still work to her advantage if she gave it some thought.

"Are we going to have some type of formal dinner?" Claire gulped. "It happens on cruise ships doesn't it? A black tie affair at the captain's table."

Claire's skeptical expression did not deter Jillian. "These are for Liana. Not all of them, but she is the reason behind this. My daughter works too hard and doesn't have much of a social life. She needs to relax and have some fun. Recreating swashbuckling pirate adventures on the high seas will get her out of her comfort zone and into a romantic frame of mind. Don't you think?"

Claire gave Delia a panicked glance before answering, "If you are looking for historical accuracy, I am afraid you won't like what I have to say."

"What do you mean? Pirates must have sailed these waters at some point in time." Jillian was counting on Claire's help to set the mood and did not like where this conversation was heading.

The erudite young woman seemed to grow taller and more confident as she spoke, "There really wasn't much in the way of piracy occurring on the Gulf side of the Keys. Hurricanes and storms caused more damage and claimed more treasure than pirates ever did. There were a few who preyed on Spanish galleons carrying gold and sliver to Cuba. The pirates of the time were not the sort of men who belong in the romantic portrait you seem so intent on portraying. They were selected from those who found themselves exiled to the Americas, cutthroats, bandits, runaways, and young men disinherited from families for nefarious reasons."

Delia could take no more. "Well isn't this just a fascinating history lesson from our resident book worm. Personally, I would have liked to check over those new recruits and make sure they passed muster, but those days are gone. I think what we are aiming for is less from the male dominated history of the time and more from the feminine perspective. After all, this is about Liana and her happiness. Am I right?"

"I believe meeting the right woman could transform even the worst rogue of a pirate. I was thinking along the lines of a womanizing rake tamed by his love for a beautiful and spirited highborn lady." Jillian would not be swayed from her version of events.

Claire countered with more factual information about the time period. "I don't think many women of means risked sailing these waters unless absolutely necessary. It would be too dangerous. If they survived shipwrecks and had the misfortune to be caught by pirates, it would not be the fairy tale ending you hope to achieve. Women who were captured were often sold into slavery or ransomed back to their family. They were the lucky ones; many others were raped, tortured, and killed."

"I think we should steer clear of history and use our exploration of the subject matter to guide our plans." Jillian gave Claire her best irritated teacher look.

"So, you have done some investigating into the era. What have you uncovered?" Claire's face lit up with delight.

Delia took several volumes out of a canvas tote. "Finally we are on the same page. Uncover is exactly the right word, and so is disrobe, undress, and strip." She tossed the research material onto a bed.

"Let's have a look." Claire read the titles aloud, "*The Pirates Blonde Booty, A Pirate's Plunder, Captive in the Keys*. These are—I see you have probed the subject matter quite thoroughly."

"Books are rather dusty and distant, so we need to move this to a more hands-on experience if we are to be assured of success." Delia's lips twitched into a sly smile.

"I take it we will all be participating in this period drama?" Claire enquired.

"Yes. This is going to be great fun for everyone, and I know we can count on your support." Jillian reached into the same bag, pulling out some loosely bound pages.

"These are the scripts Delia and I have put together outlining everyone's role. We wrote some general dialogue but also left room for improvisation. Shane and Charlie were hired for their expertise in staging productions, and they will also be our acting coaches."

Claire perused a few pages. "If you are looking for my opinion, I should spend some time going over this material more thoroughly."

Delia was about to disagree when Jillian caught her eye. "There are some people who might need convincing. Perhaps it would be a good idea to have Claire's endorsement." Jillian handed her the novels. "In case you have any questions, it's always best to refer to the source material."

"I better get back to the galley and finish lunch. I promise to give this proposal the due diligence it deserves." Claire rushed out of the room, leaving behind a very pleased Jillian.

*****

Taron told his crew of would be mariners to explore the ship while he considered how to impart several weeks worth of sailing knowledge and experience in a single day. Crashing into the scantily clad object of his desire only strengthened his resolve to see this journey through to its completion. He had held Liana in his arms for a brief instant, and the urge to keep her there was overwhelming. Taron was left wondering if she had ever received the love she so desperately needed.

After the door to Liana's cabin had shut, he felt the keen sense of loss that had been absent from his life until recent days. If he was to demolish the physical and emotional barriers that separated them, the real Taron Royce would have to take centre stage. He needed to prove to her that the man she first met in Key Largo was an imposter.

Liana was examining the rigging of the foremast sail when he called out to her. "Could I have a word please?"

She turned to face him. "Royce, if this is about this morning, it's already forgotten. No harm done."

"That's just it, Liana," he angled himself closer. "What if I can't forget?"

"I know you are a man who is used to getting what he wants from women, but you're just going to have to deal with disappointment where I am concerned. We have formed an alliance, nothing more."

"If you think the only thing I want from you is sex, you are sorely mistaken. You felt something more during our embrace, and it scares the hell out of you." He watched her battle to stay in control as the silence stretched between them. "Liana, you don't have to be afraid. All I'm asking for is a chance. Will you give it to me?"

She looked at the hand he offered while nervously shifting from one foot to the other. Her trembling fingertips brushed against his just as voices approached. The moment was lost and she backed away.

Taron quickly masked his disappointment and addressed the group. "After inspecting our splendid ship, are there any questions?"

Scarlet batted her eyelashes. "Don't get me wrong, I do like what I see. But why the jeans and T-shirt? What happened to the pirate gear you had on yesterday?"

Taron managed a taciturn reply. "Practicality won out for the day, Ms. Channing. The leathers don't have the necessary give for some of the vigorous activities we will be engaging in this morning. Is there anyone else with a question?"

Charlie timidly raised his hand. "I wondered about those big orange floaty things at the front and back of the ship. Do you use them when someone falls off, and does that happen very often?"

"Those are the MOB stations which stands for Man Overboard. I have never had reason to deploy such apparatus in all my years of sailing." Taron locked eyes with Liana. "As your captain, protecting my crew is my number one priority. Nothing untoward will happen to any of you while I am at the helm."

Charlie's fixation persisted. "Don't you think it would be a good idea to have a demonstration? We should all probably familiarize ourselves with important life saving equipment."

Taron did not dismiss the man's concern outright, reckoning a drill might be in order given Liana's propensity for mishaps. "I believe something could be arranged for another day."

Shane also tried to alleviate his friend's anxiety. "Since no one is volunteering to jump off the ship, I'm wondering how dangerous the deck might be if someone wearing high heels were to be pushed—er—slip? We could rename it the SWOB, Snarky Woman Overboard."

There was uproarious laughter as everyone imagined how satisfying it would be to give Delia that shove.

"Alright, if there is nothing else, let's begin our lessons." Manning the sails will be the most important duty you will perform." Taron moved to the mainmast and patiently described how the rigging and winches worked the sails while repeatedly demonstrated the basic procedures.

The winches controlling the lines to the canvas required two people to work them. One to turn the handle and tighten the rope while the other took up the excess line with gloved hands. Raising the sails would require strength, but little in the way of finesse. Disengaging the cable when the canvas needed to be lowered was a trickier manoeuvre. Injuries could easily occur if they released too quickly, and the ship would be adrift until the sails could once again be hoisted.

Taron knew everyone was trying their best, but it was a struggle. He was beginning to think they would never weigh anchor. Frustration was bubbling over when Shane added some levity to the proceedings.

"You'd think the guy who named the ship would have avoided his crew having to say something about the Wicked Wench's winches. The winsome woman worked the Wicked Wench's winches." He gave Scarlet a lingering glance and a naughty smirk.

"Charlie, remember all of those tongue twisters we used to practice during our warm ups in acting classes?"

His friend managed a nod and forced a grin through clenched teeth.

Shane scratched behind his ear and laughed. "You know Captain, this is just like a live stage production. We are the actors trying to play the parts of sailors, and you have the role of our esteemed director. Let's hope tomorrow's matinee performance goes well given our lack of rehearsal time."

Shane's innocent comment gave Taron some much needed inspiration. He told his rookies to pretend they were confident sailors. Encouraging them to embrace the concept saw things dramatically improve for everyone but Liana. She would not let herself go, trapped in a prison of her own making. He had no idea how, but he was determined to set her free.

The Wind At Your Back

"The first step towards getting somewhere
is to decide that you are not going to stay where you are."
J.P. Morgan

Trevor scanned the deck of the schooner from his hiding place in a thicket of saw palmettos. His body twitched as he became increasingly agitated by the motionless vessel. The sails were being raised and lowered, but the damn ship had not moved all day. What the hell were they doing? His boat was now fully loaded and ready to go, but he could not risk being spotted by the passengers.

Lowering his binoculars, he turned to the older man standing next to him. "Why are they still anchored? They travel a mile from shore and just sit there. It's like they are waiting to haul us over when we pass by."

"They have no clue we are here, or even less likely, what our plans are," his father replied.

"I don't like it. The brunette on board the ship is the same woman who backed into me in the parking lot. It has to be more than a weird coincidence. It's a sign, and I'm sure it means trouble." Trevor lived each day in the shadow of fear. He was constantly on the lookout for evil omens in the hopes of avoiding an untimely demise.

His father's acerbic voice cut through the humid air, "And what if she does spot you and remember? You were a stranger driving a van and nothing more. You really should try to live up to your last name. Bravery is needed in our line of work, and it is something you are sorely lacking. The ship will be gone soon. Then you and I are free to get on with our business."

His father was right. It would not be long before they had an obscene amount of money, and no one was going to stand in their way.

*****

Taron was unwinding from his sailing tutorial when Greg joined him in his quarters. A recap of the day's events was necessary if they were to have any chance at smooth sailing. According to his friend, the mapping had gone well.

"We have reconfigured the new route to keep us closer to shore. I made arrangements to dock at Islamorada tomorrow afternoon. Jillian had a berth reserved at Key West which is the half way point of the trip." Greg paused. "There is still the issue of the geocaching club. Tom insists a desolate island be included as a stopping point to accommodate their adventures."

Taron relished the thought of getting the sister act off the ship for a few hours. It would give everyone some peace and quiet. "It is easy enough to drop anchor and use the motorized skiff to get the treasure hunters ashore. Chart the course alteration tomorrow."

As Taron recounted the challenges at the sails, Greg's expression turned grim. "You are really going to try and sail her with a rookie crew?"

"Everyone seems determined, so I am honour bound as their captain to help them succeed. I propose we keep sailing times brief and weigh anchor only when weather forecasts are benign. If we travel during the early morning and late afternoon hours, winds should be at their lowest point. I do not foresee setting any speed records on this voyage."

"I will also be on deck to help carry out your orders. Between the two of us, we might just be able to pull this off."

Taron knew Greg would support him no matter what tomorrow's sail had in store. Knowing there was at least one person he could rely on, no matter what hardships stood in his way, changed who Taron was and how he approached his life. He was certain Liana had never been the recipient of such unwavering faith and could only speculate on the positive impact it would have had on her. He wanted to be that person for her, and if the last few days were any indication, it was never too late to change course.

Thinking about Liana seemed to be enough to draw her to him. A forceful knock preceded her resounding battle cry. "Royce, we need to talk!"

Taron bowed with a flourish of his arm after opening the door. "Not what a man likes to hear, but do come in. My humble abode is at your disposal."

Liana rolled her eyes at him and entered with Claire following behind. She turned to Greg who was set to leave. "Please stay. Claire has some disturbing news which impacts all of us."

"Well, I'm not sure exactly where to start. Delia and Jillian took me into their confidence today, and I brought the evidence with me." Claire emptied the contents of the bag she was clutching onto the bed.

"The sisters are planning a historical re-enactment of sorts. It seems there will be more of an emphasis on the acting than any actual history. Captain, I am afraid they are eager to see you back in the leathers, and Liana, you are to have a starring role opposite their leading man."

Taron's casual interest morphed into intense curiosity as he inspected the reading material. "It appears there are some racy novels and something called *Romancing Liana*. What are they up to?"

Claire began to nervously pace the cabin. "It seems you will be in the spotlight of a production with a very common theme. A man and a woman meet, although more accurately, a pirate captures a princess. They fall in love, and then they get busy—um—very busy from the looks of it. Not that I have looked very carefully."

Liana grabbed the script. "Hell, no! They are so not getting away with this."

Claire lowered her gaze. "I'm so sorry Liana, but I am afraid they are set on accomplishing their objective. They have acquired a very bold selection of period costumes, and we have all been assigned parts."

"This is not going to happen on my watch. I am putting an end to those two and their scheming." Liana hopped off the bed.

Taron lay a gentle hand on her arm. "Let's not be too hasty. We should take a minute to consider this more carefully. Given our access to this classified information, we might be able to outwit the pair. Forearmed is forewarned as they say."

He tilted his head toward the door. "Greg, don't you have some charting that needs to be finalized?"

"I do?" His friend's creased brow was soon replaced by a knowing look. "Yes, I do. I'm going to do that important mapping right now. Claire, you also have things to deal with in the galley. Urgent kitchen things that need sorting."

The pair were on their way before Liana could protest. While seeming more amused than annoyed by the clumsy exchange, she issued a warning to Taron, "If you really want to prove yourself to me, the games have to stop."

Taron lowered his head in mock shame. "I beg your forgiveness." He patted the spot next to him on the bed, managing a very sincere smile. "What do you say we conduct a more thorough investigation of the subject matter?"

Liana glowered at the mattress and then at Taron. "Royce, if you think that you are going to get me to..."

"Exactly my point," Taron interjected. By the look on Liana's face, he narrowly avoided having his face marred by a handprint and hurriedly continued, "We need to think about this carefully if we are to circumvent the enemy. We are in this together, remember?"

Liana reluctantly sat on the edge of the bed. "Yes. I do recall our partnership. Let's have a closer look."

"This one appears to have the most relevance to our dilemma, *Captive in the Keys*." Taron managed to stifle his laughter as he read, *"The eyes of the princess smouldered with defiance as she pressed the blade against the brutally handsome pirate's throat."*

"It does seem to have an all too familiar ring to it. Let's see if we can't find a more romantic moment." Taron flipped to a new page and continued, *"Their passion was ignited and she burst into flames as his potent manhood..."*

"Enough!" Liana's face was aflame. Red was definitely her colour.

Taron tried to summon a small measure of self-restraint, but failed miserably. "Quick question. Given your own experience, are those flames more like a small kitchen fire or the volcanic eruption at Pompeii?"

"It really depends on the— I can't. I mean, I can— and I have. Can you just stay focussed for one minute? We need to put an end to all of this nonsense."

"Rest assured, I can last as long as you require." Taron's wink and impish grin were greeted by another flush of her cheeks.

He was beginning to have an effect on her, and it would take being hit by a fully loaded freight train to stop any of this from moving ahead. The problem was his nemesis, Jillian. Taron needed to outsmart her while ensuring Liana did not get hurt in the process. He remembered Greg telling him about his most recent undercover operation. It was exactly what was called for, a sting. All Taron had to do was convince the woman sitting next to him.

"Let's take a minute and think this through. Your mother has been single-minded in trying to secure your happiness, has she not?"

Liana's attention was still riveted on the book he was holding. "That's putting it mildly. She is like a dog with a bone. Not a really big dog, but one of those little yapping ones." She snatched the romance from him, madly waving it in the air. "I say we bury these books and put them both on a very tight leash."

"I disagree. I think we should to send them on a trail with a different scent."

"What the hell are you trying to say?" Liana's temper flared.

"There are two ways to go about this. In the first scenario, we give Jillian what she wants, playing the roles precisely as she has written them."

"You and I are not going to have sex to please my mother." Liana eyed the mattress warily.

Taron hiked an eyebrow. "You seem fixated on that topic. Does it have anything to do with the virile man sitting next to you?"

"Keep this up, and I am seriously going to rethink whose side you are on."

"Yours and only yours, darling. If we play along with your mother, she achieves her goal, thereby ending her attempts to secure your happy ending. There is also a more devious option that would liven things up a bit."

"I'm not even sure about the first choice, but let's hear the second one," Liana grumbled.

"Your mother seemed quite perturbed when you listed my alleged misdeeds for her which leads me to believe she sees her captain as a handsome hero and not a libidinous ne'er do well."

He leaned back on his elbows and turned to face Liana. "Perhaps we should exaggerate the lascivious nature of the pirate, and the leading lady could thoroughly enjoy his ministrations." He raised a hand to ward off her protests. "It's only purpose would be to thwart your mother's schemes. If I am right, as your Aunt Delia is so fond of saying, your mother would concentrate her efforts on keeping us apart."

"So, we would only be acting out these assigned roles?" Liana sounded doubtful.

Taron's reassuring grin turned mischievous. "Hmm, staying detached and not letting your emotions get in the way. It would take some imagination and letting go of inhibitions to make it all believable. I am not sure you have what it takes."

"You think I am such a control freak that I can't make this work? I can loosen up and have fun. We are going to beat Jillian and Delia at their little game, and I am going to prove you wrong." Liana left in a huff.

She was absolutely glorious when her pent up emotions were unleashed. Liana had just agreed to spend their days flirting, and he hoped nights would be spent doing much more. It had been a very satisfying twenty-four hours for Taron. He could not argue with the wisdom of motherhood when it brought him closer to what he desired.

Taron rested his hands behind his head as his thoughts drifted to memories of his own mum. She had always maintained a positive outlook, finding the perfect words to encourage her boys when they were faced with seemingly insurmountable problems. One of her favourite expressions was an old Celtic blessing. He hadn't thought of it in years—how did it go again?

'May the road rise up to meet you. May the wind always be at your back...' He could never remember the ending, but he knew it stood for the hope that your journey in life would be trouble-free.

His mother's undying love had eased the way through life's many challenges. Undying. It was the crux of the matter. The two people he loved most had been torn from him. He was still tormented by the images of his bloodied hands holding his mum and brother. Taron had been unable to protect them from the coward who snuffed out their light. He would never be able to forgive himself.

While the memories of happier times seemed to fade with each passing year, he was always able to conjure up his mother's ocean blue eyes and hear her sweet-sounding voice. Taron knew she would tell him to follow his heart, and it called out to Liana. Perhaps the tide had finally turned and the love that had been taken from him was about to be restored.

*****

Another unexpected problem surfaced with the dawn of a new day. It was easily solved, and informing the individuals involved would be the most enjoyable part of Taron's to-do list. The sisters were finishing up breakfast when he entered the salon with Claire at his side.

Jillian gave them a warm welcome, "It looks like we have a glorious day for our first sail. Doesn't it, Captain?"

"The weather does seem quite favourable, and how astute of you to mention today's sail. It is precisely what I want to talk to both of you about. Let's help Claire clear the tables and head back to the galley."

They met up with the actors-turned-sailors below deck. Shane urged his friend to reconsider his decision, "It's not too late. You can still call it quits."

Charlie waited until the women moved into the galley before lowering his voice, "I don't belong at the sails, and I may have a way to handle Delia. I'm going to try one of Dr. Krane's techniques. Don't worry about me. I'll be fine on my own." He nervously glanced between Taron and the small kitchen before following him into the battle zone.

"Captain, what's with this little get together? I assume it has something to do with short and shaky here." Delia levelled a scathing glare at Charlie.

Karma was about to catch up with the horrid woman. Taron happily delivered the news. "Charlie asked to be relieved of his duties above deck, and I have agreed. Unfortunately, his departure leaves the crew at the sails short handed."

As usual, Jillian was eager to be helpful. "I could pitch in, but I would need time to get caught up. Practice makes perfect, you know. Maybe Greg could indulge me in some private lessons?"

"I'm sorry to disappoint you, but there will be no crash course because we must sail today. Claire has spent weeks researching historical ships. She is the logical choice. As captain, I am hereby promoting her to the status of sailor."

Taron extended a hand to the beaming bibliophile. "Congratulations, lass. You will be assisting Greg at the mainsail. He is eager to bring you up to speed."

Claire was out of earshot when Delia expressed her reservations, "So, Charlie is going to take over the cooking and cleaning? It seems like a big job for such a little man."

Before the man on trial could say anything in his defence, Taron interjected, "You are right, Delia. It is too big a job for a person inexperienced with domestic chores, and that is why he will not be alone in his endeavours."

"Captain, if you are saying what I think you are…"

Delia was shocked into silence when Taron hung an apron around her neck. He bestowed the same honour on Jillian and Charlie. "You have all been appointed to the housekeeping department of the Wicked Wench."

The sarcastic sister clenched her fists in anger and scowled at Taron. "You can't be serious. We are now the help?"

"Deadly serious, and I will leave you to sort out the details. My presence is required at the helm."

Taron stepped out onto the deck as Shane was finishing a rousing soliloquy from Moby Dick. It was undoubtedly an attempt to inspire confidence in his fellow crew members, but the sombre faces staring back at him suggested it was not the best choice. He strode to the raised quarterdeck at the aft of the ship and took his place behind the wheel. His position gave him an unobstructed view of the sails and surrounding water.

Casting one last worried look at Shane and Liana who stood at the foremast, Taron recited a quick prayer and gave the orders to set sail. He kept the ship aligned with the shore, guiding her into the light winds. There were a few tense moments when the breezes picked up, but they were soon fully underway.

Tacking the ship into the wind was now Taron's responsibility, and the crew was able to take a brief respite. There were excited conversations and delighted laughter in the joy of the moment. Scarlet was leaning over the side rail with her arms extended out to the water. Jillian had abandoned her newly assigned duties in order to resume the role of protective mother, and she was pointing out something to Greg. Taron's eyes sought out Liana. He was pleasantly surprised to find her gazing back at him. The upward turn to her lips transformed into a brilliant smile. It was a start.

The sea breezes were very accommodating, and they arrived at their destination sooner then anticipated. All that remained was to secure the sails and engage the engine to bring them safely into the marina. While their first foray as sailors was almost over, Taron found himself filled with trepidation. He had spent too much time at the mercy of the sea to discount any such presentiment. Taron's gut told him he needed to be on the main deck. He called his first mate to the helm. Greg already had his sail down and arrived at the quarterdeck just as a sudden wind shear caught the aft sail.

Shane lost control of the winch as the halyards suddenly released. Liana was tossed onto the deck. She managed to brace her legs against the mast, but was hanging onto the rope as if her life depended on it.

"Bloody buggering hell!" Taron leapt over the railing onto the deck and ran to her side. "Let go, Liana." He dropped behind her and reached around, stretching his arms over hers.

"Liana, you have to let go." There was no response, and the line continued to slip through her fingers. Her arms were shaking from the strain as Taron desperately tried to pry her hands loose. Gloves. Why wasn't she wearing any gloves? He saw the unmistakable reddish tinge of blood on the rope.

Taron rested his cheek against hers, whispering an impassioned plea, "Liana, I'm right here. Please, let go."

She exhaled a breath, collapsing against his chest. He wrapped his arms around her and tried to comfort her with soothing words. Taron barely heard the voice of Jillian behind him as his pulse thundered in his ears. He had failed in his obligations as captain and broken his promise to protect his crew. Liana was hurt, and he was to blame.

Helping Hands

"As you grow older,
you will discover that you have two hands,
one for helping yourself, the other for helping others."
Audrey Hepburn

The shock of the moment quickly dissipated. Jillian took charge, escorting her daughter below deck. Tom met up with them as they descended the stairs and began fawning over Liana in an attempt to alleviate his guilt. He had retired to his bunk after being overcome by a bout of seasickness when the ship started moving.

"Liana, I'm so sorry that I was absent in your hour of need." He reached out to take her hands after she sat down on a bed.

"No! Not my hands." Liana directed a pleading look at her mother.

In a rare moment, Jillian was dialled into the psychic mother's hotline. "Tom, you can help us by finding a first aid kit."

He ignored her request and tried to settle in next to Liana. Jillian was not in the mood for his nonsense, pulling him up by the arm and shoving him out the door. "Take your time."

Liana tried to process what had taken place as her mother fussed over her. It had all gone wrong in a heartbeat. The force of the winch spinning out of control had knocked her to the deck, and then Royce was at her side. He had definitely prevented a more serious injury, but a glance confirmed he had been visibly shaken. Fear filled his eyes and his hands trembled. This was not the cocky, self-assured exterior he presented to the world. Standing before her was a man who was vulnerable and afraid. Afraid of what she wondered?

"Sweetheart," Jillian interrupted her thoughts. She shifted toward her mother who was studiously examining her abrasions. "Your right hand doesn't look too bad, but the one gripping the line got the worst of it. It will have to be cleaned and bandaged. I'm sorry, but it will hurt when I disinfect it."

"It's alright, Mom. I've dealt with more intense pain than this." Life had taught Liana that the discomfort of a physical injury could never compare to the damage inflicted by emotional suffering.

"This one feels pretty good." She opened and closed the fingers of her right hand. "All things considered, I guess I was pretty lucky. It could have been much worse."

"Yes, it could have been if not for the timely actions of our captain. It amazes me how he was suddenly there the very second it all went wrong. We owe him a real debt of gratitude."

Claire entered the room with a tentative and sympathetic smile on her face. Much to Liana's relief, she was the one who had found the first aid kit. Tom would be on a long and fruitless search. Jillian quickly took the medical supplies from the young woman.

"Let's get your hand bandaged and tuck you into bed so you can get some rest." There was no denying Jillian when she was in full on mothering mode, and Liana surrendered to her tender loving care. True to her word, Jillian folded her into the bedding. Her mother mumbled something about finding Tom in order to prevent any further heroics as she left.

Claire also excused herself. She was heading out when she spied the aquamarine on Liana's dresser. She picked it up and examined it more closely. "I don't think I have ever seen such an exquisite specimen. I am surprised you brought one along since you don't seem like the superstitious type."

"The stone is a mystery to me. I have no idea who left it in my purse." There really was no end to the withdrawals that could be made from this woman's bank of knowledge. Liana found herself wanting to know more. "Does it have some special healing property?"

Claire chuckled. "Goodness, no. The word aquamarine is translated from Latin and means 'water of the sea.' Roman legend says it originated in the treasure chests of mermaids. They called it the sailor's gem and believed it would ensure safe passage if stormy seas were encountered. I know many a venerable seamen back in Boston who believes those legends and carries one for luck. I would love to tell you more, but I must get changed."

Liana's breathing quickened as her mind raced through the possibilities. It had to be Royce. He left the gem, hoping it would provide her with some type of mystical protection. The man had rescued her twice, rushing in without fear or hesitation. He cared for her, and Liana had no idea what to do with that realization.

*****

Anger. Taron felt it course through him. He was angry at the fickle wind, the sodding ship, and most importantly himself. Shrugging off Greg's attempt to talk, he stormed into his room and slammed the door behind him. He stalked the room like a caged beast before suddenly letting loose. Taron swept the nautical charts and instruments off the table and hurled a tumbler against the wall. He watched the glass shatter into sharp fragments and felt his heart follow suit. The GPS was about to receive the same treatment when Greg ducked his head and set foot in the cabin.

"Whoa! Ease up there, Taron. I had a feeling there was going to be a meltdown. Get control of yourself, and we can talk this through."

"I don't want to talk. What's done is done. Life has again seen fit to taunt my ineffectual attempts to ensure the safety of anyone I care about."

Greg shook his head. "You are not going down that road again. I was there, remember? I had to watch you self-destruct in the weeks after the murders. I saw my best friend's little brother take his temper out on himself and everyone around him. You need to pull yourself together."

"Pull myself together?" Taron pointed to the mess on the floor. "Like that shattered glass, the broken shards of Taron Royce were never mended. I have managed quite an effective illusion, creating the impression of someone who is confident and whole."

Greg resolutely faced the raging tempest standing before him. "As captain, you took every possible precaution. It was a random gust of wind, a one time thing. You can't continue to blame yourself for every terrible thing that happens in this world."

"You're wrong, mate. I do not hold myself accountable for the misfortunes of all, but I will not stand by and watch the suffering of those I love."

Greg glanced at the wall separating them from Liana's room. "Don't tell me you've fallen for a woman you met three days ago? You are standing on the edge of a cliff my friend, and you had better be sure about the next step."

"Never been more sure of anything in my life." Grabbing a small case from his dresser, Taron wrenched the door open and left.

He was about to knock on the polished wooden entry of the adjoining cabin when a faint noise issued from within.

"Liana?"

The voice became louder and more urgent. "Help! Please, somebody help."

Bloody hell, not again. Taron turned the knob and pushed. Nothing.

Bugger it! Why was the blasted thing locked? "Liana, it's me. Open the door."

"Royce? I can't move. I need help."

Taron launched into action, stepping back and barrelling into the door with his shoulder. He lurched forward as the timber gave way and nearly landed on the bed with Liana. She was trapped under what appeared to be every blanket on the ship.

"Thank God! Jillian has hospital cornered me into the bed. My arms are too weak to work myself free. I really can't move. Could you—untuck me?"

Taron's relief spilled over into a quick-witted reply, "I am happy to assist, but I was hoping you would eventually ask me into your bed not out of it."

The gleam in her eye told him his jocularity was well received. "Save the teasing for later, and get me out of here."

Liana tried to wriggle herself loose, but Jillian had her completely immobilized. Taron managed to pull the tightly compressed bedding out from under her without lingering on any of her curves. Tempting as it was, his duty was to free Liana from her forcible confinement. Lifting her shaky arms out from under the covers, she gradually sat up.

"The last thing I remember is nodding off after Claire left. Jillian must have come back and shrink wrapped me into the bed, locking the door behind her. It's bad enough that she treats me like I am five years old, but now she has to swaddle me like an infant."

She held up her left hand which was encased in miles of white gauze. "My mother has kept another one of her many talents a secret, mummification. Could you pull up a chair and help me get this off?"

Taron delicately ran his fingers over the bandaging before pausing to ask her a simple question, "Do you trust me, Liana?"

She found herself unable to answer but extended her hand. He selected a pair of scissors from the first aid kit and carefully cut a small slit in the cotton.

Liana expressed her gratitude while he was unravelling the layers. "Thank you for having my back today. It seems you are destined to be my gallant rescuer as you so aptly put it."

"If that is what the fates have in store for me, I would happily live out my days. The sad truth is that I arrived too late to prevent your injuries." Taron's shoulders slumped and a pained expression contorted his face.

"Seriously, Royce? How is what happened to me your fault?"

He picked up the case he had dropped and took out a small jar of ointment. "As captain of this vessel, I am answerable to any of the ills that befall my crew. I should not have agreed to set sail with a rookie crew.

113

People were managing under ideal conditions, but no one had the experience to deal with anything untoward. As a result, there was damage done—to you."

"I was injured, but it happened because of my refusal to let go of the rope. My actions were my own."

Liana gently stroked his cheek, and he closed his eyes. It had been far too long since he had allowed anyone to comfort him. He put his hand over hers as she angled his face back to her.

"Taron, please look at me." He lifted his gaze. Her tender expression nearly did him in.

"You've done nothing but fulfill your promises to me—to all of us. The captain is keeping his crew safe, and Taron Royce is proving himself to me. I don't know if I can ever give you what you want, but you have earned my friendship."

He managed a half-hearted smile. "Then will you allow your friend to take care of you, Liana?"

She held out her injured hand again, and he gently stroked the salve onto her lacerated skin. He paused when he saw her flinch.

"This is an herbal concoction my brother swore by. He used it as a healing balm for a variety of cuts and abrasions. It will sting less as I work it into your skin."

"You have a brother? I can't imagine having two Royce men to deal with."

"It's not something you need to worry about." Taron tried to stay focussed on the care he was providing.

Liana sensed his unease and tried to redirect the conversation. "I would like to know more about the aquamarine you left in my purse."

He stopped re-bandaging her hand and looked up at her in confusion.

"Yes, I know it was you. Claire filled me in on the details. I suppose you thought I could use some good luck after everything that happened in Key Largo."

"I was hoping it would prevent any further misadventures, but it looks as though the legends were only tales told to soothe the anxieties of loved ones. The jewel failed you as much as it did me."

"Failed you, in what way?"

"The gem originated with my mum. She was an amazing woman who was devoted to her family. Mum put her teaching career on hold to raise Daniel and me. She immersed us in the classic literature and theatre she loved. My dad had simpler tastes and preferred to live his life outdoors. He was a fisherman in the small seaside town where we lived. Despite their apparent differences, they were deeply in love.

'Mum worried incessantly whenever he was at sea, and purchased the jewel for him. He didn't believe in superstitions but carried it to help ease her mind. While it did lessen her fears to some extent, she always kept a watchful eye on the weather. As fate would have it, there was one morning when Dad rushed off and left it behind. The boat and all of the souls on board were lost in a squall that afternoon. My father was the great love of her life, and Mum never fully recovered from the loss."

Liana said nothing, patiently waited for him to carry on with his reminiscence.

"When my brother took up sailing, Mum tried to discourage him, but he won her over. She passed the aquamarine on to Daniel. It kept him safe during many sailing adventures and was always in one of his pockets while at sea. He didn't have it with him that night. I often wonder..." His voice faltered and the words caught in his throat.

Liana ran her hands along his shoulders and rested her head on his chest. "Taron," his name was a tremulous whisper. No other words were spoken. They sat together breathing the same air and feeling the same hurt.

He stroked her hair as he continued. "There was so much blood. Mum was gone by the time I got there. I held her and tried to will her back to me, but it was too late. I heard voices telling me my brother was still alive, and I needed to be with him. They were the three most dreadful days of my life, waiting and hoping before he finally died in my arms."

His tears were now flowing freely. Liana cupped his face with both hands gently wiping them away. "Taron, I don't know what to say. I'm sorry, just seems so inadequate. No words will ever be enough to take away the hurt."

"They never found the monster who took them away from me. The villain could have just taken what

116

he stole from the house. Instead, he shot them and never looked back. I should have been there, Liana. I could have done something to prevent it. They were expecting me to have dinner with them, but I backed out at the last minute for a date."

He looked away from her then, swiping his eyes and hoping to dismiss the dreadful feeling of hopelessness that swamped him whenever he thought of his family. He had blamed himself for so long, and even though he had been told time and again that it wasn't his fault, his heart didn't seem to agree.

"Taron, no. You can't blame yourself."

Taking her left hand in his, he ran his fingers back and forth over the gauze. He had put his own desire to have her near him ahead of sound judgment, and she had paid the consequences. Taron wished it was just a simple mistake, but his selfishness could have cost her much more than an injured hand. He stood up, wondering if he should stay away to keep her safe.

"You should get some rest. I need to go into town and pick up some materials to fix the door." Taron attempted one last feeble smile.

"Wait. I—I couldn't let go of the rope."

"Yes, I know. Your injuries are proof of the tenacity in your grip and your spirit."

"It's not just about the rope. Taron, I can't let go."

"Liana, you are afraid of falling, and the thing you need most in this life is the certainty that someone will be there to catch you when you do."

117

Glancing at the broken door as he left, Taron wondered whether he was indeed the right man for the job.

*****

After adding a few stalks of celery to the soup bubbling on the stove, Jillian cringed as she watched Charlie's attempt to chop carrots. He was trying his best, but his learning curve would be a steep one.

Liana's injury meant the vacant spot at the sails needed to be filled. The captain insisted pairings practise together before any final decisions were made. Tryouts were currently being held which meant Claire was needed above deck. Jillian had overcome her doubts about Taron after his earnest attempt to save her daughter. It was once again all systems go with her plan.

She hoped there would be no need for her to reconfigure the teams. It would make sense to pair Scarlet with Shane as they seemed to be showing a mutual interest in one another. It would also keep her hands off the captain. Tom was not likely to remain upright for long on a rocking boat, but a job above deck would keep him away from a recovering Liana. Jillian needed to give a more permanent solution to the nauseous, wannabe boyfriend more thought.

She turned her attention back to her cooking partner when he uttered an expletive. He missed the carrot he was trying to dice. The poor man resembled a woodsman wielding an axe more than the sous chef she needed. Delia was nowhere to be found, disappearing into the shadows once work was mentioned. It was probably for the best since her sister's verbal barbs would find a jittery target with unerring accuracy in such a restrictive space.

Charlie kept his head down and his mouth shut as he returned his full attention to the task. Regrettably, quiet moments never seemed to last long on the ship. Delia hurtled into the room without spilling a drop of the drink she held.

"Great timing. We could use some help getting supper ready. Why don't you grab an apron?" Jillian's answer came in the form of a disbelieving stare from her sister. "Or not—um, could you give Charlie a hand?"

Delia closed in on her quarry. "What are you hacking up there, little man?"

His bold, but ill advised reply caught Jillian off guard. "I may be short in stature, but I have a huge..."

"Charlie, language!" Jillian cracked an egg with more force than she had intended, sending pieces of shell into her brownie batter.

"If you would let someone finish for once, I was going to say I have a huge heart. It is going to come in handy where your sister is concerned."

He turned to Delia. "I think you are a woman who needs a whole lot of loving. That is just what I am going to do, drown you in hearts and flowers."

"Why you pipsqueak—" She dove over the counter grabbing Charlie by his apron. A bag of sugar was sent cascading onto the floor.

He was ready for her, arming himself with a nasty looking butcher knife. "Listen up! You might use your words as weapons, but knives are sharper and do more damage."

Delia snatched the weapon away. Charlie's sudden burst of bravery was sure to get him mortally wounded. Jillian slipped into the infinitesimal space between them. She used the only weapon she had available.

"Who wants to lick the spoon?"

Her sister dropped the knife when Charlie eagerly accepted the peace offering. Jillian wiped beads of perspiration from her brow with the edge of her apron. She would finish the evening meal before setting her assistant straight regarding the futility of his approach. A starring role in this particular version of hell's kitchen would not further his acting career one bit.

Comrades In Arms

"You can discover more about a person in an hour of play than a year of conversation."
Plato

Jillian decided a group breakfast would be the perfect way to lift everyone's spirits. The small cafe had the casual and relaxed ambience she always enjoyed. Animated conversations were briefly suspended for a quick mouthful of pastry or sip of coffee. It was a beautiful day in the tropics, and everyone seemed to be enjoying themselves—well, almost everyone. The sun was already shining too brightly for Delia's liking, so Charlie held a parasol over her while she ate. His ability to finish his meal one handed was a feat of dexterity. Delia offered him bites of food, but his tightly closed mouth said 'no' more emphatically than any words could.

No one seemed in a hurry to leave as they gathered under the coffee shop's green awning. The group was ready to begin the stroll back to the ship when Jillian announced Delia would be accompanying her on a short detour. She needed to obtain some essential items the kitchen was lacking. Her sister insisted Charlie tag along since he was now part of the culinary team, and someone needed to carry the bags.

The Islamorada Grocers was more like a general store of days gone by, stocking a large assortment of items from edibles to hardware. Jillian would have loved to explore, but they were running out of time. The ship would be leaving at noon which gave them only twenty minutes to get back. She had to hurry her companions along.

Delia's assignment was to replace the sugar lost during her skirmish with Charlie. Jillian occupied her culinary apprentice with the promise of hanging the knives within easy reach if he found the appropriate hooks and screws. She successfully kept the two adversaries apart while she expeditiously assembled the items she needed.

At the checkout, Jillian heaped praise on the store owner for packing their purchases in brown paper bags. She was babbling on about the necessity to be eco-friendly and how plastic bags were the scourge of everyday shopping when Delia tugged on the sleeve of her shirt.

"Let's go, Sis. We don't want to get left behind. I would not put it past our captain to set sail without us."

As they emerged into the blinding mid-day glare, Delia realized she had left her sunglasses on the counter. She turned back and collided with a man sprinting out of the store. Delia stumbled but remained upright. Years of balancing on sky high stilettos had its advantages. The mystery man dropped his bags and fell to his knees.

"You clumsy idiot. Watch where you're going," the downed man shouted.

Before Delia could retaliate, Charlie put down the groceries and hauled the man up by his collar. "You stupid jerk, who do you think you are? Apologize to the lady!"

"When I see a lady, I'll apologize. Get out of my way shorty." Delia held Charlie back as the stranger grabbed his bags. He hurried off to a van idling at the curb.

"What a rude young man." Jillian watched as the vehicle accelerated down the street at a reckless speed. Bad manners and bad driving, hopefully the lout would receive his comeuppance one day.

*****

Liana successfully escaped her mother's notice by situating herself in the middle of the walkers as they left the cafe. As she watched the cab carrying the culinary triple threat disappear into traffic, she gave the aquamarine hidden in the pocket of her shorts a pat of gratitude.

Taron led the way back to the ship. He set a leisurely pace which allowed everyone to enjoy the view and settle their hearty breakfast. Liana was hoping to share a private moment with him and picked up her pace, matching him stride for stride.

"You're awfully quiet this morning. Is something wrong?"

"There is nothing amiss. I am just enjoying some quiet contemplation." Taron glanced at her left hand. "Keep applying the salve. It should be much improved in a few days."

"Thank you for leaving it with me. I also appreciate your looking after me."

"It was the least I could do. As much as it pains me to say, I would like to put an end to our game of doctor and patient." A twinkle of amusement returned to his eyes. "Although, I would be willing to give you a physical should you require it."

The trademark grin and innuendo-laden flirting were back. Much to her surprise, Liana had missed it. "That's more like it. The saucy Taron Royce returns."

"I thought you would prefer a return to some formality given my emotionally charged confessions." He paused, looking somewhat uncomfortable, but carried on, "I am sorry if I took things too far. Liana, I did not mean to burden you with my suffering."

She took his hand and locked their fingers together. "It's fine. I'm glad you confided in me. There are some things I want to tell you as well."

"Hey, Liana. Are you excited about the activities your mother has planned for us this afternoon?" Tom barged between them forcing their hands apart.

Much to her relief, Taron did not relinquish his place next to her which forced the nuisance to her opposite side. "I wouldn't say excited is the right word. Any ideas what she has planned?"

Tom bounced along the marina's boardwalk like a happy puppy. "She is being pretty vague about it all, but I understand your role is more passive than was originally planned given your unfortunate injury. I have been assigned a very heroic role now that I have my sea legs."

When he tried to take hold of her bandaged hand, Liana quickly tucked a strand of hair behind her ear. Tom eyed the two of them suspiciously and threw Taron a dirty look as they boarded the ship.

Their second attempt at sailing went without a hitch much to everyone's relief. Her mother was on the move as soon as the anchor imbedded itself in the ocean floor. Jillian was eager to begin the evening's entertainment, rushing everyone through supper. Liana's nerves were once again getting the best of her, and she ate very little. Her mother declared there was no time for dessert, hurrying the women into the salon.

It had been transformed into a makeshift dressing room and seemed to be the point of sale for wicked wench wear. Scarlet surged ahead of everyone, quickly selecting a dark violet gown with a plunging neckline. She had her eye on a crimson ball gown, but it would have sent Shane into a panic. Delia chose a mock necked, black dress with an embossed design resembling snakes or was it vines and flowers? Liana couldn't be sure without getting much too close for comfort.

Claire was having a difficult time finding something suitable. The lacy creation Jillian chose for her had the embarrassed young woman tugging on the material.

"My goodness, Scarlet. Couldn't you find any dresses with a little more coverage in the chest area?"

Liana should have known this was the work of her friend. "So, we have you to thank for the lingerie line of princess gowns." She directed a chilly stare her way. "What were you thinking?"

"I was thinking you need to get a man. The business suits and blouses buttoned up to your chin are not going to cut it. You should choose something that says I'm fun and flirty, not frumpy and frustrated," Scarlet reproached.

"Then why does my mother get to wear—what exactly are you wearing Mom?" The image of her mother in skin tight suede pants, knee high boots, and some type of flowing tunic would likely disrupt her sleep for many nights to come.

"Since I am part of the action, I chose more athletic garments. I like to think of this as my bad ass mama outfit."

This was not good. "Mom, why don't you give us some hints about our after dinner entertainment?"

"It's nothing that choreographed. Charlie and Shane thought we needed some team building activities, so we are having a tournament of sorts. You and Delia will be our royal patrons. The rest of us will be competing on behalf of your respective kingdoms. I have it all arranged. You don't have to worry about a thing except getting dressed. We also should do something about your injured hand."

Claire handed Liana a pair of dainty silk gloves which ended at her wrists. "I think they will nicely accessorize your dress and add to your royal bearing. A lady often gave her knight a glove before he took a long journey or engaged in battle. He proudly wore it as a symbol of affection, hoping he would eventually win her hand. It could also represent a variety of other things such as, faith, loyalty, trust, and honour."

Her mother chimed in, "I think it would be a very romantic gesture for you to give one to your chosen champion. It's probably best to keep the glove on the hand you hurt for the sake of appearances."

Jillian passed her a pale blue dress with a fitted bodice and a flared skirt. "Time for the princess to dress the part and then go meet her suitors. Don't be long, dear."

Liana turned from side to side as she stood in front of the mirror. She had never really played dress up as a child, yet here she was, a grown woman ready to take on the part of a fantasy princess. Silencing the judgmental voice in her head, she would allow herself this moment. She would pretend to be the beautiful girl. The girl who was wanted and loved.

As Liana emerged from the salon, she heard Taron grumbling to Greg about the disparity in their costuming. "How is it you get to wear modern garb, while the rest of us struggle within the confines of period costuming?"

"When you figure it out let me know. I have no idea why Jillian wants me in a police uniform. None of this has anything to do with my life as a plainclothes detective except the badge."

"If I were to hazard a guess, I think she wouldn't mind seeing you in just your badge."

Taron's laughter caught in his throat when he spotted Liana. Heat flared in his eyes, and she felt an answering flutter in her chest. The man could have any number of gorgeous women falling at his feet with the raise of a dark eyebrow, but he saw something special in her. Her stomach twisted in anticipation, and she waited for him to show her the way.

Jillian was not as patient, giving Taron a verbal nudge. "Captain, don't you have something you want to say to Liana—something complimentary?"

Greg interjected on his friend's behalf when there were still nothing from the awestruck man, "Liana, you look beautiful." He elbowed Taron in the side. "Doesn't she?"

"Stunning. Stunning is the right word." Taron took a step toward her but was shoved aside by his competition.

Tom bent to kiss Liana's gloved hand before taking her by the arm. "Might I have the pleasure of escorting the fairest lady in all the realms to her seat?"

Liana gave Taron a wistful look as Tom led her to the staging area. Two of the salon's upholstered wing chairs were positioned on the raised quarterdeck which had been transformed into a royal platform. The competitors were positioned behind the two empty seats. Her mother ushered everyone to their places and took over the proceedings.

"I have..." she paused and then corrected herself after a cough issued from where Shane and Charlie were seated, "We have decided a casual introduction to our costume drama would be an excellent starting point. An improvisational tournament of arms will be held in honour of our royal patrons, Princess Liana of the White Kingdom and..." Jillian hesitated.

Delia stood and proudly proclaimed, "Queen Delia, overseer of all things dark and unpleasant."

"Yes—well, I guess we can call it the battle between light and dark. I will be refereeing the event as well as participating. The teams have been chosen, if there are no objections," Jillian did not wait for a response, "on with the show, as they say."

Shane was the first to step forward. "I will be fighting for the honour of the White Kingdom. Is there an offering from a fair maiden that I may carry into battle?"

Scarlet pulled a sheer purple scarf from her cleavage. Shane bowed and tied the scarf to his belt.

Charlie stumbled his way over to Delia. "Is there something you want to hand over?"

She acknowledged him with a condescending sneer. "You'll get yours when the time is right. Now get on with it."

The two men shook hands and proceeded to entertain everyone with their swordplay. Liana had to admit she was impressed. They exchanged dialogue from their stage show while weaving around the deck. The duel was evenly matched and unhurried with each man getting in his fair share of hits. They performed to the amusement and applause of almost everyone.

Delia shouted at her champion, "Short stuff, catch." She hiked up her skirts and kicked her leg forward, sending a Manolo Blahnik, faux snakeskin stiletto skittering across the deck. Her aunt had excellent aim when it came to footwear, and the red shoe landed directly between the two actors.

Shane gasped and fell. He clawed his way along the deck in his haste to retreat from 'that' colour. It was as if the shoe had reverted back to its reptilian form, chasing him across the ship.

Jillian sounded her whistle. Scarlet rushed off the dais flinging the shoe back at Delia's head. Her aim was accurate, but the woman in black deftly caught it with one hand before placing it back on her foot. As Charlie made his way past her, Delia muttered, "You're welcome."

Her mother regained control and drew everyone's attention to the large target affixed to the main mast. "The next contest symbolizes the battle between old and new. I will be representing the ancient skill of archery." Jillian picked up her bow and arrow and curtsied to her daughter. "Detective Sloan will demonstrate modern marksmanship using his 9mm Glock 22 semi-automatic handgun."

Holding his gun in one hand, Greg pointed it at Delia. He faked a shot with a quick upward flip of his wrist. "Delia."

The deft pacing of the earlier sword fight was lost, and this part of the show dragged on. Liana knew her mother had never picked up a bow an arrow in her life. It took several rounds for her to even get close to the target. A bullseye would be miraculous and take her the rest of the trip to accomplish. Greg's attempts were equally bad for someone whose life presumably depended on shooting accuracy. The two seemed preoccupied with making excuses for each others shortcomings and giving each other advice on how to improve. Greg stood much too close to her mother, helping position her arms. Tom's nausea seemed to be contagious and Liana looked around for the bucket they used to swab the deck.

Delia also had her fill, marching off the platform. She took Greg by surprise when she grabbed his gun and fired one shot into the bullseye. "One for the dark side. Game over and on to the main attraction."

Jillian was mortified. "Delia!"

Her sister carried on nonplused. "Given the waning light, Scarlet and Claire will not have a chance to demonstrate their prowess at arm wrestling. It is on to the grand finale. Tom, a knight of the White Kingdom and the champion of Princess Liana, will fight Captain Royce, a filthy pirate trying to kidnap her royal highness."

Taron vehemently objected, "Oi, I'll have you know cleanliness is important to me although dirty thoughts…"

Delia slapped a sword onto his chest before he could finish and handed the second one to Tom. "Yadda, yadda. Fight to the death you two. Give Liana a good show."

"No, no, Delia. This is all wrong." Jillian intervened once more. "Boys—I mean men, over here please.

They did as they were told and stood before Liana.

"As princess, you select your champion. The offer of your token will signify your choice." Her mother had both men kneel and bow their heads.

Liana knew she was expected to give one of her suitors a glove. Jillian told her to keep her damaged hand covered while offering up the other one. Her thoughts flashed back to the previous night. There would be no more hiding her hurt from the man who had so genuinely shared his own. She slowly peeled the glove from her left hand while thinking about the damage done to both of their hearts. Claire was right. The glove was a symbol. Taron trusted her enough to share the darkness of his past, and she would return that belief.

"Taron."

She put a hand on his shoulder and held out her glove. Liana's breath caught as she saw the answering conviction reflected in his eyes. It was a look that held out hope for the future—their future. Taron gently took her injured hand in his and ghosted his lips along her fingertips.

The two combatants took their places on the main deck. Taron had reassured her that he was well versed in fencing techniques. The private academy he had attended included it as a compulsory credit in their athletic program. Right now none of that seemed to matter. Her heart was beating wildly as he made the first move.

Extending his right arm, Taron slowly circled his sword with a small movement at the wrist.

"For the hand of the princess, en garde, Master Hern."

Tom bent both knees and crouched down. He gripped his sword with both hands while swinging it wildly above his head in large circular movements. Liana could not believe her eyes. He looked as if he was trying to trim the overhanging branches of some invisible tree.

Taron asked the question which seemed to be on everyone's mind. "Master Hern, you do not seem to be overly familiar with swordsmanship?"

"Yes I am. Get on with it."

Taron swept his blade upward as he lunged forward. Tom countered with a wild swing that went wide as the pirate ducked underneath it. The momentum of the stroke carried Tom past his opponent. Taron spun on his heel, tapping the unsteady man between the shoulder blades for a point.

Tom shrugged his shoulders several times and twisted his head from side to side. "I guess I need a little time to warm up. I'm just a bit rusty."

"I've all the time in the world, Hern. Perhaps we should stand closer and begin with both of our blades pointed at each other. I suggest you attack. I will then parry, and you riposte."

Liana took great pleasure in Tom's confused expression.

Her champion was chivalrous enough to want a fair fight and simplified the move. "You go first. I defend myself, and then we go at it."

"Ah, very good." Tom leapt forward and managed an overhead slash with his two handed grip.

The captain easily defended his position catching Tom in mid-swing. It threw him off balance and sent his sword clattering onto the wooden boards.

As Tom retrieved his weapon, Taron rested the tip of his sword on the deck, folding both hands over the hilt. "Hern, where did you say you learned fencing?"

"I didn't, and it's not fencing. It is sword fighting like in Super Smash Brothers." Tom casually swung his sword over one shoulder. "It's such a cool game and much improved from the Legend of Zelda Skyward Sword."

"Hern, are you saying a video game is the only experience you have?"

Tom gave an affirmative shake of his head.

134

"I must call this bout a draw for the sake of good sportsmanship and proper etiquette." Taron backed away.

"Ha! If you forfeit the match, then I win the hand of the fair princess. Tom began walking toward Liana.

No, no, no, not good. Liana frantically tried to make eye contact with Taron, but he already had Tom by the arm.

"Sorry mate, I don't think so. I suggest you prepare yourself to be bested by the dastardly pirate."

It was a declaration of war. The battle of modern gaming technology versus ancient skill at arms raged on around the deck. Tom leaped through the air with his elbows wildly flapping while Taron performed a graceful dance with practiced skill. He scored point after point which only served to infuriate Tom into more frenzied attacks.

Delia was overcome by fits of laughter in between sips of her tequila. "Oh, this is priceless. It's the lumbering caveman competing against the dexterous pirate."

Jillian grimaced at her sister before stepping into the fray and blowing her whistle. She told the combatants to take a short break.

Tom glanced at Liana while wetting his lips and slowly taking his shirt off. "I seem to be quite overheated. I think my technique will improve if I cool down a bit." He stretched his arms over his head, flexing his biceps."

Liana was frozen in disbelief and embarrassment. Delia tipped toward her and mumbled, "Alright princess, time to even up the match. The winner has obviously been decided, and this now becomes a glorious spectator sport."

"Delia, what are you saying?"

"I think the saying 'the gloves are off' applies to shirts as well. Our captain seems to need a little encouragement in that department. Go forth and disrobe the man."

"I will do no such thing," Liana huffed.

Her aunt snickered, "Oh, I think you definitely want to, and it would send a clear message to Tom and your mother."

Jillian seemed to be delighted with the proceedings. That was enough to make up Liana's mind. She took a deep breath before sweeping down the stairs and over to her chosen champion.

Taron watched her approach with a puzzled but hopeful expression. "Liana?"

She leaned into him. "Time to play our little game and send my mother a clear message. Follow my lead, pirate." Liana began to tentatively unbutton his shirt, glancing over her shoulder to gauge Jillian's reaction. Her mother was watching them carefully, but she did nothing more. This needed to escalate.

Liana ripped open the rest of his shirt, sending buttons cascading onto the floor. Her actions did not have the desired effect. Taron's eyes shone with amusement.

136

"You think this is funny, Royce? This was your idea, remember? Start playing your part."

"Liana, I…"

He did not get a chance to finish. Liana seductively ran her fingers over his shoulders, and the black silk fluttered to the deck. She slid her hands over the muscles of his bared chest.

She looked up at him expectantly, speaking in a hushed but clipped tone, "Are you just going to stand there? You are a pirate not a gentleman. Do something, dammit."

"Such language coming from a princess. I would hope someone of your royal lineage would have a more refined comportment.

He wrapped his free arm around Liana's waist and pulled her in tight. His hand wandered lower, finding the curve of her derriere. He gave it a squeeze and then a gentle caress.

The shrill sound of a whistle was followed by Jillian shouting, "Captain Royce, hands off my daughter."

They broke apart and Liana was ushered back to the quarterdeck by her mother. Delia gave her a nod as she returned to her seat. "That's much better. Am I right?"

Liana did not reply. She would never give her aunt the satisfaction of agreeing with her. Catching sight of Taron walking over to Jillian, she returned her attention to the staging area.

He extended his sword arm off to one side as he bowed to her mother. "If you recall milady, it was you who assigned me the role of pirate. It really was perfect casting, and I shall endeavour to live up to your expectations. I will also do my utmost to ensure your lovely daughter is more than satisfied with my performance." He winked at Liana.

The scandalized look on her mother's face was priceless.

Tom was seething with repressed rage as Taron approached him. The underdog appeared to have a new strategy in mind. He closed the gap between them and began using his body more than his sword. He made a rather clumsy attempt to trip Taron by getting an ankle around his foot. When it failed to throw him off balance, Tom tried to kick his opponent's legs out from under him.

Shane quickly interceded. "Master Hern, bad form. This is a sword fight not a kickboxing match. I will have to black card you, and the win goes to our captain if you don't follow the rules of engagement."

Liana knew Tom would not be reasonable and accept defeat. The man was relentless, and well—an idiot. He dropped his sword and ran at Taron, taking a swing. His aim had not improved, but he now had his adversary pinned to the railing. Taron supported his arms on the banister and kicked out with both legs, knocking Tom backwards. That seemed to be it for both men. An all out brawl broke out. Greg and Shane jumped into the action, but they could not get between the two antagonists.

The sound of a gun shot pierced the quiet evening air, and all activity crashed to a halt. Delia stood stock still. She was an imposing presence with one hand on her hip and Greg's pistol aimed at the sky. "Enough! And this boys and girls, is why you never bring a sword to a gunfight."

Smoke and Mirrors

"Life can only be understood backwards,
but it must be lived forwards."
Soren Kierkegaard.

Trevor trudged toward the drop off point on Lignumvitae Key. The site provided the perfect cover. It was remote and contact with visitors was unlikely. The lone dock led to the botanical park's interpretive centre which was the starting point for guided tours of the island.

A shoreline composed of limestone outcroppings made accessing a landing point difficult, so father and son paddled in by canoe. A short scramble across the stones saw them at the boundary of the virgin tropical forest. It did not take long before they were struggling through thick stands of gumbo-limbo, strangler fig, and poisonwood trees. Trevor felt a shiver creep up his spine. Limbo, strangler, poison—everything in this hostile environment seemed to have an ominous name.

Errors in their line of work often resulted in lethal consequences, and Trevor could not keep his morbid thoughts at bay. The roots of strangler figs wrapped around host trees, reminding him of veins and blood vessels clinging to human skeletons. The poisonwood trees were no better. Their mottled black and brown bark resembled some horrific skin disease in its final stages. He could not resist running his hand along a trunk and found it was remarkably smooth despite it's sickly appearance.

The battalions of mosquitoes were the worst part of the expedition. They were intent on extracting every last drop of blood and seemed impervious to the industrial strength repellant both men had liberally applied. Father and son found themselves swatting with every step they took. The reality of living and working in the tropics was not the paradise so enticingly portrayed in glossy travel brochures. Beyond the exclusive resorts lay a harsh world where the laws of mother nature prevailed. Like the crocodiles hidden in the mangrove swamps, his father was the top predator. Trevor's future was guaranteed as long as he reminded at Richard's side.

The duo was almost at the assigned coordinates when they crossed paths with a tour group. His father had concocted a simple but effective ruse in case contact with authorities occurred. Richard deftly handled the conversation with the park official. He was a wealthy nature lover who had been granted a private tour of the island in exchange for a large to donation to the site. Trevor was posing as the interpretative guide in a stolen uniform. The warden seemed content with their explanation and left them to their task.

A short hike led them to the pick up point. Trevor cut through the underbrush with a machete and piled the goods into backpacks. The cumbersome load made the journey back more time consuming, but it was uneventful. Trevor heaved a sigh of relief after they set foot on the yacht. They would cruise to Key West under the cover of darkness before heading out to meet the buyers. The goods would be exchanged from boat to boat during the dead of night to minimize discovery. The thought of several big pay days in his immediate future helped alleviate some of his deep-rooted anxiety.

On rare occasions, Trevor's conscience still called to him. It was of some comfort to know he had not inherited his father's innate cruelty. Richard Hyde was nothing more than a name on a birth certificate for most of Trevor's life. Tired of her husband's criminal activities, his mother packed up and left when he was just a toddler. It would have been easy enough to blame the hardships of life on his biological father, but in all honesty, Trevor had never really given it much thought. While his initial reaction to Richard's attempt at contact was shock, his curiosity eventually got the better of him. Trevor agreed to meet his father, hoping it might give him closure and set him on a healing path. He had no such luck.

The man he met wore expensive suits and had extravagant tastes. There was no hint of the ruthless criminal Trevor would later discover. His father presented himself as the epitome of contrition, begging his son for forgiveness. It was a very convincing act, and Trevor decided to give the man one week to make amends. It was ample time for the master manipulator to ensnare him in his web of lies. The promise of a huge financial reward was too tempting for the impoverished young man to pass up.

Catching his reflection in the window of the packing room, Trevor barely recognized the weary face staring back at him. The young man who had vague notions of right and wrong had been slowly corrupted by his father's greed. Like the tree swallowed by the strangler fig, he was left with a hollowness in his soul.

He emptied the backpacks onto a long metallic table as the boat began its slow journey south. The need for pristine conditions had been drilled into him by his father, and he kept the workspace free from any contaminants. As he retrieved the paper bags from the Islamorada grocers, Trevor recalled his encounter with the imbecilic tourists. The haul had been a small one and easily fit in two of the brown paper bags he had taken from the counter.

Reaching into the first one, he pulled out a bag of sugar. What the hell? His confusion gave way to full blown panic as he emptied the second sack and found more sugar. Son of a bitch! This was not happening. He must have picked up the bumbling woman's groceries after their collision. Instead of four kilos of cocaine worth a hundred and fifty grand, he had six bucks of sweetener. Trevor was a dead man if his father found out. Richard would have no qualms about maiming his own flesh and blood for a mistake of this magnitude.

Pulling out his cell, he did a quick internet search. His chest felt constricted and sweat began to trickle down the back of his neck while he waited and hoped. As the information popped up on the screen, he could not believe his luck. Sugar was often used as a bulking agent to dilute an order. It was one of the tricks of the trade in the world of illicit drug dealings. No one would be able to tell by looking at the product, and it would only be a minor irritant to those ingesting the drug.

Trevor assembled a line of plastic bags and began the task of dividing the merchandise into the portions the buyers had ordered. He mixed the sugar into the cocaine before repackaging it. His father was always the lead in an exchange. If Trevor could keep his fears under control, no one would be the wiser. It would be as nature intended. Only the fittest would survive.

*****

Taron was shut away in his quarters, contemplating the mess he had made of things. Liana had gone in search of some ice and the ever elusive first aid kit while he sat with his head in his hands and a heavy weight in his heart. There were no excuses for his violent actions. He knew engaging in fisticuffs with Tom was more than the need to protect Liana from the advances of an insufferable admirer. The hatred he harboured for the wrongs of the past had never been

144

put to rest. The smallest spark was all it took to explode the carefree exterior he had perfected.

Living under the illusion that nothing mattered had been all too easy. Allowing himself to care meant all he valued could be lost in the blink of an eye. He had not been willing to take the chance until now. Liana's arrival heralded a return to genuine emotions. She brought hope back into his life, and by doing so, the anger he had tried to banish was also unleashed.

A knock at the door signalled Liana's arrival. She had not yet changed and looked every inch the angel come to save him from the misery of his own self-loathing.

"It looks like it's my turn to play doctor." Her teasing words contradicted her concerned expression. "Over here, please." She positioned a chair under the overhead light fixture.

"Let's get a better look at the damage to your face." Liana carefully examined the bruise blossoming on his left cheek. "This is an easy fix. I am positive there will be no permanent damage to lessen your appeal to the ladies."

Taron followed her lead and tried to make light of the situation. "If I told you about the other places it hurts, would you offer to kiss them better?" He tapped a cut above his lip.

"Keep dreaming, Royce." She grinned as she placed an ice pack over the bruise.

Taron covered her hand with his. "There really is no need for you to waste your time tending to nothing

145

more than minor scrapes and contusions. I can fend for myself, and you should try to salvage the rest of your evening."

"Seriously? You want me to go spend more time with those crazies after that display of—I have no idea what I just witnessed."

"I think the best word to describe the events of this evening would be buffoonery. If you are referring to the part I had to play in the grand finale, then disgraceful would be an appropriate choice." He winced as Liana began to dab at small cuts with some antiseptic.

"Please accept my humblest apologies for behaving like a scrapping school yard ruffian and not the man of honour you selected as your champion." Taron pulled the glove she had given him out of his pocket.

"I accept your apology, even though it's not necessary, but I won't allow you to return my token. I made a choice today, and I stand by it. You are the only person who has been honest with me. It's time I do the same."

"Liana, whatever you have to say can wait."

"No, it can't. I'm tired of all the lies. I can't go on pretending everything is fine. Taron, I want—no—I need to be honest with you, and it's not going to be easy."

"I meant it when I said I was a good listener. You can tell me anything." He entwined their fingers and slowly stroked the back of her hand with his thumbs.

She exhaled deeply. "My strained relationship with Jillian goes deeper than her interfering in my life. She is my birth mother and gave me up right after I was born. We only reconnected a few years ago. My adoptive parents died in a car accident when I was very young. My earliest recollections were of moving from one foster home to another."

While her face betrayed nothing, Taron felt her fingers tense around his. He squeezed her hands in silent support.

"I understand the pain and the anger you are feeling, but that is where the similarities end. You mattered to someone. You can take comfort in the memories of a home, a family, and being loved. I had nothing like that to anchor me and help me find my place in the world. I quickly discovered no one was who they appeared to be, and nothing was as it seemed. If someone did tell me the truth, it always served a purpose."

Taron recognized the haunted expression in her eyes. Her heart had been orphaned just like his. He wondered who had been dealt the cruelest blow, the man who had a deep and abiding love wrenched away or the woman who had never known such love in the first place.

"Case workers told you a placement would last only to have it fall apart a short time later. People told you the right family was out there waiting, but no one ever showed up. They were stories adults told kids to make them feel better. None of it was true. It was all just smoke and mirrors. I learned to trust no one but myself in order to survive, and that's what I did. I survived my childhood."

He whispered her name and leaned in until their foreheads were touching. She took a moment to gather herself before pulling away and forcing a smile.

"I do have a memory that started off as a happy one. Not long after I went into care, they took me to see a traveling magician, hoping it would cheer me up. It was a wonderful night. I was mesmerized by a magical world where anything seemed possible. Rabbits popped out of hats, and ladies who vanished from trunks reappeared from behind velvet curtains. I went home believing I could do the same magic. By reciting the magician's exact words, I was convinced that I could conjure the perfect mom. But every time I opened my eyes, I was alone.

When I got a little older, I found a book in the library that explained the secret world of magicians. None of it had been real. It was just more trickery. There was no magic in the world, and there was no happy ending for me. Those things were meant for other people not the little girl no one wanted."

Taron's heart ached for her. The people in her life had all abandoned her. He knew only too well what Liana had done to survive. She had pushed her feelings aside to protect herself. If the pain was dulled, it allowed you to carry on with the pretence of a life. Somewhere along the way, she had also lost sight of herself.

"Taron, please say something. I've said too much?"

"Shush, no you haven't."

He walked her to the cheval mirror in the corner of his cabin. He wrapped his arms around her as she stood gazing at her likeness.

"Liana, tell me what you see?"

The tears she had been fighting began to flow. "I don't really know. I see an ordinary woman in a beautiful dress pretending to be more than she really is."

"Liana, look again. What do you see?"

"I see—I see an orphan. I see someone who was looking for a home but who no one wanted. I see a lost little girl."

Taron tightened his hold. "Let me tell you what I see. I see a woman who has the strength to hold onto a rope when no one else can. I see a woman who is smart enough to see through the deceptions of others and brave enough to face the likes of Delia. I see a woman who is a caring enough to give an angry man a second chance. There is a passionate heart beating underneath her beautiful exterior."

Taron slowly turned her toward him and tilted her chin up with his thumb. He saw doubt emanating from her topaz eyes.

"My darling, I know you don't believe any of these things yet, but I do. Let me be your mirror until you can see the truth for yourself."

"Taron, what if I never do?"

"I will be here to remind you. I won't give up on you. What remains to be seen is whether you will give me a chance?"

Liana took a step back, and he thought he had lost her. Instead of fleeing, she looked up at him and paused. She slowly reached out and skimmed her fingertips over his injured cheek. The gentle brush of her lips followed.

She whispered one word, "Yes."

Truth Be Told

"If you want to tell people the truth,
make them laugh, otherwise they'll kill you."
Oscar Wilde

Delia and Jillian had been summoned to a meeting with the Captain which left Charlie and Shane in the galley trying to prepare dessert. Charlie was struggling with the recipe while his friend was trying to extricate himself from an apron adorned with mint green cupcakes. Only a master escape artist could undo the knot that Jillian had tied.

Shane finally gave up and began griping about his additional chore, "I don't see why someone else couldn't help with this. I know nothing about cooking."

"Scarlet and Liana are working on some special project, and Claire is helping the captain prepare for his meeting with the sneaky sisters. I wouldn't complain if I were you. I have to be the brains of this operation while you get to work the motorized equipment."

Charlie tried to focus on the baffling task of deciphering the instructions. Beating and whipping seemed a tad harsh, and he did not see suitable instruments of torture lying around the kitchen. Shane appeared equally confused. He had no clue how to work the mixer he held in his hands. He plugged it in and played with the switches, revving it up to full speed and back down again.

"Powerful little thing isn't it?" He grinned and continued to play his version of kitchen motor sports.

"Stop messing around and go find me a bowl."

Charlie poured the scant contents of the sugar canister into a measuring cup. It wasn't enough. He remembered the sweetener they had bought at the grocers and emptied the paper sacks. Several plastic bags containing a white powdery substance fell onto the counter.

"Shane, come here. Does this look like sugar to you?"

"It does remind me of the stuff my Gran used to decorate her awful rum cake. It was a special kind of sugar. I think she called it powdered. She shook it all over the nasty thing to make it look pretty and taste better."

Charlie was doubtful about Shane's advice, but they were running out of time. "I guess sugar is all the same. I say we go ahead and use it in the recipe."

Both men returned to the task of making the cookie dough. A minor incident involving Shane's overzealous speed control resulted in the beaters splattering a decorative pattern across Charlie's face and chest. He was not amused and encouraged his buddy to locate a rolling pin while he cleaned up. It was a fruitless search because neither of them knew what one looked like. The instructions said the dough had to be flattened so they improvised. Charlie found a bottle of Delia's vodka and began to pummel away at it.

Shane was trying his best to cut out heart shapes. "What is it with Jillian and all this romance stuff? I don't see why the cookies can't be round."

Charlie wiped the sweat from his brow and took a short break, relieving his thirst with a chug from the rolling pin replacement. "She is going to decorate them with everyone's name and has some kind of fun activity planned. Fun was her word not mine."

He offered the multi-purpose kitchen utensil to Shane who also took a swig. "Someone should really set Jillian straight. She is going about things the wrong way where Liana is concerned."

"I've got more than enough on my plate with Delia's therapy, so you can take that on." Charlie began searching through pots and pans for something resembling a baking sheet. He reasoned it might be similar to a sheet of paper and narrowed his search to things that were flat.

The two men were soon crouched side by side, staring into the oven window in eager anticipation of the end product. The timer sounded and Charlie donned the oversized mitts to retrieve their confections. They both looked at the contents in dismay.

153

Charlie was the first to comment on their results, "Do you think Jillian would believe us if we claimed they were anatomically correct hearts?"

"Maybe they taste better than they look." Shane poked at one of the blobs. "On a positive note, I think we could turn this into a great reality show. How does *Comrades in the Kitchen* sound?"

An oven mitt to the head was his answer.

*****

A quick glance in the mirror revealed that Taron's bruise was stained a menacing shade of black and blue. It was a vivid reminder of the anger he was trying to cast aside. He ran his fingers over the darkened skin as he remembered the promise Liana sealed with a kiss. They had both been painstakingly honest with each other, and she was willing to give him a chance. Their plan to outwit Delia and Jillian would involve more duplicity. He would not add to the lies and betrayals Liana had endured.

He had discussed his concerns with her after breakfast, and she readily agreed with a change in strategy. There was a new lightness and ease to her bearing, and it made Taron more determined than ever to help heal the hurts life had inflicted upon her. He needed to confront the sisters.

The blackened eye added an extra touch of menace to the pirate garb he was once again wearing. Liana had encouraged him to adopt the fearsome personae once more. He would extract the truth by whatever means necessary. Should he fail, and he secretly hoped that would be the case, more entertaining plans were to take affect later in the evening. The winds were indeed shifting, and a dramatic turnaround was about to take place on the Wicked Wench.

Taron was startled from his introspection when Delia barged into the room. The door was slightly ajar which was enough of an invitation for her to enter. Jillian followed in the wake of her sister's blustery entrance. Fashioning his fiercest scowl, he approached them.

"Ladies, how good of you to join me. Have a seat." Taron gestured toward the two chairs he had placed in front of an antique desk.

Jillian refused his invitation. "Captain, we are very busy organizing the events for tonight so just get to the point."

Anticipating her reaction, Taron pointed to the chair and firmly ordered her to sit. Delia had already taken her place and seemed to be eagerly anticipating whatever he had planned. He hoped he was exuding a dark and authoritative air as he faced Jillian.

He began by flaunting his supposed seduction of Liana. "Let me start by saying I had the pleasure of spending a rather intimate evening with your captivating daughter." He paused, allowing the words to sink in and smirked with satisfaction when Jillian's eyes bugged a bit. "Liana and I both have questions, and only you two seem to have the answers."

True to form, Jillian tried to sidestep the issue. "Captain Royce, as your employer and Liana's mother, I insist you refrain from any more of these so called intimate activities."

Her reaction was precisely what Taron had hoped for. "Ms. Barton, is that not why you hired me? Am I not here to make sure Liana completely and thoroughly enjoys every moment on board my ship?"

"I won't allow it. I'm going to have a talk with my daughter."

Jillian tried to get up, but was pushed back onto her chair by her sister. Delia's wicked grin spoke to how much she was enjoying the proceedings.

"As for my being in your employ, this should resolve the matter." Taron reached behind his back while maintaining eye contact with Jillian. He handed her a small square of paper.

She furrowed her brow in confusion. "I don't understand? This is a cheque made out to me."

"How astute of you. As you can see, it is the exact amount you paid me to take part in this charade. This is a full refund of my salary. Consider it termination of my employment."

Jillian would not go down without a fight. "Captain, I will not accept this money."

"You can and most certainly will. If it were up to me, I would borrow Greg's gun and forcibly march you into a bank in Key West to make the deposit. Liana felt you might be resistant. If that is the case, the money will be donated to a college fund for deserving youth in the foster care system. Either way, I am a free man and no longer subject to your whims."

He stepped behind the two chairs, leaning between the sisters. "Let me tell you both how this is going to play out. I am now in sole command of this vessel." He slowly and forcefully articulated the next few words, "This is my ship, and I now give the orders. Are we clear?"

Jillian had been shocked into silence while Delia emitted a half-suppressed snicker. Before either one of them could form a reply, Claire cautiously entered.

"Captain Royce, please excuse the interruption. I checked the ship's library and found a few of the books you requested. I can always get the rest of them at our next port of call. Greg also asked me to bring you some information."

He took the materials from her. "Thank you. I am sure these will be most helpful."

Claire anxiously glanced between Taron and the two women before making a speedy exit.

He sat on the edge of the desk and carefully perused the sheets of paper before reaching around to turn on a metallic floor lamp. Taron aimed the bright beam of light directly at the sisters.

"This is very intriguing information, but it leaves me with more questions than answers. It seems my personal information has been accessed without my prior consent or knowledge. There are also details about my daily routines that could only be discovered if

I was under some type of surveillance. I believe the more colloquial term would be stalking."

His eyes hardened. "It becomes even more disturbing when I find out that my credit history and bank accounts have been accessed. The two names on the requisition forms are Louise Sawyer and Thelma Dickson." It took everything he had to keep a straight face. "I have an overwhelming need to know one more thing." He paused for effect before turning to Jillian. "Are you Thelma or Louise?"

She snatched away the papers. "How did you get your hands on this? I put a secure password on the file."

"Liana found the tablet you carelessly left in the galley. It was unattended and logged on to a page displaying a delicious looking recipe for seafood gumbo. She brought it to my attention, and let's just say, having a friend in law enforcement has its advantages."

"Greg did not hack into my accounts. He would never do something so devious and malicious," Jillian scolded.

"One might even call such an act prohibited or unlawful. It seems an invasion of privacy is easier to dismiss when the shoe is on the other foot. Am I right Delia?" Taron tapped her royal blue sling back with the tip of his black boot.

Delia threw both of her hands into the air. "Alright Captain, we surrender. Greg should read us our rights. I think a pat down is also in order. I strongly suspect a paring knife is missing from the galley, and Jillian was last seen in the vicinity. He should probably give her a thorough going over."

"Unless your recipes include banned substances among their ingredients, culinary misdemeanours do not fall under Greg's jurisdiction. Although, he has been known to make a fuss over a badly baked pie." Taron was ready to put the proverbial icing on the cake.

"Seeing as you have been apprised of my financial details, I believe quid pro quo is called for. It seems I was correct in assuming an undertaking of this magnitude would require exorbitant expenditures."

He handed Jillian a copy of an invoice. "The procurement of this stately vessel comes with the staggering price tag of one hundred thousand dollars per week."

Delia choked. "Jillian! What the hell is the matter with you?"

"Clearly the funds did not come from your sister. Tell me Ms. Barton, how does a Massachusetts high school teacher access such a vast sum of money?"

Jillian's breathing became laboured and she clutched her chest. She had been forced to the rim of precipice. What remained to be seen was whether she would jump or be caught.

"What exactly are you implying? I did nothing illegal like rob a bank or sell drugs from my kitchen. I can assure you all payments have been made, and no laws were broken. I have had enough defamation of my character for one day. I am finished with this." She stood and pushed past Taron.

"Before you go, I have a parting gift for you." Taron retrieved the books Claire had given him. "I took the liberty of expanding your personal library beyond the historical romance you seem to favour. Some nonfiction highlighting the native flora and fauna should broaden your literary horizons."

Jillian grudgingly took the volumes. "*A Guide to Venomous Snakes and Dangerous Insects, Poisonous Plants in the Keys, Wilderness Skills for Beginners.* What's this all about?"

"I am personally saddened that your selfless devotion to Liana's happiness has not allowed you to participate in the geocaching experience to the extent you had planned. In order to remedy the situation, I am hereby revoking your self-proclaimed status as cruise directors. Liana and Scarlet are now in charge of all leisure activities on the ship. Removing the burden from your duties will allow you to devote more time to your hobby."

Jillian seemed on the verge of total collapse. "Captain, the only word that comes to mind is mutiny."

An icy stare accompanied Taron's rebuttal, "And I have three words for you, walk the plank."

Since there was no response forthcoming, Taron continued, "For a mutiny to be successful, it does require the instigators to outnumber the crew. I am sorry to inform you one more person has defected. Tom was very motivated to fill Liana in on the sites you were going to visit. He had hoped geocaching would be a more prominent part of the trip. We will be able to make many of the proposed stops without significantly altering our course. Sadly, we have already sailed past the one on Lignumvitae Key.

'Tom was also under the false impression that Liana would be accompanying you on these excursions. Unfortunately, she will be much too busy with her new role as entertainment co-director. Your lovely daughter will also be assisting me with many of my duties. I like to think of it as job shadowing and look forward to helping her get acquainted with my considerable talents."

Jillian was about to speak, but Taron interjected, "I know exactly what you are going to say. I recognize my plans for Liana leaves you short handed. I would not want to put you in a risky situation, so I think a complement of three treasure hunters is still in order. Since you find it very difficult to be without your sister's company, Delia will be added to the landing party."

"Captain, you may have won this round, but I am not done with you yet." Jillian stormed out of the cabin.

Delia lingered after her sister's hasty departure. She appeared to be deep in thought. Taron was standing with one hand on the door when she finally made a move toward him.

"I had hoped I was right about you, Taron Royce. As much as I love my sister, she really doesn't have a clue where Liana is concerned."

She slithered over to him and gave his chest a few quick taps with her open palm. "Glad to see you finally put the big boy boxers on under your man pants. Good for you."

Taron dipped his head to her ear, "Truth be told, nothing comes between a man and his leathers."

"Even better for Liana," Delia smirked and left.

Games People Play

"Just play. Have fun. Enjoy the game."
Michael Jordan

Taron and Liana were discussing his interrogation of the sisters as they made their way across the deck for the after dinner entertainment. He openly expressed his doubts to her.

"Given Jillian's resistance to cross examination, I fail to see how gaming is going to aid our cause. For lack of a better term, she is one tough cookie. Unless Scarlet has acquired some form of truth serum, the odds are stacked against us."

"I think you will find that is exactly what Scarlet has done," Liana teased.

They caught up with the party planner as she exited the salon with two bottles of tequila. Scarlet hoisted both flagons in salute.

Her grin was as wild as the night they were all anticipating. "Are you both ready for operation Mama Drama?"

"As ready as I'll ever be when it comes to confrontations with my mother," Liana replied.

She felt Taron's reassuring hand on her back. "Remember, I am in full control of the ship, and the rules of the game have changed. Everyone is with you on this."

The two actors had emerged from below deck. Charlie gleefully rubbed his hands together. "The captain is right. I am definitely looking forward to playing my part in our little production."

Shane added his support, "It's time we make some waves where Jillian and Delia are concerned." Scarlet's groan turned into a squeal when he tried to pinch her backside.

Liana was the first to spot the plate of oddly shaped baked goods Shane was holding.

He caught her staring and explained, "We had some problems in the kitchen. Dessert didn't turn out exactly as planned."

Charlie picked one off the plate. "The cookies are supposed to be hearts. Jillian is planning some kind of special early Valentine exchange."

Shane suddenly blanched and hurried away to the main deck.

"Sorry, I forgot. It won't happen again," Charlie called out to his friend.

He turned back to the others. "The lead up to Valentine's Day is the absolute worst for him. Everywhere you look it's red. Our therapist thought Shane would be able to avoid the colour out here. The trip was also supposed to keep his mind off the holiday. He doesn't usually leave the house for a couple of weeks, and it is a real setback for him."

Preoccupied with their conversation, no one noticed Delia barreling down the port side of the ship until she shoved Charlie out of her way. "Alright, somebody said there would be drinks and insults. Let's get started."

The group of friends followed her to a comfortable assortment of pillows and blankets. There was a lone chair in the circular grouping and two swords lay off to the side. The bottles of liquor and plate of cookies were placed in the centre. Everyone took their seats with the notable exception of Liana's mother.

The amiable chatter and intermittent laughter ceased when Jillian emerged from below deck. She was wearing one of Scarlet's provocative gowns and tentatively approached the group. Liana silently congratulated herself on the choice. A tight fitting corset and strapless design ensured an ample amount of cleavage was on display. The billowing layers of white chiffon making up the skirt would impede any forward motion. Liana tried to assume a neutral appearance, but the upward turn to the corners of her mouth exposed her true feelings. There was no way her mother was going to make a hasty exit from tonight's proceedings wearing that dress.

Taron whispered in her ear, "Is the favour you asked of Greg related to your mother's attire?"

Liana nodded in response.

"Would you care to explain?"

She could not hide the amusement in her voice, "Let's just say, payback is going to be a bitch."

Liana escorted her mother over to her seat. "Mom, you look fantastic." She gestured toward the chair. "This will serve as your throne. It also provides the best view of the festivities we have planned for our lovely guest of honour. You are our queen for the night."

The assistance of both Liana and Scarlet was required before the miles of chiffon were draped around a seated Jillian.

Her mother anxiously glanced around the circle. "I don't understand. Why am I the only one dressed this way?"

"Well, it really bothered me that you didn't get the opportunity to wear one of the beautiful gowns during our tournament. I decided to make it up to you. Just relax and enjoy yourself, Mom."

Liana motioned for Scarlet to begin. "Welcome one and all to games night on the Wicked Wench. To get us into the right mood, I have planned a few rounds of a game called *Never Have I Ever*. Here are the rules. Someone says something that is not true about them. If what the person says is true for you, down your drink. There is no need to explain yourself unless you are challenged. Any questions?"

Jillian's hand shot up. "I only see tequila. Where is the white wine? A Chardonnay would be nice, but I could also get by with a dry Pinot Grigio."

"Sorry, no white wine spritzers tonight. You'll have to suck it up and drink it down." The playful glint in Scarlet's eye belied her intimidating tone.

Liana knew there was no way her mother was going to abdicate her throne. Jillian would rather jump into shark infested waters with a paper cut than reveal her secrets. Hopefully, the mellowing impact of the alcohol combined with their gamesmanship would get her mother to tell all.

Scarlet got the first round underway. "Never have I ever stalked a man."

Delia quickly downed her shot of tequila while her mother had a more squeamish approach. She was about to take a reluctant sip when her sister reached over and tipped the shot glass up. Jillian gagged and sputtered requiring a vigorous thumping on her back to keep her from becoming the first casualty of the evening.

"Don't worry, Sis. The first time isn't always the best. You just have to keep at it."

Scarlet snickered while gesturing at Shane to take his turn.

He boldly asserted, "Never have I ever fired a weapon."

Delia and Greg were quick to down their shots. Jillian lodged a formal complaint, arguing Shane obviously meant a gun and not a bow and arrow. Despite a prolonged defence of her claim, she eventually conceded and gulped down her poison with a shudder.

After a few more rounds, Jillian called a halt to the game. She slipped off her chair, landing in a heap of gauzy fabric when she tried to reach for the dessert. "Time for me to have my fun. Charlie, be a dear and slide over the plate of cookies."

He gave the plate a forceful kick, scattering the sweets around the inner circle.

"No! Not my cookies." Jillian picked up the one closest to her. "Where are my hearts? I asked for hearts and these are not—what are these?" She looked at the amoeba shapes and sighed. "Never mind, they are ruined now that they have deck dirt all over them."

Charlie apologized on behalf of the baker boys, "They ended up being a little tough."

He illustrated his point by vigorously slamming a cookie against the weathered boards. While the concrete confections showed no evidence of damage, Liana was certain she spied a new gouge in the wood.

Scarlet cleared her throat and announced the final game, "I think everyone is familiar with the game Truth or Dare, so I will not be going over the rules."

Her mother looked terrified while Delia seemed to be brimming with sinister intent.

Charlie began by calling Delia's name. "Truth. How did you learn to fire a gun? Your dare is to spend the rest of the evening," he lingered on the next word, "barefoot."

The image of her aunt skipping through a field of daisies with naked feet was too much for Liana. She was about to take a voluntary swig from one of the bottles to rid her self of the unwanted image when Delia swore allegiance to the truth.

"A few years ago, I was having a long distance affair with a wealthy Texan. He would fly me out to his isolated ranch and insisted I learn how to handle his weapon properly. What else was there for a woman to do in the middle of nowhere? I practised for hours each day and got quite good at it. I found that if I denied myself for too long the technique suffered."

She leered at Liana. "Am I right?"

Taron jumped in before she could retaliate. "Delia, to you once more. Truth. Where did Jillian get the money for the trip? The dare is to demonstrate your alleged mastery of weapons in combat with Charlie."

Taron was about to reach for a sword, but Delia was already on her feet. Jillian tried to help her sister, but was clearly listing off to her starboard side when she tried to stand. Taron caught her by the elbow, but failed to keep her balanced. She collapsed forward onto the deck. Their sozzled pretend queen crawled toward Delia, grabbing her by the ankle.

"Not fair. She's never played with swords."

Delia had no chance to deliver a lewd reply as Charlie approached her with a weapon in each hand. "Have no fear your drunkenness. I know how to level the playing field."

He pointed a sword at Delia's toe. "I assume you are going to insist on wearing those."

"They never leave my feet!" Delia scoffed.

"Slap a pair on me and it should make us even." Charlie offered proof of his sincerity when he took off his socks and shoes, wiggling a naked toe at his opponent.

Liana came prepared and slid a box over to Delia. The champion of pricey footwear opened the package and found a pair of her Gucci pumps inside.

Delia grabbed one and crouched down to appraise Charlie's feet. "Well, they are on the small side. If this works, it's going to be a very tight fit." She gave him an obscene smirk as she tried to wedge a shoe onto his foot.

Jillian was still stretched out on the deck and seized the heel with one hand. Delia pushed while her sister pulled. As much as they tried, there was no way the shoe was going to fit.

The comical scene had Liana cracking up. "It seems that in our version of a fractured fairy tale Cinderella loses and the evil stepsisters win."

She was laughing so hard tears had formed. Tears of joy. She had always wondered what those felt like. She glanced at Taron who was staring at her with his own accompanying grin. He had eyes only for her, ignoring the absurdity taking place in front of him.

"What?" she questioned.

"Just taking it all in. You seem truly happy. The smiles and laughter are dazzling, and you are more resplendent than ever."

"Liar!" She slapped Taron's arm and giggled.

Liana Taylor didn't giggle. She had never felt safe enough to truly enjoy the moment and she found herself genuinely enjoying this one—the silly games of youth everyone took for granted.

Taron glanced at the shenanigans before turning back to give her a devilish grin. "I wonder who is going to assume the role of Prince Charming in this rendition?"

Right on cue, Shane dropped a second box at Charlie's feet. Delia's adversary tossed the lid aside, slipping on a pair of squared heeled Mary Jane's. They were a perfect fit.

Charlie confessed, "I'm going to be in a play next month. It is an authentic Shakespearean production where men will be playing every part. I was cast in the role of Katherine Minola and brought the shoes with me so I could break them in."

"Enough with the asinine chit chat. I'm ready to crush this pesky little bug under my foot once and for all." Delia grabbed a sword and stepped away from the group.

Her opponent followed, taking precarious steps in his three inch heels. The battle began, and Delia quickly gained the upper hand. Her nimble movements compensated for her lack of swordsmanship. Charlie was handicapped by his foot work and wobbled to and fro despite his sobriety. Delia used her longer reach to lure him in and spun out of range after making contact.

"What's the matter Mrs. Doubtfire, having trouble keeping up?" Delia threw her head back, and a maniacal laugh echoed out to sea.

Liana was rapidly losing faith the fight would end in a win for their side. She shifted toward Scarlet. "He's losing."

Her friend responded in a conspiratorial tone, "Just wait, not for long."

The words were barely out of Scarlet's mouth when Charlie began to move with greater alacrity. Delia was forced to retreat with each of his masterful strokes.

"I was under the impression Morticia Adams was more skilled with a blade." Charlie whirled around her and connected with several consecutive strikes.

Scarlet gave Liana a nudge. "Charlie has been practicing in the shoes since he came aboard. He has been toying with her and is now going to move in for the kill!"

He did not disappoint. With one forceful downward swing of his blade, Delia was unceremoniously dumped onto her backside. Charle kicked her sword out of reach and quickly moved in to end the match. He raised his arm to deliver the final blow, but it never came. Delia took off a stiletto and pointed the heel at him.

"Don't come any closer. I have a Christian Louboutin, and I'm not afraid to use it."

Before she could react, Charlie plucked the shoe from her hand. Delia stood up on one foot as her adversary rushed to the side of the ship. He gulped and held the shoe out over the water. "Give it up Delia, or I'll drop it."

Delia took a tentative hop forward. Her speed was limited as she desperately tried to avoid contacting the deck with her naked appendage.

"Don't make me do it. This poor shoe has served you well and does not deserve a watery grave."

Her aunt had no choice. She conceded defeat to the cheers of everyone. Congratulatory slaps on the back welcomed Charlie back to the circle. The sarcastic one had been defeated—for now.

Liana was up next and directed a query to her mother who had been repositioned on the chair. "Truth. Where did the money for the ship come from? Your dare is to join Greg in a dramatic reading." Liana held out a bookmarked copy of *Captive in the Keys*.

Jillian squared her shoulders before standing. She smoothed out the layers of her dress and took the book from Liana.

"Mom, you will be doing the reading while Greg acts out his part. The passage has been highlighted for you."

After taking a deep breath to collect herself, Jillian began, "Enthralled by the rise and fall of her ample breasts, her rescuer reached out his hand. He ran a finger across the creamy expanse of skin exposed by her low cut gown."

Jillian flung an arm across her chest and slammed the book shut. "Liana, I can't."

"Mom, truth. How did you pay for the ship?"

Her mother opened the book again. "He lifted her hand to his mouth, pressing a kiss to her wrist. His soft lips traced a path up her arm and along her shoulder, lingering at her pulse point before biting— "

Jillian buckled under the strain, grabbing Greg's arms on the way down.

The gallant detective called a halt to the dramatic performance. "I think your mom has had enough daring and drinking for one night. She is thoroughly sloshed."

"Am not," Jillian slurred.

She grabbed the bottle of tequila as Greg helped ease her onto the deck and took a swallow before falling back onto the pillows.

Liana could not remember a time when she had enjoyed herself more. She wasn't sure if it was a sad commentary on her past, or a good omen for the future. Perhaps it was both.

Sadly, they had not yet received an honest answer from Jillian. The evening had literally come full circle.

It was back to Scarlet. "Liana, truth. What are your feelings for Taron? The dare is a sword fight with me."

What the hell was happening? Scarlet mentioned none of this to her. Liana had been duped and backed into a corner. The truth was not an option given the feelings she was developing for Taron. She felt a knot form in her stomach as she picked up the sword. Liana would never manage this on her own.

Relief swept over her when Taron whispered in her ear, "My brave lass, you can do this."

Scarlet began to giggle as she swung her sword. She could not move her feet and the weapon at the same time. Liana was in a similar predicament. She was able to take a step and swing the blade, but she ended up in a pose resembling a still life. Their lack of success prompted Shane to move in behind Scarlet.

Taron pressed up against her back and wrapped his arms around her. The comforting reassurance she felt in front of the mirror was absent. The emotion threatening to overwhelm her was the one she had so assiduously avoided whenever he managed to get close.

"Alright there, Liana?"

She managed a garbled, "mmhm."

"You are gripping the sword too tightly, loosen your hold." Taron reached out and covered her arm with his. He helped her turn the blade with the slow motion of his wrist.

"You see? Just like that." As he nuzzled her ear, the scruff of his chin rubbed against her cheek.

"Let's take a step forward together. Lead with your right foot and keep your sword pointed up." Taron held her securely with his left arm, gradually guiding her forward. He demonstrated how to swing the sword with a slow up and down stroke.

"That's much better. Are you ready to try?" He loosened his hold on her.

She was no longer sure whether she wanted him to stop or go on forever. Liana tilted her head back and saw eyes that were filled with adoration. She couldn't take much more.

"Yes," came out on a breathy exhale.

Liana took a tentative step toward her friend. There was a noticeable improvement in Scarlet's performance. She was eager to give it her all and boldly brandished her weapon. Liana remained cautious and often found herself in a defensive position. After a few more attempts at sparring, she was ready to accept defeat.

Shane suggested a new tactic before Liana put her sword down. "Let's give it a go with a more experienced partner. What do you say?"

Scarlet tossed her sword to Taron, and he awaited Liana's decision.

"I guess I can take one more stab at it," she chuckled.

Taron guided her through a few basic manoeuvres and praised each of her efforts. Liana's resolve strengthened with each parry. She began to feel energized and was soon on the attack.

"That's it, Liana. Trust your instincts."

The goofy grin on his face told her he was enjoying this as much as she was. She knew he was holding himself back and waited for the final blow. It never came. Taron surveyed the deck and suddenly dropped his sword.

"The others seem to have retired for the evening. Perhaps we should go in as well?" He began walking toward the salon.

This was not over. She was having the time of her life. Darting out in front of him, she placed the tip of her blade under his chin.

"And just where do you think you're going, pirate?"

"Liana, what are you playing at?" His eyes sparkled with amusement.

"I'm not playing, and it's not funny. Pick up your sword." She made the words sound as threatening as she could.

"Never let it be said that Taron Royce backs down from a challenge." He bowed to her. "Ladies first."

"Who says I'm a lady?" She came at him with full force. It was not done with elegance or finesse, but she put everything she had into it.

Taron appeared overjoyed and encouraged her to vent her frustrations. "That's right, get angry. After all, I am the dangerous scoundrel trying to steal you away."

She growled and lunged forward again. The sound of steel clashing against steel pierced the night air.

"I don't think the brave heroine has what is takes to properly defend herself," he taunted.

Liana got as close as she dared. Gripping the hilt of her sword with both hands, she hoisted the weapon skyward. Taron's blade met hers at the apex of the swing. He gradually forced both weapons down until they were face to face.

"Well played, but I cannot allow myself to be bested by a beginner. My reputation would be in tatters. Admit defeat, princess."

Liana hesitated for a split second, and it gave him the opening he needed. A quick flick of his wrist had her sword clattering to the deck. She tossed aside any notions of a fair fight. Sashayed her hips seductively, she moved in on him. Taron dropped his gaze to her lips. Liana took full advantage, discretely placing her foot behind his ankle. A quick jerk forward was all it took to trip him up.

"Looks like I win, Captain."

Staring down at the muscular body laying at her feet, Liana found herself entirely too warm and short of breath. She tried to tell herself it was the exertion of the sword fight and nothing more.

"Well done. I concede and hope the lovely victor will grant me mercy."

Taron propped himself up on and one elbow, extending a hand to her. As she pulled him to his feet, her emotion-fuelled strength caught them both off guard. He stumbled into her, and their eyes met in a heated stare.

He repeated the challenge she had issued to him, "Are you just going to stand there?"

Taron's expression was passionate and intent in a way Liana rarely experienced, yet he remained unmoving and silent. The impossibly supportive man was leaving the choice up to her. Liana was tired of pretending the attraction she felt did not exist. The air was thick with unresolved tension, and she was done playing games. All she wanted was to wipe that infuriating smirk off his face in the most delicious way possible.

Liana gave herself over to the moment and crashed her mouth into his. Her move clearly caught him by surprise. There was a split second of hesitation before she felt him unleash his emotions. She knew Taron was trying to be a better man, but there was nothing honourable about his kiss. The bold and brazen attack on her mouth sent a thrill coursing through her. She valiantly fought to keep pace, but this was a battle she was more than willing to lose. The last of her emotional restraints gave way just as her legs threatened to do the same. She felt a strong arm encircle her waist as a hand tangled in her hair. Floating and weightless, she melted into him.

Taron's lips were still caressing hers when he exhaled.

"Liana," he whispered her name with an awe and reverence she and never heard.

"I know," she softly replied.

Liana tried to hold onto to the magic of the moment, but the sound of voices drifting out from the salon reoriented her to time and place. Reluctantly stepping out of Taron's embrace, she took a few unsteady steps before disappearing into the darkness.

Hopes and Fears

"May your choices reflect your hopes, and not your fears."
Nelson Mandela.

Greg watched Jillian shuffle her way across the deck. She was wearing a pair of her sister's pricey sunglasses and guzzling coffee from her water bottle. Even though it was clearly a wretched post tequila sunrise, the poor woman was determined to accompany the geocachers.

Tom explained that the island they would be exploring was remote and devoid of any human inhabitants. He declared himself leader of the expedition based on his full year in the Boy Scouts. The outdoorsman was confident that his childhood training would be enough to ensure everyone's safety. Given the grandiose claims about his sword fighting prowess, Greg could not send the trio of treasure hunters into the wilds on their own. Taron felt his concerns were unwarranted, reminding him that Delia's killer glare would send any potential predators scurrying in the opposite direction. The detective knew the more likely scenario would require him to shoot Delia in order to protect some poor endangered creature of the forest. He would honour his oath to serve and protect.

The group started their trek in good spirits, but the heat and unforgiving terrain soon sapped their energy and enthusiasm. Delia bellowed her grievances with every step she took. Given the decibel level, Greg was certain there were tourists on a Florida beach wondering if the faint cry they heard was human. Her rants were focussed on the detrimental impact of stagnant water on Italian leather.

"I can't believe your only worry is about your shoes. There must be something out here that makes you shake in your boots?" Greg threw an irritated glance over his shoulder.

Delia fired a shot in return. "Did you just come up with that atrocious pun Detective Dimwit, or have you been saving it for days?"

"Lies, she can't cope with people who lie. Isn't that right, Delia?" Jillian finally ended her self-imposed silence.

"My dear sister, I think I have made my regard for the truth very clear."

Greg tried to keep his questioning on track. "It's an admirable quality to have, Delia. But it does leave me wondering why honesty is so important in your life?"

"Living your life with someone who lies is like the swamp we just travelled through. You have no idea where to put your next step because things are constantly shifting under your feet. You are always off balance and never know what to do or say to save

181

yourself. It's a life filled with uncertainty and fear unless you find someone who helps you stay on solid ground."

Delia reached out and gave her sister's hand a squeeze. "Early in our sisterhood, we decided there would be nothing but honesty between us. The only breech of that trust has been Jillian's secrecy around the money for this trip."

"It's not a lie. I just can't tell you right now. My memories of yesterday night are a bit hazy, but I do recall Liana smiling and laughing. She was so happy. I can't take a chance she will find out. What's done is done. If the facts come out after we are back home, then so be it."

"While I commend your loyalty to both your daughter and sister, it is a huge amount of money to invest in a two week vacation." Greg continued to try and guide Jillian toward a disclosure.

"This is more than a holiday. Liana is my whole world, and there is nothing I wouldn't do for her. If the money I spent ensures her happily ever after, then it is worth every penny."

"I don't know much about your daughter's past other than she spent most of her childhood in foster care. I can't imagine that it was a very easy life for her." Greg motioned to their desolate surroundings as he spoke, "I'll bet it was a lot like trying to survive under these harsh conditions. Predators are quick to take advantage of any weakness, and prey are constantly on alert for danger."

"Is there a point to this tale of the wild, nature boy?" Delia's words dripped with sarcasm.

"Yes there is. Even the most deadly creatures can be misunderstood. While there are numerous snakes on this island, we will most likely not see a single one. They prefer to maintain a safe distance from any potential threats. Snakes strike out to defend themselves only if you encroach into their space. The best course of action is to take a step away. The threat and fear are reduced, and everyone happily co-exists."

"Did you just compare me to a snake?" Jillian scolded.

"Sis, it's what I have been telling you over and over again. You are trying too hard, and Liana is not ready. She fights back because she is scared. You need to give her some space before you chase her away permanently."

"All I want is Liana's happiness even if the price I pay is losing her all over again." There was a profound sadness in Jillian's voice.

Any hope of further revelations ended when Tom announced they had reached their destination. Jillian joined him in the search for the cache while Greg spread a blanket and unpacked their lunch. He tossed Tom's empty backpack aside and was about to tuck into the sandwiches when he heard cries of, "We found it."

His curiosity got the better of him, and he went to investigate the prize. Tom was hunkered over a small plastic container while Jillian was signing what appeared to be a log book.

"Where's the treasure?" Delia grabbed the waterproof box from Tom and shook it. "There should be some gold or jewellery in there. Am I right?"

"Haven't you been paying attention? There is no treasure chest filled with gold doubloons." Jillian forced a smile.

"You mean that's it? We sign the damn book and go home? What kind of idiots labour for hours to leave an autograph." Delia seized the book from her sister. "Oh look, you two aren't the only ones. It seems there is one other moron."

Tom held his phone at arms length and stood next to Delia. "We take selfies to commemorate our find and post them online. It will be quite an honour to find a cache as difficult as this one."

"If you take a picture of me looking like this, we will be signing the guest book at your funeral." Delia stomped back to their rustic picnic.

Greg was right behind her, pausing when he glimpsed movement near Tom's gear. A sandwich was thrust into his hand before he could investigate. Lunch was a quick affair, and Tom's version of clean up was even speedier. He rolled everything in the blanket before stuffing it into his backpack.

The journey back was a quiet one. Tom finally ended the silence, defending their efforts. "Delia, I understand your disappointment, but geocaching is a lot like life. It's the experience that matters. You never know exactly what you will find around the next corner. It could be something exciting, beautiful, or terrifying."

Jillian supported her trekking partner. "Sometimes there is a small trinket or token left behind. It's nothing of monetary value, but it links you to a fellow adventurer. Tom, do you remember when we found the cute Foghorn Leghorn Pez dispenser at the Rhode Island cache?"

Tom shuddered as he answered, "Yes, I do. It turned out to be highly collectible, but I couldn't bring myself to part with it after everything we went through. The cacher who left it near the farm had one sick sense of humour. We were chased back to the car by the rooster patrolling the barnyard. I may still have a few scars on my ankles from his vicious beak. Who knew something with feathers could run that fast?"

Images of Tom being run down by enraged poultry had everyone laughing. Their merriment was brought to an abrupt end when a shot rang out in the distance.

Greg reacted swiftly, drawing his gun and telling everyone to get down. An inspection of the area turned up nothing, and he hurried back to his startled comrades. They marched back to the beach in obedient silence. Greg knew the shot he heard did not come from the rifle of a hunter. It had been fired from a semi-automatic weapon, and his gut told him they were in serious trouble.

*****

The relief Trevor felt after last night's hand off was erased by his current state of consternation. The exchange went exactly as planned, and no one suspected anything was amiss. First light saw them back at supply runs, picking up goods from the more isolated islands in the Keys.

As much as Trevor hated to admit it, the scheme his father concocted was a brilliant one. Given their proximity to the major centres of supply and demand, the illegal drug trade flourished, and local authorities were constantly on the lookout for anyone roaming remote areas. Hiding the drugs near geocache sites allowed for the perfect cover. They used the names on their fake ID's to sign the log books and took photos at the cache to further corroborate their story.

While the risk of discovery was low, the trip would be a test of his physical endurance and what little courage he had. It was no surprise when Richard refused to accompany him. Trevor's foul mood worsened when he imagined his father lounging on the yacht while he risked his life. This was no walk in the park. Trevor was hiking through unforgiving wilderness. His stumbles and missteps were punctuated with curses. Besides venting his frustration, he hoped vocalizing his presence would chase away any deadly threats lurking nearby.

An involuntary shudder ran along his spine as he recounted his father's delighted descriptions of the snake paradise he had entered. He continued to take pleasure in Trevor's fear and discussed the potential horrors of this particular outing in excruciating detail. There were cottonmouth pit vipers lurking in the marshes and tree branches, diamondback rattlesnakes in the drier areas, and the small, but deadly, coral snake seemed to find a home in any environment.

His senses were in overdrive, and the need for self-preservation dogged his every step. Trevor's progress was agonizingly slow given the precautions he took. He plodded along stirring the ground litter in front of him with a long stick and often stopped in his tracks to glance up at low overhanging branches. While it was unnerving to think of so many snakes expertly camouflaged, the possibility of a reptilian aerial assault made his blood run as cold as the serpents he feared. His free hand reassuringly patted the gun concealed in his shoulder holster. If threatened, he would not hesitate to take out whatever impeded his progress.

Trevor had the old man to thank for his escalating fear. His father had insisted they watch a movie where everyone was stuck on a plane full of snakes for their evening entertainment. Richard gleefully watched his son squirm in anticipation of the dangers he would be facing today.

Trevor was almost at the cache site and itched to see the end of this expedition. Damn! The all-consuming urge to scratch began again. His curiosity about the unusual bark on the tree at Lignumvitae Key meant he was covered in an irritating rash which no amount of medicinal cream was able to relieve. Richard delighted in Trevor's misery, telling him only an absolute fool would touch a tree called poisonwood. The blunder once again allowed the golden father to remind his tarnished son that he would be nothing without him.

The sound of something large thrashing in the nearby waterway had Trevor reaching for his weapon. The only thing worse than a possible snake encounter would be a confrontation with a croc or a gator. While Richard had an obsession with all reptiles, he revered the crocodile as the ultimate predator. There was only one law the champion of evolution lived by and that was eat or be eaten. His father had a similar outlook on life. If Richard ever had to choose between protecting his son or saving his own skin, Trevor would be the loser each and every time.

Despite the greater weight he was carrying, Trevor felt lighter on the return trip. He relaxed his vigilance, and in doing so missed the faint path leading him back to his boat. He had travelled a considerable distance before he noticed his mistake. Richard would not be forgiving about any delays, but Trevor carefully retraced his steps back to the trail. The sound of approaching voices and rustling footsteps sent him into a panic. What the hell was going on? He should be alone on this desolate speck of land. Trevor crouched low in the undergrowth, hoping his fatigues provided enough camouflage.

A flicker of recognition crossed his awareness as the sound of the unwelcome visitors neared. It was a female voice, and she did not sound pleased. As the group came into view, he recognized the clumsy woman from the Islamorada grocers. Trevor had to be the unluckiest bastard on the face of the planet. Comprehension was slow to dawn, but he eventually realized the moronic tourists must be in possession of the misplaced cocaine.

Son of a bitch! The Keys would be crawling with cops if the drugs had been turned in and an active drug operation was suspected. The terror of his surroundings was soon forgotten as he imagined the repercussions of his father's wrath. He needed to think this through from the safety of the yacht.

Once the conversation had receded into the distance, Trevor ran through the decaying vegetation heedless of any dangers or obstacles. The full backpack limited his agility, and his boots seemed to find every tree root and divot as he fled. He was almost at the canoe he had hidden in the reeds when a nasty misstep caused him to stumble and fall. From his prone position he was certain he saw something slither through the tall grass.

He stood on shaky legs while removing his gun from its concealment. Survival was the only thought on his mind when a faint rattle issued to his left. He fired and ran. Arriving at the shore, he doubled over, gasping for air. When he finally looked up, he saw his father scanning the island from the deck of the yacht. This was bad. Trevor had drawn attention to himself and their operation. He was reminded of Richard's words before he handed over the gun. If Trevor had to use it,

189

there had better be a body with a bullet in it. He was a dead man.

*****

Taron found himself stroking the canvas of the sails as he replayed the events of the previous night. While there had been hints of Liana's growing attraction, he was unprepared for her burst of passion. He had begun the evening with the hope that she might allow herself a brief moment or two of unguarded emotion. The earth shattering kiss that ended the night caught him totally by surprise.

A sultry voice returned him to the present moment, "Hey sailor, what are you thinking?"

He did a quick about face. Liana stood behind him with an easy smile gracing her exquisite lips.

"I find my thoughts preoccupied with the bold actions of a dark haired temptress." He moved closer; she did not back away. "I may need to recreate the experience to ascertain whether the reality was as delectable as I remember."

"Play your cards right, and I just might be willing to help you out. What position would you like me in today, Captain?" She lowered her lashes and rested a hand on her hip.

He gasped in mock surprise. "Ms. Taylor, are you flirting with me?"

Worrying her bottom lip, she leaned in. "Maybe?"

He lifted a hand to her waist, but she whirled out of reach. "Rest assured, any flirting would be most welcome and reciprocated wholeheartedly."

Scarlet effectively doused any sparks when she emerged from the salon. "I'm not interrupting anything between you two am I?" The look on her face was more amused than apologetic.

Taron's libidinous thoughts were put on hold as the rest of the crew spilled onto the deck. The morning's agenda involved a short sail to Great White Heron Wildlife Refuge where they would anchor just outside of its boundaries. Scarlet, Claire, and Shane were eager to do some snorkelling. They hoped to spot sea turtles nesting in the area. Once their afternoon fun was complete, the ship would head back to pick up the geocachers.

Scarlet and Shane wanted to try working the mainsail, and Claire joined her new partner at the aft mast. Emboldened by his abilities during last night's antics, Charlie had volunteered to assist her. Taron assumed his position behind the helm, motioning for Liana to join him.

"I find myself in desperate need," he paused for effect, "of a first mate this morning."

She closed the gap between them. "What are you up to?"

"Ensuring you continue to have the adventure of a lifetime." Taron removed one hand from the helm and took a step back allowing her to replace him at the wheel.

Her eyes widened and her words came out in a rush, "You want me to steer the ship? It wouldn't be safe. What if something happened?" She began to back up, her previous confidence gone.

Taron put his hands on her shoulders, ready to chase away her misgivings. "I seem to recall a lass who knew nothing about sword play, yet bested a notorious pirate."

She glanced back at him. "We were just having fun. This has real life consequences."

He stood firm. "I have every confidence in you. Do you trust me to see you through this safely?"

Indecision and fear flitted across her features before she turned to the horizon. She inhaled deeply and squared her shoulders.

"Alright Captain, tell me what I have to do."

Taron stepped in behind her. The tension in her arms made them stiff. "Relax your hands and work with her, not against her. Try this. Close your eyes and feel the rhythm of the vessel moving under your feet."

He wanted her to feel the same freedom and exhilaration that flooded his senses when sailing. She had every right to experience the happiness and love she had been denied. Liana began to relax against him, and their bodies swayed in time with the ship's movement.

"That's it. Focus on the horizon and hold her steady. I'm going to let you go." He tried to ease his arms away from hers, but she tightened her hold.

"Taron, don't you dare. I can't."

He pressed his body against hers. "I'm right here if you need me." He leaned his mouth next to her ear, "Liana, just let go."

It was beyond any happiness he could have imagined. Standing on the deck of a majestic ship, he sheltered the woman who had begun to unlock his heart in his arms. He was the luckiest man alive.

"I'm doing it. Taron, I'm sailing the ship." Liana's delight bubbled over in a fit of giggles.

She turned her smiling face up to the sun as her hair streamed behind her. Liana had emerged from the confines of her self-imposed cocoon and taken flight on newfound wings. It was dazzling. She turned to gaze at him with the most candid expression of pure happiness he had ever seen. Taron wanted to sear it into his memory for all time.

"I never doubted you for minute," he winked.

The end to his bliss came all too soon. The snorkelers literally jumped ship as soon as the anchor dropped. Taron planned to use the Man Over Board equipment to bring them back on board. Charlie was adamant that he take part in the all important emergency preparedness drill. He disappeared below deck to begin supper preparations after reassurances that he would not be left out.

Liana settled on an oversized chaise lounge. She ran her hand along the canvas of the neighbouring seat, shooting him a meaningful look. "I was hoping you had a minute."

"You're certain you don't want to join your friends?" Taron kept his tone casual as he made his way over to her, secretly rejoicing at the opportunity to spend more time together.

"I could put on my bikini and join them if you are so eager to get rid of me."

Taron bent down and twirled a strand of hair around one finger. "Perhaps you could don your swimwear and rejoin me on the deck."

"I was thinking more along the lines of some iced tea and sympathy." Liana was back to business as she offered him the beverage which he reluctantly accepted before positioning himself on the vacant chaise.

Her attention was briefly diverted by the excited voices of the swimmers. "It seems Shane and Scarlet are getting close. She is planning a special night in Key West to help him get over his fear about Valentine's Day."

Taron had come to recognize when Liana was being evasive. It only served to heighten his interest. "I am certain you did not arrange this private time to discuss your friend's budding romance. What is it that's troubling you?"

She looked down, fiddling with a stray thread on the seat. "I need to ask you something, but I'm not really sure how to go about it."

He reached for her hand. "I have nothing to hide, ask away."

She appeared on edge and stumbled over her words. "I—I wanted to know about the women. I mean—you told me it's a one night kind of thing for you—so it's all very casual?"

Taron managed to keep his bewilderment contained and took his time answering. "While this is not the conversation I had in mind, women have never been a conquest for me. Anything openly offered could be freely declined." He knew she was trying to work something out and hoped it was about furthering their intimacy after last night's heated kiss.

She let his hand drop. "So, you don't form—attachments. It's a no strings kind of thing, right?"

"Liana." He gently took her hand again, waiting for her attention. "The man sitting next to you is not the principled son and brother from years ago. As much as I would like to revive him, he died the day Daniel took his last breath."

She shook her head. "I'm sorry. I didn't mean to bring up those memories for you again."

"It's fine. We need to talk about this if it is bothering you." He opened his arms to her and she scooted her chair closer, nestling into his side.

"I managed to get through my days numb to anything but the most basic sensations. The perception of pain and pleasure remained, but they were bereft of any enduring emotions. If you don't love, you never feel the anguish of loss. It is the creed I have lived by for far too long."

Liana ran a hand along his chest. "You were never in love after the tragedy?"

"There was one woman. I was very much in love with her. We were happy for a time, but the feelings I had for her slowly transformed into something ugly and possessive. I became obsessed with losing her. I deluded myself into thinking the jealousy and anger signified how deeply I loved her. Looking back, I don't blame her for leaving me."

Liana turned her sorrowful gaze up to him. "You closed yourself off. The one night stands meant no entanglements."

"I wish I could speak about it in the past tense, but the need to possess and protect is still there. The fight with Tom served as a stark reminder. I would hate to see you look at me with fear in your eyes."

She lifted her head. "Taron, I am not afraid of you. You have been nothing but patient and honest with me. You have kept your distance and not rushed me into anything."

"I struggle to keep those old instincts from resurfacing. The more I feel for you, the more I fear that I will become that man again. You deserve so much better, Liana."

"If you are talking about the person I met in Key Largo, then yes, I do. You were the embodiment of all the men who have hurt me over the years."

Taron tightened his hold and let her continue.

"My early romantic experiences did not end happily. The new girl in town usually attracted a lot of attention, and I was a naive teenager who was hungry for affection. I let myself believe all of the promises whispered in the throes of passion. Things got old very quickly, and the boys disappeared along with their vows of enduring love. I had my heart broken a few times before I finally figured things out."

Taron whispered into her ear as he softly stroked her hair, "You no longer believe in love?"

"The fantasies of a starry-eyed teen are long gone. I don't know what scares me more, falling in love or never feeling that way about anyone. Taron, what if it's been hidden away for too long, and I can't find my way back to it?"

"You're wrong." He cupped her face in his hands. "The woman I know has a generous and compassionate heart with a tremendous capacity for love. Liana, there is always hope. Never give up hoping things can change for the better."

He reached out to clasp the back of her neck, pulling her face down to his. The kiss began softly. He felt as though he were holding his breath, afraid to break the tentative connection they had slowly been establishing. Taron felt her answering smile as she opened to let him in. He welcomed everything she offered him. It was a blissful give and take that reflected how well the broken pieces of Liana Taylor and Taron Royce fit together.

They pulled away from each other as Charlie's shouted, "man overboard, women overboard."

Liana's chuckle fanned her warm breath across Taron's face, and it was sweeter than any ocean breeze.

"Darling, I'm afraid the real world is calling."

She hid her face in his shirt. "Make him go away. I'm not ready to go back."

The faintest whisper from her lips was louder than any song of the sea. "Your every wish is my command," he told her.

The Home In My Heart

"A little misery at times, makes one appreciate happiness more."
L. Frank Baum

The past twenty-four hours had been the ultimate test of Jillian's indefatigable spirit. Her quiet despair was suddenly accompanied by an unfamiliar weight. She pried open one eye and groaned when she saw the pair of ruined Prada boots on her chest.

Delia was sitting on the edge of her bed, massaging her aching feet. "These," she scowled while pointing to the twisted remains of her footwear, "are a reminder of today's sacrifices in the name of sisterhood. If you can offer me the unadulterated truth about the money for the trip, I will call us even."

Jillian buried her head under a pillow, hoping the saying 'see no evil, hear no evil' might have some protective qualities. "I will be much more personable after some sleep. We can talk about this in the morning."

She should have known her sister would not go down without a fight. Delia reached over, yanking the

199

pillow out from under her head. A sly grin was the only warning she got before Delia whacked her across the face with it.

Grabbing her own feathery weapon, Jillian retaliated. The fluffy fight to the finish managed to cover every inch of their cramped quarters. An explosion of plumage put a halt to the bogus hostilities, and they collapsed onto their respective beds in fits of laughter.

"Remember how much my mother hated our play fighting. She always seemed to catch us after we had wrecked something she had deemed irreplaceable."

"I remember Eve always seemed to interrupt just as I was just about to claim victory." Jillian ducked as a pillow whooshed past her.

Delia's words took on a sombre tone, "I can still hear her syrupy sweet voice reminding us proper ladies did not behave in such an uncivilized manner. It was always about appearances with my mother. Nothing else mattered."

"Her remarks still haunt me too. The sugary coating did nothing to hide her malicious intent. If we ever gave her any real trouble, she would have shipped us both off to boarding school the minute Dad's back was turned." Jillian's eyes burned with unshed tears and her voice cracked, "I did end up there, pregnant and alone. I should have never let her convince me to give up my baby."

Delia sat down next to her. "I believe your advice to me was to leave the past behind. You and Liana can still travel toward a happy ending together if your next step is the truth. It hurts me to see you follow in my mother's deceitful footsteps."

"You can't compare my hopes and dreams for Liana to Eve's treachery." Jillian felt a stabbing pain in her heart.

"I know you mean well, but you are manipulating the situation just as deftly as she ever did. A house built on lies will never survive the storms of life."

Jillian knew her sister was right. Their bond was forged from the strength of honesty, and they had endured life's hardships together. She needed to be truthful with her daughter. What remained to be seen was whether they would all survive the consequences.

Delia was about to retrieve some liquid encouragement when Liana appeared at the door.

"Hey, I was just wondering how you were doing? I heard it was quite the foot race home." She held out a bottle of aspirin. "I thought you might need this to help ease any aches and pains."

"Your timing couldn't be better. We were just talking about you. Come have a seat." Liana took the space Delia vacated.

"Before either of you begin, I have something I need to say. Mom, I don't agree with how you orchestrated this whole thing, but today was a good day. In fact, it was probably one of the best days of my life. Thank you for making it happen."

"Sweetheart, that's wonderful!" Jillian embraced her daughter. Liana had finally found some genuine happiness, and she was about to snatch it away.

She summoned up her courage and continued, "We were just reliving some childhood memories. I don't think I've ever told you about our summer visits to your grandfather's log cabin."

"No you haven't. It sounds a little too rustic for your taste, Delia."

Her sister kept quiet, letting Jillian take the lead.

"We both have the happiest memories of the time we spent there. It was always just the three of us who made the journey. Eve would never set foot in such an isolated and primitive place. Delia and I felt like we were leaving the world behind. We called it the enchanted forest.

'Your grandfather always made sure we had the most fantastic adventures. We often spent the whole day pretending. Whether it was wizards and warriors or kings and queens, we chased each other through the trees before retiring to our castle. The warmth of a fire in the massive hearth heated the common room, and light shone from the kerosene lamps. The whole cabin was aglow, inviting you in."

"They sound like wonderful memories, but why are you sharing them with me now?" Liana looked confused.

Jillian clasped her daughter's hand. "Delia and I still visit twice a year to celebrate Dad's birthday and the anniversary of his passing. It's where his spirit still lingers. I feel it in the trees of the forest and the stone and wood of the cabin. Every time the front door opens on those creaky hinges, I can still see him standing there with his bright smile. His heart was so full of love, and he was such an amazing man. I should have never doubted him, but I did. He was denied an incredible granddaughter, and Liana—oh sweetheart—you lost so much."

A steady stream of tears stained Jillian's cheeks. "I wanted to try and give you back just a fraction of that love and happiness. I would do anything if I could just go back in time and change things, but I can't. Liana, this was the best I could do."

Her daughter's discomposure was evident in her creased brow and tight-lipped query. "Mom, what did you do? Is this about where you got the money for the trip?"

The finality of the moment nearly undid Jillian. There would be no turning back once the words were spoken. Delia instinctively responded to her distress and quickly moved into position beside her.

"My beautiful girl, I love you so very much. You mean more to me than anything in this world. The money for the trip—it came from the sale of my house."

Delia was the first to regain the power of speech. "Jillian! Oh, for the love of God."

Liana swayed and her hand slipped from Jillian's grasp. The seconds ticked by in shocked silence. Her voice quavered as she stood on tremulous legs, "No, you didn't." She shook her head back and forth. "You didn't give up your home for me. You need to get it back."

Jillian was living her worst nightmare. She tried to reach out, but Liana pulled away. "Baby, I can't. The deal is final, and I move out the week we return. Please try to understand. It is only a house. When I lock the door for the final time, I will be leaving behind the empty shell of a structure, nothing more. Home is in your heart. It's the comfort and the happiness you feel when you are truly loved. Liana, let me do this for you."

"You love that house. Your life savings are invested in it. Mom, now you have nothing."

"Liana, I love you. I still have everything that matters, you and Delia. I would happily live out my days on the street if it meant the three of us could always be together."

Liana's gaze was fixed on the door. Jillian knew she was getting ready to run and did the best she could to prevent it.

"You don't need to worry about me. I have made temporary arrangements to stay at a hotel. I am sure something will turn up because these things always work out."

Delia's eyes shimmered as she patted her sister's hand. "You will do no such thing. You are going to come live with me."

As Jillian turned to embrace her sister, Liana bolted from the room.

"No!" Jillian leapt off the bed, but her sister quickly pulled her into a hug."

"You have to let her go. My dear sister, I promise she will get through this. We all will."

*****

Liana tore out of the room and sprinted up the stairs two at a time. Tripping on the last step, she scrambled onto the deck on her hands and knees. It was all too much. Her mother's sacrifice was too great. Righting herself, she sprinted to the side of the ship. There was nowhere to run. She was surrounded by ocean.

As she paced alongside the handrail, Liana thought she heard someone calling her name. It sounded so far away. Her body was trembling and her eyes were blown wide as she turned toward the sound. Someone was drawing closer, too close. She desperately tried to take a breath, but her chest felt like it was being squeezed by some massive unseen force. Her stomach was rolling with nausea as she launched herself past the shadowy figure, rushing to the opposite side of the ship. The adrenaline pumping through her system overwhelmed her senses. She had to get away.

Just as she put a leg over the railing, powerful arms surrounded her and pulled her back. "Liana. Liana, my love. It's Taron."

The voice was calm and reassuring. Taron. He had come to her rescue again.

"Darling, you need to breathe. Give it a minute, and it will be over. I promise."

The unfamiliar sensations of being safe and protected wrapped around her as securely as his arms. She collapsed onto the deck. As her panic eased, she felt Taron release his hold. He placed her hands on his chest, covering them with his own.

"Breathe with me." He inhaled and exhaled deeply, encouraging her to do the same. "Just like that."

She focussed on the slow rise and fall of his chest. The rhythmical heartbeat under her fingers was strong and steady.

"Shhh, my love. I won't let anyone hurt you. It's just us Liana—just us."

It could have been minutes or hours that passed. Time no longer mattered as she was rocked in Taron's embrace.

"She sold her house." Her words began quiet and flat, but gained in volume as she spoke, "Jillian gave up her home to pay for the ship." Like tearing off a band aid, she hoped it might hurt less if she said it quickly.

"My mother will have nothing left when this trip is over. Nothing. It's too much and I'm not…" She could no longer choke back the sobs.

"Liana Taylor, don't you dare tell me you are not worth such a magnanimous gesture."

She gripped the fabric of his shirt. Drowning. She was drowning in pain and he was her lifeline.

"Jillian told me she gave up her home so I could find my happiness. She thinks it was a fair exchange.

That's the irony of it all. I had just finished telling her I finally had the best day of my life. Now look at me. I'm shattered. She made a poor investment banking her life savings on me."

"Don't do this to yourself, Liana. You have had a shock and need time to make sense of it all."

She looked into the fathomless depths of his turquoise eyes and saw no judgment only compassion and understanding.

Taron put a guiding hand on her elbow and helped her stand. "Let's get you back to your cabin."

She fell into him and burrowed her face in his neck. "No. Please don't leave me."

"I'm not going anywhere. Shall we head back to my quarters then?"

She nodded her consent and leaned on his arm. They took each step together.

Walking into his room, Liana knew there was one more thing she needed. "Taron, would you mind getting the wooden box on my dresser."

"Not at all. You'll be alright settling yourself in?"

"Yes, just hurry back."

She eased herself down on the bed and drew a patchwork quilt over her. Curling into herself, she squeezed her knees into her chest. She was overcome with the need to make herself as small as possible. If she could wink herself out of existence, maybe the fear would disappear as well. A bone-weary exhaustion settled in as the physical sensations began to fade, but the continuous loop of negative thoughts continued.

She had humiliated herself, and Taron had witnessed the full extent of her imperfections.

She felt a warm hand begin to rub her back. The box with her treasured remembrance was placed in her hand, and she curled her fingers around it.

"I'm sorry," she murmured.

"Why on earth are you apologizing? There is nothing to be sorry for."

"Yes, there is. I lost control and what you saw is the real me. I'm a mess."

She felt the warmth of his hand caressing her face as he crouched next to the bed.

"Never be ashamed to show me what you are feeling."

Liana wiggled sideways, making room for him. He stretched out next to her and pulled her into his arms.

"How long have you been having the panic attacks?"

She rested her head on his chest, needing to hear the reassuring rhythm of his heart once more.

"They come and go. I thought I was rid of them once I opened the doors to The Wayfaring Swan. I was finally in control of my life. My choices were my own and there was a consistent routine to each day. Jillian came along and upset the order of things. Her intrusions were always so unsettling. The anxiety has been building, but I've never felt anything like I did tonight."

She looked up at him with the barest hint of a smile. "You were amazing. You knew exactly what I needed and—" Her voice hitched as the realization hit her. "You've felt this way too, after the murders."

He nodded slowly. "Yes, I did. But my anguish manifested itself in a different manner. It felt more like a blackness which rolled in and engulfed me."

"What did you do?"

"Like you, I tried to ward off the feelings. Escape came in many different forms. I drank too much, fought at the slightest provocation, and shut myself away from the world." He tried to sound nonchalant, but there was a pain underlying his tone.

"Was there no one who tried to help you?" It hurt to think of him battling his demons alone.

"Greg was there for me when I was at my worst. He would come round to sober me up and drag my sorry arse out to the boat. We would spend the day sailing. Things seemed easier out on the water. I found myself looking forward to the trips, and that is when I recognized the error of my ways. Liana, you can't keep fighting off the darkness. You have to move toward the light. Like a sliver of sunshine forcing it's way between two battered planks of wood, you try to find the smallest beacon of hope. You keep moving toward it, and one day you will find yourself standing in brilliant sunshine wondering how you got there."

"And when was that for you?"

"Today, when we were sailing, and I held you in my arms."

"Taron, I don't know what to say."

"Then don't say anything." He dipped his head and pressed his lips to hers. She relaxed into the kiss, savouring the taste and feel. He was giving her everything, and it felt like home. She murmured her contentment, and he answered with a sigh.

"Mmm, I like the way you kiss." She was floating in a blissful haze.

"I assure you the feeling is mutual. My lips are always at your disposal. Feel free to indulge yourself whenever you wish," he teased.

"I really should wipe that smug look of self-satisfaction off your face." Liana tipped her head to the side to look at him.

"I think I would thoroughly enjoy myself if you did."

She marvelled at the number of times this man had beaten back her fear and returned her peace of mind. The day ended exactly as it began. She was happy.

Trying to stifle a yawn with her hand, she was caught by her ever watchful protector.

"I think you need some sleep." He got up and tucked the quilt around her.

"Not yet." She opened the box and placed the feather in the palm of her hand. "You were right, it is a swan feather. It's the last one. I don't want to forget but…"

Liana hesitated, caught up in the sadness of her memories. She focussed on her breathing as she watched Taron delicately brush a finger along the plume.

210

"I have scattered the others around the world during my travels, but I just can't seem to let this one go. This trip seemed like the perfect opportunity. I wanted this last one to take flight on a breeze over the open water."

Taron closed her fingers around the precious memento. He kissed her forehead while smoothing back her hair. "You will know when the time is right. As for tonight, there is no need to discuss anything further."

Like she had done so many nights before, she tucked the feather under her pillow. It always brought her relief in the sweetest of dreams. Breaking the ties binding her to the pain of the past, she would soar on white wings until wakefulness brought her back to earth. As she drifted off to sleep, she heard a wish for her to sleep well and have pleasant dreams.

She did both.

A Small World

"Little things make big things happen."
John Wooden

The ship had set sail at first light and was now safely docked in Key West. Delia could not have been happier. She had returned to civilization and there would be no domestic chores, slogging through swamps, or sword fights for the rest of the day. It was a disgruntled group of travellers who joined her for an early morning shopping expedition. Her mangled boots needed to be replaced and that meant a pilgrimage to the ultimate shrine for designer shoes. Her toes tingled in anticipation.

In stark contrast, Jillian remained despondent after her staggering confession. While Delia was impatient to see a return to her perky optimism, she knew it was too soon to try reconciling mother and daughter. She managed to convince Greg to join them, hoping that the presence of the unattached detective would help ameliorate Jillian's somber mood. He was trying his best to engage her sister in conversation, but there was no response. This was serious.

As they aimlessly wandered the streets of Key West, Greg was the first to voice his displeasure. "Delia, are you sure we don't need the GPS to locate this store? I don't understand how '!' can be the name of a business?"

"And what would an out of style police officer know about the latest trends?" Delia gave Greg a haughty look before enlightening the group. "The most exclusive stores have adopted a minimalist philosophy. Names have gone from one word to a single letter. The next step is self-explanatory to any sophisticated buyer."

She noticed Charlie taking a few steps back before he joined the conversation. "I think Delia can sniff out the leather of those fancy designer shoes from miles away, so I'm not worried. She is like those pigeons with the little notes attached to their legs. They always seem to find their way home."

Finely tuned reflexes allowed Greg to duck behind Delia before she could retaliate. She made very little effort. It had been a lot of walking, and her feet were getting tired.

Jillian finally spoke up when a display in a store window caught her eye. "Delia, these look very sensible, let's stop here and replace your boots."

The offensive offerings elicited a derisive retort. "Those are Birkenstocks. Do I look like some tree hugging environmental do-gooder?"

"I think they are a very practical choice in footwear." Jillian cast an encouraging look at Greg who had accessorized his brightly patterned board shorts with the aforementioned sandals and a pair of white sport socks.

Any further debate on fashion versus functionality was halted when Charlie exclaimed, "We found it."

As Delia breezed her way into '!', she felt like an expatriate returning to the motherland. She was home.

Jillian and Greg collapsed into the plush seating. Charlie was hot on her heels, shadowing her around the store. He seemed to have an inordinate interest in the merchandise. She grabbed his arm just as he was about to reach for a gold, sequin-encrusted Dolce and Gabbana.

"Don't touch them with those sweaty palms. The moisture and salt will compromise the structure of the leather. Why aren't you resting with those two?" She pointed in the direction of their weary companions.

"The shoes I bought for my debut in the Taming of the Shrew are rather plain. I thought I might find something jazzier. The sixteenth century gowns will come just above our ankles so I thought…"

Delia held out the price tag on the pair he had been admiring.

"Shit!" escaped before Delia could clap a hand over his mouth.

'Keep your voice down you troglodyte," Delia muttered.

Unfortunately, Charlie had already drawn the attention of the sales assistant.

She turned and addressed the clerk, "He's having a little religious experience. You know how it is with the Gabbana's."

"Darlings, I've had people faint dead away when the new Alexander McQueen's arrive. Works of art, you know."

"It is so nice to meet a fellow devotee." Delia glanced at his name tag, "Victor."

A pair of black ankle boots with silver skull zipper pulls were added to Delia's collection. Charlie was pleased to hear the golden pumps he coveted came in a size nine extra wide. Delia was quick to take advantage. She agreed to pay the shoes, guaranteeing the future indebtedness of short and stocky.

She caught Victor sliding an appraising eye over Charlie as he wrapped their purchases. "I know a boutique around the corner where you could get a sexy little dress to match these."

Charlie bashfully replied, "I already have a gown to wear for my performance."

"You perform on the stage in women's clothes?" Victor stared at him in amazement.

"Not yet, but this time next month, I will be making my debut."

Victor tapped a finger against his cheek. "You don't seem the type, but who am I to judge? There is a great club on First Avenue if you want to take those little gems out for a trial run. I'm sure an impromptu performance could be arranged."

"That sounds great!" Charlie beamed.

Delia stood behind her obtuse friend and rolled her eyes.

Victor gave them both a wink as he tucked a business card into their purchases. "If I'm not around, tell them you're my friends. You will be well looked after."

*****

Further down the street, Trevor was anxiously drumming his fingers on the table of a sidewalk cafe while sipping a beer. The casual conversations suspended in the humid tropical air could not distract him from his worries or his pain. Pressing the cold bottle to the abrasions on his wrists helped soothe the sting. His father had forced him to wear handcuffs during the trip to Key West as a reminder to control his itchy trigger finger. Richard had not decided whether further disciplinary measures would be necessary after they reboarded the yacht. Watching Trevor squirm every time he dropped a hint would provide his father with a full day's entertainment.

He cast an uneasy glance across the street each time a patron exited the gilt edged door of the tobacconist. Richard was going to take his time. He would slowly savour the aroma of each expensive cigar before making his purchase. It was a happy coincidence that the contact point for their regular buyers also

216

fuelled his father's addiction. Images of Richard dying a slow and painful death from a variety of nicotine induced diseases helped Trevor pass the time. He was daydreaming about a particularly gruesome end when he heard a familiar voice.

Damn. How could anyone be so unlucky? A hurried look confirmed his suspicions. It was the loud mouthed woman from the grocers and the geocache site. As the group made their way past the pub, Trevor quickly dropped to his hands and knees and hid under the table. The arguing voices had barely faded into the distance when his father's shout sent another chill racing down his spine.

"Son! Why are you crouched under the outdoor furniture like some twitching rodent?"

"Sorry, father. You know how clumsy I can be. I dropped my cell and couldn't quite reach it."

"Well, get out from under there. We have serious business to discuss."

In his rush to comply with his father's demand, Trevor lunged forward and fell. He caught his father's disgusted expression as he rolled out from under the table.

"I bought you shoes with velcro instead of laces so you wouldn't trip over your own two feet. You need to fasten them for that to work. Now, get up."

Richard held out a hand. Of course, he would use his left arm knowing how much Trevor hated the repulsive tattoo stretching from his elbow to his wrist. An offer of help was never what it seemed when it came to the old man. The ink hinted at a savage and secretive past that Trevor hoped would never be revealed. As he got to his feet, his face was inches from the lidless crocodilian eye embedded in the hilt of the ornate dagger. The point of the knife pierced a bloodied heart with the words "occidere aut occidi" carved into it. Kill or be killed. The words bound him to his father more securely than any metal restraints ever could.

"Change of plans for tonight, son. The head of the organization has requested a meeting. We take the boat out after midnight and rendezvous at sea." Richard's lips twisted into a sinister smile. "The big boss never comes out to meet his minions. There must be an enormous deal coming our way."

*****

As Taron watched each person come through the patio doors of the Inn-Chanted Evening, he recalled sitting alone at another table after Liana stormed out. The cantankerous tourist he rescued in Key Largo was now a distant memory. She had been transformed into the remarkable woman who now held his heart captive. While he longed to show her an unforgettable night, he was unsure how to proceed. Scarlet had reserved an extra room at the Inn, but Taron had no idea if Liana was ready for such intimacy.

"Deep in thought, I see."

Taron immediately jumped to his feet and held out a chair for her.

"Thinking only of you."

218

Liana skimmed her hand along his forearm. "I missed you too."

"I take it Scarlet made her way back to the ship?"

"Yes. She said something about running lines with Charlie and Shane." A worried expression accompanied her words, "Is it really necessary to have someone on board the ship at all times? Greg has notified the local authorities, and there is no proof of any criminal activity."

"All the more reason to take the necessary precautions. An increase in patrols is unlikely given the lack of tangible evidence. I trust Greg's instincts. If he says we need to be on the look out for trouble, then that's what we do."

The waiter approached their table, halting any further discussion on the matter. Taron set out in a new direction after their orders had been taken.

"How did you and Scarlet manage to pass the time in my absence?"

"Just doing a little shopping. Scarlet still had a few loose ends to tie up for tonight. I did not just say that! Knowing her, she just might use some rope." A blush made it's way to her cheeks. "Let's just say she has devised her own therapeutic plan for Shane. It involves red lingerie and a Valentine themed room. She is either going to kill him or cure him."

Taron tilted his head as he laughed and saw an innocent looking white bag hidden under the table. He bent over to get a closer look. *Fashion for Passion* was embossed on the paper. "I see you also made a purchase. Would it be ill advised to request a quick peek, or were you planning a private unveiling at a more leisurely pace?"

"What if I were to offer you an invitation?"

The provocative tone in her voice set his heart racing as did the hand she discretely placed on his knee.

"I would wholeheartedly accept and delight in envisioning the many ways such a generous gift could be unwrapped." He reached for her hand in a playful gesture, and then pressed a tender kiss to her fingertips.

"This is working, isn't it?"

"If you are referring to the arousing images competing for my attention, consider your task accomplished."

"I mean this." Liana gestured at their surroundings. "I was worried that once we left the fantasy world my mother created things might change between us. But it hasn't. This still feels right."

Taron silently berated himself for not considering how anxious she must still feel. Of course, their shore leave would be unsettling. Life on the ship had sheltered them from the concerns of ordinary life. The passing of each day only served to strengthen what he felt, but this was all so new for Liana. He found himself once again reaching for her hand.

"Never doubt my feelings for you. I know our relationship began in a contrived manner, but rest assured I would choose you no matter the time or place. What I'm trying to say is—I mean—" Taron suddenly felt like an awkward teenager, waiting for the inevitable rejection. "I want to ask you something."

Liana gave him an inquisitive stare.

"Might I request the pleasure of your company this evening?"

"Are you asking me out on a date?"

"I am."

The delay in her response and the playful glint in her eye unsettled him.

"I'm sorry, but my answer is no. I already have plans for this evening."

Taron found taking his next breath difficult.

"You see, there is this good looking sailor in town just for one night. I have made some very special arrangements, and I would hate to disappoint him."

"Disappointment would not even begin to describe the depths of his despair. He is a most fortunate man indeed." He exhaled in relief.

Liana dropped her gaze to the table and nervously toyed with her napkin. "There you go again. You always find the right thing to say in any situation. I'm not confident putting my feelings into words. Until a few days ago, I was still trying to hide my emotions. I guess what I'm trying to say is…" Her words trailed off as she looked away.

"As opposed to my proclivity for verbiage, you would like to express yourself with actions?"

"Yes," she answered.

"I accept, and I look forward to a perfect evening." He gave her a reassuring smile.

"I do want it to be perfect. Taron, you have been so devoted in your efforts to make this a fantastic experience for me. I know I didn't make things easy for you at the start, and I just want to show you how much I appreciate everything you have done for me."

"Liana, you don't have to…"

She touched her fingers to his lips. "Shush, let me finish. I've never had anyone come close to understanding me the way you do. I was attracted to you from the moment we met and it did scare the hell out of me." Her hand slipped to the side of his face. "Thank you. Thank you for not giving up on me."

"Never." He kissed her wrist.

Their food arrived and the rest of the conversation flowed as easily as the wine. There were so many things they were eager to share with one another. Taron found no detail was inconsequential where Liana was concerned. Her every word held his rapt attention.

They were about to share a luscious slice of key lime pie when they heard a woman's voice ask, "Liana? Liana Taylor is that you?"

Liana warmly greeted the newcomers. "What a pleasant surprise. You two are on holiday again?"

"You know us, we can't seem to stay in one place for too long. There is so much of the world to still explore." The sprightly senior gave Taron a warm look.

"Judy and Bill this is my…" she paused, unsure how to introduce him.

Taron stood and reached out to shake hands. "Taron Royce, it's a pleasure."

222

"Can't stay more than a minute or two. We are off to find the buoy marking the southernmost point in the continental United States. You now how Bill likes to document these milestones with a photo op." The affable couple beamed at each other.

"Judy and Bill were very special clients of mine. I arranged a holiday in Tahiti for them."

Bill voiced his disapproval, "A holiday, is that what you call it? This incredible women gave us a fortieth wedding anniversary we will never forget. Renewing our vows in front of the most glorious waterfall as the sun set over the distant mountains. It was everything we had ever dreamed about and more."

Judy agreed with her husband. "It is still the most magical moment we have ever had, and there have been so many with this wonderful man."

Bill returned the loving gaze of his spouse. "Even after all these years, there is nothing I wouldn't do for my beautiful bride. I love her as much today as the very first time we met."

A peal of joyful laughter rang out. "William, don't you mislead this lovely couple. Our story was not love at first sight."

"I do remember a few colourful words were exchanged as I tried to get your hand out of the drain. Going after the friendship ring that muscle-bound jock gave you, what were you thinking?" Bill gently massaged her wrist as if the incident had just occurred.

"Luckily, I did. A dashing hero came to my rescue. It just took me a little while to figure it out."

Judy pulled Bill along by his arm. "Come along dearest. We've taken up enough of their time. You two lovebirds enjoy the rest of your afternoon."

Liana waved goodbye before turning her attention back to Taron. "They really are the most devoted couple. I'll have to fill you in on the rest of their story one day."

Taron's mind was preoccupied with thoughts of the future. He could see the next forty years clearly unfolding with Liana at his side. Lovebirds. It was a very fitting description. Taron Royce was indeed in love.

To Have and Have Not

*"You can't get away from yourself
by moving from one place to another."*
Ernest Hemingway.

Ten more minutes until Taron arrived for their date.
Liana was having difficulty keeping her jitters under
control and fussed with her hair for what seemed like the
hundredth time. An updo was a drastic change for her,
and she worried it might all collapse in a gust of wind.
More pins were needed, just to be sure. That was the real
problem, she wasn't sure about anything right now.
While she had promised Taron a perfect evening, she
had very little experience to drawn upon. Liana did not
plan dates. She just showed up at the appointed time and
place.

Thinking about all of the women Taron had dated
sent her stomach rolling. She had tried to conjure the
most romantic setting she could, but now worried it
might be too much. Dammit! She dropped the earring
she was trying to fasten with shaky fingers. After taking a
few steadying breaths, she managed to secure the delicate

pearl. She did a final check of her appearance in the room's full length mirror, shifting her position so she could check the front and back of her dress. The navy bodice was sleeveless and form fitting to the waist. It flowed into pleated panels alternating with a gossamer fabric. The delicate ankle length dress wafted around her when she took a few steps and spun. At the very least, she felt like she looked the part of elegant leading lady.

One week with Taron was all it took to drastically alter her neatly arranged world. He had shown her moments of pure joy and she craved more. Tonight was about new beginnings and a future they would move toward together. There was no pressure. None at all. A sharp knock roused her from her thoughts. Her date was here. She took one last glance in the mirror before letting him in.

"Hi." It was all she managed to stammer as she took in the man framed in the doorway.

Navy pants were paired with a crisp white shirt and a pale blue tie. The sleeves of the shirt had been rolled up to expose tanned forearms. She allowed herself a moment to fully admire him. After finishing her thorough perusal, she glanced down at her own dress. "We seem to be a matched set. How did we manage to co-ordinate the colour of our clothes?"

"It seems our connection extends to all things. Although, I fail to see how a mere mortal could compare to your ethereal beauty?" His eyes were actively engaged in roaming her body.

Any other man would have received a tongue lashing, but this was Taron. His look of total reverence told her that he meant every word. Oh, no! She was already thinking about that expert tongue. Giving her head a shake, she tried to pull herself together.

"Let me just get my purse and we'll be off." As she picked up her clutch, she noticed that Taron had one hand positioned behind his back. In a grand gesture, he swept out his arm and presented her with a single lavender rose.

"I'm afraid its loveliness pales in comparison, but I believe I can rectify the situation." He broke the stem and tucked the floral tribute behind her ear. "Much better. Its beauty has now been well and truly complemented."

Liana laced her arm through the bent elbow he offered as they exited the room. They found Shane standing in the hallway anxiously pacing in front of Scarlet's door. He opened his mouth to say something, but there were no words.

Taron slapped him on the back. "I hear you and the lovely Ms. Channing have a big night planned?"

"I'm afraid Scarlet has done all the planning. I have no idea what she is up to."

Liana knew exactly what was waiting for him as did her date. Taron enthusiastically rapped on the door, and it immediately swung open. Scarlet had gone all out. It would be the ultimate test of Shane's endurance. Her lust-filled gaze raked over the terrified man as she beckoned him in with the curl of a finger. Scarlet toyed with the sash of her fire engine red robe and drifted back to the bed which was covered in red silk sheets. The rest of the room was bedecked in crimson roses and candles. Liana felt it was an appropriate colour for her friend to be wearing. The fire department would either be called to perform CPR or douse the flames when the room when up in smoke.

Before Shane collapsed, Taron gave him a solid shove imparting some final words of advice, "Best get on with it mate."

"Holy crap," were the last words of the condemned man.

Liana burst into laughter as soon as the door shut. "Do you really think that was necessary? I mean you didn't even give the poor man a chance to decide his own fate."

"I was merely giving a decent fellow a nudge in the right direction."

"I think it was a gigantic shove which is more Jillian's style," Liana teased.

"Let me make one thing very clear. The only rule for this evening is no more talk about your mother. Tonight is about the two of us."

The love struck couple crossed the patio and followed a well worn path to the seashore. They emerged through an opening in the palms and flowering shrubs. Liana watched as Taron took in the view of an idyllic oceanside scene. A pathway formed by glowing candles ran across the beach. It led to a small linen covered table flanked by two chairs and surrounded by lit torches.

228

She glanced at him apprehensively. "Well, what do you think?"

"Dining at the water's edge as the sun sets. It is perfect."

Her efforts were rewarded with a soft kiss. Liana sighed in relief.

Slowly lifting one leg, she reached down to remove a shoe. She then pointed her other toe and flicked off the remaining pump. Taron was mesmerized by her every move. He quickly removed his own footwear and rolled up his pant legs. She took his hand in hers and walked them to their private rendezvous.

The candles on the table flickered in the gentle ocean breeze as they indulged in a sumptuous entree. Liana savoured every sensation from the leisurely sips of wine trickling down her throat to the feel of the waves gently lapping at her toes. After their meal, they basked in the glow of the setting sun. The blazing colours of tangerine and crimson reflected the fire in her heart. This was the best night of her life.

Even though it had started with a crazy mishap, nothing had ever felt so right. There was no slowly getting her feet wet when it came to Taron Royce. She had plunged in head first and found herself completely immersed in the depths of his affections. Liana could actually feel the warmth of the water rising around her, and it flooded her senses. The reality of the situation slowly permeated her thoughts. She looked down and saw the edges of the white table cloth floating in the deepening current.

"Taron, I think we're sinking." Her voice held a hint of laughter as the absurdity of the situation registered.

Her ardent admirer was finally roused from his musings. "Bollocks! The tide is upon us. Don't move."

Taron swiftly made his way around the table. Before she could protest, he gathered her in his arms and carried her to dry land, following the path to the informal seating she had arranged. Blankets and pillows sat under an ancient mangrove. The sprawling branches had been adorned with paper lanterns.

As he gently released her, Liana slowly slid down the length of his muscular frame. She found it difficult to leave the warmth of his embrace and kept her arms locked around his neck. Her date was in a more playful mood, seizing the opportunity to lift her in his arms. A small squeal of surprise preceded her delighted laughter. He whirled her around as she clung to him.

Liana's hands drifted to his chest after he set her down. She gave him a lighthearted slap. "Idiot."

"Guilty as charged, but I am your idiot and yours alone."

"Well, you are not alone. I have made quite a mess of things. For someone who has been on a ship for a week, I should know more about the ocean."

Taron settled beside her on the makeshift pallet. "Ms. Taylor, I do believe you fully intended to be swept into the arms of your dashing escort. I quite enjoyed this unexpected turn to the evening."

Liana gave him a warm smile as she reached for her clutch. "Given that my gallant hero has once again come to my aid, I have a token of my appreciation for all of his efforts." She retrieved a small box and shyly presented it to him.

He carefully extracted a pair of silver cufflinks from the tissue lining the interior. They were a perfect replica of an antique schooner's helm.

"Liana." He seemed overwhelmed by her gesture.

"I know you probably won't wear them. I mean, not many men do anymore. They caught my eye when I was shopping, and I thought of you—well, more like us. Sailing the ship was such an incredible moment and I thought they would be a reminder of…"

Taron's impassioned kiss put an end to her nervous ramblings.

"Hmm, I take it you approve." Liana would never tire of the way this man kissed her.

"Will you help me put them on?" He rolled down one sleeve.

The quizzical arch to her eyebrows called for an explanation.

"I know wearing a dress shirt is a bit old school, but I felt our first date deserved something special. Unfortunately, I did not have the proper closures with me, hence my shocking display of bare arms," he said with a wink.

Somehow she had been able to find exactly what he needed, and the thought made her shiver. She managed to fasten the cuff links with trembling fingers. As she closed the last clasp, Taron gently cupped her cheek.

"I find myself also in possession of a gift." He reached into his pocket and pulled out a small velvet bag with a drawstring closure.

"When did you have time to buy anything?"

"I ran an early morning errand while you were still sleeping. Go on, open it."

Liana tugged on the golden threads, emptying the contents of the pouch into the palm of her hand. Grasping the end of a silver chain, a delicate necklace dangled from her fingers. It was a rose compass with four diamonds embedded in the silver band, one for each direction. A familiar blue stone was in the centre.

"Is that your brother's aquamarine?" she asked in amazement.

"It is now yours, and my sincere apologies for borrowing it this morning. I always felt it needed a setting befitting its history and brilliance. I was fortunate to find a jeweller who was a willing accomplice in my romantic cause. He finished it just in time." Taron ran his fingers down along the silver strand. "Daniel and I gave my mother the necklace. Mum saw the compass as a symbol that my brother and I would always find our way back to her no matter where life's journey took us. I suppose having both keepsakes with me is my way of honouring their memory."

"It is stunning, but I can't." Liana was overcome with an emotion she dared not name. "This is too precious. You shouldn't part with it."

"Liana, please do me the honour." He took the chain from her and gently placed it around her neck. "It is exactly where it belongs." He reached out to hold the pendant in the palm of his hand. "My home, my happiness, and my love all come together in your heart." Taron let the compass fall into place and covered it with his palm.

"I love you, Liana."

Her pulse was pounding a furious rhythm as she let the words wash over her. She closed her eyes and tried to steady her breathing. Despite the cooling night air, she felt feverish. The choice was hers. Liana could surrender to the fear those words evoked, or she could seize happiness with both hands and fight to hold on. She surged forward and captured Taron's mouth in a possessive kiss.

Had she been standing, her legs would have buckled. Instead, she found herself sinking into the man who loved her. Taron relaxed back into the pillows and began sifting through her hair. He was mumbling something as his fingers began a sensual massage.

"Liana, why are there so many pins?" Taron removed a few of the metallic hindrances, freeing some of her tresses from their confinement. He twirled a few locks around his fingers as he scattered tender kisses across her closed eyelids and cheeks.

"I find myself very conflicted as to which is softer, these silky strands—or this spot, right here." His lips moved to place an open mouthed kiss below her ear.

"No, I'm wrong. I think it might be this delectable spot." He nuzzled at her pulse point, and she arched her neck to allow him better access.

Liana had indulged in her own fantasies this past week and was ready to satisfy them. She opened her eyes and began to remove his tie.

"Taron?"

"Mmm, what darling?"

"You have tiny anchors and sails on your tie."

"Do I?"

"You're adorable."

"Not what a man wants to hear in a heated moment."

Taron turned her in his arms until she was the one leaning back on the pillows. There was nothing innocent in his seductive gaze.

"While the dress is lovely, I am curious as to the other gift I have yet to unwrap. Perhaps you could give me with a few clues about your purchase."

"Well, there are satin straps."

Liana felt his hand slip down the silky fabric starting at her shoulder. This was a sexy little game and she was all set to play.

"Yes there, and the lace starts…"

"Right about here?" Taron's nimble fingers followed the line of material outlining the curve her breasts.

"Colour?" His voice became low and demanding.

"It's a deep blue and has a shimmer."

"Like the sea?" His breathing was becoming ragged.

It was Liana's turn to grab fistfuls of hair as he continued his explorations. She could feel his hand rising and falling as her own breath quickened. It was the most exquisite form of torture.

"There are matching panties and—oh!" Any remaining thoughts fled as Liana felt Taron's hand splayed across her stomach and on a downward path.

She was being throughly seduced while still fully dressed. She felt cherished and loved, but wanted more.

"Liana." His hand suddenly stilled.

"Don't you dare stop."

"I must. It seems my spoke has thrust its way into the opening of your pin."

"Not the words I would have chosen, but—ouch! Taron, my hair."

"Darling, don't move. My cufflink seems to be well and truly caught in your coiffure."

Taron was trying to disengage himself, but he seemed to be having great difficulty. "Could you just turn a bit in this direction." His free hand grabbed her bottom, and he flipped them over.

Liana found herself staring into blue eyes which were much too amused for her liking. "Not funny, Royce."

What was undoubtedly a witty retort was interrupted by the ringing of a cell.

"Really, you brought your phone?"

"It must be Greg. I told him I was to be summoned only in the case of a dire emergency."

"Oh, no! Aren't you going to answer it?"

"I can't seem to reach into the pocket of my trousers with my hand trapped in your hair. Would you mind?"

Taron continued to try and release his cufflink while she fumbled in his pocket.

"If you could just twist a bit to the right. There, I think I've just about got it."

"Liana—that's not my phone."

"No, it's not—is it?" Her ardour soon gave way to disappointment. It would have been a glorious end to the night.

"Liana," a strangled whisper escaped on Taron's exhale.

She reluctantly removed her hand and gave him the phone. His frustration equalled her own.

"Blast it! Greg Sloan is a dead man." Taron scanned the incoming text.

"It's your mother. She's been arrested."

Worry replaced Liana's irritation as Taron worked his cufflink loose. A myriad of unpleasant possibilities filled her mind as they hurried back to the Inn. She went inside to let the staff know their date was finished while Taron made his call from the deserted patio. She was on her way to the bar when she felt a hand on her arm.

"Buy you a drink gorgeous?" The unkempt man next to her reeked of alcohol.

"Thanks, but no thanks." Liana tried to brush past the drunken fool, but he blocked her.

"What's your hurry, baby?" The lowlife reached out to touch her hair.

Liana took a step back.

"Where are my manners, I'm Trevor. What's your name?"

She stood her ground and remained silent.

"Oh, you're a shy one. I'll bet it just takes a couple of drinks to bring out your wild side." He swayed back and forth, clearly unsteady on his feet.

Liana had travelled the world and was well versed in discouraging the advances of men who were much tougher than this idiot appeared to be. She would have no problems ridding herself of the nuisance.

"What's say we forget the bar and head upstairs?" He grabbed her by the arm.

Taron's outraged voice blasted across the room. "Get your hands off her. Now!"

"It's alright. I've got this." Liana turned toward her date which allowed the inebriated reprobate to grab her by the waist.

Taron crossed over to her in a few easy strides and pulled the drunkard away. "You stupid son of a bitch."

"Hey, it's over. Let's just leave." Liana put a hand on Taron's arm.

"If I'd known you liked it rough—" He did not get a chance to finish.

Taron exploded. His first punch solidly connected with the man's jaw. He staggered but did not go down. Taron kept coming at him until the drunk crumpled to the floor. The sights and sounds of the room fell away as Liana helplessly watched the violence unfold before her.

All she saw was an enraged Taron. She could not believe her eyes.

Liana forced out a cry when she spotted blood. "Taron, no!"

She desperately pulled on the back of his shirt. "I need you to come back to me. Taron, please!"

He had promised to always be there for her, and Liana knew he would not let her down. Her words penetrated the anger which had consumed him. Taron's body went slack and he fell to his knees.

He looked up at her with a pained and bewildered expression. "Liana?"

She put a comforting hand on his shoulder as she crouched down in front of him. "Hey, it's over now. Everything is going to be fine."

Liana tried to wrap her arms around him, but he stood and stepped back. He looked down at his hands. They were balled into fists and his knuckles were bloodied.

"What have I done? I'm so sorry." Taron turned and disappeared before she could get to her feet.

She, of all people, knew better than to chase after him. He would find no relief from his emotions by running. This was not how she imagined their picture perfect evening would end, but it was all too predictable. Liana had once again been abandoned to face the night alone. She would do what she did best, pick herself up and carry on.

"Excuse me, Miss? I think you lost this during the tussle." A kindly guest held out her necklace.

"Thank you." Liana graciously accepted it before scanning the room.

"Did you see what happened to the man who was punched?"

"He seemed to be in a great hurry to leave. I wouldn't worry about him."

Liana would not give the drunk who had ruined her date a second thought, but she was relieved the police hadn't been called. At least, Taron would not be sharing a cell with her mother. Greg would clean up whatever mess Jillian had gotten herself into. She needed time to think and made her way back to the beach.

A full moon had risen, sending shimmers of light dancing across the dark waves of ocean. She still had a tight hold on the compass as her hand found it's way to her heart. Liana pressed the cool metal against the warmth of her body and thought of him. A devoted son, a loyal brother, and the man who loved her. She would not let him down. Somehow, she would help him find his way back. Back from the darkness. Back to her.

Midnight Madness

"Freedom lies in being bold."
Robert Frost

Jillian seemed to be repelling everything in her life including the errant pea she was chasing around her plate. She scowled at her sister just before forcefully impaling the wayward legume. All of Delia's attempts to lift her spirits had failed. Jillian had officially hit rock bottom. The only option left was to drown her sorrows. Mission accomplished. She no longer had a clue how many glasses of wine she had gulped down with her supper.

She should be ecstatic. Liana was on a date with Taron. All of her efforts were finally paying off, but she was miserable and filled with doubt. What if yesterday's confession had gone too far, and she had done irreparable harm to her relationship with Liana? She would have nothing left. Finding her daughter and atoning for her mistake had been her sole purpose in life. The thought of filling that void filled her with dread.

Delia felt the solution to her problem was a simple one. Jillian needed to loosen up and let her hair down. She tugged on the strands of her short bob. It was a style she had worn for years. Everything about her was practical, traditional, and outdated. Looking around at the other diners, she was the only one wearing a pink long sleeved sweater on a sultry tropical evening. Her sister was right. Jillian needed a fresh start, but change took time. It didn't happen overnight, or did it?

Sensing she was honing in on a life-altering revelation, she continued her line of thinking. Motherhood was the complete antithesis of what she had hoped it would be. Her decisions always seemed to leave her daughter frustrated and angry. If every inclination she had was wrong, it stood to reason she should do the opposite. It was brilliant and surely the answer to all of her problems. She would be anti-Jillian, the madcap mother.

She was eager to get the fun started and Delia seemed to be in the same frame of mind.

Her sister turned to Charlie. "Let's see what this far-flung little town has to offer. Think you can get us to Victor's club?"

"It shouldn't be hard to find. First Avenue is the main drag like Victor's card says. A short walk and some cooling night air might be just what some of us need." Charlie cast a sideways glance at Jillian.

In an effort to prove him wrong, she raised herself by placing her palms on the table. Delia put a steading hand on her arm as she wobbled. Jillian definitely needed to stop drinking. No, that was wrong. If she truly believed her new theory, more alcohol was needed.

"I need to get very, very sloshed. Tom, you and Claire should come along, the more the merrier."

The five ship mates spilled out onto a street overflowing with weekend revellers. Several navy vessels were in port which added hundreds of sailors to the throngs. While it promised to be a fun evening, Jillian was beginning to feel a little too clear headed for her liking. She surveyed the vicinity and quickly found a target.

"I need a little break and something to quench my thirst." She did not wait for a group consensus and barged her way into 'Gin and Bare It.' She was already seated by the time the others made their way inside.

After their drinks arrived, Charlie began to squint and rub his eyes. "Delia, there seems to be something a bit off about this place. It looks like two people at the bar are naked?"

Everyone looked to where he was pointing.

Delia was the first to comment, "Well, would you look at that."

The couple in question turned around.

"God no, don't look! It's stark-naked seniors night," she sputtered before slapping a hand over her sister's eyes.

Jillian was quick to pry her sister's fingers loose and take a closer look. Charlie was studiously examining the tops of his shoes while Tom and Claire raised their glasses and snickered into their drinks.

The couple exchanged a meaningful glance as they approached.

"I can tell this is your first time here. It's quite the place isn't it?" The butt-naked man made eye contact with Delia.

"Most people miss the clothing is optional part of the sign. My husband is a lawyer and always reminds people to read the fine print. Although, on nights like this, he does leave his legal briefs at home." The woman's laughter made her wobbly bits jiggle even more.

The couple proceeded to share a series of groan worthy puns which included packing the bare necessities for their trip and uncovering the naked truth about Key West. Jillian had enough and took advantage of the distraction to make her getaway. She needed to strike out on her own if she was going to rediscover herself.

As she slipped through the crowd, she tried to give off a nonchalant air. The unassuming school teacher in her wanted to tell the naked people to not sit down because they could catch a cold—or worse, but the madcap mother would not allow herself to think like some goody two-shoes. She confidently held her head up as she marched to the washroom. If she hadn't been keeping her eyes up—way up, she would have missed the sign which brought her to a stand still. Body painting.

Her gut told her to ignore it and return to the others. She was about to move on when she remembered her goal was the ultimate about-face. Classic artists often painted nude portraits, and some framable art work would be a nice reminder of this momentous turning point in her life. Jillian boldly marched through the entrance ready for whatever the night had in store.

*****

Delia turned to tell her sister they should head out and found herself staring at an empty chair. She quickly mobilized the group into a recovery mission and hoped a drunken Jillian was not baring her soul, or anything more, to anyone who would listen.

The search party came up empty handed. A distressed Delia decided they should split up and hit the streets. They would meet in one hour at Victor's. Delia held out the faint hope that her sister might find her way there. Insisting he knew the way, Charlie shoved Victor's card into the hand of one very insulted geocacher. The bickering twosome raced toward the nightclub while Claire and Tom went in the opposite direction.

As they made their way through the crowded streets, Delia tried to reassure herself that the always sensible Jillian would not succumb to all of the alcohol she had consumed. Dropping Victor's name, she pushed her way past security at the door to the club.

She was not going to let anything stand in her way including the man dawdling behind her.

"Stop gawking and hurry up," Delia shouted as she fought her way to the bar.

She was trying to attract the attention of the bartender when the relentless pest tugged at her sleeve.

"Um, Delia. You know how we were over dressed at the last place? Well, I think we are a little under dressed for this one. The women here seem to be all glitz and glamour—and very tall."

Delia took a moment to scan her surroundings and inhaled a sharp breath. "What did you say the name of this place was?"

"The Main Drag. It's very clever because this street is the main drag. Get it?"

Delia gave him a sharp tap on the back of the head. "Idiot! I get it, but apparently the man who occasionally parades around in women's shoes doesn't. Take a careful look around and rethink drag."

"I really didn't think I would see you here, my darlings."

They both turned to see a stunning women in a red sequinned, body hugging dress.

"Wow! That's some dress you are wearing." Charlie's hand was grasped in a firm handshake.

Delia shook her head in disbelief. Her companion was clueless. "It's Victor. Remember your Dolce and Gabbana's?"

"Damn! Is that really you, Victor?"

"Actually, I prefer Victoria when I am in drag."

Delia rolled her eyes and snickered. "You're going with Victor and Victoria. Isn't that a bit old school?"

"You have to give a nod to the classics every now and then. My stage name is actually Victoria Secret."

She raised her vinyl clad leg onto the top rung of a bar stool. "My performance has a more modern bent to it. As you can see, the boots are kinky."

Charlie ogled the bright red thigh high boots which ended in five inch heels. "You walk around in those things?"

"I do more than that, and you might as well learn from the best. Let me get you seated by the stage."

Their table proved to be an excellent vantage point with a great sight line to the front door. Delia could keep an eye out for her sister while her sidekick watched the show. The house lights dimmed and the music began. What followed was a spectacular display of high heeled dexterity the likes of which Delia had never seen. Her skills paled in comparison.

Charlie happily tapped a sneaker clad toe as he hummed along. Their enjoyment of the show was interrupted by a sudden commotion at the door. Delia gaped in horror. A bubble gum pink confection was bobbing and weaving its way to where they were seated.

She cried out, "Dear God! Jillian what have you done?"

Her sister's features registered confusion before transforming into delighted recognition. She screeched, "Dee Dee! I thought I lost you," before toppling over and covering Delia in layers of tulle.

Charlie managed to haul Jillian's backside onto a chair, but her upper half collapsed across the table. Delia grabbed her sister by the hand and noticed her bare arms.

Jillian caught her staring. "I cut the sleeves off. Snip, snip—all gone."

She pushed off the table and thrust her arms out toward her sister. "Wanna know why they're all pink? I'll give you three guesses, and it's not a sunburn."

Before Delia could reply, her sister grinned and held out both hands. Pinching her fingers together, she bent her wrist downward. "See, this is the face." There was an eye on the side of her hand and her blackened fingers resembled a beak. 'And this—is the neck." Jillian performed a series of undulating waves with her pink limbs, animating her creation. "I have flamingo arms."

She was positively giddy. "You know what else?" She motioned them closer. "I am all flamingo—everywhere." Her eyes widened and she dropped her gaze to emphasize her point. "I had my whole body painted, and the nice artists found me this lovely pink tutu."

Jillian unceremoniously hoisted a leg onto the table. "I also have bird legs." The skinny black outline of a long avian appendage topped a layer of white paint.

"You were right, Dee Dee. I need to loosen up. The body painting people chose a flamingo because it means socializing and having fun. They made me free as a bird."

Delia had always believed that timing in life was everything, and Jillian's desire to fly free coincided with Victoria announcing the start of karaoke.

"Me first, pretty please." A pair of flamingo arms were held out to their host.

Delia tried to grab her sister by the waist, but she could not get a firm grip on all of that tulle.

Victoria easily lifted Jillian onto the stage. "Let's welcome our first performer of the evening. Who do we have here?"

Jillian stuttered the first syllable of her name before hesitating, "I'm—I'm—the Flaming Flamingo, and I've never done anything like this before."

Victoria urged on the skeptical onlookers. "Come on everybody, let's encourage our little bird to sing."

The audience applauded while Delia pulled out her sunglasses and shrank down as far as her chair would allow.

Her sister grabbed the microphone from their host. "There is a song that I love to sing." She whispered to Victoria and the DJ before continuing, "I need some help with it, and I would like my devoted sister to join me."

Before Delia could protest, Victoria grabbed her by one arm while Charlie firmly held the other one. They manhandled her onto the stage. She found herself caged in with no means of escape.

Victoria enthusiastically introduced them, "The Main Drag proudly presents our opening karaoke act, "Flaming Flamingo and…"

Delia stood silent and fuming.

It was Charlie's turn to take centre stage. "Welcome—Ivy—Poison Ivy. Give her a chance; she kind of creeps up on you."

Delia turned on her adversary. "Your shoes go back tomorrow."

As the first notes began, Delia saw Tom and Claire emerge from the crowd. Astonished looks soon gave way to snorts and chortles. She watched in horror as Tom retrieved his cell ready to document her utter humiliation.

Jillian was already moving in time with the music. She began to sing as she danced around her sister gracefully waving her pink arms. Delia raised her hand in a move which was more threatening than rhythmical. Charlie quickly thwarted the impending assault by taking her hand and spinning her into a dance. Her sister continued to sing and motioned Claire to join them.

As Delia swung Charlie off to the side, she saw Victoria reaching into a trunk at the back of the stage. She gave Jillian and Delia large feathery fans and then draped Charlie and Claire in pink boas.

Jillian hugged her sister around the waist and marched her around the stage. "Delia, look! The audience is singing and dancing with us. No one is disappointed in me, and everyone looks so happy."

Wild applause encouraged Jillian to flap her fan behind her while leaping across the stage. Delia found herself being twirled from one partner to the next as she tried to get closer to her sister. A sly grin made its way to Jillian's face as she slowed down her gyrations. She held the mass of plumage tight to her chest and shuffled from side to side. If Delia had not been staring at her feet, she would have missed the tiny pearl buttons skittering across the polished floor.

Jillian dropped the fan to expose the beautifully painted pink feathers covering her naked breasts.

"Wee, I'm flying."

She jumped off the stage and flew out into the night.

*****

Greg could hear the raucous chorus of complainants as he burst through the doors of the small Key West police station. He squeezed past the familiar faces on his way to the front desk. The beleaguered desk Sergeant had a shaky hand on his revolver while his assistant was aggressively wielding a stapler.

"Sarge, I say we kill them all if they don't shut up. Show no mercy," the woman shouted.

"Stand down. I don't think there is a need for weapons. I am Detective Sloan of the Boston PD. I've got this." He turned to face the rabble. His shrill whistle silenced the group. "Not one more word from any of you."

Greg showed the officer his badge. "I understand my friend Jillian Barton has been arrested. I am here to clear up any misunderstandings, and then we can all go home."

Sergeant Lane scratched his head. "I don't know about your friend, but we have someone calling herself Flame in our holding cell."

Greg tried to exert as much authority as he could. "Maybe it's best if you have the accused brought out. I would like to hear the charges and her explanations."

"Rachel, you go get her. I am not facing that fan again. She has wicked aim with that thing."

The assistant added a letter opener to her free hand. "You owe me a week off for this, Sarge."

It was not long before Jillian emerged clutching her plumage. Her irritated expression quickly transformed into one of relief when she saw Greg. "I knew you'd find me. Greg, they have it all wrong and..."

The Sergeant did not allow her to finish and began rattling off the charges. "First, we have possession of stolen property. The label on the assault weapon says it belongs to Victoria Secret."

"That's me." Victoria strutted toward the desk. "And it's not stolen. It was on loan for her performance."

Greg wondered why the obvious solution had not occurred to anyone. "Jillian, give the fan back, and we can have one charge dropped."

"I can't."

"Now is not the time to argue. Give back the fan," Greg stated firmly.

Jillian took a step toward him and whispered, "I can't because they think I'm naked. I'm not you know. I have the most beautiful pink feathers. It's called body art."

Sergeant Lane spoke up. "Ma'am we don't think, not unless we really have to."

He turned back to Greg. "Charge number two was obvious after I was hit over the head with the feathers. Indecent exposure. This also led to another simple assault charge."

Greg had already removed his button-down, handing it to Jillian. He held up the fan while she quickly put on his shirt.

"She is now fully clothed, and the item in question has been returned. I don't imagine the plumes did any permanent damage. You mentioned another assault charge?"

"According to the arresting officer, he gave chase to a partially clad woman streaking down the main drag.

Delia squawked when Charlie elbowed her and said, "Told you."

The sergeant ignored them and continued, "The accused resisted arrest and assaulted the officer while he was trying to handcuff her."

"Greg, don't believe them. He threatened to pull out his gun. My flamingo got angry and took it from him."

She raised her arm, and her fingered beak gave him a quick peck on the cheek. "See, she likes you."

"Which brings me to the most obvious charge, public intoxication."

The detective in him wanted to let Jillian and her alter ego contemplate their folly in a jail cell. Greg Sloan, the compassionate man, sighed and tried to free her.

"Let me ask you this, Sergeant. Do you really want an arrest report on file stating that one of your officers was disarmed by a 5 foot flamingo?"

"Greg, I'm five foot two."

"Not really the time to argue, Jillian."

"I see your point, Detective Sloan, but I can't overlook the drunk and disorderly behaviour of the accused. Any ideas?"

"You could remand her into my custody with my personal assurance that she will not cause any more problems."

"Done. Now, I suggest you leave before I change my mind. You all better be on the first boat out of Key West in the morning."

Greg followed the deflated group out of the station. The door closed on the final words of Sergeant Lane. "I never want to hear the words naked and gun in the same sentence again. Let's make that an office rule, Rachel."

In My Darkest Hour

"Life can only be understood backwards,
but it must be lived forwards."
Soren Kierkegaard.

Trevor bobbed and weaved his way through the throng of people as he tried to find his way back to the marina. If he did not return to the boat in time, the actions of the irate man at the Inn would pale in comparison to his father's wrath. He spotted the yacht and looked up to the heavens to thank whoever might still be watching over him. The gratitude he felt was quickly extinguished when he found himself gaping at the accursed ship once more. Even in his disoriented state, there was no mistaking it. He staggered backwards at the sight, stumbling into a stack of crates.

The fall jolted him back to awareness, and Trevor finally made the connection. The woman he had been so drawn to at the Inn was the same one who had crashed into him in Key Largo. She was also a passenger on the loathsome vessel silently dogging him like a colossal harbinger of doom. Nothing had gone

254

right for him since that accident. Fate seemed determined to take him off the path to rich rewards and send him down the road to hell.

The tingling hairs on the back of his neck signalled trouble was on its way. He managed to stand up and tried to regain his bearings. A full moon looming large in the night sky illuminated the docks. Trevor felt too exposed and vulnerable. His instincts told him to remain hidden, but he knew his father was waiting. The words 'you can run but you can't hide' taunted him on his mad dash along the walkway.

Trevor took a moment to look back as he clamoured aboard the yacht. Patterns of light and shadow danced across the boats as clouds began to caress the face of the moon like ghostly fingers. The ship he so feared was cast in a silver glow. It shone like a beacon of salvation in the dark waters surrounding it.

His father was uncharacteristically forgiving about Trevor's inebriated state. Richard assumed his son deserved whatever punishment had been meted out. Trevor's problems meant nothing unless they interfered with his father's plans. The huge deal in the offing had the normally composed man giddy with anticipation. His incessant chatter had Trevor imagining ways to shut him up permanently. The ideas were there, the courage was not.

Richard cut the engine when they closed in on the GPS coordinates. They watched and waited as the night sky clouded over into an inky blackness. A single spotlight suddenly winked into existence. The motor was restarted, and they moved toward the gently bobbing light. The whole scene reminded Trevor of something which he couldn't quite place. His rum soaked brain made a connection with a movie about a lost fish. Whatever it was, he could not shake the feeling that following an enticing light in the dark would lead to lethal consequences.

Trevor managed to avert his gaze just as a blinding array of lights flashed in the darkness. His eyes adjusted to the glare as they swung around to align with the much larger vessel. The crew made quick work of securing the yacht. Father and son were greeted by several brawny men sporting automatic weapons slung over shoulders and a variety of knives and ammo tucked into belts. It looked more like an all out war than a midnight rendezvous to discuss the mutually beneficial exchange of goods and services.

They were escorted to a dimly lit cabin below deck. Trevor could barely make out the small human shape seated in what looked like a comfortable recliner. The clapping of hands caused an overhead fixture to shed light on the room and the situation. Trevor's mouth gaped open in shock. The big boss was a little old lady.

His father revealed nothing and conducted himself with his usual aplomb. "May I say what an honour and pleasure it is to finally meet you. I am Richard Hyde, and this is my son, Trevor Bravery."

Trevor could not suppress his nervous laugh. The rhythmical clicking of knitting needles suddenly stilled.

"Something funny young man?" The silver haired matron peered over her oversized black glasses. Her steely gaze had Trevor instantaneously choking back any further comment.

She introduced herself as Mrs. Bruno, motioning Trevor and his father toward the two empty chairs facing her. The man with the pistol served tea and cookies. She took a dainty sip before continuing the exchange of pleasantries.

"It's so nice to see a father and son find a common vocation. There is no one more trustworthy than next of kin in a business like ours. It was my late husband who passed running the cartel on to me. People had their doubts, but any voices of discontent were soon silenced."

Trevor followed the dismissive way of her hand to the bodyguard. He patted his gun as he glared at the duo. Trevor gulped and turned his attention back to the widow. There was something familiar about her. It was tantalizing close, and he wished his mind were clearer.

"Burgers!" He blurted out the word to the mortification of his father and the amusement of the drug lord.

"You own Bruno's Burgers. Wow, it's so great to meet you. I would have never guessed Bruno was—well, you. Your diners have the best burgers. The cheeseburger has the most incredible flavour. It's so cheesy. A lot of places skimp on the cheddar, but not you."

Richard seemed to have developed a sudden tick on the left side of his face. "You'll have to excuse my son. He is not quite himself tonight."

Mrs. Bruno paused to count the stitches on the baby sweater she was knitting. "I am very proud of both organizations. They have both been very profitable. My late husband and I started with one restaurant in Florida, and the chain is now nation wide. As the head of any successful business will tell you, keeping customers satisfied is the number one priority."

She directed a shrewd look at Trevor. "The secret to my food is the quality of the ingredients. It keeps loyal patrons coming back for more."

The old lady was beginning to make Trevor sweat. It was like she knew something he didn't.

"I have managed to do what my beloved husband only dreamed about before his untimely death. My restaurants are a very convenient location for all types of take out and deliveries if you catch my drift. Consider yourselves the wholesalers who gather the raw ingredients. You sell them to me, and I serve up a first class product to my customers."

She directed an impudent wink at Trevor. "Do you see where I am going with this young man?"

"I think so. You put the coke in the burgers. It's what makes them taste so good, and why everyone comes back for more."

Trevor glanced at his father. He was pinching the bridge of his nose as his cheek continued to twitch.

"Nice try, but that's not it. A good chef is the key. They are always tasting the ingredients to ensure everything is just right. I have a reputation to uphold in both of my business ventures."

She began to cast off her knitting. "Still nothing to share? I hoped you would be more forthcoming. Things might just go easier for you if you confess."

Trevor suddenly knew where this was heading. Things were about to get very real, and none of it would be suitable for family viewing.

"Every kilo of product that comes into my possession is stringently tested for purity. It seems I purchased a batch that was not up to snuff in more ways than one." She leaned toward Trevor and tapped one of the needles on his cheek. "I do not take kindly to anyone who tries to swindle poor old seniors."

"Still nothing?" She forcefully run the metal point across his face, impassively watching the welt form. "You cut my cocaine with sugar."

Trevor managed to squeak out a single word, "Shit."

He knew this was beyond bad when his unflappable father swore and dropped his tea cup. The man never lost his cool.

The drug kingpin continued in her honeyed voice. "When pests become a problem in my restaurants, they have to be exterminated. Normally, I would have my security waste both of you, but then I would be out my money and the drugs. Right now, I find myself unable to serve my loyal customers and that is the real crime."

259

She motioned for them to stand. Trevor somehow managed to do what she asked despite his shaky legs.

"I am going to give you forty-eight hours to get me the product I paid for. Don't bother trying to find me when time runs out because I will know exactly where you are. If I were you, I would also think twice about squealing to the cops. It is very important to keep your hands clean when working in the kitchen. The authorities have never caught me violating any infractions."

The ill-fated duo had their weapons returned before they were ushered over the side of the ship. As soon as Trevor's sneakers landed on the deck, he was shoved up against the railing. Richard's hand wrapped around his neck as a gun was pressed to his temple. His vision began to fade and flickers of light sparked behind his tightly shut eyelids. Passing out was not a kindness his father would permit. He eased the pressure on Trevor's windpipe, allowing him to gulp down some vital oxygen.

"I know you don't have the smarts or the courage to try and outwit your dear old dad. Make no mistake, it is the only reason you are still alive. Answer the next question very carefully because it could be the last thing you ever say. Where are the drugs?"

"I don't know."

Trevor was once again staring at the vile tattoo. There would be blood, but not from a stabbing. He winced and waited for the end.

"Not the answer I was looking for, son. I am going to ask one last time."

The cold metal was digging into Trevor's scalp as his father increased the force of his grip. He began to stammer out his story in barely coherent fragments. Richard was able to piece together some of the facts which seemed to appease his murderous intentions. His father needed him alive if they were to have any chance at saving their asses.

Recovering the goods seemed like an impossible task, and no supplier could generate the amount needed in such a short time. They would have to rely on Trevor's ability to recall the voices and faces of the people he had bumped into at the grocers. He knew they were in Key West, but where and for how long? Their chances were slim to none.

After pulling into the slip at the marina, Richard went below deck to formulate a plan. Trevor was tying off the boat when he heard a woman singing something about families and being together. As they got closer, she was babbling on about flamingos when a very familiar voice told her to keep her beak shut. The tone of irritation and superiority was unmistakeable. It was music to Trevor's ears.

*****

Ghosts from the past had once again come to haunt Taron Royce. The spectral entities beseeching him for atonement were not conjured by the scotch he had consumed, but by his actions. Another violent outburst ended in remorse for deeds that could not be undone. While the dead had been laid to rest long ago, he was unable to find peace in the present. Taron's anger lived on, devouring his moral fibre like an insatiable beast. He glanced between the empty glass in his hand and the half-full bottle of scotch at his side. Moderation was something he seemed to be incapable of achieving.

Thankfully, Liana had found the words to prevent a more heinous act. If he had killed the boorish drunkard to protect her, it would make him no better than the faceless murderer who had changed his life forever. He would let the woman he loved go before he allowed his anger to taint her as well.

He sensed her presence before she emerged from the shadows. Given the fury she had witnessed, he could not fathom why she would seek him out rather than retire to the safety of her cabin. To make matters worse, he had failed to live up to his promises. She deserved so much better. He indulged in a large swallow straight from the bottle before letting his eyes meet hers.

"I had a hunch you might be here. It's the perfect vantage point for our dedicated captain to ensure his ship is safe and secure." She paused, waiting for his response. When none was forthcoming, she hesitantly enquired, "May I join you?"

"Suit yourself." Taron motioned to the steps leading to the quarter deck.

She made her way to the top stair and sat next to him. He could not mask the tension he was feeling as he tried to avert her gaze. There was nothing he could say to right the wrongs forced upon her this evening. Instead of taking her in his arms and begging her for forgiveness, he sat in stony silence.

When Liana made no move to leave him to his misery, he finally spoke. "If you are waiting for me to come to my senses, I'd wager you will be here for quite some time."

She turned toward him with a determined set to her jaw. "I will not let some loud-mouthed fool ruin the best night of my life. I had plans to end the evening in the company of the amazing man sitting next to me, and that is exactly what I am going to do."

She slipped her arm through the crook of his elbow and laid her head on his shoulder. "I'm not going anywhere, Taron."

He tipped his head against hers. "I'm sure you could find better company than a brooding sailor. Perhaps your time would be better spent freeing your mother from her incarceration." He felt her hand reach up to brush aside a stray lock of hair from his brow.

"No need to worry that handsome head of yours. I went back to our room to change and grab my things. Greg sent a text saying it had all been sorted. They should be back soon."

"Our room. This is not how either of us imagined our first date would end." He leaned forward, running his hands through his hair. "Liana, I don't know what to say. Any apology would be woefully inadequate given what I put you through."

"You don't have to ask because the answer is obvious. Of course, I forgive you. The real question is can you forgive yourself?"

"No, I can't. There is no excuse for my violent behaviour tonight. The urge to protect you was overwhelming, and I let my anger get the best of me."

He exhaled a long breath before continuing. "I can't forgive and forget the past either. The bastard is still out there living his life without a care in the world. I once believed that I would be content if he were held accountable for his crimes, but I was wrong. I am ashamed to admit I still want vengeance. I need him to feel the pain he inflicted upon me."

And there it was, he had laid his soul bare and shared the darkest part of himself. The revenge he sought was to take a life for the lives he had lost.

"You need to stop this, Taron. I am not like the woman who left you. I won't give up as easily as she did. I am willing to fight for us even if it's you I have to battle."

Her lovely face took on a look of stubborn resolve. This incredible woman was a force of nature. Her fiery spirit burned brightly no matter what adversities she faced.

"My brave and beautiful, Liana. I don't deserve you."

"Taron, you deserve every moment of happiness you can get. Please don't keep punishing yourself because you survived and they didn't. You and I both know it would not have made any difference if you had been there that night. The madman would have murdered you as well. He was a crazed thief who stole away your family. Don't let him take your heart as well. It's not what they would have wanted."

Tears shone in her eyes as she pleaded, "Please, let me help you."

She was right, he had not been able to let go of his guilt. It was still lodged deep within him and he had been unable to shift it on his own. He needed Liana to shine a light on his darkened soul and show him he could be a better man. Taron put his arms around her and pulled her close.

"My heart is safe because it is no longer in my possession. Tonight I gave it to you and that is where it will stay until I take my last breath."

While he yearned to hear the words, he could see the love she felt for him shining in the depths of her wondrous brown eyes. She melted into his embrace. They sat in tranquil silence until the song stylings of one very tipsy school teacher filled the night air. Liana groaned and hid her face in her hands.

"And on a different note, albeit an off-key one, it seems your mother has overindulged once more." His mouth curved into a wry smile.

Liana's delighted laughter greeted the weary party goers. Taron was convinced it was the sweetest sound he would ever hear.

*****

The bickering and singing stopped when Jillian saw Liana. She rushed onto the ship and flung herself at her daughter.

"Oh, my little hatchling, you found your way back to the nest."

"Mom you're…"

She did not let her daughter finish. "Happy!"

Jillian whirled around her with her arms held high. "I'm happy." She began another song and dance.

"I would have gone with drunk," Liana chuckled. "Um—and you're wearing Greg's shirt because you were cold?"

"No, silly girl. Your auntie Dee Dee will fill you in because Greg and I are leaving now." She gave her daughter a quick kiss on the cheek. "Nighty, night."

Jillian charged across the deck. She felt Greg's arm catch her just before she plummeted down the stairs. After regaining her balance, she hurried past her cabin and barged into his room.

She turned and gave him her best sultry stare. "Aren't you coming in, Detective Dangerous?" The pleasant buzz of fruity cocktails lingered, and Jillian was not ready to shed her new found freedom. Shedding— that sounded like a splendid idea.

"You seem to have mistaken my cabin for yours." Greg hesitated in the doorway.

"No mistake. Not ready for bed, unless you want to join me?"

"Yes—I mean no. I should get some sleep and so should you. Me, here in my bed, and you down the hall—in your bed—alone."

Greg made a move to step around her, but Jillian quickly blocked his path. She put a hand on his chest, forcing him backwards.

"Tonight, I am all things flamingo. Did you know they mate for life?"

"Interesting, but I really need to get some rest. It's been a long night." Greg appeared to be studiously examining the paint on the ceiling.

He was more reluctant than Jillian hoped, so she gave him another shove towards the bed. "They try to get the best mate. Do you know how?"

She did not wait for his response. "It's a dance."

Jillian lifted her arms out to the side, slowly raising and lowering them as she circled her target. "The ladies spread their wings and show off their feathers to the boys. It's the flamingo dance of sex."

She began to hum while swaying back and forth. "Know what else, detective? Love is the best drug. Jillian began to sing as she rubbed her feathers against him.

"Jillian, this is highly inappropriate."

The lyrics were a bit hazy, but she continued to sing as her hands roamed his body. Greg still seemed unwilling to participate, and this was not going to be a one woman show. She needed to up her game. Jillian dropped to a squat putting her at eye level with his belt buckle. She slowly stood up while grinding her hips against him. It sent Greg into full-on retreat. The backs of his knees hit the bed, and she gave him the final push he needed. Jillian pulled the oversized shirt over her head and liberated her feathers.

Her mouth was inches from his when the door suddenly opened.

Liana screamed, "Oh my God! What the hell is going on in here?"

Jillian threw an irritated glance over her shoulder. There would be no testing her newfound wings, her flight had been grounded.

*****

It took the combined strength of Liana and Delia to pull her mother off Greg. Her aunt shepherded Jillian out of the cabin while she stayed behind to seek advice from the newly freed man.

"I know this is not really a good time given what just happened, but I need to talk to you about Taron."

"I don't think sleep is going to come very easily for me tonight so fire away." Greg rubbed a weary hand over his face.

She gave him a brief recounting of the events at the Inn before revealing her thoughts. "I'm worried Taron won't be able to control his anger or resolve his guilt unless he finds closure. Is it possible to reopen a cold case?"

"Liana, I can see how deeply you care about him, but what you are proposing would do more harm than good. Taron and I worked day and night to try and solve the crime. There was very little physical evidence left at the scene. One witness was dead. The other lay unconscious in the hospital. Daniel did come around for a few moments and seemed desperate to say something. Taron managed to decipher some of the details despite his grief. It seems the killer had a bloodied knife with a few Latin words tattooed on his forearm. Taron spent every waking moment at the station going through thousands of mug shots. He was like a man possessed, and it was a terrible thing to see. If you want to help him, find another way."

She left Greg's room unsure about what to do, but clear on where she needed to be. Liana made quick work of her nightly routine. She placed the swan feather in her pocket before slipping into Taron's cabin. Bare chested and wearing an old pair of sweatpants, he had fallen asleep before he could get under the covers. Liana tucked herself next to him and drew his arm over her shoulder.

She laid her head on his chest, listening to the rhythmical drumming of his heart. The sound was so strong for such a fragile organ. It was all too easily stilled or broken. Its steady beat abruptly increased to a frantic pounding as his body stiffened. He began to twist and turn. She heard him mumbling about saving someone. Flexing her fingers against his chest while softly speaking words of comfort, Liana tried to ease whatever nightmare had taken hold.

"I will die before I let you hurt her," he shouted. He awoke screaming her name.

"Hey, I'm right here. You were having a bad dream, that's all."

Taron wrapped his trembling arms around her. "Liana, you're safe?" He sounded so broken and afraid.

"Yes, I'm fine. You are not going to lose me." His body sagged against hers and his muscles loosened.

She gently ran her hands along his chest while continuing to reassure him.

"I have a bedtime story that might help. A frightened woman locks herself away thinking it will keep her safe. A brave and devoted sailor comes to rescue her. Despite the challenges she throws at him, he will not give up on his quest. His valiant efforts achieve the impossible. He wins her trust and banishes the fear. He loves her, and it is his love that gives her the courage to face the future. The tale of their loneliness ends, and the story they write together begins."

His lips met hers in a tender kiss of gratitude. "I do love you, Liana."

She kept watch over him until he drifted back to sleep. After pressing a tender kiss to his forehead, she slipped the feather under his pillow.

"I love you too," she whispered.

Dawn of a New Day

"Forgiveness is the final form of love."
Reinhold Niebuhr

Taron woke to the dull grey of dawn staking its claim as the darkness grudgingly receded. Liana was sleeping peacefully in his arms. The light slowly transformed the shadowy objects looming in the cabin into their innocuous daytime counterparts. He tightened his hold, unwilling to let the real world intrude on his bliss. A few short hours ago, he was certain he had lost her, but Liana had not shied away from the truth and embraced all that he was. The soft body pressed against him was proof of her commitment. He was equally determined to conquer his demons and prove himself worthy. While they had started this journey of self-discovery together, the road to absolution was one that needed to be travelled alone.

Liana began to stir and inched closer to him. The dark brown hair cascading over her shoulder begged for his touch, and he was powerless to resist. Taron burrowed his face into her neck as he tried to block out the muted noises of the marina slowly coming to life. His deepest wish was to exist in this moment forever, and he tried to commit every sensation to memory.

"Mmm," Liana purred. "I was having the best dream. Care to make it a reality, Captain?"

She arched her back and brazenly rubbed against him. It was a vivid reminder of the amorous attention he had hoped to lavish on her throughout the night. As tempting as it was to surrender to his impulses, he had plans for a slow and thorough seduction. It took every ounce of self-control he had to pull away.

"Darling, as much as I would like to fulfill your fantasies, I need to get the ship ready to leave port."

She rolled over and directed a cheeky look his way. "You read my mind again. I think hoisting a sail is a very good plan."

Taron groaned. "Is that really what my witty remarks sound like?"

"Yes. Now, answer the question." A smile twitched at the corners of her lips.

"Under different circumstances, I would eagerly devote all of my attention to satisfying your every need. If you recall, Greg managed to secure your mother's release with the promise of leaving Key West at first light." Taron leaned closer, his mouth just below her ear, "She seems to have thwarted our plans once again."

A grin lit up Liana's face. "I'm pretty sure you could call us even in that department after last night."

They both dissolved into unrestrained laughter as she recounted barging in on her mother and Greg. As

Liana continued to fill him in on the details, he toyed with her tank top. The necklace was missing.

"You took off my gift," he could not hide the disappointment in his voice.

Liana stilled his hand with her own. "I did no such thing. The clasp is a bit loose, and it came off during the tussle at the Inn. It's an easy fix."

The happiness of the moment faded as Taron's thoughts drifted back to his family. The failure of the necklace to remain fastened symbolized the tenuous connections to those he cared for. The fragile threads holding two lives together could easily be torn apart when life took an unexpected turn. Liana was his treasure, and he would not lose her. There was nothing more important to him than protecting and caring for the woman he loved.

He felt Liana's fingertips trace the worry lines on his face, and he leaned into her touch.

"Hey, this does not mean we are broken, you will lose me, or whatever else is going on in that head of yours. You know I'm not someone who believes in magical tales, but the story you told be about your mother's belief in the compass proved to be true. It found its way back to me even before I knew it was missing."

"You're right. Liana Taylor, the optimist. I love seeing this side of you."

"If I am more hopeful, it's because of you. I am so grateful for everything I have right now." She tucked her head under his chin. "I meant what I said last night. Nothing is going to come between us. I won't let it."

The conviction of her words had him believing it as well. If anyone could alter the course of fate, it would be this indomitable woman.

"I will do my utmost to arrange some private time for us this evening. But for now, the new day awaits."

Liana flipped onto her stomach and groaned into her pillow. He climbed out of bed and made his way across the room.

She lifted her head. "Maybe tonight, we could see a little less of our honourable captain and a whole lot more of the libidinous pirate."

He was back at the bed in two easy steps, pinning her beneath him. "I can assure you Ms. Taylor, it is well within my expertise to handle more than one wicked wench today."

He heard a small gasp as his teeth tugged on her earlobe. "Until tonight, my love."

A pillow hit the wall next to him as he exited the cabin.

*****

Charlie had been left on his own in the galley and was confidently buttering toast. Everyone was up with the birds except their dancing flamingo. She seemed immune to the chirping of her avian cousins. Thankfully, Delia was also absent and likely standing guard over her sister. Having witnessed last night's antics, he felt sorry for poor Jillian. She would have difficulty looking anyone in the eye, but that was exactly where he was going to keep his line of vision. He really needed to keep his mind out of the feathers—no— gutter. Not feathers, mind out of the gutter, Charlie.

After finishing his last task, he began to organize the condiments Claire had requested. Charlie wanted to make it to the salon in one trip, so he loaded his arms with as much as he could carry. The sack of sugar on top of the pile hit the floor and burst before he made it to the door. Shit!

He grumbled to himself as he emptied his arms onto the counter. There had to be more sugar left. He reached into the darkened cupboard, catching a brief glimpse of snakeskin as he took out the last bag. Charlie shook his head and chuckled. It wasn't like Delia to misplace one of her precious shoes unless she was more plastered than he thought. He poured some sugar into a small container before returning the bag to the proper shelf. Claire came looking for him just as he was sweeping up the last of the spill. Those assembled in the salon were eagerly awaiting breakfast. She told him to hurry.

The captain was discussing the itinerary for the day when they arrived. A morning sail would take them to Big Pine Key. There was a secluded island just off the coast where the ship would anchor for a few days. Even though this had turned into a working vacation, Taron felt that it was high time they all relaxed and enjoyed themselves. Charlie nodded his head in agreement as he grabbed a plate.

The sound of singing interrupted the morning meal and all eyes turned to Delia.

"Not what any of you are thinking. She was sound asleep in our cabin when I left her."

Charlie was about to indulge in another forkful of pancake when he recognized the voice. "I think it's Shane, and he's singing something about red wine."

"Whoever it is sounds entirely too happy," Delia griped.

The door to the salon swung open and Charlie's suspicions were confirmed.

"Morning all, we are back and ready to start the day." Shane lingered on the 'red' part of the word while wiggling his eyebrows.

"Roses are red, violets are red, and my darling Scarlet is red." He grabbed the sexy blonde who tried to wriggle free while he showered her face with kisses.

"Violets are blue, you ass."

"They are red today, you gloriously snarky woman." No one was more shocked than Delia when Shane planted a kiss on her cheek. "In fact, you could say it's a red letter day for me."

His friend no longer had a problem saying 'that' word. Charlie puzzled over the reasons behind such a miraculous cure. It might be something he could try to rid himself of his water phobia.

"Thanks to the beautiful woman standing next to me, I am a new man." He unzipped his jacket, revealing a burgundy T-shirt emblazoned with the words, *Proud to be a Redneck*.

"You are such an idiot. Do you even know what that means?" Delia snapped.

"I think it has something to do with these." He leaned into her and pulled down collar of his shirt, revealing a trail of bright red hickeys.

Delia palmed her face and turned away.

"That's right. My name is Shane Redmond, and I am cured."

*****

Liana watched Taron guide the skiff back to the ship after ferrying the last of the passengers to the island. Delia had asked Liana and her mother to stay behind. Apparently, her aunt had plans for them to resolve their differences. Liana refused to take part in anything until Taron returned. They would face whatever her aunt had concocted together. She exhaled an exasperated sigh. A leisurely afternoon on the beach would have to wait.

Delia slapped a sword into Liana's hand just as she stepped out of Taron's hug. She supplied her hungover mother with the same weapon. Jillian's haggard appearance suggested any fight would be short lived. The pallor of her face rivalled Delia's, and her constricted features suggested a pounding headache lingered. In the glare of the mid-day sun, she looked more like a frail woman who had been beaten down by life rather than the feisty mother who wrestled all adversities into submission.

Jillian seemed equally uninformed about Delia's plans, and her inexhaustible patience for her sister's antics seemed to be at an end. "Are you going to tell us what this is all about? I am really not in the mood for company or combat today."

Delia carried on as usual, refusing to accept the opinions of those around her. "The mother and daughter stand-off ends today. I don't care if the result is death or dismemberment. You two are going to have it out, here and now."

Taron reminded her that the swords had blunt edges before directing a worried look at Liana.

A roll of Delia's eyes was accompanied by an exasperated sigh. "Fine, verbal sparring it is. I'm sure it will be more entertaining for the spectators and very cathartic for the combatants. Degrade, defame, and disparage at will."

Jillian and Liana were finally in agreement. Neither made a move, and they both gawked at the instigator.

"Nothing from either of you? Let's see if I can find a topic that will start things off on the right note." Delia pursed her lips and tapped a finger against her chin. "Here's one. Angry daughter rejects her mother's obsessive attempts to bring her happiness. Discuss."

Liana pointed her sword at Delia. "I am not angry."

Jillian took a few unsteady steps toward her sister. "I am not any of those things."

"Seriously, mom!" Liana redirected her outrage. "Take a closer look at yourself. You have tried to push

278

me toward your version of happiness since the moment we met. In case you are wondering, it feels a little like this." Liana gave her mother a shove with both hands.

Taron shouted from the sidelines, "That's the spirit, Liana! Go after her."

She gave him a quick smile before turning back to her mother. "Your dream is nothing more than childhood fantasy. A girl finds her Prince Charming, they get married and have kids then live happily ever after. I'm sorry my life doesn't fit the fairy tale, but I am not some lonely and unwanted woman. None of this is necessary. You do not have to buy me a man."

"Liana, I did no such thing. I purchased the experience of a lifetime for you." She gave her head a quick shake. "I mean us."

"Sis, cut the crap. You arranged all of this so Liana could have sex." Delia turned a shrewd eye to Taron. "I hope you are giving it all you've got. She did sell her house after all."

Liana boldly made a run at her aunt, swinging her sword from side to side. "Shut the hell up, Delia! Leave Taron out of this. It's not his fight."

"There is no need to be rude to your aunt. Apologize right now." Jillian was clutching her forehead. All of the shouting appeared to be getting to her.

Liana turned and stalked back to her mother stopping when she was inches from her face. "No!"

Jillian teetered as she took a step back, raising her sword into a defensive position. "Stop acting like a child."

"Then stop treating me like one." Liana tapped her mother's blade lightly.

Delia jabbed Taron's side with her elbow. "Now, that's more like it. Am I right?"

The exertion caused the rapid return of colour to Jillian's now flushed cheeks. "Maybe I treat you that way to make up for the past."

"I don't want you to make it up to me. I am not some mistake that has to be fixed. Yes, foster care was tough, but many people have been through hard times. It is not what did the most damage. You did."

Liana advanced, releasing all of her pent up anger. "You didn't want me. She emphasized each word with the furious strike of her blade. "You—gave—me—away."

As she took aim for a final strike, Jillian dropped her sword, leaving herself defenceless. "No, baby. I gave you life."

Liana didn't understand why her mother had surrendered. This wasn't over. "Yes, you gave birth to me. But then you had a decision to make, and you chose to give me away."

"You know Eve left me with no other option."

Liana's shoulders sagged and her lips trembled. "You were supposed to fight for me because that's what mothers do. But you didn't, you let me go."

"Sweetheart, I made the right choice when it mattered most." Jillian broke down into uncontrollable sobs. "I chose to give you life."

The shocking truth was finally exposed. Liana felt her world spinning out of control. "Oh my God! You were going to have an abortion."

Jillian grabbed her daughter's hand and held on tightly. "No! It was never what I wanted. I've kept the pain to myself for all these years, but no more. It was Eve. She made the decision for me. I was young and inexperienced, but I knew it wasn't what I wanted. What she tried to do was unforgivable. Everyone should have the right to choose when destiny leads to a fork in the road."

Delia tried to move toward her sister, but Taron put a hand on her arm. "Why would you keep something like that from me? Jillian, my witch of a mother was going to force you to have an abortion."

She turned her tear-streaked face toward her sister. "I'm so sorry, Delia. She threatened to send you away, and I couldn't cope if you were gone for good. I loved you and Dad so much. I needed you both in my life. I was only sixteen, and I didn't understand the truth until much later in my life. Our father would have loved his grandchild more than anything in the world. Eve knew a baby would jeopardize her future and the stranglehold she had on our family."

Liana tried to free herself from her mother's grasp, but Jillian's strength had returned. "You were a threat that needed to be eliminated. There was no room for tender sentiment in Eve's cold and calculating heart."

This was all too overwhelming. Liana was desperately trying to make sense of each distressing revelation. "You didn't go through with it. I'm still here. I don't understand why you kept this a secret."

"I was too ashamed to tell anyone. I still am." She fell at her daughters feet. "Liana, I said yes. The appointment was booked. I was going to go through with it." Jillian's voice broke as she wiped away a tear, "Is there anyway you can possibly forgive me?"

Liana saw hope briefly flicker in her mother's anguished stare.

"I don't understand what I am supposed to forgive. This is all too much to process." She turned to Taron for support in all of the confusion.

He gave her an encouraging smile. "I suspect there is more to Jillian's story."

"There is." Jillian blinked her eyes shut and took several shuddering breathes before continuing, "The day before the procedure was scheduled, I knew there was no way I could go through with it. I had to get away from Eve, so I ran. I phoned Uncle John and Aunt Margaret from a friend's house, and they came to get me. I told them that Eve was up to her old tricks, making life difficult for me. Other than Delia and I, they were the only people who saw past the polite mask Eve put on with her make up. It was summer break, so I didn't have to worry about excuses for school. I never told John and Margaret about the baby and only stayed long enough to think of a plan."

"I do remember something about them asking you to come for a visit. You were gone for two weeks. Eve insisted I was not allowed any contact." Delia gripped Taron's arm.

"The only calls our aunt and uncle took were from Dad. They were worried Eve would try to use you to get in touch with me. I needed time to work up the courage to confront her. Dad and Eve picked me up when I was ready. I managed to corner my stepmother before we left for home. I told her if she forced me to terminate the pregnancy, I would tell Dad everything. I was bluffing, but she didn't know that."

"Delia, I'm so sorry. I lied to everyone. It hurt me so much to do it, but I had to protect my baby. You know the story from there. She did end up getting rid of my little girl, but not in the way she had planned."

Taron put his arm around Delia shoulders. Her tears were now flowing freely.

"You stood up to Eve on your own. Jillian, she made you suffer for that, didn't she?" Delia's pain resounded in her words.

"It doesn't matter. It is was all worth it in the end." She turned to her daughter.

Liana was stunned. Her interpretation of her mother's choice had defined the entire course of her life. The decisions she made reflected her staunch belief that Jillian had not loved her enough to keep her. She had been wrong. The truth stripped away the last of her defences, and she saw things clearly. The life Liana was living was an illusion that she had created.

She dropped to the deck and took her mothers hands in hers. "You wanted me. Mom, you fought for me."

"Sweetheart, yes. Then, now, and always."

Liana Taylor was not the girl no one wanted. Her mother had battled to keep her safe from the very start. It was the ultimate expression of love and it deserved an equal act of forgiveness. She flung herself into her mother's arms, clinging to her with a fierceness that startled them both.

Jillian rocked her back and forth, smoothing the hair off her face with one hand. "Shush, baby. Don't cry. Your mom is right here, and she loves you so much."

The tightness in Liana's chest released. Everything she was feeling burst forth like the sudden onset of a powerful summer storm. Rather than drown in an enormous wave of emotion, she found herself lifted up toward the heavens. Wrapped in her mother's arms, she let her body sag and her muscles become slack. She was safe and loved. Liana Taylor was no longer the abandoned little girl. She was the cherished child.

"I love you too, mom." Saying the words could not compare to experiencing them with every part of her being.

"And I do forgive you. For nothing and for everything."

Fates Collide

"There is no remedy for love but to love more."
Henry David Thoreau

If they survived the next twenty-four hours, Trevor would make sure he never set foot on another tropical island. As he trailed behind Richard, the old man recounted his son's numerous failings. He tried to make the best of it by mimicking his father's facial expressions and wildly gesticulating arms. Taunting him behind his back was risky, but Trevor was running on adrenaline and caffeine. Not a good combination for a man with a jittery constitution and a gun.

Trevor had been up all night keeping the schooner under surveillance. His father managed a good night's sleep after devising what would hopefully be a successful recovery mission. Richard concluded that the ship had been travelling to the same geocache sites. It narrowed down where the tourists might be heading and allowed them to follow the larger vessel at a discrete distance. His father was brimming with smug satisfaction when the antique ship anchored at another cache site.

They had watched several people go ashore, but there was no way of knowing if anyone was left on board the antique ship. Richard decided any attempt to storm it during daylight hours would be too risky. They would spend the time locating a small delivery of drugs on the island. If his father's scheme to retrieve the cocaine onboard the ship failed, Trevor hoped the paltry offering might buy them a stay of execution. It was probably wishful thinking, but he was desperately trying to hold on to what was left of his sanity.

Once they retrieved the merchandise from the cache site, they would return to the yacht and wait. Their best chance for success, and ultimately survival, was to attempt a coup in the predawn hours while those on board were still sleeping. They would force one person to lead them to the drugs and then make their getaway. It all sounded too easy. While Trevor had his misgivings, he would continue to follow in his father's footsteps. There simply was no other choice.

*****

Liana felt Taron's arms circle her waist as she surveyed the coconut palm in front of her. She had spotted it as the skiff made it's way to shore. Unlike the surrounding trees, it's trunk curved out over the water. Exposed to the elements, it had adapted rather than surrendered. A survivor. It was perfect.

"Darling, what are you thinking?"

"This is it. This is
excitement ran dow⌐
the hand holding tʰ

Taron dropped hⁱ⌐
shoulder. "Are you sure?"

"Now that I've taken the ⌐
with my mother, I need to make ρ
well." Liana opened her hand, revealing heⁱ

She swept her finger along it. "Look how ⌐
and flexes, but doesn't break. A single feather looks
fragile, and yet it has such strength. You would never
think something this delicate would allow its owner to
fly, but it does. Just like her, elegant and resilient."

"Who was she, Liana?" Taron rested his cheek
against hers.

"She was my wayfaring swan. I stumbled across
her when I was eleven. She was resplendent even in the
dingy little enclosure holding her captive. Her white
feathers shone so pure and bright. I couldn't stay away.
I had to get closer, close enough to touch them. I
wanted to see if the feathers were as soft as they
appeared—but before I could touch her, she looked at
me."

Turning around in Taron's arms, she gazed into
the eyes that had enthralled her from the beginning.

"She tilted her head left and right, as if she was
trying to figure me out. She didn't turn away, not like all
the others. I was the little girl no one wanted to see,
broken and hurting, angry and afraid. People looked the
other way, so I learned to hide the ugly emotions and

face they wanted to see. Little by little, day
became invisible to the world, and in the
I lost myself."

er eyes brimmed with tears as she carried on,
she saw me and didn't turn away. She looked at
like she knew exactly what was in my heart. She
nderstood. We were both trapped, and she helped me
find my way out."

"How?" Taron gently brushed his fingers along her
arm in a gesture of comfort.

"After school, I would visit her on my way home. I
told her about my day, and sometimes I made up
stories. Liana the brave and her magical swan would go
on grand adventures together. The more I talked, the
more I found myself opening up about my feelings. I
told her things that I couldn't say to anyone else. It felt
good to have someone listen to me. Slowly, I got back
in touch with who I really was."

Liana ran the feather along her cheek as she
continued to reminisce. "I loved going to see her and I
think she enjoyed it too. She seemed so excited when
she saw me, making these odd little noises and bobbing
her neck as she walked the fence. She was my only
friend. And then…"

The tears began to flow as the pain resurfaced. It
felt so real again, but she needed to confront her
memories. She needed to face what she had done.

"Something in the shadows of the surrounding
trees must have spooked her. She felt threatened and
lifted herself up to flap her wings. I don't know why I

hadn't noticed it before, but part of her right wing was gone. Even though I was only a kid, I knew what they had done to her. It was no accident; she had been broken—mutilated. It's called pinioning. They do it to birds so they can't escape to the wild. She would never fly."

She paused to compose herself. "Taron, we were both so broken. She was born to fly, and someone stole that from her. People are meant to love—to feel things, and that was taken from me. My heart had been cut out just like her wing had been severed."

"Liana, I'm so sorry," he whispered in her ear and nuzzled her cheek as he tightened his hold.

"Don't be. I betrayed her. She offered me friendship and love, but I left her behind. All of the pain came rushing back when I saw her wing. It was too much, so I panicked and ran. I gave up on her. I was no better than the people who had done the same thing to me." There was a bitter sting to the words. She had deemed her action unforgivable.

"That's not the worst of it. I realized my mistake and went back the next day, but she was gone. I never saw her again. My best friend disappeared and I never got to tell her goodbye—or say that I loved her. And Taron, I did love her."

She looked at the treasured remembrance in her palm. "I collected quite a few of them during our visits, but this is all I have left of her. I've had it locked away all of these years, but it's not mine to keep. I need to set us both free."

Liana brushed away the last of her tears as her eyes scanned the horizon. She would release her suffering into the world along with the feather. She turned and took the few steps to the tree, climbing onto the trunk. Her plan was to straddle it and shimmy out over the water. She was slowly moving along the roughened bark when she heard Taron's worried voice.

"Are you sure this is a good idea? Darling, don't take this the wrong way, but you have been known to take the occasional spill."

She looked down and saw him following along beneath her. God, she loved him. He had not given up, no matter how much she pushed him away. The insight she gained from her mother's revelations showed Liana that her isolation was largely self-imposed. She had prescribed a test everyone was destined to fail. Everyone but him. Taron would always find a way to support her. His love was the security she needed to move forward with her life.

"I really think that's far enough, Liana. You can catch a breeze from there, and it will carry her out over the water."

"Taron, I can do this." She heard him gasp as she swung both legs to one side of the trunk. Her reassuring gaze seemed to ease his concern and his shoulders relaxed.

"Of course, you can. I'm just sharing in the joy of the moment." He was trying so hard to bolster her confidence, but she knew him well enough to hear the uncertainty in his voice. He could be just as protective as her mother, and the thought made her giggle. Taron was right. This was a joyful moment.

She pressed a kiss to the feather before releasing it into the clear blue sky. "Fly, my friend. Fly and be free."

The feather rode the gentle current of air, and Liana's heart soared right along with it. What she failed to take into account was the onshore breeze which predominated during the day. A sudden gust had her precious plume swirling back over the island.

"No! Taron, it's going the wrong way." She crawled back along the trunk as the feather drifted through the trees.

"It seems she has her own direction in mind. It's a great view from here. Why don't you climb back down?" Taron was anxiously circling below her.

She turned to do just as he had asked, but then paused. The little girl in pig-tails longed to fly away just as much as she had wanted it for her swan. Liana was all grown up, but there was no reason she couldn't make her wish come true. Glancing down, Taron was still standing below her. His worry seemed to fade away as he saw the happiness in her smile.

"Taron, I'm going to jump." Before he had a chance to protest, she let herself fall.

It was not the romantic catch she had in mind. She landed on him with a thud and he fell back onto the sand. Liana ended up sprawled across his chest.

"My love, give me a little more warning next time. Wouldn't want to damage any vital organs, particularly…"

She covered his mouth in a lazy kiss before he could finish whatever titillating comment he had planned. An upward thrust of his hips let her know where his thoughts were headed. Her chuckle was silenced when the kiss intensified. The waves washed over them in a slow and easy rhythm as the cool water soothed the heat their body contact sparked. Liana's toes curled into the sand, and she lost herself in the passion she was feeling.

Taron rolled them over until she was pressed into the wet shore. He propped himself up on one arm. "Has the brilliant princess truly fallen for the humble pirate?"

"Yes, I love you. The princess loves the pirate, and Liana is hopelessly in love with Taron."

Another enthusiastic kiss followed her declaration. Every physical sensation was magnified by the love she felt for him. Lifting her hands, she slid her fingers through his hair and pulled him closer. Their passionate encounter came to an unexpected halt when a large wave surged over them. Liana squealed and found herself sputtering sea water as she was hauled upward by two powerful arms.

"Dammit! Are you alright, Liana?"

She blinked away the salty drops clinging to her eyelashes and saw anxious blue eyes staring back at her. "I'm more than alright. I've never felt better, and I'm in no rush for reality to intrude." She tipped her head toward the group gathered further down the beach.

Taron massaged his forehead before running a hand through his hair. "We probably should head back before your mother sends out a search party. I think we can enjoy a leisurely stroll as long as you stay within her line of vision." He took her hand and they splashed their way through the edge of the surf.

Liana tried to take in the beauty of their surroundings, but found her gaze continually returning to the man who had changed her life. She never thought she would recover what she had lost so long ago. Yet, here he was. Someone who had seen the faintest pulse and steadfastly cleared the rubble of pain and fear to expose the love still steadily beating in her heart. Her friend, her love, the hero her mother had tried to create.

Preoccupied with her thoughts, she did not notice their saunter had slowed to a standstill. Taron seemed to be inspecting the mud at his feet.

"Are you looking for buried treasure? I'm absolutely certain I've found mine, but if you're not sure, I can help you search."

Taron did not reciprocate her teasing and there was a note of longing in his voice. "Our walk reminded me of summer weekends spent beach-combing with Mum and Daniel. As we looked for interesting tidbits, I noticed something about the sand. Each time the water receded back into the ocean it left a different pattern behind. My brother and I called it sand sighting. It soon became our favourite pastime. It was like cloud gazing, and we took turns guessing what the different formations might be.

'When we were old enough to understand, Mum explained that it was a give and take between the elements. The water removed a layer of sand and brought it back with the next wave. She told us there was a balance to all things in nature, light and dark, life and death, even love and hate. My mother believed people complemented each other in the same way, calling them soul mates. Mum hoped I would find mine one day. She would have adored you."

Liana was awestruck. "You think that's what we are, soul mates?"

"I do. We both felt a deep connection right from the start. I believe some higher power was trying to give back the love we both lost. You needed to be held as much as I needed someone to hold. You provided exactly what I needed to heal, and I was able to do the same for you. If that is not destiny, then I don't know what it is."

Liana threw her arms around him and buried her head in his shoulder. He stroked her hair as she collected her thoughts. A week ago, she would not have agreed with a single word he just said, but now, she had no other explanation as to how she could feel so much in such a short period of time.

She tipped her head up to him. "I believe again."

"Believe in what, my love?"

"Magic—destiny, whatever unseen force brings two people together and keeps them on a journey to love and happiness."

His characteristic smirk found its way to his lips. "Be careful, Liana. You are starting to sound an awful lot like your mother."

Taron ran down the beach before she could answer. She watched him splash through the water and took a moment to revel in how carefree she felt. He turned and gave her a wink, before diving into the ocean. She was only too happy to chase after him.

*****

Taron could not remember a time when the sea did not hold his heart in thrall. He knew her more intimately than any woman and entrusted her with his safekeeping despite her mercurial moods. What seemed so placid and serene one moment could instantly rise into a turbulent force of destruction. The turquoise water stretching to the horizon could no longer compare to the beauty and love he felt for another.

He found his gaze continually wandering to shore. The sight of Liana stretched out on the sand was more enticing than any siren's song. As he emerged from the water, she lifted her head and gave him a sultry smile. Rather than watch his approach, she returned to the studious examination of her reading material.

"Did you enjoy the view?" he teased.

The ensuing silence demanded a more daring action. A quick shake of his head had the water clinging

295

to his hair cascading onto her back. He delighted in her surprised squeal and managed to jump back when her arm snaked out to grab his leg.

"I just dried off after our swim. Keep the water to yourself." The sparkle in her eyes betrayed the annoyed tone of her voice.

Taron dropped down beside her and continued his quest to arouse a more enthusiastic reaction. He traced a rivulet of water as it ran from her shoulder to the diminutive scrap of fabric covering her bottom. The goosebumps forming in the wake of his fingers told him exactly how much his touch affected her. Seeing her in the gold bikini she had unveiled earlier did unspeakable things to him.

"Now is not the time or place. We are surrounded again."

The disappointment in Liana's words matched the exasperation he felt. If three was a crowd, then ten was a full fledged invasion. Delia had set up her encampment in a shady spot which allowed her to observe everyone on the beach. She was draped in a hammock with her usual drink in one hand. Out of necessity, Jillian was also shunning the sunning and had settled on a blanket next to her sister. The rest of their friends were scattered along the beach, enjoying their island sojourn.

"Taron, I know you are as frustrated with the situation as I am, but we have to make the best of it. We can't just wish them all away or order them back to the ship. It pains me to admit this, but I should have indulged my mother in her romantic fantasy for a little longer."

She flipped to the cover of *Romancing Liana.* "If I had read more, the two of us would be alone tonight. We were rapidly approaching the climactic moment in the story."

His fingers danced up her arm and along her shoulder before he whispered into her ear, "Darling, nothing in their story can compare to the astounding climax I have in mind."

"Please! You're going to kill me with those lines. I will make sure you live up to every one of your innuendos. Right now, all we have is their version of events." She handed him the manuscript.

He read for a few minutes and then suddenly stopped. "Tom and Greg play officers who board the ship in a rescue attempt. The pirate captain is unable to defeat them. He jumps ship and takes the princess hostage."

He glared at the pair responsible for the egregious writing as they relaxed in the shade. "I take great umbrage at their characterization of me as a coward."

"You are missing the point. The two of us were supposed to be stranded on this island. It's the last geocache stop on the trip. Mom even mapped out a quest for us."

She turned a page. "Take a look at this. Only my mother would draw a map with tiny footsteps. It ends at the treasure chest with an 'x' underneath it."

Taron carefully examined the text and noticed some of it had been crossed out and rewritten. His smile broadened as he read aloud, *"The pirate uncovered the bountiful treasure hidden in the chest of the princess while she was busy handling his sword. They pillaged and plundered for the rest of their lives. The End."*

"It does not say that?" Liana leaned over and peered at the offending lines. "I think it is safe to say this was a last-minute edit by my aunt."

Taron glanced back at the makeshift campsite. "I am ready to dislodge Delia from her self-appointed role as queen of all she surveys."

"Pretty sure I remember our last attempt at a hostile takeover failed."

Taron hoped the smile he gave his love was as naughty as his thinking. "Darling, I think it's time you fulfilled your earlier promise to bind us together physically."

Liana's startled brown eyes met his. "Taron! I am doing no such thing with an audience."

"My dear, you really must focus. I am merely accepting your prior offer to introduce me to the frightful contraption hanging from the trees. In order to do so, we must evict the current occupant."

"It's called a hammock. Two people can share if they position themselves correctly."

"I am willing to experiment with any position you like."

Her playful giggle followed the suggestive wiggle of his eyebrows.

"I do like the sound of that." Liana jumped to her feet. "If we sneak up behind her and grab the mesh, Delia's butt hits the sand before she knows what happened."

"By all means, let's go have some fun."

*****

Taron woke to find his limbs tangled with the woman he loved. It was the perfect afternoon in paradise. He tried to prolong his happiness, but a sudden cramp in his calf begged for immediate relief. He extricated his hand from under Liana's shoulder and began to massage the offending muscle. Her body responded instinctively, and she tried to pull him closer in her sleep. The resulting wave of motion flipped the hammock, landing them in the dirt.

"Bloody hell!"

His irritation was short lived as he felt soft curves pressed into to him. He basked in the sensual delight.

"What happened?" Her eyes looked down at him in confusion.

"It seems hammocks are more dangerous than they appear. Wouldn't you agree, Delia?"

Liana's delighted laughter rang out into the quiet evening air.

It was too quiet. Why was Delia not making some lewd remark about taking a tumble or who comes out on top? Liana sensed Taron's unease and rolled off to one side. He pushed himself into a sitting position and scanned the beach. Everyone had vanished.

299

"My guess would be alien abduction, but I'm pretty sure they would beam Delia down the minute she opened her mouth." Liana seemed more amused than concerned.

Taron surveyed the campsite and spotted a note tacked onto a tree trunk.

"I think the conspicuous absence of our fellow travellers has a Jillian feel to it." He retrieved the message, and they read it together.

We decided to let you sleep since you both looked so peaceful. Supper is in the hamper, and extra blankets are next to the hammock. Call if you need us. See you in the morning. Love, Mom.

"It seems your mother is determined to conclude her romantic epic as planned." His provocative stare had Liana dropping her eyes back to the note.

"There is a bit more here. It looks as though someone added it in a hurry. It says…"

She blushed furiously and held the page out to Taron. There were hastily scribbled words below her mother's writing.

Condoms are with the napkins. Delia

"What is with my family? This is beyond mortifying." She groaned and palmed her face.

"Liana, I fail to see the problem. A romantic night away from prying eyes is exactly what we were planning."

"That's what bothers me. I wouldn't be surprised if a pair of binoculars were trained on us at this very moment." She turned her gaze toward the ship on the horizon.

Taron looked up at the tree branches. "I can arrange the articles we have on hand into something more secluded. I seem to recall an inspired setting on a beach in Key West."

"It was the perfect night until we were interrupted." Liana arched an eyebrow.

"We better not leave anything to chance then." Taron turned off his cell and pitched it onto a nearby blanket.

They busied themselves draping blankets over the mosquito netting Delia had insisted come ashore. Pillows, towels, and the quilt Jillian had left behind finished off the cozy interior. It was a blanket fort to rival anything Taron had created with his brother.

A light supper accompanied by cups of lemonade followed. Taron insisted they forgo any of the libations in the hamper since they were already besotted with each other. Liana was unusually quiet as they ate and took much longer than necessary to repack the leftovers.

As much as they were both ready to indulge in their passion, Taron knew she was battling her nerves. He also found himself overthinking the intimate night which lay ahead of them. His gaze landed on the manuscript as he tried to come up with a way to put them both at ease. It was the perfect solution.

He waited until Liana returned from her task before assuming the role of dashing scoundrel. Taron narrowed his eyes and donned a sinful smirk.

"It seems your cowardly retinue has abandoned you to face the fearsome pirate alone. Cut off from any rescue, I now hold the fate of the courageous princess in my hands. Will she be able to maintain her bravery or will she beg for mercy?"

There was brief second of hesitation before she followed his lead. "The thought of being marooned on this island with a man whose reputation is so scandalous does give me chills."

She gave her lower lip a gentle tug while holding his heated stare. "Unfortunately, the brief cooling effect is not enough to ward off the intense tropical heat." Grabbing the hem of her oversized t-shirt, she pulled it upwards slowly exposing inch by inch of creamy skin.

It had the desired impact. Taron's desire flared with an intensity he had never known.

"I will bargain for my release by offering myself in trade." Liana pulled the garment over her head and tossed it aside.

"Tonight, I am yours."

"What are you saying?" He quickly dropped all pretence as he tried to discern if his assumption was correct.

"Taron, it's time to make good on all of those promises. Go get the napkins."

*****

Liana squinted and tried to focus her vision in the darkness. The dying embers of the fire no longer shed any light or heat into their hidden sanctuary. She inched closer to Taron, pressing every part of her body against his warmth. Happiness and love permeated her entire being as she lay next to him. Tonight was more than a physical act; she had bared herself body and soul surrendering herself completely. It was the most intense experience of her life.

There was no longer any need to hold back in anything she said or did. Taron saw through to the core of her being and refused to turn away. By exposing the parts of herself she felt were too damaged to reveal, he showed her what she refused to believe. She was beautiful. He accepted and loved her as she was. There was no need to be better, stronger, or braver. She was Liana Taylor and that was enough.

As she thought about the day, Liana had trouble believing any of it had happened. It felt more fantasy-like than anything her mother could have come up with. Her fingers outlined the contours of Taron's face, reassuring her that he was very real.

The feather light kiss she placed on the lips of her lover earned her a lazy smile in return. "I'm sorry for disturbing your much-needed rest. I couldn't resist."

"Never apologize for waking me in such a delightful manner." His broad smile reached the crinkles at the corners of his eyes. He was happy—truly happy, and the knowledge swelled her heart.

She returned his smile, wondering what he was thinking. Taron had lived up to every seductive promise, but had it been everything he had hoped for? She suddenly felt very vulnerable and looked down, nervously pulling threads from the quilt.

He must have sensed her unease, tilting her head up with a finger under her chin. "What is it?"

Liana saw only love shining from his eyes, and it gave her the courage to ask. "Was it—was it what you thought it would be?"

His face remained soft, but gave nothing away. Closing his eyes, he remained silent. Her pulse accelerated as she waited for his answer. She tried to offset her rising anxiety with a light tone.

"Alright, why is the man who always finds the right words suddenly so quiet."

He turned toward her and propped his head on a hand. "Liana, tonight was the most profound moment of my life. I—I…" He paused and closed his eyes again, struggling with what he wanted to say. "There are no words to capture what happened between us. What I feel for you. I can't…" He stopped again, and she covered his lips with hers.

"Good because I feel the same way." She gave him a sleepy grin.

"It's still early. You should try to get some more rest. Yesterday, must have been emotionally exhausting." Taron trailed his hand down her arm.

"I'm fine. It felt good to totally let go."

"I recall two times. Would you care to make it a third?" A smile dangled on the corner of his lips.

Liana couldn't help the blush that stained her cheeks at the reminder of how passionate the night had been. "That confident in your abilities, Mr. Royce?"

He sat up abruptly, the blanket pooling at his hips. "I don't remember hearing any complaints. I do recall you making some delightful sounds when I..."

She leaned in and cut him off with another slow and full kiss.

One more thing would make her bliss complete. "Will you watch the sunrise with me?"

Taron stood and pulled her up into his arms. "I can think of no better way to begin the day. Now and always."

They pulled on some clothes and emerged from the shelter.

A disembodied voice in the shadows took them by surprise. "It looks like you two are in the wrong place at the wrong time."

A dark figure approached, levelling a gun them. "A cruel twist of fate, is it not?"

Devil of a Time

*"If you aren't in over your head,
how do you know how tall you are?"*
TS Eliot

Liana's heart hammered in her chest as her mind desperately scrambled to make sense of what was happening. They were being held at gunpoint by an insane man who seemed to materialize out of thin air. As much as it felt like some bizarre dream, their plight was all too real. The shock had temporarily incapacitated her, but the urge to flee now took hold. She turned her eyes to Taron whose hardened glare was locked on the gunman as he clenched and released his fists. Liana knew he was ready to fight, but there was nothing either of them could do.

The would-be assailant oozed his way towards them like an oil slick spreading across a pristine body of water. Liana saw stealth and cunning in his comportment and realized he was not a man who would be easily caught off guard.

"It seems I have interrupted a lover's tryst." The thin line of his mouth transformed into a corrupted smile.

Taron stepped in front of Liana shielding her as best he could. She tried to force her way past his arm, but was no match for his adrenaline fuelled strength.

"Happy endings are in short supply this morning, and you two are standing in the way of mine. No time for tearful goodbyes." He aimed the gun at Liana's head. "The gentleman in me says the lady goes first."

"Father, no!" A second man careened out of the trees.

The older man gave him an irritated glance. "Son, did I just hear you give me an order? You were to meet me back at the skiff."

"You can't kill them. I mean—um—it might not be in our best interest if you did. They could be more valuable to us alive. We don't know what the old woman has planned. Two hostages could come in handy if she doesn't get the cocaine or sends the cops after us."

The father considered his son's request while looking up to the heavens. "You are finally making some sense, Trevor. There might be hope for you yet. Put some cuffs on the man while I keep my eye on his girlfriend."

Liana immediately recognized the younger man. He was the drunk who had accosted her at the Inn. The look on Taron's face told her that he had formed the same conclusion. Recognition also darted across

Trevor's features as he approached them. He said nothing as he fastened the restraints. Taron's muscles trembled with the strain of maintaining control.

When Trevor moved away, she realized there was only one set of handcuffs. She would remain free. Liana frantically surveyed their surroundings for anything that might be useful and saw Taron's phone. He had tossed it on the blanket near the hammock. It was too far away. Any attempt to reach it would draw the older man's attention and fire.

"Trevor, you lead with the brunette. The boyfriend and I will follow you."

Instincts from the past focussed her harried thoughts. A small glimmer of hope occurred as they neared the picnic hamper on the beach. She took a sidestep toward the blanket and twisted her foot under the edge of material. There was very little in the way of pretending as she tripped and fell.

"Don't shoot, it was an accident. I'm such a klutz and this happens all the time. I didn't see the blanket in the dim light, and my foot got caught."

Taron picked up on her ruse and tried to prolong the distraction. "Darling, you are most likely still suffering from the after-effects of your concussion. It has only been a week and most people…"

"You shut up." The father pressed his gun into Taron's side. "As for you, girlie, keep your balance or it will cost you dearly. I am not a man to be trifled with."

Trevor jerked her into an upright position and muttered, "No one messes with Richard Hyde if they want to stay alive."

Liana had accomplished her task and would not risk any further attempts to secure their freedom. They proceeded along a trampled path of vegetation to a small section of beach. Trevor withdrew another pair of cuffs from a duffle bag on the skiff and secured Liana's hands.

Four people barely fit into the small boat. It made the journey across the water safely, but bobbed precariously as Trevor tied it to the yacht. He kept a gun trained on them while Hyde climbed aboard. Taron was followed by Liana. Unable to use her bound hands to steady herself, she struggled with the last step of the ladder and lurched forward. Hyde caught her before she fell onto the deck. Liana stiffened and fought back the urge to scream when she saw the tattoo on his arm. There was no mistaking it from the description Greg had provided.

"You really are a clumsy woman aren't you? You also seem to be cursed with unimaginably bad luck."

Liana lifted her head and met the lifeless eyes of a man who was no longer in touch with the human part of himself. He was a cold-blooded killer who was no different from the predators lurking in the waters around them. Her mind struggled to grasp the implications of their latest misfortune. While Taron had vowed to conquer his need for revenge, life seemed determined to keep him on the path to self-destruction.

They were ushered below deck by father and son. Trevor secured one of Taron's cuffs to the post of a massive oak headboard while his father kept an eye on Liana. When her turn came, Hyde shifted his attention to Taron, badgering him with questions about the lay out of the Wicked Wench. Trevor had difficulty attaching her restraints to a brass railing on the wall. He turned his back for a moment and she seized the opportunity, deftly depositing the item she had retrieved into the pocket of his cargo shorts. Liana's gaze dropped to his feet as she drew back. Her sharp gasp drew Trevor's attention.

She tried to cover as best she could, "Ow! You twisted my wrist."

Taron gave her an agonized look. Before he had a chance to respond, Hyde swung around to face her. "You better toughen up, girlie. Your pain has just begun. Keep your mouth shut or I will do it for you."

Trevor pulled some duct tape from his bag. He was overruled by his father who lectured him on the ineffectiveness of using it to muffle noises. Hyde had something more lasting in mind should they cry out. No further action was taken, and Liana felt a wave of relief when both men left the room. The sound of a radio told her there were other ways to keep any calls for help from being heard.

Taron tried to give her a reassuring smile, but his eyes were robbed of their usual mirth. "How are you holding up, my love?"

Liana reached out her hand. "I'd be much better if your arms were wrapped around me."

He stretched out as far as he could, and while their finger tips barely touched, it was enough. "I'm so sorry, Liana. It seems I court disaster at every turn. I will find a way to get you out of this."

"Don't you dare go there. The psycho had a gun pointed at us. If you had tried anything, we would both be dead. We will find a way to free ourselves. I refuse to believe fate would bring us together only to have it end it this way."

His eyes brightened. "You have a tremendous amount of faith considering the dire nature of our circumstances."

Tears glistened in her eyes as she stared at her hand. "She came back to me." Liana opened her palm to reveal the swan feather.

Taron's disbelieving stare moved from the feather to her face. "How is that possible?"

"I don't know. I looked down and saw it stuck to the velcro on Trevor's shoe." The wonder she felt allayed her fear. "She came back. Somehow, against all odds, she came back. Taron, it has to mean something."

His voice was steady and sure. "It does, my darling. It means we must have hope. We will make it home, alive and together."

Liana nodded her head in agreement. Like the feather she held in her hand, they had been blown off course. They could allow themselves to be buffeted by the storm that had descended upon them, or they could find the strength to take control. There had to be a way out.

"Alright. We stay calm and come up with a plan." Liana uttered the words with every ounce of conviction she felt.

Keeping their emotions in check was the key to survival. It would be a Herculean effort for Taron. The minute he saw the tattoo his temper would get the best of him. By letting him know, she could help him try to come to terms with his emotions.

"I need to tell you something before we make any plans. Greg told me about the tattoo. It was on the arm of the man who murdered your family. He described the horrible thing and said it had some Latin words on it."

"Occidere aut occidi. Why bring that up now?" Taron looked puzzled.

Liana braced herself for what was to come. She knew with absolute certainty he would put himself in harms way to protect her from the tragic end that had befallen his family. Resisting the temptation to seek his revenge if an opportunity arose was another matter. He had clawed his way back from his rage and despair once, and she would help him do it again. She would not lose him.

"Liana?"

"I saw it. The man who killed your family. It's Hyde."

It took a moment for Taron to fully absorb her words. Anger flared in his eyes and his face contorted

312

into a tortured grimace. The menace in his voice terrified her.

"He has taken everything from me. I will not let him have you."

Taron made a futile attempt to wrench himself free from his shackles. He jerked his arm back, writhing in unrestrained fury. He was like a wounded animal fighting to free himself from a trap before the hunter returned. His growls and shrieks were raw and primal.

Icy fingers of pain reached into Liana's chest and squeezed her heart. She could not bear to see him in such anguish. Any hope still left in his soul needed to be rekindled before it was smothered by a blanket of hatred. Tears burned behind her eyes as she cried out his name and begged him to return to her once more.

"Taron, I need you. Please, I can't do this alone."

He suddenly stilled and sank to the floor. Taron's darkened eyes met hers and she held his gaze trying to see the truth of his thinking. His voice was low and tight as he reined in his fury. "I will protect you with my life. If he tries to hurt you, I will find a way to kill him."

She closed her hand around the feather. The villains were not going to win. Not this time.

"It won't come to that. I've already set something in motion. It's not much of a chance, but it's something."

"What has my brilliant lass done?" The slightly raised corners of his mouth told her that he was coming around.

"The magic books I told you about may have shattered my dreams, but they taught me a thing or two. Perfecting a few sleight of hand tricks had its advantages in the system."

"Does this have to do with your bogus stumble on the beach?"

"I had to work quickly and didn't find much, but I managed to grab some of Jillian's silly princess napkins. If at least one finds it way from Trevor's pocket to someone on our ship, they might figure out the connection. I heard Hyde mumbling about a riskier plan because they had wasted time and it was now daylight. Those bastards are going to raid the ship in order to reclaim their drugs. Everyone we love will be at risk."

Taron's eyes held a steely resolve. "Don't think the worst. Greg has a weapon and is one of the most street wise detectives on the force. If anyone can keep them safe, it's him."

"Don't forget my mother. She may not have access to a gun but you know how fierce she can be. Those two don't stand a chance against Jillian in full on protective mama mode." She gave him a tentative smile.

Taron reached out for her again. "I love you, Liana"

"I love you too. We will make it." She held out the hand holding the feather. "Believe."

*****

THE WAYFARING SWAN

The peaceful morning had Delia feeling uneasy. Whenever there was smooth sailing on this trip, stormy seas seemed to follow. She had elected herself to maintain law and order, recognizing the need for leadership in Taron's absence. No one else would be as ready for the other shoe to drop as she would. Jillian and Greg were off to see if the ardent lovers needed anything. Thinking about all of the captain's boasting brought a smirk to Delia's lips. Hopefully, Liana's needs would have been met several times by now.

As she made her way onto the deck, Delia tried to keep her salacious thoughts in check. Shane and Scarlet were standing at the rail, and she was thankful for whatever caught their eye. They had been slobbering all over each other since the miracle cure. The ship of fools had somehow been transformed into the love boat. Delia's next mission would be to arrange some alone time for the conventional detective and her sister. Her mind was churning with all of the possibilities as she followed the ardent couple's line of sight. A yacht was approaching in a very erratic manner. The man behind the wheel was frantically waving and shouting.

"What's he saying?" Delia had difficulty hearing anything over the music blaring from the boat. She cast a worried glance at Shane.

"He says his boat is disabled and he needs help. He wants to tether it to ours and come aboard. What do you think we should do?"

Delia could spot a lie a mile away, and nothing about this seemed right. "I don't like it. I say we don't let him."

Tom had been packing gear for the day's island adventure and now joined them. "Scarlet, go tell Claire we need her. She is in the galley with Charlie."

The frail looking man provided additional information as he navigated the vessel closer. He told them he was on his way to Big Pine Key to pick up his son. The boat had engine trouble and started drifting shortly after he set out. Without anyone to help, he was not strong enough to work the anchor.

Delia's lie detector was in overdrive. Claire hurried over to the group, and to no one's surprise, knew about the tricky rafting at anchor procedure. The newcomer also seemed very knowledgeable about connecting two boats at sea. They decided to secure the yacht, but the stranger would remain where he was while they tried to help him. Delia felt a surge of pride as the novice crew managed to attach the fore and aft mooring lines to the schooner's cleats. They were literally patting themselves on the back when she noticed the visitor making his way onto their ship.

"No one has given you permission to come aboard. What do you think you are doing?" Delia yelled.

The unsuspecting passengers were all focussed on the man slowly making his way toward them. Delia watched as he reached into the pocket of his jacket. He had his gun drawn before she could utter a word.

Another voice from behind told them to freeze. Who the hell was going to move with a gun pointed at them? She turned and watched a sopping wet fool pull a weapon out of a plastic bag. The ladder had been left in the down position after the skiff had gone ashore, and the second intruder must have used it to clamber onto the ship.

The older and drier of the two men took charge, ushering them into the salon. They were lined up on one side of the room and told to slide their phones across the floor. Delia nodded to the group, and they followed her silent command.

Once the task had been accomplished, the mastermind of the operation spoke, "I have had a very trying morning, and my patience is wearing thin."

He aimed his gun at Delia. "Where is my cocaine?"

She was not about to let some obnoxious intruder threaten her. "What the hell are you talking about? You have clearly boarded the wrong ship. Do we look like a bunch of drug dealers to you?"

"Father, they are clueless. If they thought the cocaine was sugar, they must have stored it in the kitchen."

"Don't just stand there, Trevor. Go get it!"

Dammit! Charlie was most likely still preparing breakfast. Delia hoped his newfound fascination with cooking was not going to get him killed. Her heart nearly stopped when she heard a high pitched scream. If they hurt her sidekick, she would murder them with her bare hands. The flunky soon hurtled back into the salon as if he was being chased by the devil himself. He had his gun drawn, but was shrieking about a snake while holding out his left arm.

"Dying, I'm dying! I knew it would be a fucking snake that got me in the end. Richard Hyde always gets what he wants, and I'm a goner."

"Pull yourself together, son. Where is the cocaine?"

"Screw the cocaine! Didn't you hear what I just said? I've been bitten by a coral snake. Those red and black little shits you told me were extremely venomous."

Claire tried her best to help. "Calm down and listen carefully. Did the snake have a yellow stripe touching a black one?"

Trevor looked at her with a stunned expression. "Sorry, but I didn't stop to take notes because I was too busy fighting for my life." He paused to catch his breath. "I don't think so, but I can't be sure."

In a lecture that would lull most students to sleep, Claire continued to explain the finer points of serpent identification. "Two snakes which are very similar in appearance inhabit the Keys. An easy way to tell the difference is the rhyme, 'if red touches yellow it kills a fellow.' I think you were bitten by a scarlet king snake whose yellow stripes are adjacent to its black ones. While the bite stings, the venom is not lethal."

Trevor's obvious relief was short-lived. "Oh shit!"

His irate father bellowed, "Now, what?"

"I found a bag when I checked the cupboards. I reached my hand in to grab it and that's when the snake attacked. I didn't have a firm hold on the bag, and it kind of—well—burst when it bounced off the counter. It landed in a sink full of soapy water."

The most delicious smile made it's way to Delia's lips. The old guy turned a shade of red which would have sent Shane running from the room had he still been burdened with his affliction. She took small comfort in the fact that nothing seemed to be going right for the bumbling criminals.

Hyde directed his fury at the group. He wildly waved his gun as he shouted out his next question, "What happened to the rest of my merchandise? There should be two more bags of cocaine—sugar. I want answers and I want them now!"

"Well that explains what went wrong with the cookies. Thank goodness no one ate them." Shane gave Delia an 'I told you so look,' pleased his culinary skills were not at fault.

"Are you trying to tell me that you used several thousand dollars worth of cocaine to bake cookies? What kind of imbeciles are you people?"

"The kind who do dessert not drugs." Delia's snark was the only weapon at her disposal.

"The last bag! Where is the last bag?"

Claire answered, "It got knocked off the counter, and swept into the trash."

"Do you know what this means, father? We're dead. That vicious old broad will snuff us out if she

319

doesn't get her drugs. She is going to turn us into burgers."

"Not now, Trevor. We need to get out of here and make sure no one follows us. Watch them and shoot anyone that moves."

Father of the year pulled out an odd looking tool and began working on the door's lock. As much as Delia wanted to wring their necks, taking action would only get someone killed. His task was swiftly accomplished and the pair took off.

Delia was at the only exit in an instant. Of course, the handle would not budge. She overheard the heated exchange between father and son, gleaning the basics of their plot. Trevor was to purge the gas tank and empty their limited supply into the sea. Daddy dearest was going to disable the ship's communications and instrument panel.

Tom managed to find something to work the hinges free and began the task. He had just removed the first one when a gun shot pierced the unsettling silence.

"No! Hurry up and get us the hell out of here." Delia was frantic.

She leapt over the fallen door right after the second hinge was popped. The last mooring line to their skiff uncoiled and slid across the deck as she raced down the stairs, fearing the worst.

"Charlie! Where are you? Answer me!"

The door to the washroom inched it's way forward. A familiar face peeked through the opening.

320

"Delia? I knew it would take more than some gun toting gangsters to eliminate you. I was thinking it might be more along the lines of a nuclear weapon."

She sprinted forward and pulled him into an enormous hug. He eventually managed to squirm his way free.

"I was coming up the stairs when I heard the shouting. I felt the best option was to make myself scarce while I tried to come up with a plan." Charlie gave a bashful nod toward the washroom. "It's always been the place I do my best thinking."

*****

Nothing seemed to be out of place, but the abandoned campsite had Greg worried. Jillian had left behind a treasure map to the cache site and was convinced Liana and Taron were on a romantic quest. She made herself comfortable awaiting their return while Greg examined the surrounding area. He followed a trail of flattened grass to a secluded beach. Drag marks in the sand indicated a boat had been pulled ashore. None of this felt right and the evidence was pointing to a disturbing conclusion. He hurried back to Jillian, arriving in time to hear a shot ring out from the schooner.

"We go back now!"

He pulled out his gun with one hand and grabbed a pale pink arm with the other. They ran across the sand to the skiff. Jillian barely had time to get in before Greg started the motor. He sped back to the schooner.

Scarlet waved them in and helped Shane tie off the small boat.

Delia was orchestrating the activity on board with enviable precision. Greg saw concern flicker in her eyes when she looked at the empty boat.

"They aren't with you?"

He tried to quell his own unease before responding. "No. The beach was deserted when we arrived. What the hell happened here?"

Delia recounted the events. Nobody knew who fired the gun, but everyone on board was fine. Tom and Charlie had surveyed the damage below decks and reported there was no fuel or means of communication. The need for immediate assistance had Greg reaching for his phone. He came up empty-handed and turned to Jillian.

"Could I have my cell back?"

"Oh, no! Greg, I'm sorry. I met Claire on the way back to your cabin and we chatted. I followed her back to the galley to get breakfast for Liana and Taron. I forgot to go back for it."

He saw the worry etched on Jillian's face and tried to reassure her as best he could given their dire straits. "Everything is going to be alright. It's in my cabin so we can still call for help." He put arm around the upset mother.

"I'm afraid that's not possible." Tom exchanged a worried look with Charlie. "Any valuables left out in the open were taken."

As much as he feared for his best friend, he needed to get everyone to safety. "We need to get help. Two of us will take the skiff to the sheriff station in Marathon. The police can handle the drug dealers, and the coast guard will evacuate those remaining on board."

Delia voiced her concern, "Shouldn't we be trying to find the missing couple?"

"You're right," Jillian said. "We need to search the island. My map was pretty straightforward, but they must have taken a wrong turn."

Greg put both hands on her shoulders. "I found signs the fugitives came ashore not far from our encampment. It's possible they stumbled across Liana and Taron."

"You think they were kidnapped?"

Greg would not voice his worst fears given the lack of evidence. As the seconds ticked by, he said nothing.

"You think they are hurt—oh God—or worse." Jillian finally broke down.

Delia moved to comfort her sister but paused after a few steps. "Hold on a minute. We could barely hear the little creep because of the loud music on his yacht. What if he was using the noise to conceal cries for help?"

"Good thinking. You need to come with me and tell the police your story. Every little detail could be important." Greg turned toward the ladder. He found a tenacious Jillian blocking his path.

"No one is going anywhere until we know where Liana and Taron are," she declared.

Delia tried to reason with her sister. "There is no time to search the island. The criminals get further away with every minute we waste. It helps no one if we run off half-cocked."

"Maybe this will help." Charlie handed Jillian a small foil package. "I found this in the galley after snake-bite-boy raced out. He reached into his pocket and threw this on the floor. It was stuck to a wad of wet paper."

She gave him her best annoyed teacher face when she saw the skull and cross bones on the wrapper. "Really, Charlie? 'Bury your treasure, mate.' The man dropped a novelty condom. How is that supposed to help us?"

Delia grabbed the prophylactic from her sister. "Let me see that? It's them. Our assailants have Taron and Liana."

The self-appointed captain was quick to defend herself. "What? I hid some protection in the napkin. It's better to be safe than sorry."

"I can't believe you put these next to my pink princess napkins." Jillian waved the offending item under her sister's nose.

Delia's smile turned lascivious. "Your napkins said she was 'waiting for her prince to come.' I figured if that was true, he was definitely going to need these."

Greg was the voice of reason once more. "I believe we have our answer. Delia, let's go."

Jillian stepped in front of him and put a hand on his chest. "You are not wasting time by getting the police involved. The bad guys have a head start. We are going after them."

"The logical choice is to involve seasoned professionals. We have no idea where they are headed." Greg tried to move around her, but she held her ground.

"I heard them say they would hit one more cache in the everglades before their buyer caught up with them," Delia offered.

"So they were using the geocache sites as a cover for their drug operation." Greg's hunch had been correct. "We need to narrow the search area."

"I think I can help." Tom handed him one of his meticulously drawn maps. "There are only a few sites in the everglades. The one closest to the shoreline and our present location is marked here."

Jillian pleaded with him, "Greg, please. She's my daughter, and Taron is your best friend. We can't lose them."

Despite the flexibility required when working undercover, Greg was very much a by-the-book cop. This was the type of crazy vigilante response that would see him kicked off the force or worse get someone killed. The choice was an easy one; he needed to do the right thing.

All Hands on Deck

"Alone we can do so little; together we can do so much."
Helen Keller

Delia watched the small boat fade into the distance as she held a hand to her forehead, shielding her eyes from the brilliant sun. Her ever-present sunglasses were on loan to Jillian who had reassured her that she would be returning them soon. Greg insisted he go alone, but the devoted mother was determined to help him find her daughter. Delia had no right to stop her because if the roles were reversed she would move heaven and earth to protect Jillian. They had stood shoulder to shoulder through all of life's adversities, and this would be no different. Delia was not about to be left behind.

"Look sharp people. Finish your preparations and let's get underway."

Charlie was the only one willing to risk incurring her wrath. "Greg said he wanted us to stay put."

Delia made her way to the quarterdeck in a few confident strides. She stood tall and faced her crew with both hands firmly placed on her hips. "I am your captain now, and I say we go after them. No one messes with my family and gets away with it."

Maintaining a commanding presence without her usual sarcasm was not as easy as it looked. Gaining support for her plan would be much simpler if people were actually looking at her. There was a sudden fascination with footwear she would have appreciated under different circumstances. Motivational speeches were unfamiliar terrain and more suited to her sister's talents. Delia swept through life exposing the cold hard truth while Jillian tidied up with hugs and encouraging words.

"It's decision time everyone. Our family and friends are in a fight for their lives. I need to go after them, but I can't sail this ship alone. If a rescue has even the smallest chance of success, we have to work together. We either move ahead as a team with a single purpose or we wait here. You each need to decide how much you are willing to risk."

Delia was ready to gamble everything but wondered if anyone else would follow her lead. She looked around and saw the faces of ordinary people who had already extended themselves to accomplish extraordinary things. They had learned to sail a ship and had survived an armed ambush. The task ahead was formidable, and the odds were stacked against them.

Her water-fearing buddy was the first to step forward. Delia swallowed hard trying to hold back the feelings welling up over his display of loyalty.

"I didn't have many lessons with our Captain, but I do remember some of what he taught me. I volunteer to work the sails."

Scarlet gave Delia a confident smile as she put a hand on Shane's arm.

"We have the most experience working the main sail. No reason to break up a good team."

Tom fiddled with something in his pocket as he took his time deciding. He glanced at Claire before pulling out a compass. "Greg took the GPS, but I still have this. I also kept copies of the nautical charts and maps to the cache sites. If we can get the ship underway, I will find our friends."

The weight of the world now rested on the smallest pair of shoulders. Other than Taron, Claire was the only one who had manned the helm for any length of time. Delia stepped aside as she moved up the stairs. Claire skimmed her delicate fingers along the grooves and nicks worn into the wheel by many a strong and confident hand. The words she spoke were barely audible.

"It's much more difficult than it appears. The Captain always used the motor to get us going after weighing anchor. It takes a huge amount of effort to steer her without it. Tacking her in and out of the wind is also tricky. He was always there to guide me and inspire confidence." She raised her teary eyes to Delia. "So much could go wrong."

Delia put a hand on each slender shoulder. "My dear, it already has. Lets try to make it right." She knew this unassuming young woman could meet the challenge. "Nothing happens unless you agree. You can do this, Claire."

Conviction slowly replaced the doubt in her green eyes. "Alright, I'll try."

"Absolutely not." Tom rushed onto the quarterdeck, situating himself next to Claire. "There is no trying because you will succeed. I will navigate from here and help you any way I can." He gave her a nod of encouragement and a shy smile.

"Wonderful, we have a helmsman." Delia breathed a sigh of relief. "Let's make this happen people."

The scramble to ready the ship began with one notable exception. Charlie stood before her nervously wringing the bucket hat he had been wearing in his hands.

"Um—Delia. It takes two to work the winch for the sail. I'm going to need some help."

"Yes, I know." She poked him in the middle of his orange vest. "It's going to be you and me, Pillsbury Doughboy." She disappeared below decks, leaving behind a gaping, newly appointed first mate.

Preparations to set sail were completed in short order. The novice crew was well versed in the routine and were awaiting further instructions when Delia re-emerged. Her new attire included a plain T-shirt, shorts, and an earth shattering choice.

Charlie's gaze dropped to her feet. "Whoa! You put on flats. This is some serious shit now!"

Delia was wearing the sensible rubber soled shoes that Jillian had insisted she pack. It was a true testament to the gravity of their predicament. Tom's calculations added more discouraging news. The ship would need to be at maximum speed if they had any hope of arriving in time to be of assistance. Jillian and Greg were travelling much faster in the motorized skiff and would make landfall within the hour. The kidnappers were well ahead of them all.

Claire patiently explained how they would need to keep the wind at their backs. The Captain never allowed them to run with full sails due to the dangers it presented. A sudden change in wind direction or an abrupt turn would be catastrophic given their lack of experience. Delia insisted there was no time to waste and her crew agreed.

Their start up was as tricky as Claire predicted. She relied on Tom's added strength at the helm to hold the ship steady as the sails were raised. The ship began to pick up speed and relief flooded the deck. Delia felt like a small miracle had been granted. It was like finding a pair of sale price Gucci sandals among December's winter boots.

They managed to sail east without incident but were now faced with performing the difficult tack north to Florida. The change of wind direction that occurred with the turn suddenly had the ship running downwind. Scarlet and Shane managed to duck under the boom of the main sail as it jibed across the deck. Delia had no such luck. She was caught off guard as the boom of the smaller sail swept her off the ship. The Wicked Wench listed to one side. It took the combined effort of Tom and Claire to keep her upright.

*****

Charlie was the first to jump into action as Claire rattled off her commands to release the sails and drop anchor. He raced to the side of the schooner. Delia was floating in the water.

"Son of a bitch! The boom must have hit her on the head. She's either dazed or knocked out."

Shane joined him at the rail, unsure how to proceed. Charlie shoved him aside and yelled, "Man overboard!"

There was no time to build up the courage to act or think about the consequences. Charlie tensed his muscles and muttered a quick prayer before he leapt off the ship.

Shane was startled into action by the bravery of his friend. "What the hell, Charlie? You don't know how to swim!"

"Man over board! Get to the man overboard station!" The bobbing orange cork yelled back.

Shane's panic stricken gaze followed his friend. "You'll never manage on your own."

"Charlie, hang on." Scarlet gave Shane a quick hug before diving into the sea.

The barrage of shouts from the ship to the water drowned out the loudest gulls. Charlie somehow kicked his way over to Delia. His vest kept them both afloat until Scarlet arrived. They sandwiched their unconscious commander between them and awkwardly made their way back to the ship. Charlie gave those still on the ship directions on how to use the MOB equipment to bring them aboard.

Delia exploded into awareness once she was safely back on deck. Her eyes bulged as Charlie's lips descended in a resuscitation attempt. She sat bolt upright, sputtering water and obscenities. "You dimwit! Why would you jump in after me?"

She grabbed him by his flotation device. "You were in over your head. For God sakes, you could have died."

"Nah, not while I was wearing this." He glanced at his life vest. "Besides, I owed you one for coming after me when the bad guys were on the ship." He leaned in and kissed her on the forehead. "You're welcome."

The close call made the precariousness of their objective all too real. A return to sound judgment was necessary, and Charlie's sensible conclusion overruled the emotions of the day. "Our part in this story ends here. We can't take anymore risks; it's not what the Captain would want. We need to stay put and hope that help arrives."

"I don't think we will be waiting for long." Tom pointed to something off the starboard side of the ship.

In all the commotion, they had not noticed the other vessel. A large yacht was bearing down on them at top speed.

This was a day for roller coaster emotions. Charlie had gone from abject terror to elation during Delia's rescue. He was grinning from ear-to-ear as he launched himself into the air waving his arms. "Over here." He looked back at his friends. "We're saved."

*****

The steady drone of the small motor was punctuated by the occasional slap of a wave hitting the side of the boat. The monotony of sound went unnoticed as Jillian was intensely focussed on mapping the route they would take once they made landfall. She had lost her precious daughter once and would not let it happen again.

The fraught silence was interrupted when Greg cleared his throat. "If you stare at that map any harder, it will disintegrate."

Jillian clutched the scrap of paper to her chest as tightly as if it she were embracing Liana. She was certain that she looked as miserable as she felt. "I can't stop worrying about them. Two days ago, my worst fear was that Liana would never speak to me again, and now I may never..." She could not say the words out loud.

"Hey, don't do this to yourself." Greg gave her hand a comforting squeeze. "I know it doesn't look good, but we have to try and stay positive. Liana is not alone. She has Taron. He will do whatever is humanly possible to keep her safe. He is fiercely protective of the people he loves, and he loves your daughter very much."

"I think she loves him too. It's more than I could have hoped for when this journey began."

"My thoughts were the exact opposite. I told him he was foolish for developing intense feelings for someone so quickly, but I was proven wrong. Liana revived a man I thought was gone forever. You did well in your profiling—I mean matchmaking," he said with wink.

"It wasn't me." Jillian slid the maps back into her backpack. "It was Delia who made the final decision. We narrowed it down to two candidates, but she was the one who insisted it had to be Taron. After all of our research, she relied on her intuition. You know, she really is much more reliable than any lie detector or truth serum you have at the station. Maybe you should hire her?"

"I don't think our bullet proof vests would stand up to the cutting remarks she throws at everyone." Greg managed a laugh. "Did she ever tell you why she chose Taron?"

"It was in his eyes. She saw an overwhelming sadness there. I tried to point out that two people who were hurting would not be the best combination, but Delia has never taken no for an answer. She also noticed the smallest glimmer of hope along with the pain and that was enough for a final decision."

A sly smile made it's way to Jillian's lips. "There is a bit more to the story. Our second choice liked to wear Crocs. Delia rebelled at the thought of future family photos, so he was a definite no."

They indulged in a brief moment of laughter before returning to their solemn contemplations. Bold actions and absolute loyalty were needed for the daunting task ahead. Jillian knew Greg would get the job done. He was a forthright man who had not coddled her with meaningless reassurances.

There was still so much to learn about him and she longed to uncover more. Uncover. She had a sudden flashback to her gyrations in his cabin. While he had deftly avoided any mention of the incident, she needed to deal with the giant flamingo in the boat. Conversation had ceased so there was no time like the present.

"Greg, I'm sorry."

"Excuse me?"

"About the other night—and you know—my dance."

The dismayed expression she was expecting did not materialize. His gentle smile and considerate manner tempered her embarrassment.

"Please don't worry about that right now. It's already forgotten."

"So it was forgettable? I mean it's not like I've done that sort of thing very often—ever." Jillian ducked her head trying to hide her embarrassment. "I suppose it could have been better if I'd had more practice." She felt her face flush and was thankful for the rosy pigment stubbornly adhering to her skin.

"Jillian, you were very alluring, but the dancing was a bit of a surprise." Greg looked away and nervously rubbed the back of his neck before meeting her gaze again. "You were also very drunk."

"And you would never take advantage of a woman in such a state. You are a decent and principled man, Greg Sloan."

"So I've been told. I'm as solid and dependable as they come. I guess the suffering I see on the streets every day makes me appreciate the simple things in life. I suppose it all sounds very ordinary and uninteresting to you." His hands tightened on the rudder arm of the motor as he turned his eyes to the horizon.

"What I wouldn't give for a dull moment right now. Oh, no! I didn't mean—well—that a steady and reliable man is dull. I like dependable. It's a very attractive quality."

She was now thoroughly flustered, but could not seem to stop herself. "It's good to know there are men like you keeping the streets safe. A man who a woman can count on—a man who wouldn't abandon her when…"

She was saved from any further mortification by the courteous detective. "I see the same strength in you. Underneath the doting mother and bubbly exterior, lies a steel core that will not be broken. You are a force to be reckoned with Jillian Barton. Let's put our heads together and come up with a plan to catch some thieves."

"I'm sure I've said enough so thinking it is."

"Jillian, one more thing."

"Yes."

"Once you've had some practice, I would enjoy another performance." Greg's expression turned from flirty to smouldering in the blink of an eye.

Jillian flashed him a dazzling smile. "I think that could be arranged, but I need to dance on two graves first."

She directed her unyielding gaze to the expanse of water stretching before them and focussed all of her love on Liana.

"Hang on baby, mom is on her way."

*****

Taron kept a watchful eye on Liana, monitoring her for any signs of distress. She seemed deep in thought as she toyed with the feather. Her measured breathing and steady hands eased some of his worry. He never thought he would find himself in this situation again—helpless to protect someone he loved. Liana had put her trust in him, and he would not fail. Not this time.

His eyes roamed the cabin looking for a means to escape before landing on Liana's troubled gaze. His disquiet had not gone unnoticed. As often as it had occurred, he still marvelled at their intuitive understanding of one another.

"I know what you're thinking, and the only idea I am going along with is one where we both survive. There has to be a way to escape." She spoke the words with absolute determination.

Taron knew bravery rarely manifested itself in epic acts of selflessness. Heroic deeds were more often measured in the daily triumphs over fear. There was no one more deserving of the title than the magnificent woman gazing at him with immeasurable love and concern. Liana had lifted the weight of negative emotion he had been trapped under for so many years. He loved her with a purity and intensity he never thought possible. If anything happened to her, there would be no hope for him. None whatsoever.

"I want that as well, but if there is a chance for only one of us to get away, you must take it." His resolve was equal to hers.

"No, no!" Liana shook her head and panic flashed in her eyes. "Taron, I won't leave you behind. I couldn't bear it."

"And I will not live my life without you." He sighed heavily. "Where does that leave us?"

"It leaves us trying to outsmart our captors. I have the beginnings of a plan." A shrewd smile formed on her lips. "I think it's time we gain the upper hand in this game of cat and mouse."

Taron gave her a curious look in return. "Given that we are already ensnared," he rattled his cuffs, "it seems the cat has won."

"Not if the mouse is patient and waits. I remember a brown tabby at one of my foster homes. He was the ultimate hunter and often left a body at the back door. I would check on the tiny victim, and much to my surprise, it sometimes sprang to life and scampered

338

away. Not all of them, but there were enough to give me hope that something small and frail could stare death in the face and survive."

We continue to 'play dead' and follow the rules of our captors while covertly resisting. If they let their guard down, it might give us the window of opportunity we need to escape. I will agree to this as along as... "

She knew where he was heading and cut him off, "Fighting back is not the answer when you are outgunned, but we can certainly try to outmaneuver them. I think our best chance is to try and gain Trevor's sympathy. He would not have saved us if he had his father's cold blood running through his veins. I look at him and see a beaten down man who is terrified. Trevor is doing the old man's bidding out of fear."

Liana's forehead creased and her eyes were fixed as if she were looking at something behind him. She blinked once and refocused. "Trevor was so different at the Inn. He was more aggressive which is out of character considering the man we met today. I think he may have a great deal of repressed anger and resentment which he releases when his father is not around. We probably can't get him to act on it but maybe we can drive the wedge between them deeper."

Taron gave her strategy careful consideration before replying, "Perhaps you're right. We focus our energy on weakening Trevor's resolve."

While Taron voiced his agreement, he knew Hyde would not be as easily duped as his son. He was a calculating and dangerous enemy. With Greg's assistance, he had spent countless hours profiling the unknown killer. His friend reckoned the murderer was motivated by power. In all likelihood, he perceived himself to be a superior being with the right to dominate those around him. Any challenge to his authority would be a fatal mistake. He was without a conscience and victims would be treated with cool detachment.

As far as Taron was concerned, Hyde was evil incarnate. Once they no longer served a purpose, the monster would snap his jaws shut. There would be no escape. His first priority was to get Liana out of harms way. As soon as that was accomplished, no one could blame him if he seized the opportunity to rid the world of such a repulsive villain. In a final showdown, he wondered who would make an appearance, the revenge driven son and brother or the loving and honourable man Liana had brought back to life.

"Whatever changes you are making to our plan, stop now." Liana scanned his face with laser focus. "I know it's not good because there is a storm gathering behind your eyes. All we need to worry about is getting out of here. Once we are free, we let the authorities deal with Hyde. I know you still want your revenge, but I can't lose you. I love you."

"You won't lose me, and we will see our loved ones again. In fact, they could be mounting a rescue as we speak."

Liana's face brightened at the mention of their friends and family. "That's the spirit. They are just as likely to walk through that door as our captors."

Before either of them could say anything more, noises from above deck drew their attention. Any hopes of a rescue were dashed when they heard the caterwauling of their kidnappers. Disappointment was still ringing in their ears when Trevor burst into the room looking terrified.

"I know that I screwed up big time by covering up the missing drugs, but what kind of a father tries to kill his own son?"

His wild eyes leapt between Liana and Taron. "He knew everyone on board was safely locked away. All I did was poke my head into the cabin to tell him I was finished purging the gas. The scumbag knew it was me when he sent the bullet whizzing past my head. It was meant to scare the shit out of me. He never misses. Let that be a lesson to both of you."

Liana murmured words of reassurance as Trevor set about releasing her restraints. "You were lucky. Your father does not seem like the kind of man who is very forgiving. It can't be easy working with him."

"Lady, you have no idea."

"Liana. My name is Liana."

"I am working for him, not with him—Liana." Trevor seemed to struggle with the familiarity of using a first name. "We are not father and son. I am a slave and he is my master."

"I guess that makes you slightly better off than we are." Liana tried to work her magic, but he ignored her as he finished his task.

Compassion seemed to be a cloak that Trevor was eager to shed, and he turned his attention to Taron. He grumbled and swore as he struggled to unfasten the handcuffs from the awkward angle of the bedpost.

"It sounds like a rough life, mate. Why carry on working for such a wretched excuse for a father?"

"I think about what it would be like to be free of him every day, but it would never work. He would track me down, and all I could hope for is a quick end. Miserable as it is, I do value my life."

"Fortunately for us, you are not your father's son." Taron cast a quick glance at Liana, and her slight nod signalled he was on the right track. "You confronted him on the island, and we owe you our lives. Thank you."

Trevor stared at him like he was a rare specimen in some exotic zoo. Gratitude was clearly not the response he was expecting from a hostage.

Taron was momentarily freed and pressed his advantage during Trevor's split second of doubt. "If you would grant us just one moment, I give you my word there will be no trickery."

Liana understood the objective and begged Trevor to comply. "Please! Let him hold me one more time. You know we might not have much longer."

Neither of them expected Trevor to agree so quickly. He raised his gun and motioned Taron toward

Liana. He swept her into his protective embrace. Taron felt her body press into his and then sag with relief. The world around him faded away. There was only Liana. He brushed her hair back with his fingers and kissed her softly.

"If all we have is a few more hours together, I would not trade it for a lifetime without you. You are my love—my everything." He reluctantly inched his body away from hers and allowed Trevor to secure his hands behind his back.

"Love will win out, Taron. I know it." Her eyes were filled with hope as she turned around to offer her hands to Trevor.

"Father told me to bring you above deck for the journey. He says you are not to speak, and you will have no food or water. The man thrives on pain and suffering so conserve your strength." Trevor marched them out of the cabin and up the stairs.

The ship was already underway when they emerged into the ferocious heat of the mid-day sun. They were forced to kneel on the deck in an attempt to make them as physically uncomfortable as possible. Mercifully, they were not separated.

Taron glanced up and saw Hyde sneering at them from the ship's wheel. Memories of that dreadful night suddenly flared with vivid clarity. As a surge of anger welled up, Liana leaned in to him. She managed to keep her face hidden behind the veil of her long hair and mouthed, "I love you."

His eyes were riveted on the angel whose love was keeping him afloat in the whirlpool of hate spiralling him into the depths of hell. She meant more to him than any chance at retribution. He would not sacrifice a future with her in order to obtain justice for the crimes of the past. Complying with the demands of the murderous bastard was his only recourse. His name would be added to a long list of unsung heroes.

While Taron vaguely registered Hyde's instructions to Trevor, he clearly heard the younger man express his disapproval.

"Father, there is no need for the hoods. They have cooperated and don't deserve any punishment."

Hyde was not a man who would be thwarted from playing his sadistic games. The black material dropped over Taron's head, submerging him in darkness. His thoughts immediately centred on Liana. He wanted to spare her any further torment, but there was no way to reassure her. He was unable to provide a comforting word, a warm smile, or a soothing touch. Tilting his head toward her, he felt something brush against him. A familiar weight settled onto his shoulder. Liana.

She believed love would prevail. He silently chanted the word with all the devotion he possessed. It was a prayer sent to the heavens in the hopes that salvation would find them both. Love. Love. Love.

Friend or Foe

"It is a man's own mind,
not his enemy or foe that lures him to evil ways."
Buddha

Delia's gaze swept across the deck as the approaching ship geared down. She immediately recognized a bespectacled woman with closely cropped silver hair. She had seen that face all too often on the menus of Jillian's favourite eatery. The spry looking senior was accompanied by several burly looking men. Delia fought the urge to fling herself overboard again. A trustworthy captain would always go down with the ship.

Once the yacht pulled alongside, introductions were made. The elderly matriarch confirmed her identity. Delia revealed only what was necessary after a rapid assessment of her options. They were an inexperienced crew who ran into difficulty and had no means of communication. Mrs. Bruno extended an offer to call for assistance which Delia summarily dismissed to the amazement of those on board both ships. She needed

ROSE SCHMIDT

the old lady to cooperate which called for the utmost in diplomacy. Too much information would make them vulnerable, but not enough would leave them stranded.

The deception Delia had endured under her mother's reign developed her uncanny intuition and the ability to recall seemingly insignificant details. Out of necessity, these skills were sharpened under extreme duress. Given the danger they had faced, no one else would remember Trevor referring to the drug lord as a vicious old broad or his remark about the burgers. The less her friends knew the better off they would be during the gamesmanship she was planning. She would be the only one to suffer the consequences if she miscalculated.

The first thing Delia needed to do was find out if her suspicions were correct. "Our family is in serious trouble, and we need to get to the everglades as quickly as possible." She baited her hook and tossed out the line. "We haven't seen hide nor hair of them since yesterday."

The silver haired matron locked eyes with her. "That is very troubling news. I am confident that I can provide assistance, but I will need more detailed information."

"I think you'll find I've got nothing to hide." Delia emphasized the crucial word with a decisive narrowing of her eyes.

"I am happy to welcome you all on board and extend my hospitality. I'm sure a chat over a nice cup of tea would be a lovely opportunity to get to know one another. My cozy little hideaway is below deck." Mrs.

Bruno was as crafty as Delia hoped and quickly caught on to her covert tactics.

While she was eager to get underway, Delia knew she was unable to put her best foot forward in the waterlogged shoes she was wearing. The drug lord granted them permission to change into dry clothes and gather a few essentials. Bewildered expressions greeted her once they were below deck.

It was Scarlet who emerged victorious in the race to ask the question on everyone's mind. "Delia, what the hell just happened out there?"

"Isn't it obvious? I landed us a ride to the everglades. I am not giving up now that we are this close. We don't have time to discuss it, so you'll just have to trust me."

"Trust you? Charlie and Scarlet could have died trying to save your ass!" Shane yelled.

Delia was sickened by the reminder and countered with a verbal slap to the face. "Don't you think I know that! Glad you can finally see red and express your true feelings on the matter."

Charlie peeked out from behind Shane's shoulder. "Hey, not dead. Not even almost dead. I say we go." A goofy smile was plastered on his face. "Who knew Mrs. Bruno from the diner ads was real? I don't know about the rest of you, but I've worked up an appetite after all that exercise. I'll bet she has some good eats over there."

Delia's personal life preserver bounced back quickly, and why not, he was still encased in his puffed up rubberized jacket. His attempt at levity had an immediate impact and tensions eased. There was a retreat to individual quarters after Delia announced she would meet anyone still supporting the rescue at the bottom of the stairs.

She forcibly exhaled several deep breaths as she shed her wet clothes and towelled off. The chilling memories of the day's events were not as easily discarded. In the absence of her faithful sister, she would carry on alone. Delia did not labour under the delusion that anyone would continue to blindly follow her lead in light of what her rash decision had nearly cost them.

After placing the unsightly deck shoes in a plastic bag, she rummaged through her steamer trunk. Jillian's practical choice in footwear would make the journey with her, but right now she would need something that created a more intimidating presence when challenging Mrs. Bruno. She thought about the multitude of churlishly delivered jokes her passion had earned over the years as she made her selection.

Her obsession's painful origins began during Eve's iron fisted rule. The unfeeling matriarch dominated her family, and Delia's heels gave her the physical stature and confidence she needed during confrontations with her mother. The minute she put them on, she was no longer the slip of a girl confronting a merciless despot. She became an equal staring down her foe.

Easing into her midnight black Manolo Blahnik stilettos completed the transformation into worthy opponent. A quick glance in the mirror told her Mrs. Bruno would meet her match today. She raised herself to her full height as a look of grim determination hardened her features. Stepping into the hallway she saw five people waiting for her at the foot of the stairs. As she walked toward them, she didn't know whether to admonish their foolishness or commend their bravery.

Charlie nudged Shane forward. An elbow to the side finally had him speaking up. "We each have our own reasons for coming along and no one is willing to let you or our friends down. We are going to trust you."

She had taken these disparate souls under her wing, and they were now family. Delia would protect them with everything she had. "Alright, if you are determined to follow my lead, let me make one thing clear. I will be the only one engaging grandma. Keep quiet and reveal nothing."

Delia turned to the one who would have the most difficulty with her request. "And whatever you do, don't piss her off."

Charlie nervously gulped down whatever he was about to say.

The strapping crew stepped aside as Mrs. Bruno welcomed them aboard. "After consulting with my captain, it seems you are indeed heading in our direction. There is no time to dawdle so we leave now."

Tom tried to hand over his maps, but she waved him off. "We have our bearings." She motioned toward the stairs leading below deck, "Ms. Barton, please join me. My crew will make sure your friends are well looked after."

Delia gave her assent to the group and turned back to Mrs. Bruno. She was scrutinizing Scarlet from head to toe.

"You were employee of the month in the Boston location. It was about eight years ago if I'm not mistaken."

"Yes, that's right. I supported my schooling by waitressing for two years."

"All grown up I see." Mrs. Bruno cast a disapproving glance at Scarlet's revealing blouse. "Please join us and we can get caught up."

Delia and Scarlet followed her below deck while the others were ushered to the ship's salon. Mrs. Bruno had effectively separated them. It would now be a battle between the two alpha females.

The grande dame began with a careful approach on common ground. "I know how worried you must be. My loved ones mean everything to me, and I consider all those in my employ an extension of my family."

Another scathing glare had Scarlet fidgeting uncomfortably while she tried to fasten a nonexistent button on her low cut top.

Mrs. Bruno covered the dainty tea pot with a knitted cozy. "I almost rejected your commendation when I saw the photo attached to your list of achievements. There were some modifications to the uniform that did not represent the wholesome family image Mrs. Bruno's has always tried to project. I was pleasantly surprised when I read your file. You were a hard worker, and your customers always left very satisfied."

Scarlet forced a smile and was visibly relieved when their host directed her next question at Delia. "As is often the case in life, people aren't always what they appear to be. Wouldn't you agree, Ms. Barton?"

"Please, there is no need for such formality. Call me Delia. I do seem to recall a children's story—something about a wolf in sheep's clothing. I found it rather far fetched. None of the sheep would have been harmed if a determined shepherd was guarding the flock."

They were interrupted as tea was poured by Mrs. Bruno's husky assistant. Delia declined the offer of milk and sugar, but helped herself to some whiskey conveniently located on an antique desk. Mrs. Bruno sidled up to her. She was apparently also on the hunt.

"I always seem to be misplacing my spectacles. I thought I left them here, but I appear to be mistaken. Funny how things don't always turn up where you think they will be." She returned to her arm chair and searched through her basket of yarn. "Ah, here they are."

She donned the black-rimmed glasses before sampling her tea. "I really should invest in that newfangled way to find lost things. I think you young people call it a GPS. I hear they now make them small enough to fit inside a pill capsule. You could swallow one and never know you were being followed."

Mrs. Bruno offered them a plate of cookies. Delia turned her down citing dietary restrictions and slapped Scarlet's hand away when she reached for one.

"My wee grandchildren love sweets, but I don't care for them myself. Too much sugar can be very bad for your oral hygiene. I am proud to say that these choppers are still my own." She bared her teeth in a feral grin before continuing, "I do like to serve my guests a little something with their tea no matter how short their stay."

Delia fired back, "I would imagine a hungry visitor could gobble down several cookies with tea. You could use another sweetener, but cutting down on sugar would be ill advised."

"You are very right about my standards. I like to keep all of my guests happy, but they frequently bite off more than they can chew. The restaurant business can be very cutthroat, so it is important to keep a watchful eye on everyone. There are always those who are looking to take advantage and bamboozle you for more than their fair share."

Scarlet was now thoroughly confused. "You don't get very far on minimum wage, so if you are talking about my tips…"

Mrs. Bruno interrupted, "No need to be vulgar. I'm sure you are very proud of them since you have them on such conspicuous display."

Delia put a hand on Scarlet to keep her seated while Mrs. Bruno's assistant whispered in her ear.

"Oh dear, my hearing isn't what is used to be. I am sorry, but I do think you earned enough to purchase some sturdier foundation garments." Having made her point, she turned back to Delia. "As much as I would love to discuss more of my trade secrets, a certain anonymity is required given the competitive nature of my business."

Her adversary wanted reassurances and Delia chose her words carefully. "If anyone should ask, I shared a cup of tea with a wise entrepreneur who was kind enough to provide us with transportation."

"There are laws to be upheld even in the world of food preparation." Mrs. Bruno eyed her suspiciously.

In the unlikely event that I am questioned by any culinary law enforcement, about—say, the sugar in your cookies." Delia arched her eyebrows. "In all honesty, I wouldn't be able to tell them a thing. I didn't sample any cookies, so I could not comment on any irregularities."

Mrs. Bruno seemed very pleased. "I think you and I understand each other quite well."

"I am also extremely grateful to receive support from a like-minded individual." Delia was truly impressed and might even have befriended the old girl if she wasn't a nefarious drug dealer.

"Seeing as you are a friend in need." Mrs. Bruno handed the walking monolith a key. "Stefan, open the cabinet."

She motioned Delia toward the array of hand guns and assault weapons which were revealed. "There are many dangers in the swamp, and you will need to arm yourselves accordingly. I assume someone in your party is familiar with shooting a weapon."

Delia was already testing the weight of a M24 bolt action rifle. "I know how to handle myself, and this is quite the piece. Perfect for taking a long distance shot, and the silencer adds that extra security."

"There are some nasty crocs and gators in the everglades, and I would be remiss if I did not offer you some form of protection. I know some people would shoot a predator on sight, but my motto is 'live and let live' unless it threatens one of your own. No one can fault you for protecting what is yours."

Delia scanned the room through the telescopic scope of the weapon. "I think you and I definitely see eye to eye on this matter."

Mrs. Bruno reached for a stack of knitting on a side table. "Before you leave, I have a little souvenir for you."

She handed Delia a knitted coaster. "Happy hunting, dears. I'm certain you'll find what you are looking for."

Their exit from the ship was perfunctory. The rescue party soon found themselves on a small strip of sand. All eyes turned from the departing yacht and gazed expectantly at Delia.

Charlie had not yet eaten his fill and was the most disappointed of the group. "They were just grilling some burgers, and I only had a chance to eat two of her pita pan specials. What kind of a friend just dumps us in the middle of a swamp?"

"The kind that is giving me exactly what I asked for," Delia replied.

Tom also voiced his displeasure, "You do realize we are way off course. The access point to the cache is nowhere near here. According to my charts, we will have to negotiate miles of swamp to get back on track."

"We wont be needing those." Delia handed him the woollen coaster. This is a GPS tracker."

Tom pulled out the device. "What's going on here?"

"Plans have changed. It seems our target has swallowed some live bait and is going after a bigger score. Stay put and you will all be safe." She uttered her final words through gritted teeth. "I'll be back."

Delia slung the sniper rifle over her shoulder before taking a few determined steps. Stealing a backwards glance, she saw that a single line of intrepid souls had formed. There was no time to marvel at their loyalty or courage. She gave them a reassuring smile before leading them into the ultimate game of hide and seek.

*****

It took several minutes for Liana's eyes to adjust to the glare of the tropical sun once her hood was removed. Hyde's ploy did not induce the terror she imagined he had intended. She had never been afraid of the dark even as a young girl. The night meant safety, solitude, and sweet dreams. Dreams of forever homes filled with family and love. Dawn was an intruder burning away the hazy remnants of peaceful slumber to expose the solidity of her sadness and pain. Monsters were not imaginary creatures living under the bed. They were living and breathing entities that roamed among the innocents in broad daylight.

The man operating the motor behind her was a child's worst nightmare. A demon whose malevolence

355

seeped out of every pore. It wrapped around the small boat hell bent on finding its way under her skin and into the very core of her being. Liana was afraid, but not for herself. Her thoughts centred on the man sitting in the bow of the boat. Taron was happiness, home, and so much more. She would fight with every ounce of strength she had to keep him safe.

As they neared the coastline, a small opening in the hammock of trees appeared. They entered the narrow confines of a mangrove channel. Hyde cut the engine while Trevor clumsily used a long pole to manipulate the boat through the shallow creek. Branches and leaves overhead intertwined to form a canopy that screened out the sunlight. The mangroves stood like sentinels on guard, flanking the snaking ribbon of water. Their enormous roots curved outwards and disappeared into the channel. They reminded her of bony fingers ready to pull them from the boat into the deadly world beyond. It was as if nature was conspiring to keep any intruders out.

Liana tried to resist the fear that was threatening to hijack her rational thinking. She needed to keep her mind clear and sharp. It was safer if she kept her emotional barriers in place. By curbing her reaction to Hyde's vicious mind games, she hoped to placate the monster. He would have no reason to attack, and Taron would not take it upon himself to protect her.

Hyde's shouts drew her attention to the wider basin of water they were now navigating. He was directing his son to a landing point, but Trevor seemed as confused as Liana. She saw nothing but a barrier of tree roots and torpedo grass. The inhospitable access meant someone would have to wade into the murky water and pull the boat to shore. Trevor was convinced he saw something move and began to describe the countless ways a crocodile could tear you limb from limb. Before he could finish, Taron whispered to him and swung himself out of the boat into the knee deep brackish pool. Hyde shook his head in disgust but allowed his son to release Taron's bonds.

Liana watched him pull the skiff to the shore, holding it steady as Trevor climbed onto dry land. Taron was clearly abiding by their plan to befriend the persecuted son. Hampered by her handcuffs, Liana wobbled when she tried to exit the boat. Taron was at her side in an instant. Instead of taking the arms she held out, he picked her up.

"Alright, darling?"

Liana had been unresponsive since the hood was placed over her head and said nothing. She knew Taron was worried by the way he tightened his grip, fingers digging into her side. He was not about to let anyone take her from him. As he carried her to higher ground, she buried her face in his chest and tried to wish it all away.

As he gently released her, she heard Hyde's, "Tsk tsk."

She fisted her hands and batted Taron's chest in frustration. "You have to stop trying to help me. If we make him angry, he might take a shot."

"I can't help myself when I see you in trouble." Taron kissed the top of her head as they clung to each other.

"Enough you two." Liana swung around to face Hyde. The look in his bloodshot eyes was one of pure hate and revulsion.

"Lover boy, you and my sorry excuse for a son haul the boat over there." Hyde pointed to an area crowded with mangroves, saw palmettos, and ferns. "Cover it up with whatever you can find. My patience is running out. Don't be long."

Taron tried to reach for her hand. "Come with me."

Hyde aimed his gun at Liana. "Back off. The girlfriend stays here."

She gave Taron a faint smile. Her gait was casual and her expression neutral as she approached Hyde. She gathered strength from frequent glances at Taron. Halting in front of the madman, she kept her head down. Locking eyes with Hyde would only challenge him and reawaken her fear. She could not afford to show any sign of weakness.

Hyde leaned in until they were inches apart. "I sense your boyfriend is the protective type. If he tries anything, I will shoot him in self-defence. While a hostage benefits us for now, there really is no need for two."

He flipped her hair over her shoulder with his pistol and then ran the cold metal along her cheek. Liana swallowed hard as the bile rose in her throat. He was counting on the fact that she would be her own worst enemy, but she did not flinch or blink.

"Liana!" The distress in Taron's voice begged her for an answer.

She cast a reassuring glance in his direction. She was quick, but it was not fast enough to escape Hyde's scrutiny. The murderer laughed. It was a shrill cackle that pierced the eardrums.

"You are afraid of what I might do to him. Isn't that right?" He levelled his gun at Taron. "I could kill him right now. Shoot him when his back is turned. He would never know what hit him."

Liana heard the safety click. Her body betrayed her efforts to remain unfazed. She felt the fear twisting her gut and constricting her throat. Her thoughts drifted back to her panic on the ship and how Taron had brought her back from the brink. Her gaze lingered on him as he worked. She watched the steady rise and fall of his chest, synchronizing her breathing to match his.

A flow of calm energy rode the current of air creating a link between them.

Unable to elicit the desired reaction, Hyde thumbed the safety back to the on position. "Much too cowardly a thing to do, wouldn't you say?"

Relief flooded her senses, but the respite was all too brief. The fetid breath issuing from the depths of his corrupted soul polluted the atmosphere around her as the mind games continued.

"Still nothing from you? Hmm—it might be better sport to wound him. He would make an easy meal for a hungry crocodile. Does he call your name and profess his love for you one last time? Perhaps he screams in agony, cursing the day he ever met you?"

Liana remained stoic. Her expression registered only passive indifference.

"You can resist all you like." His voice was low and full of malice. "When I tire of my fun, I will end it. Neither of you will leave this swamp alive. Now make yourself useful and go help them. We need to get moving."

As Liana drew closer to the two men, she overheard Taron telling Trevor their friends on the ship would summon help. He also divulged that Greg was a cop who had figured out the connection between the geocache sites and an active drug operation.

She cautioned them both, "Keep working. Things are taking too long and Hyde is getting frustrated."

Trevor broke off a few more palm fronds as he explained their new predicament. "No one is going to find us because the trail to the cache site is further down the channel. Father is on edge because he has something bigger in mind and that means trouble. We need a huge score to settle a deal with one of our buyers. The everglades are a haven for drug runners. I am guessing the old man is looking to steal from another supplier. He's playing a dangerous game, and it's going to get us all killed."

Liana was certain the cavalry was on its way with her mother leading the charge. The crucial element to their survival was time, and she would steal as much of it as she could. "We need to stall anyway we can."

Trevor put the last of the camouflage on the skiff. "There is no we. If I get caught, I go to jail for the rest of my life. I would rather take my chances out here—with him." He walked back to his father.

Liana looked at the debris covering the boat. A plan began to form. She knew her mother would be moving heaven and earth to find them. They needed to help her with the search. Jillian had developed extraordinary tracking skills during her geocache adventures. While Tom relied on his instruments, her mother liked to closely examine her surroundings.

A hurried whisper to Taron was all she could afford, "Leave a trail. Do whatever you can."

She grabbed two palm leaves as they made their way back to Hyde and dropped the fronds in the drag marks left behind by boat. While there would be no trail of breadcrumbs to follow, she hoped the detestable man would meet the same fate as the witch in the children's tale. The flames of hell were surely the ending he deserved.

Trevor refastened their handcuffs as Hyde circled them. "We now leave the civilized world behind and enter nature's killing ground. It is ruled by the strongest and smartest hunters. The timid and weak serve only one purpose, supporting the food chain." Hyde pointed a scrawny finger at them. "The two of you stay alive for as long as I find you useful."

As they began their trek, the smell of the fresh salty air gave way to the odour of damp earth and decaying vegetation. Trevor reluctantly led the way with a reconfigured GPS. Liana and Taron followed with Hyde at their backs. They would be blazing a new trail which worked to their benefit. Footprints left clear indentations in the thick mud and plants were easily snapped as they splashed through the water of the marshes. Hyde was intent on the prize he was seeking, causing him to overlook the crucial evidence they were leaving behind. Liana provided an additional distraction as she swatted at mosquitoes with some of the leaves she plucked.

The hostile environment eventually took its toll. Struggling through the water and muck was physically exhausting, and the humid air depleted any strength that remained. Everything around them was slick with moisture, and their clothing was soon soaked. Progress through the swamp slowed. Hyde was forced to stop and rest in a small clearing.

He glanced at his watch and took his anger out on Trevor. "Time is slipping away. We need to be out of here before the sun sets. They are slowing us down."

"It's the handcuffs. They might have better balance and be quicker without them."

"Are you suggesting we let them go?"

"I could cuff her to me. You could do the same with the man. We set the pace and they have to keep up."

"That's two good ideas you've had in one day. Try not to over extend yourself, son." Hyde's mouth curved into a sarcastic grin.

Trevor walked over to them, freeing Liana first. He shielded her from his father's line of sight and offered her a water bottle before unfastening Taron's restraints. Liana surveyed the area as they took turns sipping the precious liquid. She saw a familiar shrub which pointed out to Trevor.

"These are beauty berries. If you rub them on your skin, the juice should help keep the mosquitoes away."

Trevor was reluctant to take her advice so she crushed some of the berries and began applying the juice to her arms. "I often travel to wild and remote locations. Knowing the difference between something helpful or toxic is crucial to survival in an unfamiliar environment. She knew progress was being made when Trevor began rubbing the berries on his exposed skin.

Taron used the man's momentary distraction to draw her attention to the trees behind them. "Go now. I will deal with them, but you need to be fast."

He wanted her to leave him behind, and she knew exactly what the cost would be. Liana kissed him with a sudden urgency. "Taron, I'm sorry." Her actions were swift and sure. She attached her dangling cuff to his unfettered wrist.

"Liana, no!" Taron's plaintive cry captured Hyde's attention.

"Well, what have we here? Isn't that sweet. The two have become one." The maniac examined the cuffs, ensuring they were secure. "It does give new meaning to the word wedlock. It also makes things much easier for me. I now have only one target to follow. If either of you decides to play hero, you will both suffer the consequences."

Taron said nothing for several minutes. She did not look his way until she felt his fingers close tightly around hers. "Liana, it was your best chance. Why would you do this?" He shook the metal bonds connecting them.

Liana squeezed his hand. "I am done running. I won't leave you."

"You are now stuck with me for better or worse." He forced a smile trying to relieve some of the tension.

"In good times and in bad." Amusement briefly flashed in Liana's eyes as she returned his smile. "Pretty sure this is as bad as it gets, so we should be fine for the rest of our lives."

Their improvised vows were interrupted by Trevor's screams. He was writhing on the ground clutching his ankle. Liana somehow managed to avoid the hole which had tripped him up. She tried to assess the damage, but Hyde was quick to take charge.

"Stand up. We don't have time for this nonsense."

Trevor tried to do as his father asked, but he crumpled back to the ground.

Liana could take no more of the man's brutality. "He can't go on, it's badly sprained and already swelling. He's your flesh and blood. How can you stand to see him in such pain?"

"The state of my family is none of your business, girlie." The murderer turned his gun toward his ailing son. "You drag me down at every turn, but no more. It's time to get rid of the dead weight."

The look on Trevor's face was one of sheer terror. He was expecting his father to put him out of his misery. Much to Liana's surprise and relief, he snatched the GPS from his son before turning to confront them.

"He stays here, but one of you is coming with me. I need help carrying the goods."

Taron leapt at the chance to save her. "I'm the stronger one, and Liana is not as sure-footed as I am."

She was not about to let this happen. Taron could not be left on his own with Hyde. His all encompassing hatred would get him killed. He had rescued her from debilitating fear. She would save him from his anger.

"He's right. He is stronger and could overpower you. I'm less of a threat and can carry what you need."

Taron's temper flared with the desperation he felt. The more he vehemently argued that he be chosen, the more he unwittingly sealed his fate. She knew Hyde would select the one he felt was smaller and weaker. It would be as nature intended.

"Girlie, grab the backpack. You're coming with me." He shouted his final orders at Trevor as he refastened Taron's cuffs. "If her boyfriend comes after us, you will wish you were dead when I get back."

Taron reached out for her as she passed by, "Liana, please don't do this."

She knew her decision was agony for him, but she couldn't turn back. "Take care of yourself. I will see you soon."

His shouts faded with every step she took. Her heart sank deeper and deeper as the swamp closed in on her. Liana would once again be facing her fears on her own.

Breaking Free

"Nothing can bring you peace but yourself."
Ralph Waldo Emerson

She was gone. Liana had willingly followed the demon into hell to keep him safe. It took every ounce of Taron's self-control to contain the all-encompassing need to give chase. His best shot at saving her lay in the hands of another. Trevor literally held the key. A lengthy stalemate with the injured man would only put Liana at greater risk.

"I'm going after her." The determination in Taron's voice left no room for doubt.

Trevor raised his gun with a shaky hand.

"Shoot me because nothing else will stop me. I will not abandon her."

"I can't let you go. If you fail, my father will punish me when he gets back. You heard him."

"I will succeed. He will not remove her light and love from the world. I will die before I let it happen again."

"Again? What are you saying?"

Taron exhaled an exasperated sigh as he looked in the direction Liana had disappeared. He needed to gain Trevor's confidence as quickly as possible, and that meant proving the kind of a man his father really was.

"Eight years ago, there was a burglary. My mother and brother were executed by a thief whose identity remained a mystery until today."

Trevor's eyes widened in shock. "No! It wasn't my father? He threatens and tortures. That's all. His days as a thief were before my time, but he never once mentioned murders. He intimidates those who stand in his way by exploiting their weaknesses."

Taron rubbed both hands over his face in frustration. "He is a liar, a thief, and a killer. His murderous urges have been diverted by tormenting you. He just held a pistol to your head. Tell me you didn't think you were going die?"

"He does that to scare the shit out of me. He gets off on it. I'm still alive which is proof he's every bit the coward I am." Trevor's gun lowered as his uncertainty increased.

Taron could see his defences were crumbling and delivered the final blow. "The only clue to the crime was a tattoo. Occidere au occidi."

"Kill or be killed." Trevor spat out the words as if trying to purge himself of their distaste.

"Think about all he has taken from you. Multiply your pain a thousand times, and you might begin to understand mine. Liana is all that matters to me. I will not abandon her. She is my last chance at happiness and perhaps yours as well."

His words finally struck a chord with the beleaguered man. "It's what the old man does. He takes and takes, until there is nothing left." Trevor's voice cracked as he directed a woeful stare at Taron. "There is no good inside me anymore."

"You are wrong, Trevor. The decency in you doesn't just disappear. Liana knew it was still there. She held out the hand of friendship, to you, her captor. You can still find the courage within yourself to do the right thing."

Taron held out his cuffs. "Prove your father wrong. Help me save her and yourself."

The fear and uncertainty etched in the lines of Trevor's face eased. He reached into his pocket and deposited the key into Taron's outstretched hands. By releasing the bonds of his captive, he had set himself free.

*****

Jillian's composure was slipping with each stroke of the paddle. There was a tightening in her chest and a lump in throat. This was taking too long and there was not a thing she could do about it. Their boat was moving as fast as the meandering waterway would allow, but it was not enough. Given their sluggish pace, Greg estimated they would arrive at their destination in twenty minutes.

While it was the logical route to take given what Delia had overheard, Jillian couldn't shake the feeling that something wasn't right. Her eyes were focussed on the banks of the channel looking for any sign that would confirm what her instincts were telling her.

The answer came when they rounded a bend and entered a small lagoon. Flamingoes. They were feeding near the shore.

"Greg, stop the boat!" She frantically gestured at the birds. "Look! The stream bed must have been disturbed and they are taking advantage of it. Get us closer."

"We really don't have time to indulge in any hunches right now."

"Greg Sloan, if you don't take us in that direction, I will wade in there myself."

"I am not going to waste time arguing. A quick look is all we can afford."

The birds scattered as Greg guided the skiff closer to shore. A marked depression in the damp earth suggested that a heavy object had been pulled from the water. Jillian's suspicions were confirmed. She sprang from the boat and immediately found the answer to her prayers.

"Liana's been here." She pointed at two palm fronds lying with their stems crossed. "Yesterday, I left her a map to the cache on the island. I marked the site with an 'x' and a treasure chest. Liana left a sign only I would recognize."

In the joy of the moment, she leapt into Greg's arms. Relief swept over her as her worst fear was abated. "They are both alive."

"Thank God! Remind me to never underestimate your mother's intuition." Greg returned her brilliant smile before releasing her from his arms.

A quick search of the area uncovered the kidnapper's boat and a trail leading inland. Jillian's keen eyes discovered a path that was deliberately being marked. She was eager to proceed, but a hand on her arm halted her forward progress.

"Why do you suppose they changed their plans?"

"Maybe they were worried someone was following them. Who knows?" She tugged his hand forward. "Let's not waste precious minutes analyzing their motives. We need to move."

"Jillian, I don't like this. We have no idea what we might be walking into when we catch up with them. Circumstances have changed, and we should take the time to rethink our approach."

"So we walk and talk. We don't have a moment to lose."

"Without new co-ordinates, how do you propose we find our way?"

"We are going to do this au natural. Not naked—I mean nature's way. You know—we follow the trail wearing our clothes. Greg, I have skills you have yet to discover. A manhunt in the wilderness is no problem."

Jillian heard her partner's soft chuckle as she took the lead. There was no time to be flustered. She was a woman on a mission and set a gruelling pace. Momentary pauses occurred only when signs along the trail were obscured. If there was any confusion about how to proceed, Jillian yielded to a greater power. Love. Her love for Liana would always keep her on the right path. The one that would bring her daughter home.

Their progress came to an abrupt halt when she discovered signs of a scuffle. Her heart was filled with dread and her voice was thick with emotion, "It looks like someone collapsed. Please, not them."

"I fell and twisted my ankle."

Greg's razor sharp reflexes had his gun drawn in an instant.

"Hey, don't shoot. I'm unarmed and I can help."

He whirled around trying to find an identifiable target. "Who are you? Where are you?"

"My name's Trevor, and I'm up here."

Jillian was the first to spot a pair of legs dangling from the gnarled and twisting branch of an ancient southern oak. Trevor straddled the limb while clinging to the massive trunk.

"I fell and sprained my ankle. Taron helped me into the tree." Trevor tried to wiggle his injured appendage as corroboration, but tightened his hold after nearly unseating himself.

Greg reiterated his question, "And you are?"

"That's not important. If you are part of a rescue, you need to hurry. Richard Hyde, my father, has taken Liana. Taron went after them." Trevor pointed to a trampled path heading north. "I gave him my gun so I needed a safe place to wait. There are too many snakes in this godforsaken swamp."

The pieces had already fallen into place for Jillian, and Greg looked like he was going to shoot the roosting bird off his perch. Grabbing him by the arm, she moved in the direction Trevor had indicated. "Since you don't seem to be going anywhere, we will deal with you later."

"I'll be here when you get back. Wait, take these. You might need them." Trevor tossed the handcuffs to Greg. "When you catch up with my father, shoot first and ask questions later."

Greg broke into a run and caught up with Jillian. "Would you like to tell me why we are leaving one of the kidnappers free to limp away whenever he chooses?"

"He's not going anywhere. His fears are going to keep him where he is."

"What makes you so sure?"

Jillian stopped and turned around. "If he wants to get down, he is going to have to use the branch underneath him. There is a python curled around it. It is well camouflaged, and you would never know it was there unless you stepped on it. We should be able to hear the scream from miles away if that happens. Hard to believe that frightened fellow is a criminal."

Another mile along the trail found them at an impasse. There were two paths that veered away from each other. Greg consulted the maps Tom had carefully drawn and argued against Jillian's choice. Hers was the shorter route, but it would lead them to another stream. The other path would bypass the hindrance all together. While Jillian had no aversion to snakes, she did draw the line at negotiating what was likely a gator-infested body of water.

Progress along the loop that skirted the waterway was slow until the trail widened It showed signs of frequent travel, and a sense of foreboding settled over the couple. The sounds of life were suddenly replaced by an eerie silence. Jillian felt like she was being watched by dozens of unseen eyes.

"Greg, I have a bad feeling about this."

Before the detective could speak or act, four gun-toting thugs rocketed out of the underbrush and surrounded them.

Jillian tried her best to provide an explanation. She thrust a map in front of the closest man. "We seem to be lost. Could you point us in the right direction?"

The assailant was momentarily stunned by her daring.

"No? How about showing us the way to the nearest ranger station then?"

"How about you shut up before we have to shoot you?" One of the goons took aim at her.

"There is no need to be impertinent. A simple no will suffice. Greg, let's be on our way."

"No one is going anywhere." A behemoth blocked the path in front of them.

The skirmish that followed was over before it really began. A shot from the trees hit the hand of the man who was threatening Jillian. He was expeditiously disarmed. The others tried to identify the source of the gunfire which gave Greg the opportunity to act. He tackled the man closest to him, cuffing his hands before he had time to recover his weapon.

Jillian backed up her partner by retrieving the gun of the wounded attacker. She wheeled around and confronted the remaining two men. "Freeze!"

One of the idiots had the audacity to laugh at her. "Or you'll what, shoot us?"

The two men turned and tried to make a run for it. They ended up face to face with a rifle and a very pissed off Delia. "She may not, but I definitely will."

A shrill whistle had the rest of her crew emerging from the tree line. Before Jillian could question her sister about their timely arrival, she was pulled into a fierce hug.

"Thank God you are alright. Where are my niece and the captain?"

"One of the men is still holding Liana hostage, and Taron is chasing after them. We have no idea which way they went."

"Well, I do." Delia swung the rifle back over her shoulder and grabbed the tracking device from Tom. "Let's go find our family and bring them home."

"You two are not going anywhere without me." Greg was using the lengths of rope Charlie had miraculously removed from his backpack to secure the hands and feet of the criminals.

"I just know we are running out of time." Jillian tucked the gun she was still holding into her belt.

The distant sound of another shot had both sisters running headlong into danger before anyone could make a move to stop them.

*****

Taron raced through the swamp, hurdling obstacles and crashing through brush. It was beyond reckless, and he drove himself to the very limits of physical endurance. Closing the gap before it was too late was at the forefront of his mind. He knew exactly what Hyde would do when he no longer had any use for Liana. The sobering thought forced another burst of speed from his aching muscles.

A marsh filled with sawgrass finally slowed his forward momentum. The razor sharp edges of each blade clawed at his arms, leaving behind bloodied scratches and triggering a flood of memories. His tortured past dogged his every step as all reason slipped away. The grass and branches scraping across his skin mutated into arms reaching out for help. The terrified faces of his family were reflected in every pool of stagnant water.

His heart was pounding and his breathing ragged when he finally stumbled onto a patch of drier ground. He allowed himself a brief moment to regain his physical strength and some small measure of sanity. As his vision cleared, he noticed the track ahead was no longer distinct. Several trampled paths led away from where he was standing. Liana's ploy had been discovered.

Without her guidance, Taron was unsure of his next step. She was the force leading him onward, and he was lost without her. When she faced her fears in the comfort of his embrace, he told her to seek out the light no matter how impenetrable the darkness. He now needed to do the same. Looking up to the heavens, he cried out for guidance to those who were long gone.

"Help me!"

The luminous path of the sun's rays filtered through the trees, leading his gaze to a patch of dirt. A flash of metal caught his eye, and he dropped to his knees. Taron carefully lifted the treasure with trembling fingers. It was the necklace—the cherished gift he had given Liana as a token of his love. She would never willingly let anyone take it from her. He was ready to surrender to his worst fears when he remembered the faulty clasp. The necklace was lying in one of the trails heading away from the clearing. Liana was showing him the way. He took off at a dead run.

His sprint slowed to a walk in the dense undergrowth of a cypress grove. Barely audible voices brought him to a standstill. He crept toward his quarry straining to hear what was being said. Hyde's threats eventually assaulted his ears.

"In case you hadn't noticed, it's just you and me. I could kill you right now. There would be no one to witness your untimely demise. No evidence you ever existed. No one to mourn your loss."

"You won't win. Taron will never give up because he loves me. Love gives you the courage to carry on even when all hope seems to fade. It is something you will never understand."

"Enough of your sentimental foolishness."

Taron watched and waited as Hyde motioned Liana toward the water. Timing was the critical element to his plan.

"You are going to cross the stream and follow the path to a stash of cocaine. Fill this, and bring it back to me." Hyde tossed her a backpack.

"Sounds easy enough." Liana's eyes darted across the ground as she bent down to pick up the pack. "How deep is the water?"

Hyde's crazed laughter sent a shiver through Taron. "Oh, its not the depth of the channel you'll need to worry about. It's the gators guarding their nests. This is the season for hatchlings. Contrary to popular belief, reptilian mothers are very protective of their young."

When Liana made no move to comply with his demand, he trained his gun on her. "The only choice you have to make is whether you take the high road or the low road." Hyde swung his weapon between a small tree leaning across the channel and the stream beneath it.

"So many questions to consider. Are you a decent climber, and will the tree support your weight? Maybe you are a better swimmer, but will the splashing attract unwanted attention?"

They were now close enough for Taron to take a shot. Hyde was vulnerable, but so was Liana. If he missed, she would pay the price. His grip on the gun tightened, but he could not pull the trigger. Words would have to be the weapon of choice. As he stepped onto the battle field of mental manipulation, his fury turned into something cold and functional.

"The only choice that needs to be made is where I put the bullet, in your head or the blackened organ masquerading as your heart."

"Taron!" Liana shouted his name and was able to take a few steps toward him before Hyde regained his composure.

"Move again, and I will turn you into the main course for the hungry hordes waiting in the water," he hissed.

Taron underestimated the impact seeing Liana in danger would have on his self-restraint. A blinding rage once again consumed him as he confronted the man who had laid waste to his life. He had dreamt about this moment for years.

"Take your shot. He won't do it." The conviction in Liana's tone drew his eyes to hers. "You know he prefers his prey helpless."

Hyde threw her a malicious smirk. "That's exactly what you are, an easy victim."

Taron understood her intentions perfectly. The element of surprise in their game of cat and mouse. "It was my mother and brother. They were alone and afraid. No one heard their screams except the man who murdered them."

Hyde looked puzzled and his attention was briefly focussed on analyzing the meaning behind Taron's words.

"Kill or be killed. Easy enough to accomplish when your victims are unarmed. Did you get the tattoo as a trophy to commemorate your heinous act?"

The revelation caught Hyde off guard, allowing Liana to make her move. She released the backpack and hurled a stone she had picked up. It flew through the air hitting the old man in the elbow. His short sleeved shirt meant there was nothing to cushion the blow. Hyde howled in pain, dropping his gun."

Underestimating his clever lass was a stupid mistake. Taron knew the cunning malefactor would not be so careless again. He needed Liana safe before he could finish it.

"Darling, over here. Move slowly."

The reprobate swiftly recovered from his shock, taking advantage of the weakness Taron had exposed. "The world is full of fools. What does it matter if I rid humanity of one or two more? Only the strong survive. Think of it as culling the herd."

Hyde's shadow seemed to lengthen and stretch toward Taron like a nightmarish monster reaching out to pull him back into the darkness. The distressed voices of his family drifted in on the rustling leaves and echoed in his head. Pleading. Beseeching. Save us.

"You were the one who found them, weren't you? You couldn't save them. You were not there when they needed you most." The words slid off Hyde's tongue and hit home.

They were the questions that had tormented Taron for eight long years. The sweat glistening on his skin took on the chill of that cold January night. The horrendous brutality and the unbearable pain washed over him again.

"I couldn't save them." His voice was barely a whisper. "They were gone. I couldn't save them."

A new voice called to him, sweet and clear. It was asking him to come back. The words wrapped around him like the caress of loving arms. They beckoned him forward into the warmth and the light.

"Taron! Taron! Listen to me. It wasn't your fault, not then and not now. I'm here. You did save me."

"Liana?"

She was standing next to him. Her beautiful brown eyes were filled with compassion and tears.

He needed to get her to safety. "Follow the trail back. I will be right behind you." His gun was still aimed at Hyde. The man was infuriatingly calm.

"No! I'm staying. For better or worse, remember?" Her stance remained defiant. "I know what you are about to do, and I won't leave you."

"Liana, it's not over until he pays for what he did. He deserves to die."

"You and I both know there are punishments worse than death. It is the great injustice of the world.

381

Innocents die while those who might deserve death live on. Condemn him to living life as the wretched human being he is. Confine him to a cell where he has no power or freedom. Take away everything he values to settle the score."

"I will have vengeance for my family. A life taken for the lives lost."

"This is not self-defence. It is a calculated kill. Please don't do this. It will haunt you—us—for the rest of our lives."

She was right. Liana would stay by his side and proclaim her love, but Taron would never fully have her heart if he committed this act of hatred. Destiny had brought him to this moment, but the choice was his. He was caught between Liana's love and light and the darkness and despair that was Hyde. Trapped in the past or freed in the future. He would honour the legacy of his family and be the man worthy of Liana's love.

When he shifted his gaze to her, Hyde's reaction was swift.

Liana screamed and Taron's world imploded.

They hit the ground together.

Love and Light

"Darkness cannot drive out darkness; only light can do that.
Hate cannot drive out hate; only love can do that."
Martin Luther King Jr.

There was no movement. Liana lay limp in his arms.

The air had been forced from Taron's lungs and he could not draw a breath until she did. If she was gone, surely his heart would have stopped beating as well. Her eyes saw what his had not. She had thrown herself in harm's way, shielding him from the piercing stab of a bullet just as deftly as she kept him from shattering under the weight of his bitter anguish.

Seconds felt like an eternity. He was finally able to choke out her name on a broken sob, "Liana."

Crushing her to his chest, he tried to meld their bodies into one. "Please, not again. Breathe, my love. Just breathe."

"Not very likely with the hold you have on me," Liana squeaked.

Taron was incapable of honouring her request as his arms acted on their own accord. Holding her securely, he lavished her with kisses. Liana was doing her best to land the occasional peck, but with little success. By some miracle, they were both alive.

"I'm not complaining, but shouldn't we be checking on Hyde?"

"It's under control," an unfamiliar, albeit friendly voice answered. "Is everyone alright?"

Rejoicing in their survival, Taron presumed Liana had not been harmed. A jolt of alarm raced down his spine. "Darling, are you injured?"

"Pretty sure I'm fine." She swayed as she tried to stand, leaning heavily on Taron's arms for support. "I'm just a little dizzy from another fall."

"There is no room for uncertainty in matters of such grave importance." Taron ran his gaze over her looking for any signs of trauma. Finding all was well, he swept her into his arms.

"Would someone care to explain what's going on here?"

The man asking the question wore a green and tan uniform and was standing over the prone and lifeless form of Hyde. He was perfectly camouflaged. No one would have noticed his advance through the brush.

Liana took a deep breathe and answered his question, "It's a long story. The man at your feet is a kidnapper and drug dealer. He held us captive and we just managed to break free when—when he…" She began to stammer as the reality of what had transpired overwhelmed her.

"When my timely arrival saved you both." Their rescuer approached and extended a hand to Taron. "Officer Logan Thorne, Florida Fish and Wildlife Conservation."

"Taron Royce." He reluctantly lifted one hand from Liana's waist, offering it in greeting and gratitude. "We owe you our lives. Thank you."

"Think nothing of it. Glad I was in the right place at the right time. I've been monitoring a crocodile nest in the area, and I hoped to tag the elusive female today.

Liana glanced back at Hyde. "So he's...?"

"Immobilized, yes. After hearing your voices, I tried to figure out what was happening before I fired. The cagey geezer has the reflexes of a pit viper. His hands were on the gun the minute your head was turned. Lucky for both of you, I'm a faster draw and I always get my gator—well, in this case, man."

Taron didn't know whether to laugh at the irony or cheer their victory. "You incapacitated him with a tranquilizer dart?"

"Yes, but don't worry. If he does start to move, I used the handcuffs he dropped to subdue him. Listen folks, I need to find a spot where my cell will get a signal so I can call this in and get us some help. Will you two be alright until I get back?"

"Absolutely, everything is as it should be." Taron pulled Liana into a fierce embrace.

She also held on to him as if her life still depended on it. He rubbed her back while whispering words of praise.

"Darling, your bravery is staggering. You saved me."

Liana's eyes glistened with unshed tears as she reached for his face. The soft caress of her fingers eased the last of his tension. "You did the same for me."

Her lips brushed his in a delicate kiss that sought comfort and gave reassurance in equal measure. It intensified into a passionate affirmation of life and love, filling them both with a joy that knew no bounds. Their reverie was short-lived as a call from the wild brought them back to the present moment.

"Don't mind us. We would knock, but there is no door." Delia's declaration was followed by her sister's ecstatic shout.

"Liana! Taron! You are both alive."

Taron stepped aside, allowing mother and daughter the poignant reunion that was long overdue. Liana ran into Jillian's open arms.

"We heard a gun shot. Liana, I thought I'd lost you."

The flow of tears soon gave way to smiles and laughter. Rapid fire questions followed, and the gist of the story was told.

Delia made her way to Taron with open arms. "Well done, Captain. You kept my niece safe, and for that, you have my undying gratitude."

"Thankfully, no one will be dying today." He braced himself for the impact of a hug that never came.

Delia's gaze was fixed on a spot behind him. She gradually raised her rifle. "I wouldn't be so sure."

Taron's movements were slow and deliberate as he turned to confront yet another threat. The crocodile had silently eased her massive bulk out of the water while they were savouring their triumph. Her intent was clear as she lumbered toward Hyde's unresponsive form. A quick glance over his shoulder was all he needed to come to a decision. Liana had stilled Delia's arm, giving him the freedom to act.

Withdrawing his gun, he slowly moved forward. Halfway to the target, his forward momentum was halted as the beast swung her jaws at him and hissed. Hyde's glassy eyes were fixed on the reptilian horror moving his way. Death was coming for him. He had no means of escape. The scourge that had plagued Taron Royce was about to be wiped off the face of the earth. All he had to do was wait.

Taron closed his eyes and opened his heart ready to welcome the relief he had been so desperate to find. A vibrating energy penetrated every cell and nerve fibre. It was the last thing he expected to feel. It surrounded him in a moment of spiritual purity that nearly brought him to his knees. Love. It was the very fabric of the universe transcending time and mortality. The love of his family had been transformed not destroyed. It remained in his heart, binding him to Liana and to every thought and deed.

The truth was a moment of stunning clarity. Destiny could be shifted by hate, but it could also be reshaped by mercy and love. There was only one way out of the darkness; one way to become whole again. A single shot fired into the air saw the crocodile plunge back into the water. Taron looked into the eyes of his enemy and saw stunned disbelief. It was finally over. He turned and walked to Liana never once looking back.

A rustling in the trees had Delia battle ready in an instant. Officer Thorne burst through the foliage and found himself staring down the barrel of a gun. The guardian of the universe would not stand down until Taron informed her the man in green was one of the good guys.

"Apologies, but someone who blends in with the shrubbery should not be sneaking up on people." Delia eyed him with suspicion.

Logan patiently explained his vocation and wardrobe choice to the two newcomers.

Jillian was quick to express her displeasure regarding the day's events. "I think the public would be better served if you left the wildlife alone and focussed on the criminal element flourishing here. We've been hijacked, accosted by four drug runners, and survived a kidnapping."

Taron watched the proceedings in amused silence. Only Jillian could dress down a man that was already so casually attired.

"I'm sure if you put your mind to it, you might be able to accomplish both tasks. You could dig a few moats and load them up with alligators. Use them like guard dogs," Jillian concluded.

Logan managed to quash his laughter by coughing into his sleeve. "I will take your gator watch under advisement, madam."

A new visitor tearing out of undergrowth had weapons at the ready once more.

"Greg!" Jillian flung herself at the detective.

Delia fixed Logan with a commanding stare. "If you are going to allow people with guns into this primeval swamp, you really should hang a bell on them." She lowered her rifle and closed the distance between them. "It really is dumb luck that I haven't killed anyone today."

"Happy to discuss your prowess with weaponry once we get you all out of here." To his credit, the man did not shy away from Delia's imposing presence.

A succinct discussion about whose authority had jurisdiction took place between the officers. Given Greg's experience with the drug squad, he was the logical choice to take charge of the traffickers until the local police arrived. He had already called for reinforcements using a cell confiscated from one of the assailants. Logan's mandate to remove any invasive species threatening the environment left him with the catch of the day. He gave Greg his personal assurance that both Richard and Trevor would be delivered to the rendezvous point.

There was no time to waste as daylight was waning. No one wanted to be caught in the everglades after dark. A short hike saw the crew of the Wicked Wench reunited once more. Taron and Liana were met with a round of enthusiastic hugs and excited chatter. Jillian tried to dissuade Greg from staying behind since Charlie and Will had their attackers trussed up more securely than a thanksgiving turkey. The dedicated detective would not neglect his duties and urged his friends to follow Tom to the designated meeting place.

The group emerged from the forested hammock and settled themselves on the beach. Taron positioned himself with his back to a palm tree, stretching out his legs. Liana collapsed next to him and curled herself under his arm.

"It won't be long now, my love. Once we get back home, we can put all of this behind us."

"I don't want to shut everything out. I will never forget what you were willing to sacrifice for me."

"It is not only about what I was willing to do. Look around you. Everyone here risked something today in the name of family and friendship. I have never been more proud of a crew and likely never will be again."

"Pretty amazing show of loyalty, isn't it, Captain?" Liana's eyes glowed with love and happiness.

Not everyone remained as faithful to the cause. Charlie set off to explore the area, grumbling that his stomach was as empty as their water bottles. Delia was eager to ensure he did not stray too far and tightened the leash.

"There should be some coconuts under the palm trees right here on the beach. If you do find one, maybe we can crack it open on your thick skull." She turned to her sister. "The idiot will probably uncover some fruit that poisons us all."

Charlie eventually returned empty-handed. He distracted himself from his cravings by recounting tales of their derring-do. His crew mates clarified the occasional point whenever a tendency to embellish events in his favour occurred. Adventures on the big screen paled in comparison to the narrative that was being told. Taron marvelled over the fact they had all survived.

His good humour failed when he heard how Delia had commandeered the Wicked Wench. "You captained my ship?"

She swaggered over to him. "Seriously? I was hoping after your night on the island, Liana would be the only one allowed to—"

"Delia!" A chorus of voices cut off her bawdy remark.

"Happy to give command back to the rightful captain." Taron accepted the hand of friendship she held out to him.

All eyes turned to the sea as the sun continued to sink toward the horizon. The coast guard cutter was the first of the rescuers to be spotted. It was soon followed by a Monroe County police boat. Launches were already on their way when Logan and Greg came into view. They carried Hyde on a makeshift stretcher, and Trevor was draped over the back of another everglades wildlife officer. He was prattling on about the size of a snake.

Taron and Liana stood motionless while the others approached their tormentor. Hyde was beginning to regain his senses and searched the faces around him.

"Him." He pointed a wobbly finger at his son. "It was all his idea. He was the brains behind all of this."

There was not a chance in hell Taron was going to let the old man squirm his way out of this. He escorted Liana over to Greg.

"This is the man who kidnapped us. His name is Richard Hyde."

Liana tightened her grip on his hand.

"I know this will be hard to believe, but he also killed Mom and Daniel. Check his arm."

Greg found the incontrovertible proof and turned to his friend. "You had a justifiable motive in self-defence and a weapon. Why is he still alive?"

"It was the right thing to do." Taron embraced his love and stepped back as the police made their way across the sand.

As Greg began to recap events, Hyde tried to implicate Trevor once more. The manipulative father lifted his head and turned toward his son.

"Trevor threatened to kill me if I didn't go along with his plans."

Delia stormed over to the deceitful miscreant. "That's him. The man who held a ship full of innocent tourists at gunpoint looking for his cocaine."

Greg filled in the rest of the story adding to the list of alleged crimes. Before the local law enforcement could question Trevor, Delia spoke on his behalf.

"I am sure this poor man has been doing his father's bidding under pain of death. Without his assistance, this heroic couple would not have survived." She gave Taron and Liana a warm smile.

Charlie whispered to Taron, "Shit! She just told a lie."

Delia tried to simplify her quickly fabricated story emphasizing key points with the raise of her eyebrows. Taron hoped the maligned man would catch on and be able to remember the details during his interrogation. He corroborated Delia's accounting as an astonished Trevor was loaded onto a second stretcher.

"A minute if you please." Delia bent over Trevor. "Take it from someone who knows, everyone deserves a second chance. Blow it, and I will make sure you spend the rest of your days waiting tables at Bruno's Burgers."

Taron gave her a puzzled look, but any confusion was soon forgotten. What began as a tempest of heartache and terror, ended in a gentle wave of compassion and love.

*****

Their crazy adventure fittingly ended at the Sea Ahead Inn in Key Largo. As they made their way from the parking lot, Liana was wedged between Taron and Jillian who both seemed determined to keep her from being carried off on the evening breeze. The owner was happy to welcome them back. A one night stay was not a problem nor was their late arrival after making statements at the sheriff's station. They would spend the night recuperating before travelling to Miami.

Their accommodations were scattered throughout the Inn with the exception of two rooms across the hall from each other. Liana found herself literally being pulled in two directions—one hand being clutched by Jillian and the other by Taron. Delia prevented a tug of war by propelling her sister though the open door of their room. She gave her niece a quick kiss on the cheek and was rewarded with a grateful smile and a hug.

Once inside their safe haven, Taron spun her into his arms. Liana had been a block of granite for twenty-four hours and she was ready to crumble. Curling her arms around his neck, she anchored herself to him.

"Taron, we almost died today."

The strength of his hold kept her upright when her legs gave way. What started as a steady stream of tears, soon turned into gut wrenching sobs. They had been to hell and back, giving everything they had in the quest to ensure they both survived. She could not tear herself away and sought comfort in the warmth of his body and his loving touch. It healed her like nothing else could.

"Darling, you are exhausted. Let's get cleaned up and get some rest." Taron carefully released her.

Holding out her hand, she gestured for him to follow. "Come with me. I need us to be together."

His concerned look told her he felt likewise. He took her hand and followed her into the bathroom. After easing their weary limbs out of soiled clothes, they stepped into the comforting stream of water. Liana couldn't seem to make her fingers work properly, dropping whatever she tried to hold. She was so very tired.

"Let me, darling."

Taron took over with careful strokes and gentle caresses. He catalogued every bruise, soothing each one with the brush of his lips. Tears mingled with the water trickling down his face as he discovered each new mark.

"My turn."

Liana trailed her lips along the path of his tear drops. Her light touch barely grazed his muscles. When she reached the cuts on his arms, her hands stilled and she traced the abrasions with her fingers. They were the battle scars each of them had gladly endured for the other. Body and soul were laid bare as they tended to each other's hurts with a profound intimacy. The pain and fear of the past were washed away with the impurities of the day. It was a fresh start for both them.

Collapsing onto the bed, Liana luxuriated in the softness of the mattress and the plush feel of the sheets. It felt like heaven to her aching limbs.

Taron crawled in next to her. "Rest easy, my love. It is just the two of us now."

As much as she wanted to give her sleep deprived body what it craved, there were still things that needed to be said.

"Taron, you didn't let him die. You gave up your revenge. Why?"

His blue eyes were filled with awe. "I don't know if I can fully describe it. It felt as though I was connected to everything. I saw things so clearly. Love is all there is, was, and ever will be. There is no room in my heart for hate. There is only the light and love you have returned to my life."

Liana placed a soft kiss on his lips. "You did this, not me."

"No. It was your faith in me that led the way. You prevented Delia from taking action."

"The wrongs of the past were yours to right in whatever way you chose. I knew the incredible man I fell in love with would make an appearance."

"And so he did, but there is something still worrying you. Tell me."

She lowered her lashes and worried her lip. "I lost the necklace. I'm so sorry. It didn't take much to release the clasp, and I hoped it might help you find me. I had to take the chance, and now it's gone."

Taron turned his head toward the dresser and smiled. She followed his line of sight and gasped.

"It can't be." Her necklace was lying to the feather. "How?"

"Divine intervention, a miraculous occurrence call it whatever you like. I think we both know the significance in all of this." Taron ran the back of his hand along her cheek. "We were meant to be, my love."

Liana thought back to the moment that had altered the trajectory of her life. "Our journey started the night you rescued me from the water. You ended up saving me in more ways than one. I was such a…"

He hushed her with a gentle kiss. "You are a beautiful, brave, and intelligent woman. I would not be parted from you then, and I never will be again. Now, let's get some sleep."

Liana rolled over and turned off the bedside lamp. She felt Taron press into her back, draping an arm over her and nuzzling his cheek into curve of her neck. A sigh of utter contentment and bliss left her lips. She never believed anyone would love her so completely. It was a dream come true. A dream she never knew she had.

*****

How on earth had she let her mother talk her into this? Liana had a death grip on Taron's hand.

He leaned in and whispered, "It will be over before you know it. Let her have this moment."

"Taron…"

Any further comment was interrupted by a firm, "Quiet everyone."

The television announcer's voice rumbled over them, "Miami Mornings is back with your hosts Katrina Call and Joe King."

Liana took a deep breath as a round of applause died down.

Joe gave the usual exaggerated introduction, "Miami Mornings is proud to bring you a story of high seas adventure, death-defying rescue, and the dramatic take-down of a notorious drug syndicate. Please give a warm welcome to the intrepid crew of the Wicked Wench."

He sent his mega watt smile in the direction of Liana's mother. "Let me first introduce Jillian Barton, the mild-mannered Boston teacher whose dream of a once-in-a-lifetime vacation turned into a nightmarish episode of cops and robbers."

Jillian's polite expression instantly shifted into one of displeasure. "Mr. King, if you had done your homework properly, you would know they were drug runners not robbers. And yes, I did organize a holiday for my amazing daughter, Liana Taylor."

Katrina dove in trying to save her co-host. "Why don't we let the fearless captain tell us how he risked life and limb to save his damsel in distress."

Taron turned his loving gaze to Liana. "I beg to differ, Katrina."

"Please, call me Kat." The women did nothing to hide her obvious interest in Taron.

"The beautiful and courageous woman sitting next to me is the love of my life. I am sure she would agree that we rescued each other." Taron flashed Liana a devastating grin.

Joe aimed his dubious charm at Delia. "I understand you and your sister hand picked Captain Royce as the romantic leading man to star opposite Ms.Taylor. It seems you succeeded in making a love connection."

Delia directed her response to his cohost, "I'm sure Ms. Kat Call has the most experience when it comes to a single woman's love life. Didn't I see you on the cover of the Town Tattler with that much younger married man? What was his name?"

Kat choked on her morning coffee while Joe tried to cut their losses. "We seem to be running out of time, so we will leave you with a Miami Mornings exclusive. Among the crew was vacationing Boston police detective, Greg Sloan. He single-handedly apprehended four men whose confessions led to yesterday's arrest of a drug kingpin."

Greg looked like he was ready to throttle the man. "I admit that I played a small part in things, but the lovely lady sitting to my right was the one who tracked them down. It was her quick thinking and bravery that got the job done."

"Greg, there is no need to be so modest." Jillian smiled at her valiant partner before turning her attention back to the co-hosts. "Shouldn't there be some kind of medal or promotion for a man who risks his life in the line of duty?"

"Kat, if that isn't the perfect lead in, I don't know what is?" The duo dazzled them with killer smiles as they handed Greg with an enormous cardboard cheque.

Kat delivered the surprising news, "Detective Sloan, there was a reward of two hundred thousand dollars for information leading to the arrest of the notorious everglade's drug runner, El Donaldo.

Greg was flabbergasted, but quickly recovered. "As a member of a law enforcement agency, I cannot lay claim to any reward." He turned to an upset Jillian. "I believe the civilian involved in their capture is the one who deserves the money."

"Greg, you can't." Jillian's voice quivered with emotion.

"I can and I will."

Liana overheard the words he softly spoke to her mother, "Go get your house back."

It was the perfect moment to end the segment, and Joe threw it to commercial.

"Well, that's all folks. Join us tomorrow for our hard hitting investigation into the explosion of pet pythons in the everglades. Wildlife officer Logan Thorne will be our special guest."

The lights dimmed and a dazed but happy group left the stage. Congratulations and hugs were exchanged as they slowly made their way to the exit. They would all be heading to a boutique Miami hotel to enjoy the final days of the trip. Captain Morgan was thrilled with the Wicked Wench's newfound notoriety. Bookings had tripled since news of their adventure surfaced, and he insisted on paying for their stay as a show of appreciation.

No one seemed ready to say goodbye. Jillian was quick to point out they were all family now which meant keeping in touch. Shane and Charlie guaranteed them front row seats for the opening of their play. Regular trips to Boston were also in Shane's future as he and Scarlet continued to explore their relationship. Delia heard a Miami PBS station was looking to add a cooking show to their roster and offered to help Charlie and Will pitch 'Comrades in the Kitchen.' Claire's sabbatical was far from over, and she was looking forward to more geocaching adventures with Tom.

Liana stood in Taron's arms as her friends slowly dispersed. They were lost in a world of their own. She no longer cared whether their tender kisses and caresses caught the attention of people leaving the studio. Their public display of affection did not escape her mother's notice.

"You two are so adorable. I think I'm going to cry." Jillian's wide smile refuted her statement.

Liana watched as Delia's arm slide around her mother's shoulders.

"This has been one hell of a ride, Sis. Someone really should write a book about it." Delia's lips curved upward, settling into a broad grin. "I can't believe any of this worked out. Nothing went according to plan."

Jillian beamed, "The best stories never do."

Acknowledgements

This book was written during a very difficult time in my life. There were many people who helped me through that and encouraged me very step of the way. I thank you all from the bottom of my heart.

My deepest thanks to Talia and Rachel who assisted me from the first draft onward. I thank you for your faith in me and your generous support. You have both taught me so much about writing, friendship, and life.

I am grateful to Cord and Joanne who made time to help me polish the final draft.

Thanks to Vila Design for creating a beautiful cover.

Website
Doterra

On guarde

mix coconut oil
dogs teeth Spray
disinfectant

Serenity - Calming

Key West once rented
Oprah has island ~~cottages on~~
off coast are cottages on
sunset key

CPSIA information can be obtained
at www.ICGtesting.com
Printed in the USA
LVOW04s2030230616
493823LV00015B/75/P

9 780995 161511